OATHKEEPER

ALSO BY J. F. LEWIS

Grudgebearer

OATHKEEPER

J. F. LEWIS

an imprint of Prometheus Books
Amherst, NY

Published 2015 by Pyr®, an imprint of Prometheus Books

Cover image © Todd Lockwood
Cover design by Jacqueline Nasso Cooke

Inquiries should be addressed to
Pyr
59 John Glenn Drive
Amherst, New York 14228
VOICE: 716–691–0133
FAX: 716–691–0137
WWW.PYRSF.COM

19 18 17 16 15   5 4 3 2 1

Library of Congress Cataloging-in-Publication Data

Lewis, J. F. (Jeremy F.) author.
    Oathkeeper : Book two of the Grudgebearer trilogy / By J.F. Lewis.
        pages cm. — (Grudgebearer trilogy; Book Two)
    ISBN 978-1-63388-054-2 (paperback) — ISBN 978-1-63388-055-9 (ebook)
    I. Title.

PS3612.E9648018 2015
813'.6—dc13

                                                                    2015000807

Printed in the United States of America

This one is for all the moms out there and to one in particular, my wife, Janet.

CONTENTS

PART THREE: A KING ARISES

PART FOUR: THE OLD SKULL LAUGHS

PART ONE

THE SACRIFICE PLAY

"Nebulous millennia in advance of the fate-fueled blow which wrought the destruction of the Life Forge and twisted the elemental magic of all Eldrennai save the Destroyer herself and those of Villok or Uled's blood, the Test of Four had long been reduced to an empty, if grand, spectacle of coronation . . . a quaint remnant from a time before all Eldrennai youth were trained in the use of elemental magic. The Test of Four existed before construction of the Tower of Elementals and the practice of Ranked Elementalists visiting all newborn Eldrennai to test them and send them to the tower for training, to the Artificer's Guild, or other less glorious fates.

By my father's era, the Test of Four had lost all meaning as a measurement of ability, transformed into a demonstrative device each new king used to display not just his command of the four elements: earth, air, fire, and water, but his creativity . . . his flair for magic. My father once described it as a myopic exercise in the flaunting of birthright and superiority—an opinion held, perhaps, because neither he nor any of his bloodline could pass it spectacularly or without artificial aid.

Such a simple test: light a candle four times, extinguishing it (once each) with air, earth, and water. For those who hold sway over all four elements: child's play. Of course, the ancient rules officially require magic to be used only once in the test, coming as it did from a time before the successful merging of elemantic bloodlines. . . . Not that the rules for the Test of Four were ever revised. A technicality, true, but kingdoms have fallen and mortals raised to godhood by technicalities.

They are never safe to overlook."

From *The Kings of the Eldrennai* by Sargus

CHAPTER 1
ROYAL CONTINGENCIES

Night birds called in the outer dark, joining a chorus comprised of tent fabric shifting in the gentle breeze and the chirps, cries, and grunts of nocturnal creatures. Rivvek loved those sounds; even the sea lapping against the pier at Oot contributed to the unscripted opus.

Combined with the scent of stale air inside the tent and the snores of another person nearby, the sensorial collage conjured memories of brighter days camping with his father the king . . . even hunting trips with his younger brother before Dolvek had become so insufferable. Rivvek had hoped his brother's encounter with Kholster would be transformative.

If it had been, Rivvek couldn't see it.

Elsewhere in the ramshackle encampment, Oathkeepers and Oathbreakers alike slept soundly, dreams little disturbed by the Grand Conjunction's approaching end.

Their world is about to change in ways they cannot even imagine, he thought, *blind to the turning of the gears in the great destiny machine.*

The great destiny machine.

Rivvek smirked at the thought of it. Once he'd believed the gnomes worshipped a literal device that wove the skein of mortal fates. When he'd realized numbers were the gnomish religion and their great destiny machine merely a codified method of determining likely outcomes, he'd been sorely disappointed . . . and then, years later as he lay healing under the care of the Vael, he'd learned to do the math.

The gnomes played a game with triangular tiles: trignom. Queen Kari of the Vael had given him a set during his convalescence. He had never learned to play well. Irka, Kholster's son—a perfect double called an Incarna—always beat him, but Rivvek remembered building patterns with the double-sided numbered tiles atop the stiff and pungent plaster in which the Vael healers kept most of him wrapped, and knocking them over to watch the trignoms fall.

The whole world was like those tumbling tiles if you knew how to look at it, and, eyes having been so painfully and thoroughly opened, Rivvek knew no other way.

My graduation approaches.

Rivvek considered his true education to have begun at the Grand Conjunction a hundred and thirteen years ago. It marked his thoughts then as clearly as the scars he'd received afterward warped his flesh. Was it fair to hold the lack of such learning against his brother? An Eldrennai who still had his magic, whose body was whole and hale?

Prince Rivvek lay in the dark, incapable of slumber, stacking up the trignoms in his thoughts, looking at them from every angle and doing the math. The first tile would be flicked over soon. It was a tile he would have given almost anything to protect, to place his hand over the tile and hold it in place safe and secure. There were three ways to stop it he could accomplish alone, but then the pattern changed, and the new designs woven into the great destiny machine spelled doom for the Eldrennai.

He wasn't sure why the Zaur hadn't started burning Root Trees yet. The math said they should. Perhaps his formulae were off in that regard, but his calculations, his own personal version of the great destiny machine, was far more accurate when it came to the Eldren Plains and the politics and machinations of the Eldrennai.

Those sums spelled destruction now. He had not yet been born when Uled had created the Aern, a race of warriors to defend against the reptilian Zaur and their magic resistance. For each new problem, it now seemed, Uled had created a new race and with each race, the path to doom had become more and more difficult to avoid.

Uled had wanted to restrict the Aern's ability to breed, creating them all male, thinking he could use low-born Eldrennai women with little magic and no connections as brood mares for his warriors, but bearing Aern, with their bone-steel and unique nutritional properties, rendered an Eldrennai female barren, often after the first birth.

Nine in ten. Rivvek saw the statistics in his head, marveling at how much cruelty could be concealed when suffering and evil were disguised as numbers.

To solve the breeding issue, Uled had created the plantlike Vael, their bodies designed to be both appealing to the Aern and easily capable of producing many Aern offspring, quite rapidly if the raw materials were available in sufficient quantities.

Two gallons of blood per infant to be awakened. . . . Words from Uled's notes haunted Rivvek, but he'd needed to know, to understand, so that he could get the numbers right. His predictive model required deadly accuracy.

On the page, everything looked like it would work, but chaos, the natural tendency for change, had not been accounted for in any of Uled's plans or designs. First came the appearance of female Aern, then male Vael.

Worse were the changes and complications brought in by individuals in power. Enslaved by Uled's magic, unable to refuse a command, or break an oath, the Aern might have remained under complete Eldrennai control forever. Given the pride and arrogance so common to Rivvek's ancestors, in fact, the entire bloodline of Villok, Rivvek was still astonished it had taken as long as it had for an Eldrennai king to break his word to Kholster, First Born of Uled's Aern, thus releasing the Aern from the spells that bound them.

From there, even Rivvek's predictions would have been wrong had he been alive to make them. In prolonged battle against a magic immune warrior race in possession of nigh unbeatable warsuits, even in limited numbers, Rivvek would have projected a complete genocide for the Eldrennai. His calculations would have failed to account for the Vael's inborn desire for peace and mediation as well as the Aern's affection and respect for them.

The six hundred years of peace they had enjoyed had been a statistical anomaly. Rivvek wondered whether other Eldrennai comprehended how lucky they had been that the uneasy truce had lasted a year, much less six hundred. Even if Dolvek, Rivvek's brother, had not so stupidly broken the truce by moving the warsuits the Aern had left behind as part of the truce, it would have ended eventually. At that time, the oath made by Kholster to slay every Eldrennai would have come into effect, and the path upon which they now walked would still be theirs. Only the date had been variable.

But, as his own scarred body told the world, there are varying levels of ruination. One can be scourged near to death, be broken, and laid waste to and still heal to emerge from the flames, if not whole, then . . . still useful.

"Kings die," he whispered, his voice breaking, the words strangled. "Fathers die." He pushed on, forcing himself through a verbalization of the hateful truth. "Everyone dies eventually. It's making sure that death has as much meaning as . . . as . . . ."

Optimize your life and you will be rewarded in the next. That was what the gnomes believed. Rivvek was certain Torgrimm, as god of birth and death, had made it happen. Would Kholster, in his new role as Harvester, do the same? For the gnomes? Rivvek did not doubt he would. For King Grivek?

Eyes closed more against that idea than the dark, Rivvek's ears perked up. His melted ear tugged against the tender flesh at his temple as he eavesdropped on the Kingsguard. Their appointed rounds kept them stationed far enough from the cluster of deiform statuary to avoid disturbing the Conjunction itself, but close enough that the brave Eldrennai could charge to their deaths in King Grivek's defense. Rivvek assumed their voices were overheard just as easily by the Vael and the Aern at Oot as they were by him.

"Now that Kholster's dead," a husky-voiced Eldrennai muttered to someone, "our King will make things right between the Grudgebearers and us. You wait and see, Dace."

Was that Thalan speaking? Rivvek decided it must be.

"You think so, Thal?" Dace breathed.

"She's not even half a hundred yet," Thalan chortled. "You think this kholster Rae'en can out-negotiate an Eldrennai king with over half a millennium on the throne?"

This then, Rivvek thought, sitting up, *is the peril of my people: arrogance unrivaled by any other race and self-deception enough to make Kilke himself blush.*

"My prince?" Sargus stirred. Rivvek opened his eyes, making out the aura of Sargus's life force more easily than he could his features in the night—another "gift" from his time beyond the Port Gates. When one stood too close to a Port Gate or wore armor made of Ghaiattri hide, one could see, as if through a thin veil, the creatures of the Ghaiattri's realm. Rivvek's sight afforded him a dual view of reality, particularly at night, the never-dark of that other place seeped into his perceptions. With it came a light that illuminated the spirits of sentient beings around him. Sargus shone as a whorl of colors, dark, rich purples wending through golds and blues shot through with the occasional bloody red or coal black.

When bending his mind to a problem, the black, red, and purple spread through Sargus, filling him up, the borders assuming jagged lines. Now he was mostly blues and golds. Colors Dolvek thought of as safer. He hadn't been able to completely codify the internal palettes of others, but the inner black was not good.

Sargus had fallen asleep reading. Blinking to focus on the real world as much as he could, Rivvek barely made out the glint of the other elf's goggles in the scant light that crept in from outside. A full moon.

"I'm sorry to wake you," Rivvek whispered.

"I shouldn't have fallen asleep," Sargus answered. "Shall I—?"

"No," Rivvek interrupted. "Let me do it. I need the practice."

Rivvek heard an intake of breath as if Sargus had been about to object, but the Artificer held his tongue.

A prince still has pride, Rivvek chided himself, *even a magic-crippled one.*

Rivvek rubbed his eyes, clearing away scratchy motes of "sleep" from the corners. He took a long deep breath, held it, let it out again.

Mustering a supreme effort of will, Rivvek forced his inner power to its utmost. Veins stood out on his forehead. His scars grew hot then aching—pain a constant chaser to the savor of his magic now—and fire raged forth: a gleaming white flame no bigger than the wisp atop the wick of a lit candle hovered above the tip of his index finger.

Warm illumination filled the tent, revealing the smiling face of Sargus where he sat in the strange folding-chair contraption of brass and leather that let him adjust the back to recline or sit up straight if needed. Rivvek didn't know how it could be as comfortable as Sargus claimed.

Thoughts focused on the bit of mystic flame, Rivvek crossed the tent and lit a lantern sitting upon a small camp table. Wiping a bead of sweat from his cheek, Rivvek scratched absently at his nightshirt, as the pain in his scars faded with the magic. The heat would take longer to dissipate, a side effect for which none had been able to provide adequate explanation.

"Find anything we missed?" Rivvek nodded at the leather tome open on Sargus's lap.

"No." Sargus closed the volume, shifting it from his lap to a nearby camp table. "We do still need to make sure we take care of the Stone Lord, just in case—"

"One son and two daughters," Rivvek interrupted. He waved to his left in the vague direction of the other Aiannai tents, the temporary homes of those who had followed him to Oot hoping their prince and their new status as Oathkeepers would save them from the Aern. "Each to inherit in an order we've already hammered out. They relayed their request via Caz's warsuit Silencer. I handled it on my last trip."

"Who took them in?"

"Is it horrible that I don't remember?" Rivvek yawned. "But with Lady Flame, the Sea Lord, Lady Air, and the Stone Lord . . ."

"That's all of the elemental council dealt with except for Hasimak." Sargus yawned despite himself. "He is more powerful than you realize. Were he to oppose us, he could still—"

"No." Rivvek pulled his nightshirt over his head revealing Kholster's scars upon his back: a diamond shape at the base of his spine with two parallel lines marking each facet, the right-angled wedges at each shoulder, and a thumb-width line along his spine. Far from the only things that marked his back, the scars of the First of One Hundred merely filled in the space not marked by the various elemental foci that dotted his back in winglike arcs in failed attempts to restore the full might of his magic.

Once . . . he cut the thought off ruefully and reached for his traveling clothes. *Once these clothes were clean and fresh.* They were rank from the multiple visits to and from Port Ammond, but he could get a change of clothes when he got there. A bath, too. He'd almost given in to the temptation to bring a cleaning wardrobe, but doing so had felt too extravagant. "We'll go with your strategy."

"It's risky. Even with the elemental lords and ladies siding with you, the people could still riot. Even if Hasimak is with us, he will never turn on his own people. If the citizens revolt . . . he has always been loyal to the crown. Longer than the crown has existed, actually, and there are far more non-magic-using Eldrennai than there have ever been. Aern have proved how much trouble opponents without magic can be. The plan is—"

"Not as risky as you think it is." Rivvek heard footsteps outside his tent flap. Two steps took him close enough to throw them open. He smiled when doing so revealed Brigadier Bhaeshal, his personal Aeromancer.

"Just happened to be in the area, Bash?" Rivvek teased.

"Finally used to your new schedule." She smiled. Dressed as Rivvek was in a traveling tunic, trousers, and boots, Bhaeshal would have made Hasimak's nose wrinkle in dismay at her lack of formal robes, but they weren't really all that sensible for long flights. "Lord Artificer." She nodded to Sargus, the light from the candle reflected in the masklike band of steel that was her elemental foci. She looked back at him with those pale white crystalline eyes, and he returned her gaze warmly.

"Lady Aeromancer," Sargus nodded back.

"Will you both be coming?"

"Perhaps I ought to stay and . . ." Sargus trailed off.

"Look after my father?" Rivvek smiled. "I wish there were something you could do to change his fate, but there isn't. I need you with me . . . to stop Hasimak from taking the throne."

"Please don't even jest about that." Sargus got up.

Rivvek tried not to let it worry him. Yes, Hasimak was the oldest living Eldrennai, but it was hard to imagine how he could be a threat to . . . well, to the Aern if it came down to it. No, Rivvek was forced to ask kholster Rae'en for assistance. It would be sad to see Hasimak go, but if that was the required sacrifice to save as many of Rivvek's people, as many of the Eldrennai, as he could. Rivvek intended to make that sacrifice and any others the gods demanded.

"Don't forget the book." He gestured, and Sargus picked the heavy tome up off of the camp table.

"My prince . . ." Sargus put a hand on Rivvek's shoulder and seemed momentarily surprised by the scars beneath his tunic, still hot to the touch even through the fabric. "Maybe she won't kill him."

"Kings die. A good king dies for his people when it is required." Rivvek's voice cracked as he whispered the words. Believing them didn't take dismiss their sting in the slightest. "You just promise me we'll make his sacrifice mean something."

They flew before dawn, sunrise catching up with them halfway to Port Ammond. The rising light lent the flowing myr grass a fiery aspect. Rivvek, carried by Bhaeshal's Aeromancy, caught himself staring down at it and remembering another departure one hundred and thirteen years before.

*

He'd been scarless then, a haughty elemental lord with command of all four elements as was his birthright. A Flamewing, like his mother, when he worked magic wings of fire sprouted from his back. A glory to behold. It had been like armor, that pride, and Kholster had cracked it.

The Aern himself, First of One Hundred, stood in the last light of the third day of the Grand Conjunction, bone-steel mail—uledinium, his people had called it, but Rivvek would never dare to refer to it as that again—denim trousers belted at the waist with knotted bone-steel chain. Even those clunky boots had seemed grand to the prince. A Vael princess named Kari (not-yet-queen), her head petals cascading over Kholster's shoulder as she leaned against him, watched Rivvek with sad, wide eyes.

"You are right," Rivvek said hoarsely. "What you say is true. My father told me I should believe your version of any history you chose to share with me and, hard as it is, I do. But, Kholster, what would you have me do? How can I fix this? My people. My ancestors. There is no excuse for what they did to you. No excuse for my father's order at As You Please. No excuse for the mistreatment of the Vael. Not for any of it. I came here ready to hate you. Maybe I did hate you at first, but now . . ."

"There is nothing you can do, Oathbreaker prince," Kholster said, his voice gentle. "But I, or my representative, will return again in one hundred years for the next Conjunction if for no other reason than that you have heard and believed. You have my oath on it."

Rivvek opened his mouth to object.

"Unasked for," Kholster laughed. "I know."

"I will find a way," Rivvek answered. "I will find a way, not to make things right, but as right as they can be."

Kholster laughed again. "Good hunting then, but I fear your quarry is long dead, if it ever existed."

"Princess Kari," Rivvek shook his head. "Is there anything I can offer the Vael other than my apology?"

"The Vael have no Litany to recite against you, Prince Rivvek." Kari smiled pityingly at him. "You are guilty of nothing in my—or our—eyes. Keep it that way and we ask nothing more. If Kholster agrees, you are even welcome in The Parliament of Ages."

Kholster nodded his assent.

"Such," Rivvek answered, "is my intent."

"No promise?" Kholster asked.

"I swear that it is my intent, but I cannot read what the future may hold . . . and accidents happen."

CHAPTER 2

BURN IT DOWN

Sparks flashed underground, pinpoints of light reflected in reptilian eyes as each rasping scrape of flint and steel briefly illuminated the scale-covered bodies of the invaders. General Tsan exulted in the percussive rhythms pounded out by the Zaurruk handlers behind him in the tunnel, their holding song keeping the massive serpents in check as they shifted impatiently, longing to strike. Cutting the air with a precise bob of his wedge-shaped head, Tsan put a foreclaw on the top of the gray-scaled firelighter's cranium just between its eye ridges.

<<You are relieved, third hatchling.>> Tsan tapped the phrase in Zaurtol with a few sharp twitches of his tail.

<<Yes, General,>> the firelighter ducked low on all fours, sprayer nozzle and striker still gripped in his forepaws, head touching the stone floor of the tunnel. The peculiar rig of glass, brass, and leather strapped to his back sloshed as he moved. <<I'm sorry there isn't enough good air for the flames.>>

<<Blackdamp,>> Tsan tapped with a dismissive flex of his tail. Just when a little firedamp might have been useful. At least it wasn't cold. The body heat of the assembled attack force helped moderately in that regard, but the magic of the Root Tree overhead was responsible for most of it.

Tsan's nictating membranes flicked up and down over his slit-pupiled eyes. Once. Twice. He peered back at the retreating firelighter. Was that one the third hatchling of the second brood of Marsis, or was he conflating him with one of the Zaurruk handlers? Bah! It hardly mattered. He waved the firelighter away, turning to his personal guard with their black scales banded by narrow stripes of iridescent blue, an odd contrast to Tsan's scales of ruddy red.

<<What's the breath count?>> Tsan tapped.

<<Three-quarters of a candlemark for the Zaur. Twice that for the Sri'Zaur,>> Kuort answered. Plenty of time. Tsan didn't know how warmbloods survived with such limitations. Unable to hold their breath for so much as a candlemark or to survive being frozen . . . it astounded him that there were still so many warmbloods in the world.

Good. Tsan's forked tongue flicked out, tasting the stale atmosphere of the tunnel. Sealing vents in active sections of the maze of underground passages that comprised Xasti'Kaur, the Shadow Road, made timing tricky at certain strategic phases of the plan, but it could also catch the Eldrennai by surprise and leave them gasping in the blackdamp if they figured out what the Sri'Zaur were actually planning before the shard-wielding assassins of Asvrin's Shades sowed confusion and death among those who had lulled themselves into a false sense of immortality.

Asvrin, Tsan thought, *I am so proud of your rise to power . . . though I am no longer your mother. You, even more than Dryga, are one to keep an eye on, if not a claw in.*

Tsan turned away from his guard, dropping to all fours and peering up at his army's current objective. The stone, far colder than the air around it, hurt the joints of his forepaws, a sign that his gender switch was soon approaching. The switch, he did not doubt, was responsible for turning his mind to children from his previous clutches . . . those he could still recall.

Tsan preferred being female; he felt more agile, more lithe, and even his scales were smoother, more supple. But the timing . . . taking the time to mother another brood at all, much less in wartime, was unthinkable. He'd had to take too many new names, stop and restart his career too many times to make that sacrifice again. Heresy or not. Anger ripped through him, speeding his heartbeat, diminishing his air reserves, and Tsan reined the line of thought in. Resisting the gender switch enflamed emotions, wreaking havoc with impulse control. Letting it happen meant peace and steadiness, but it would have to wait.

Filling his mind with an inferno, scourging his mind of all distraction beyond his current purpose, Tsan deliberately slowed his heartbeat. Eyes half-lidded and lazy, he channeled the confidence he'd felt at Na'Shie when he had successfully cut off all hope of aid to the Eldrennai from the human kingdoms beyond the Sri'Zauran Mountains. One last step and the way would be prepared.

But first the flames. He stretched his jaws wide, pops of temporary dislocation music to his auditory receptors.

<<Brazz,>> Tsan tapped, lingering on his Prime Flamefang's name. He'd done as he'd promised the alchemists back home, had given their Zaur firelighter and his accompanying device a chance. He was unsurprised that they had failed. Still, there were numerous ways to start a fire—a few extra for Sri'Zaur such as Brazz. *I may need his help with more delicate matters before the week is out . . . but first we burn the Vael.* Wedged head angling up like a hound sniffing the air, Tsan crept in closer to the mass of tree roots exposed by his Zaur's tunneling. Digging a foreclaw into the wood, he chuffed as the tiny root hairs wriggled away from him in a futile attempt at escape. The Vael Root Tree was as weak as a human in its way.

Tsan's humor died when the sap welling up from beneath his black claw was a honeyed amber color. The youngest Root Tree, yes, but transmuted enough, even at this early stage in his root taking, to have a different sap from the rest of its race, the Vael.

It would have so much easier to get the warlord's Vael blood sample before the battle even started, Tsan mused. *Alas.*

What Warlord Xastix wanted with samples from the Weeds, scarbacks, and stump ears, Tsan did not know. He did not need to know. His place was merely to deliver the blood and, if possible, a treaty with the Weeds. None of that, of course, erased his desire to know.

<<Get Brazz up here.>> General Tsan snapped his claws in the vague direction of the three guards nearest him. After a brief bit of shuffling, an older Sri'Zaur with yellow scales marked by zigzagged lines of fiery orange padded near.

<<You want something burned, General?>> the Sri'Zaur clicked softly, rising up to stand, bipedal, when he reached his commanding officer. <<Move aside and let Brazz start you a nice warm fire.>>

Move aside? Tsan's anger flared, accompanied by a sharp abdominal pain. *How dare that old—*

Ah. Eagerness. Tsan recognized the gleam in Brazz's eyes and released his ill humor, his battle calm reasserting control of his emotions. Fire was the barren old reptile's life, his only love; why not let him do his job and admire him for his dedication? Had he not burned Na'Shie? <<Very well. How long?>>

Brazz withdrew a flask from one of the pouch-like pockets lining the leather vest that hugged his chest tightly, matching the lines of his form. Sulfur and citrus odors bit the air as Brazz uncapped the flask. He wafted the elixir beneath his nostrils, savoring its acrid aroma before downing its contents in one long pull.

Tsan resisted the urge to demand one of the alchemical flasks then and there.

Patience, he chided himself, *or they must all reveal your heresy or share the guilt.* Tsan knew commanders who would, but no . . . it was enough that his soldiers overlooked the ruddy red of his once-black scales and what that color change meant. He would approach Brazz about an alchemical remediation on the old Flamefang's sleep cycle. Tsan peered over the assembled Zaur and Sri'Zaur, entertaining a premature notion about commandeering a flask from one of his newer Flamefangs. But . . . no, best to go to Brazz directly. Dragonvenom was useful for its effect on a Flamefang, true, but it had other, less well-known uses. . . . Uses with which he knew Brazz to be well acquainted. And Brazz wouldn't ask any questions or wag tongue or tail about it.

Why staving off the gender switch remained heresy, Tsan understood up to a point, but he refused to let such foolish convention keep him from seeing this war to its end. Why forbid females to fight, especially since his venom was so much more deliciously toxic when he was female? It had made sense when they had first fled into the depths to recoup their strength and even in the years between wars when repopulation was vital, but during the war, when the ranks already brimmed with eager soldiers thirsty for Eldrennai blood?

Tsan watched hungrily as Brazz returned the empty flask to his belly pack. The Sri'Zaur's eyes lit from within as the dragonvenom worked its magic, blue flame spreading from his slit pupils to his orange markings, filling the corridor with light. How Tsan envied such—

Later, Tsan told himself. *You still have time. First, burn the Weeds. Focus!*

<<How long?>> General Tsan repeated.

"Not long," Brazz cackled, wasting breath in a series of grating hisses as he reached into a separate pouch belted to his abdomen and began withdrawing pawfuls of dark powdered metal, which he tossed onto the roots, letting it coat them as much as possible. "Not long. Just a little seasoning to kindle our hate. Help it bite. Help it spread. The Zaurruk will breach the surface when I signal?"

<<Of course!>> General Tsan tapped harder than he'd intended.

Brazz opened his mouth to say or ask something but clamped it shut as if thinking the better of it. He offered the general a respectful throat baring in its stead.

<<Get on with it.>> General Tsan turned away back to his troops. <<Don't forget,>> Tsan tapped as he left Brazz to his work, <<Warlord Xastix wants the blood of a Vael brought to him as soon as possible. Captain Dryga has already gone racing homeward with the blood of an Aern and an Eldrennai. Let's make sure we're the ones who complete the warlord's set. Yes?>>

And then it will be me who is gifted with a shard as a sign of the warlord's trust, not Dryga.

Dryga, I should have crushed your egg. I wonder if I will regret not having crushed Asvrin's, in the end . . .

A hundred enthusiastic vibrations washed over him, banishing the thoughts. His forked gray tongue tasted the air with relish.

<<To His secret purpose,>> some of the Zaur were tapping.

General Tsan chuffed, surrendering to their enthusiasm by tapping out the same message. It was so nice when Kilke's plans aligned with his own. Tsan had wanted to burn a Root Tree ever since he'd discovered the Weeds could grow them, and now he had orders to burn several, if needed. No ill-timed quirk of biology would stand in his way. He refused to allow it.

*

Sleeping soundly on a bed of moss, Prince Kholburran stirred. He reached out for Malli, possessed of a distinct notion she had gotten up to patrol. His lips twitched up at the corners in a reassured smile when his fingertips found her shoulder, the warmth of her smooth bark reassuring at first, but then not so much. If Malli was still in bed, then what was that noise?

Sensing motion as Kholburran rolled off the bed, the lichen-covered ceiling responded with a soft glow of mixed blues and yellows, casting an uneven green illumination over the sparsely appointed room. Running a hand through his spiky red head petals, Kholburran yawned, widely exposing the thorny protrusions from his unpruned dental ridge that had earned him his most hated nickname.

"Come back to bed, Snapdragon," Malli purred, still half-asleep.

Kholburran snorted, amused by the giddy pardons love granted so lightly. The rotted nickname did not sound bad in the slightest when Malli used it. As a sproutling, he had wondered whether pruning and scoring his dental ridges like some Vael did would put an end to the nickname, but it seemed too painful and vain. He knew back in the slave days Uled had required it, considering the undifferentiated ridges to be a flaw, but Kholburran liked his mouth better without any useless carving.

"Do you hear that?" Kholburran whispered. *Was hear even the right word?*

Malli came awake in an instant, rolling out of bed and seizing her heartbow in one swift motion. One of the many things he loved about her was how she paid attention to his instincts even though he was a boy-type person. She understood he wasn't some fragile thing to be protected and hidden away until he was old enough to Take Root. She—

"Take Root." Kholburran surveyed his surroundings in the increasing illumination, his jade eyes, seemingly without iris or pupil, taking in everything. At first he'd thought it was a sound that had awoken him, but now that he was paying full attention, it felt more like a vibration . . . as if he were trembling all the way down to his core wood, not violently, but enough to notice.

Kholburran paced the room, toes squinching in the moist mossy carpet. He stopped, closing his eyes. Turning slowly in place, reaching out, senses open, he quested for some inkling of what disturbed him.

Uncle Tran was getting better at being a Root Tree, but he was still learning. The rooms within him tended to feel sparse. His beds clung low to the ground more like drier raised extensions of the soft mossy carpeting than mattresses and sheets. He finally had proper doors, serviceable utilitarian things with no locks, but they worked. The shelving, what there was of it, ran more along the lines of conveniently placed and proportioned bumps-on-a-log than the elaborate craftsmanship of the Twin Root Trees Hashan and Warrune where Kholburran had grown up.

Kholburran counted to seven before opening his eyes. Had anything changed?

A thin line of sap ran down from the edges of the room along the join between ceiling and wall. Sap? What was Uncle Tran trying to do? Grow windows? Kholburran ran his thumb and forefingers together, his own sap-like sweat slick beneath them, the piney scent filling his nostrils.

"No," Kholburran hissed under his breath. "No no no no."

Trees in The Parliament of Ages cry out when they burn, passing the news of the fire ahead of the flame.

Having never traveled beyond his homeland, Kholburran didn't know whether all trees reacted to flame in this way or if the local trees had learned it through proximity to Root Trees and Vael over the years. Kholburran had felt this sensation, so different that he felt it in his chest as a pang of general anxiety rather than actual noise, before, and it was very close to what he sensed now.

"You too hot, Snapdragon?" Malli asked. "Are you sick or something? You're sweating."

"I'm sapping defensively." Kholburran dashed to the wall where his wooden warpick was propped. Boy-type persons were not permitted proper heartbows, but Kholburran had tried anyway, beseeching his uncle for a gift of living wood. Instead of a limb suitable for shaping into a heartbow, as Kholburran had hoped against hope, Uncle Tran had given him a branch obviously meant to become a melee weapon. Kholburran had tried to convince the wood to grow into a sword or an axe. Either would have been fine, but the weapon flatly refused to thrive in any form other than a warpick. As result, he'd named it Resolute (Mr. Stubborn when he was aggravated) and done his best to learn how to use it.

Sweeping Resolute up and onto his back where it hung in place despite their combined lack of bone-steel or Aern blood, Kholburran placed one donkey-like ear against the wall, splaying his hands on either side of his head. The vibration shook his dental ridges.

"Great Xalistan," he mouthed. The cry of burning tree was coming from Uncle Tranduvallu.

CHAPTER 3
THE FALL OF TRANDUVALLU

Zaurruk burst through the ground, the inrush of oxygen fueling the blaze that engulfed Tranduvallu's roots with explosive intensity. Plumes of smoke and fire rose around the bodies of the massive serpents as rank after rank of Zaur poured out of the underground tunnel system wreathed in the scent of wood smoke.

<<Kill all but one!>> General Tsan pounded on the ground, his words amplified by the tails of his personal guard as they echoed the same message one beat behind his. <<To His secret purpose!>>

His infantry, comprised mostly of unnamed Zaur, poured out after the Zaurruk, the first rank shielding Brazz and a dozen other Flamefangs, each clad in leather multi-pocketed vests and belly pouches identical to Brazz's. Zigzag bands glowing blue fire marked their yellow scales with the infusion of dragonvenom and pyrotechnic potential.

A Named Zaur approached, leading Tsan's deep walker. Its rock hide grated against the ground as it moved. Waiting for four unnamed Zaur to likewise bring his personal guard their mounts, the general laughed at the first screams of Vael in pain: an enemy's agony ever the delight.

Once all five beasts were in place, Tsan and his guard mounted in unison, springing onto the backs of their deep walkers and slapping themselves into the chain harnesses with practiced synchronicity. Twenty other riders rode up into position. The rock hide of their eyeless mounts looked deadly enough in shades of granite, the hardened protrusions along their shoulders, knees, and sides lending them an air of invulnerability—juggernauts of the deep. Tsan and his guards' mounts served as more threatening examples of the breed than those ridden by lesser Sri'Zaur, each with skin like obsidian, the front of their deep walkers shorn clean of hair where other mounts sported lengths of braid from the smooth surface where, on some other animal, a head might be.

The attending Zaur handed Tsan his Skria, its four-foot blade heavy in his hands, hurting his wrist. *Already?* Tsan cursed inwardly at the tenderness of his joints. *I should have more time than this. I need to get some blasted dragonvenom!* Not that the alchemical mixture would make his joints stop hurting. Only allowing the transformation would do that. Ironically, he would have been able to wield the Skria fine as a female, it was only in transition when—

<<General Tsan?>>

Too distracted to recognize the speaker, Tsan shook off his personal preoccupation and ordered the charge, galloping up out of the tunnel, into battle.

Aboveground, smoke, fire, and chaos reigned. Brazz and his fellow Flamefangs belched sprays of liquid fire upon the bark of the still-growing Root Tree. Scattered Vael coaxed spouts of water from the nature spirits dwelling in nearby reservoirs, directing them carefully toward the flames only to watch the water go from liquid to steam with no sign of quenching the blaze. Other Vael fired deadly arrows from their heartbows, kept aloft by what Tsan could only assume were more of the annoyingly cooperative spirits with which Uled's third race showed such an affinity. Tsan hated the way the Weeds could cheat the bonds of earth and soar the air like the Eldrennai . . . not, of course, that he hadn't come prepared.

*

Kholburran had imagined many things happening when he raised the alarm. Being cornered by his own bodyguards was not one of them. Malli stood between him and the door, a gentle frown on her lips. She'd abandoned her usual beaded midriff-baring top and doeskin leggings for a beautiful suit of leather armor worked in brown and green with golden leaflike highlights.

Functional and attractive. Leave it Malli to redesign the ceremonial armor of the Root Guard into something in which one could actually fight, even if it did look like it might be harder to breathe with so much surface area covered. Kholburran mourned the way it disguised Malli's curves, the way the helmet covered her orchid petal hair, but not as much as he hated not being allowed to have a similar suit of armor. He didn't care how hard it would be to breathe with that much material covering his bark. He wanted to fight. But . . . girl-type persons fought and boy-type persons grew into big strong Root Trees and pollinated. Such was the way of things.

"Tran is burning!" Kholburran shouted. "We can't just stand here!"

"And we're making plans to get you safely back to Hashan and Warrune as soon as we have a clear exit, Snapdragon," Malli explained patiently.

That's not what I meant, he thought. Kholburran knew Malli was trying not to sound condescending. Trying was not the same as succeeding, however. Hearing a noise behind her, Malli stepped clear of the door, silently drawing the longsword belted at her waist. She resheathed it when Arri, Lara, Mavyn, and Seizal filed into the bedroom, all clad in armor similar to hers.

"But I can fight, Molls." Kholburran unslung his warpick. As deadly as it looked with its lacquered dark wood, Malli gave it the same sort of glance one might give a sproutling's dolly.

"I know you can," Malli cooed. "Of course you can. I spar with you, and you're not bad, but if you die here we'll have lost two Root Trees."

"It's not fair that I can't fight just because I'm a boy-type person." Kholburran regretted the words as soon as he'd uttered them.

"That's not the only reason, my prince," Arri interrupted. "It's that you are a royal boy-type person. If you were anyone else I'd happily petition Queen Kari for an exemption. But, and it pains me to say this—"

"I'm more useful as a Root Tree," Kholburran snarled, dental thorns bared.

There it was, the irkanth in the shadows, now out in the open for all to see. Of course, they ignored it. They were girl-type persons. Girl-type persons always got their way.

"I'm just trying to say—" Kholburran began. He stopped. Only Malli was bothering to look him in the eye, the others seemed . . . embarrassed by his outburst, looking at the walls, the floor, the door, or his bare chest. He let it go.

"We've got to leave!" Faulina shouted as she burst into the room bringing with her the scent of burnt roses. Scorched green sap ran across her smoldering breastplate from a nasty wound to her left shoulder, the pauldron hanging loose where something had sliced through the strap that secured it to her armor.

"The rest of the Root Guard?" Malli asked.

"They can't make it, Captain." Faulina shook her head. "There are hundreds of Zaur and some of them . . . I've never seen Zaur do what some of them are doing. I've never seen Zaur as big as some of these. They have troops that spit liquid fire that won't scrape off and others who—"

*

<<Archers,>> Tsan pounded, <<Fire!>>

A volley of crossbow bolts peppered the moonlit sky. Heartbow-wielding Weeds scattered, some avoiding the barrage, many crying out as the cruel shafts pierced armor and bark. Tsan didn't care whether the archers hit the flying Weeds or not. He was far more interested in the layout of the Vael city. So far, this one seemed astonishingly basic. He'd counted six outposts—glorified tree forts by his assessment—in the largest of the Redwoods and Grove Oaks surrounding the Root Tree at their center.

Four of the six were already burning, and the natural wooden walkways where branches from different trees merged together to form an easily navigable overhead route linking them to the Root Tree were engulfed in flame. He and his cavalry had already charged twice into the fray but were hanging back now until they were needed, resting the deep walkers. Tsan had been prepared to lead the charge up any one of the trees if needed, the six long-splayed toes of their mounts granting them access to routes not available to more traditional land creatures, but it had proved disappointingly unnecessary.

A great hissing cheer went up amongst his soldiers as the Root Tree shifted, dropping several feet to the base of the tunnel beneath it then falling northward with a loud creaking thump that shook the forest floor.

"Root Tree down," one of his guards laughed.

Was that one second hatchling of the Twelfth Brood of Ixxant or first hatchling of the Second Brood of Naxxint? Tsan couldn't keep them straight with all the competing battlefield odors obscuring their pheromones.

Kuort, Tsan's most senior guard, drummed his claws along his Skria to get Tsan's attention. Once he had it, Kuort wordlessly pointed a sap-slick foreclaw at one of the still-standing outposts where a squad of Sri'Zaur with mottled scales and light armor clung to the bark of the tree. His Gliders weren't quite as stealthy as Asvrin's Shades, but against the Weeds . . .

<<Archers!>> Tsan thumped. <<Maneuver Six, toward the closest unburning outpost!>> He paused three beats for them to shift their aims. <<Fire!>>

Tsan's grip tightened painfully on his Skria as some of the airborne Weeds flew back toward the outpost to avoid the deadly crossbow bolts. One young Weed, flowing white head petals flouncing about her head in the night air, drew close enough, and one of the mottled-scaled Sri'Zaur pounced, leaping free of its lofty perch, webs of skin between its front and rear paws drawing tight and catching the air. At the last possible moment, the Weed seemed to sense the danger, spinning and gaining altitude . . . not in time to evade the Glider, but to let loose a curse as the airborne Sri'Zaur sunk its fangs into the Weed's throat and thrust the tips of its Skreel knives under her breastplate in a reverse-gripped double-thrust.

As the Weed fell from the sky, the Glider leapt free aiming for another flying target. Seconds later, the rest of its squad was in the sky as well.

Oh, Maker, Tsan thought warmly, *you designed us to be so mighty and we . . . we have made such improvements.*

*

"—who look like twisted Jun Beasts," Faulina continued. "Who knows what else. Tranduvallu is lost, we—"

A sudden shifting of the room cut her off as the floor dropped several feet out from under them. All the Vael except Malli lost their footing and dropped flat, the impact inflicting bruises and, in Arri's case, a broken arm.

"What the hells—" Kholburran began only to curse as the room shifted again sending all of them sliding along the floor to smack into the far wall.

Malli leapt between Kholburran and the wall, shielding him, protecting his head as best she could with her chest, cradling him. Kholburran's sap froze at the loud snap when Malli struck one of Tranduvallu's knob-like shelves. Hoping it was only her heartbow, knowing it wasn't, Kholburran pulled free once the room came to a halt. Knickknacks and tokens from their travels to other Root Cities dotted the wall-now-floor in broken pieces.

"You okay, Snapdragon?" Malli wheezed.

Her heartwood is cracked. The words skittered through his mind, an unwanted assessment, automatic just like Malli had trained him. *Arri is going to insist we leave Malli behind. I only have moments to—*

"Her core is compromised. We have to—" Arri started.

"We don't leave Malli. Help me get her back to Hashan and Warrune," Kholburran cut her off, "or you will have to fight me all the way there. At every turn I will bite, scratch, kick, or try to escape. Help me get her back there and I'll do everything I can to make the journey quick and easy."

"But her heartwood—" Seizal started.

"Is something I can fix when we get her back to the Twins." Kholburran's voice was even, deadly.

"Only if we . . ." Malli's voice trailed off, eyes closing in pain.

"Well," Kholburran smiled at her, "who else was I going to marry. If you're willing?"

"Wait. I think I can—" Malli moved to try to stand, an increased flow of sap and moisture from her exposed cambium seeping from the edge of her breastplate where the dark core of heartwood was exposed with a further crack.

Kholburran had never seen a Vael faint before, but Malli went down with a sharp intake of breath and low grunt.

Grabbing his crumpled shirt from a corner of the room, Kholburran tied it around Malli's waist using the remains of a broken chair to stabilize her and (hopefully) prevent any further breakage.

"We ought to leave her," Arri said standing over him, hand resting close to the wedge-shaped scars that marked the bark over his shoulder blades. "I know you've been spending a lot of time with her . . . em . . . gardening . . . but—"

"She comes with me or I don't go." The color in Kholburran's jade eyes developed a whorl of amber at their center. "I swear it."

"You boy-type persons," Arri said, shaking her head. "I don't know what goes on in your handsome little heads. All right. Calm down, Snapdragon. Don't go all mock-Aern on me. I'm the one trying to save your bark." She sighed, looking back at the other Root Guards. "Faulina, you and Seizal pull up that moss bed for a stretcher. Snapdragon, you stay right behind me or Lara at all times. Mavyn, you take up the rear. Let's go be stupid and hope Xalistan is with us."

"Not Dienox?" Kholburran asked.

"Dienox is already against us." Mavyn spat.

"We're hunted now," Lara agreed. "It's Xalistan for us and Gromma for Molls."

*

Sandwiched between protectors, Kholburran couldn't help checking over his shoulder to ensure Malli was still suspended on the remnants of their mossy bed between Faulina and Seizal. She lay on her side, the vinous color of her heartwood obscured by his makeshift attempt at arborism, but he couldn't help but see it jutting out sickeningly just below the base of her breastplate in his mind's eye.

Can I really heal that? he thought in dismay.

Marriage was rare among the Vael, more so among the royals, and even less common with princes expected to Take Root. It bound them together and made them one far more literally than the matrimonial joining amongst other races. Kholburran was counting on the rejuvenating effect it had on both germinator and pollinator, renewing both individuals physically as it reworked them . . . optimizing the pair for pollination with each other— resprouting them as hybridizations of what they were before.

But that wasn't all there was to it; their spirits became linked so strongly that injuries to one could wound them both. That link would extend Malli's life tremendously, making her nigh immortal once he eventually Took Root. As a Root Wife she would be his voice and his caretaker, deciding who could use his pollen to produce sproutlings, and his strength would be her strength.

It was a price Kholburran was willing, even eager, to pay. But would Malli want that for herself? He knew she liked him, hoped she loved him as much as he loved her, but it was so hard to tell with girl-type persons. They were so intent on the physical, on . . . gardening. Saying whatever they thought he wanted to hear and then . . .

True, Malli had never shown any interest in proper pollination, just in being together the way Aern and Vael were together . . . and that certainly couldn't produce any sproutlings between two Vael. It was pleasurable and fun, but was that all it was to Malli? He didn't think it was. Even so, this wasn't how he had intended to propose; he'd hoped she would handle that part, though he'd begun to fear she wasn't thinking along those lines. . . .

"Eyes forward," Lara snapped as she drew and fired over Arri, who moved, sword at the ready in her left hand, killing a Zaur as it came lurching out of a nearby passage. "You just might get the chance to use that warpick of yours."

Kholburran winced at the stump of Arri's right arm, where she'd hacked it off at the break.

"What?" Arri asked, noticing his gaze, "you weren't planning on marrying me, too, were you?"

Kholburran shook his head, flushing.

"Then don't worry about my limb. It will grow back all on its own. Though I wouldn't mind a little gardening myself if you're interested."

Kholburran frowned at that, but Arri wasn't looking, already crawling out the door, and the others were trying not to laugh.

All in good fun, Kholburran tried to remind himself as he followed her lead. *She doesn't mean anything by it.*

The seven Vael walked behind Arri through off-kilter hallways, Zaur showing up with greater frequency as they neared an exit. When they reached the kitchens, Kholburran stepped over the body of Hildi, one of his other Root Guards. Three of the cooks were clustered in an unmoving stack against a central island. Dead. One of the cooks seemed to have been killed by Tranduvallu's fall, her head crushed by impact. Hildi, however, was festooned with crossbow bolts. Had she been trying to reach him even after receiving such terrible wounds?

Kholburran guessed he would never know.

Hope I'm worth it, Hildi. I'll do my best to be.

"We're not taking her, too, Snapdragon," Arri hissed, misunderstanding his look.

"We're in luck," Seizal whispered as they clambered over the cluster of cabinets and cooking equipment that blocked the exterior door. "All we have to do is clear this and we should be able to make a run for it."

As if in response, a blast of liquid fire hit the wooden obstacles from outside, and it burst into flames.

"You were saying?" Arri snapped.

Gods, help us, Kholburran prayed.

CHAPTER 4

A DEATH GOD'S TEETH

Cadence Vindalius knelt on her grass meditation mat sweltering in a heat she knew was somewhere else. Warmth bloomed across her cheek as if she leaned too close to a bonfire. Black hair shot through with red and orange streaks clung to her sweaty neck, the ends slowly turning purple (a little more each day) even though she'd cut more than half of it off. She looked up and saw moonlight rather than the cracked stone ceiling of her small dorm cell.

Treetops and fire.

"What are you seeing, Cadence?" The rough voice of Sedric, the dean of the Long Speaker's College, called from only two feet away, but the sound faded as it reached her. She looked back and could barely see him. In his place appeared wavering images of Vael in some sort of armor carrying a wounded Vael between them. As her concentration increased, the stink of roses and pine mixed with suffocating smoke hit her nostrils.

Sedric, with his hawkish features, salt-and-pepper beard, and ornate Long Speaker robes, telescoped away from her, growing more distant with each heartbeat. He walked around in front of her, soft brown eyes peering into her violet-specked gray ones, squinting. "I see flames reflected in your eyes. Where are you?"

Flames? She gritted her teeth, grinding them as if she were crunching god rock. Heat rose up around her, this time of her own making.

That's right, you useless idiot, Hap's voice spat in her head. *Burn him and get out of there. Find me and I'll get you what you need. You belong to me and you know it. Who cares the others are dead? Less of a split that way. Leaves more for us.*

She knew it wasn't really Hap, just her idea of the man who had been her kidnapper, her master, and (eventually) the father of her son haunting her thoughts. Dean Sedric explained (at times repeatedly) it was a sort of sickness that happened from time to time in Long Speakers who possessed more than one talent of the mind.

"Cadence!" Sedric said more sternly, and she drew the flame back, letting it go quietly like coals burned down, almost out, but still glowing and dangerous under the ash. "Can you tell me what you are seeing?"

She couldn't. It wasn't long sight as it had been described to her, more like she was riding in the back of someone else's mind, not understanding or clearly interpreting the information flooding into her. Was that even possible?

37

"It's gone upside down or sideways," Cadence muttered. "The furniture has all fallen up against the door and it's burning. He's going to risk it anyway."

"Risk what, Cadence?" Sedric pleaded. "Who?"

"I don't know," she growled. "It's all out of focus."

*

"Okay." Arri knelt awkwardly over a broken water jug, trying to dampen herself as much as possible, before—

This is dumb, Kholburran thought to himself, *I'm hardier than she is. Slower to burn or wilt. I'm already dripping with sap. I should be the one to bust through the wreckage. She's only got one arm!*

Billowing clouds of black poured from the flaming mass of broken furniture blocking their exit. Heat and smoke choked his lungs (air bladders, really), so he shut them down, but that wouldn't help him breathe with all this smoke and ash covering his bark. He stared hard at the wood and fire-choked doorway, the smoke and fumes stinging his eyes, generating more sap to cover them and lending everything a gauzy out-of-focus cast. Hildi's corpse caught his eye.

There's no one between me and the door. Kholburran and Arri noticed it in nearly the same heartbeat.

"Snapdragon, don't!" Arri shouted.

Snapdragon did.

Sweeping his warpick over his head the Vael prince charged the fiery obstruction, bringing the thornlike head of Resolute down once, twice, three times. Each blow cracked and splintered wood, but the mass of debris refused to move. Steam hissed off his outer bark, but his sap was cooking off first.

Still safe, he told himself. *Not burning.*

With the next few blows, chunks of debris broke loose, but the increased airflow only strengthened the flames. Sending gouts of fire rushing up, enveloping Kholburran as he continued to strike and kick the mass. A high creaking touched his ears, his movements growing harder to make. His outer bark, the soft pliant layer that did such a good job of mimicking all the tactile pleasures of Eldrennai skin, pulled taut, cracking.

Gromma, his eyes widened with fear. *I'm drying out!*

A spark of fire lit upon his arm and caught.

*

Welts raised on the back of Cadence's hands, spreading to her forearms, right shoulder, side, and cheek from the heat as whoever she was touching charged the flaming debris. This was wrong, utterly wrong, Long Speaking was from Long Speaker to Long Speaker or established through eye contact, and even then it had to be a willing connection. This remote link was . . . was . . .

"No!" she screamed, pushing the heat away, sucking it out of her burns and thrusting it away, not here, but there. Wherever there was. With a victorious cry, the mind she'd been touching (Snapdragon? Was that really a name?) burst through the blockage tumbling out onto the ground. Safe, for the moment, on parched dry dirt in black grass where fire had already spent itself and spread elsewhere.

How do I break free of this?

The slap caught her by surprise. She blinked to find Dean Sedric standing over her, ready to strike her again with his open palm. He looked like a man who'd just soiled his breeches and was afraid he might have to give a repeat performance before he got to the latrine.

"I'm back." She coughed, rubbing her jaw, doubly glad to feel no sign of the welts that had raised there. "I couldn't pull loose of his head." She didn't realize she'd been smelling a deep forest until, odor gone, the scent of grass mat, sweat, and incense resumed their normal places in her olfactory palette.

"Does your jaw hurt?" Sedric asked, his voice gruff. "I'm sorry, but I couldn't get through to your mind. Where were you?"

"My jaw never hurts." The last time she'd felt any pain in her mouth at all was when Kholster had extracted her cracked and broken molars—teeth she'd damaged crunching god rock to enhance her Far Flame ability in a futile attempt to kill him—and generously replaced them with some of his own.

That had to be why when the death god died or, rather, when the new death god rose to power, Cadence Vindalius had felt it in her gums. If crunching god rock was "twisting crystal," what did one call having a deity's teeth rooted and living at the back of your jaw?

"A different tactic then. I apologize if this seems redundant," Sedric said, visibly relaxing back into his role as stern-faced educator. "But could you confirm for me where exactly you believe yourself to be now?"

"Back home." Cadence patted the grass meditation mat at the center of her cold stone room.

Sedric frowned, brow furrowed as if her answer was insufficient.

"Fine." She rolled her eyes. "In the Long Speaker's College."

He kept staring at her, hands clasped behind his back.

"In the Guild Cities . . ." Cadence watched the older man closely for a sign that she had said enough. "On the lower continent. Just south of Bridgeland. What? What? I know where I am."

"I know where I am . . . what?" Sedric trailed off, a faint smile on his lips.

"Sir," Cadence scoffed. "I know where I am, sir. Aldo's name, Sedric. Is this really the time for . . ." she trailed off. "'Emotional responses may become muted when a Long Speaker overextends him or herself. It may become necessary to provoke an emotional reaction to assess the extent of the fatigue in trainees,'" she quoted at him.

"As you do not seem to have overextended yourself," Sedric nodded, his eyes twinkling, "do you feel up to trying again? I believe you were Far Seeing, though your lack of control and the volatility of your powers (due probably to the crystal use) did produce rather unusual effects."

That last part sounded like bird squirt to Cadence, but she let it go. The old man was immensely fond of telling her whatever he felt he needed to so that she would try something and then explaining it correctly later (at length) and assigning a reading selection about it that explained far more than she'd ever wanted to know about the subject upon which he prevaricated or glossed over during a practice session.

"This time try to let your mind go," Sedric continued. "Don't reach out for any one thing. Be a seed on the wind, drifting wherever Aldo takes you. Some find that asking him for assistance directly helps focus their minds. So try that if you like. Can you do it?"

Cadence closed her eyes. Body weak from adherence to the days of detoxification rituals and techniques the alternately demanding, kind, and cold elder Long Speaker had given her to do, Cadence cleared her mind and started again at the first circle of expansion.

First inward to feel the core of herself then outward again by degrees. She froze in the middle of the twelfth circle of expansion, her consciousness hanging at the very edge of visual surroundings ready to break free. A cold stone square with nothing more than a cot, a candle, a change of clothes, and the meditation mat. By design, the room encouraged initiates to be bored with it, to force the mind to let go of the body and see beyond.

You can't do it, Hap's voice spat in her mind. *Not without crystal. Sell them those Aernese teeth and you could buy all the rock you want. I don't know what you've let that stuffy old worm stick in your head, but you ain't nothing special without a little taste. Just a load a meaningless useless visions. Useless like you, you stupid, dried up—*

"Ignore the voice and focus," Sedric said gently. "He isn't here and he isn't a Long Speaker. He represents your doubts and your self-loathing. If you feel inadequate, he will tell you that you are. No one can cut you as deeply as you cut yourself."

Cadence fought the surprise she felt every time at Sedric's knowledge of the inner workings of her mind. If he dealt with the same inner turmoil, he would not say, but she decided it did not matter. She was so glad someone understood, she was willing to do whatever it took to make him proud.

"It's not unusual for the most powerful of us to have a touch of madness. Especially when they and their abilities have been so abused for so long. It will take more time before we know how bad the damage is, but so far your talent is impressive even taking into account your crystal twisting."

"Talent?" Cadence looked up from where she knelt on the mat, its coarse construction ablating the worst of the cold from the stone floor, but leaving basket-weave patterns in her skin through her cotton initiate's robes all the same. "I have no talent without—"

Sedric frowned, his only other response a turned back as he walked to the room's tiny door.

"I'll try again," Cadence said at once. "Don't leave. Please, I—" She caught herself. "Please, sir, let me try again."

"Self-doubt is your greatest enemy." Sedric turned back. "You will learn your limits in time. Now I am determining what those limits are for myself. I have evaluated many students. Do not presume to tell me whether or not you have talent." He gave a gravelly half-chuckle. "Try again. If it helps, start out by picturing yourself in the womb. It is warm and comforting and you are safer there than you will ever be again in life."

Visions formed at the outskirts of her mind, but only random phantasms that came without sense or meaning. They fit together somehow . . . she knew they must, but she couldn't see it. *Please, Aldo,* she prayed, *let me see something. Something important. A vision Sedric can use to gauge my abilities like he wants. He says I have a gift. Please, help me unlock it.*

"The girl with the death god's teeth requests a boon." Aldo's voice rang in her mind and in her ears. It reminded her a little of Sedric's voice, but colder. "A favor I find amusing and intriguing to grant. So be it. A vision Dean Sedric can use to judge the extent of your skills and then the unlocking of those talents. If Kholster ever asks, I do hope you will point out that I did exactly and only what you asked of me."

"Ah!" She hissed as a new vision drew her in and pushed her down, her mind erupting and opening as pieces of a puzzle snapped together in her brain.

*

Twisting and writhing in the dark, Cadence tore with her egg tooth at the wet sack of protein from which she must emerge or die; the tiny thing with rust-colored scales she had become in this vision burst free into the sultry atmosphere of the egg crèche. Tasting the air with a minuscule gray tongue, she/it sensed danger. Fighting the urge to eat the rest of her shell casing while it was still fresh, the newborn quested, her (his?) yellow eyes barely open, for the source of alarm.

Behind you! hissed a voice in her mind, high, haughty, and filled with hate . . . but accurate.

The newborn spun, skittering to the right, sliding back between the wall and the rough apple-sized egg of another Sri'Zaur struggling to be born. A wedge-shaped head darted after her, reptilian death wrought in miniature, striking once, but missing. Chemicals flooded the little newborn's brain; every nerve ending screamed for Cadence to flee, to run, to hide, to—

Up and over your fellow broodling's egg, the voice snapped. *The egg tooth is much better than our claws or teeth now. Your brother is big, but stupid. Eat him first and then your egg.*

Scrabbling up and over the nearest leathery sac, tiny claws finding easy purchase in the rough brown casing of her yet-to-be-born brood mate's current home, the newborn started in terror when she was greeted with the hissing jaws of the larger broodling. Striking despite her fear, the newborn used her egg tooth like a mighty horn, first to batter then to pierce. Her brother scratched and mewled, but the newborn could see, as if on a set of designer's schematics, where to strike to find blood and bring death. As she feasted upon her brother, the voice in her head chuckled, soft as a whisper.

Eat the brains and heart, then move on to our other brothers, the voice ordered. *If you kill all twelve and emerge as sole survivor we get to pick a name. I refuse to be called second hatchling of the Twelfth Brood of Lagara.*

Hunt.

Eat.

Devour.

Tired, clawed, and bitten, the slight reptile small enough to fit into a human's cupped hands emerged from the crèche, slick with dark blood. Even the voice in her mind sounded tired. Both breeds, Zaur and Sri'Zaur, were born speaking three languages: Tol, Zaurtol, and Eldrennaic. One in ten thousand hatchlings stepped out to face the crèche guardian, a sole survivor of his clutch . . . but only one in ten thousand years of births and deaths hissed, "I am Xastix" before killing the crèche guardian, too.

*

"Xastix," Cadence coughed as the vision released her. "Who?"

Her ears popped, followed by the same sensation at the center of her skull. Bright sparks of light swam before her eyes. As they cleared, the room drew into a level of pristine clarity the likes of which she had only ever experienced twisting crystal.

Eyes wide, Sedric backed away.

Panic.

Fear.

Power.

Hate.

But not from Sedric. Well, not all from Sedric. Just the first two. The last two were—

Sedric, she meant to speak, but thought instead, *I had a vision and—*

Without meaning to, she sent the vision directly to his mind, showing him, letting him feel exactly what she felt and saw.

"A moment, child." He reeled. "Be still. Let me process this."

And to prove you are not limited to the past . . . , Aldo's voice echoed.

Cadence screamed as her mind jerked free of her body and flew across the Junland Bridge and just beyond Castleguard where four Aern ran from King Mioden's knights.

"The Aern," she choked both on the knowledge that filled her mind and the words as she tried to speak rather than think them at Sedric. "Four of them. Overwatches. They're going to kill them. Tell the kholster of the Token Hundred at South Gate. They belong to Rae'en. I can see the connection stretching all the way to Oot."

As she spoke the words, the world went away, but as it did, the panic left her, replaced by a muted calm.

*

"Overextended at last." The old Long Speaker knelt over the young woman, grimly checking for a pulse. She was warm under his hands, feverish in fact. He found her heartbeat: a faint but steady rhythm beating far more steadily and slower than his own racing heart. She would live. Terrifying as she was, she would survive. *If I let her.*

"Curse you, Kholster," he muttered, forcing himself to his feet, back creaking as he rose. "Leaving me this with which to contend."

He paced slowly around the unconscious woman counterclockwise, chanting very softly in Yvagg, a language he had created solely as a linguistic game when he was a novice. "*Ossec issep ojeg roh. Ilmer issep ojeg soh.*" The words meant very little, merely a mnemonic device to focus his mind, but they helped to make his actions seem mystical, and he was used to them. Speaking the phrase had become a well-worn path through his mind to exactly the portion upon which he needed to call.

Cadence rose lightly into the air, levitating over and settling gently upon her small cot. The old Long Speaker gazed down at her, his face contorted with indecision. If he let her live she would be trouble, but she had been entrusted into his care by the Aern who had scant days ago become the god of death.

He uttered a few more words, extending his left arm. Air rushed around his hand, sending his sleeve flapping. A loud snap sounded, and a long, thin staff appeared in the air. It materialized core first, the outside slowly forming counterclockwise. When it was complete, the staff was six feet tall and held at its tip a cat's-eye stone the size of a hawk's egg, black with a vertical vein of gold running through it. He dug his staff's steel-capped bottom into the trainee's meditation mat and muttered in an irritated tone, "Tell the kholster of the Token Hundred at South Gate? Because they are within walking distance, I presume. Bah! If there is one thing I cannot abide, it is young Long Speakers who do not accept that the world is much smaller than they presume it be."

He turned the staff's eye to face him and peered into it deeply. A small horizontal slit opened in the center of his forehead, revealing a stone exactly matching the one mounted on his staff. When he spoke, a blue nimbus surrounded it, glowing more brightly the longer he continued. "From Sedric, dean of the Guild City Long Speaker's College and Possessor of the Seventh Eye to whomever is currently stationed at the North Gate Relay." He pictured the predetermined geometric shape currently used to designate North Gate. "I have it on . . . good authority . . . that four young Overwatches who have recently passed through your gate have or will shortly run into trouble in Castleguard. You are to relay this information to the kholster of the Token Hundred on the Dwarven side of the gate immediately."

Blue light, visible only to those with Long Skills coalesced around the staff's head, then fired into the air. The energy pierced the wall along the most direct path to North Gate and vanished into the night. After a few moments, the Third Eye closed, and the adrenaline rush that accompanied all successful transmissions pulsed through him.

He paused.

Technically that was sufficient. Technically.

Sedric gazed down at Cadence's slowly breathing body and considered his Seventh Eye. Most Long Speakers had a Third Eye. Advanced Long Speakers had a fourth and perhaps a fifth for discreet communications and for projecting boards and game pieces for the various amusements in which the idle rich liked to engage with one another over long distances. If the Long Speakers used these moments to glean bits and pieces of information from the unprotected minds of the merchants and royals to whom they sold their services at the same time . . . well, that knowledge was kept within the Long Speaker hierarchy, so whom did it actually harm?

Each stone or crystalline eye was implanted into the psychic space every collegially trained Long Speaker housed in their brain, a practical merging of magic and mental power.

Only those with the most calculating, focused minds could survive the implantation process, and though Khalvadian Long Speakers had been long renowned as the best, the Hulsite school of training was finally coming into its own, largely because of Sedric's rise to power in the Guild Cities' school.

Few had a Sixth Eye; it was reserved for messages so secret that no chance of interception could be risked. The Sixth Eye allowed a handful of Long Speakers to communicate directly mind to mind, instantaneously. It was also incredibly draining.

Only three Long Speakers in the whole of Barrone possessed a Seventh Eye. One was the Guild Master of the Khalvadian Long Speakers Guild; the second was the Headmaster of the Khalvadian Long Speakers Academy. The third was Sedric.

The Seventh Eye burned like a tiny sun, so bright it was difficult to look at. At times, its presence drowned out all surrounding thought, granting sweet yet disturbing moments of complete mindquiet.

Sedric's own father had died trying to accept the Seventh Eye, but Sedric had succeeded where every Long Speaker in fourteen generations of his family had failed. The Seventh Eye was a weapon, pure and simple. It was also the reason the rate for Sedric's services was twenty times that of a Revered Master Long Speaker.

Sedric calmly invoked the eye but did not open it. Even so, it illuminated the stone cell with a hellish red light. A thin crimson line pulsed an inch above his wispy eyebrows.

It could be used to kill, to maim . . . it could also be used to purposefully burn out another Long Speaker's abilities. And yet Kholster had placed this woman in his care, under his protection, to be trained . . . not handicapped and discarded.

"Hells," he cursed, dismissing the Seventh Eye. "Hells. Hells and triple hells besides. I'll likely boil in the Bone Queen's bathwater for it, but . . ."

He opened his Sixth Eye and reached directly into the mind of the Head Long Speaker positioned at the Castleguard Relay: *Cassandra, this is Sedric, dean of the Guild City Long Speaker's College and Possessor of the Seventh Eye. I ask this very respectfully as you are a Revered Master Long Speaker and Possessor of the Sixth Eye, not to mention the fact that your mother is a Possessor of the Seventh Eye, my senior and mentor: What in all the Maker's creation is going on up there in Castleguard?*

CHAPTER 5

DEATH WALKS ALONE

Under the same moon, deep in tunnels hidden from its light, reptilian hordes clashed with rank upon rank of sentient Aernese armor beneath West Watch. The death god, Kholster, formerly the leader of the Aern, walked among them. Kholster moved through the three main prongs of battle winnowing the souls of the fallen. He hurled spirits of the dead into the Horned Queen's clutches without comment, question, or pause. Each step took him to a new dying mortal.

None saw the grim-faced deity in his bone-wrought armor until their souls were gripped in his pale white gauntlets beneath the crimson scrutiny of his warsuit's crystalline eyes. He did not wonder whether they knew there was a face behind that Irkanth skull helm with its leonine lines and curving horns. The Harvester came when needed, warpick across his back.

It hadn't always been that way. Only days ago, he'd been burning, wounded by Ghaiattri flame through the bond he'd shared with Bloodmane, his warsuit . . . his former warsuit. Over the six-hundred-year exile since the Sundering, they had grown apart, a chasm that only widened when it came time to redeem Kholster's oath to slay his former masters, the Eldrennai . . . the Oathbreakers. Bloodmane had believed that a way should be found to forgive them.

That rift had become strong enough that when he'd finally been reunited with his warsuit, his second skin, when Kholster touched the armor with his hand, his palm had sizzled. Used to being able to flow back into his armor if slain, the warsuit protecting and preserving his soul until his body could be repaired, the bones stripped of meat, interred in the warsuit and the warsuit filled with blood, protein with which he could rebuild his body, Kholster had not realized the true extent of the problem until the last moment. When the fire slew him and his soul pulled free, rocketing across the miles between him and his warsuit, as his soul touched the warsuit, he had begun to burn, to Bloodmane's dismay.

Torgrimm, the god of birth and death, had stepped between them, giving Kholster the option to choose his death or Bloodmane's. When he opted to die rather than slay his own creation, Torgrimm had presented Kholster with a second opportunity, to fight Torgrimm for a portion of his power and then use that power to try to set right a wrong growing within the heavens.

In many ways, being a god was no different than being Armored and First of One Hundred. Variations of temperature meant nothing to him. But as he trod from death to death, his path led him not only into the dark tunnels where the warsuits of his former people the Aern waged war upon the reptilian Zaur, but to the jungles of Gromm where the envenomed fangs of an hourglass spider found the unprotected flesh of an explorer's ankle, aging its victim to dust, to a sickbed in Darvan where the God Speaker's husband lay stricken by the weeping reds, and elsewhere to harvest the souls of peoples and in places of which Kholster had not even dreamt when he had been mortal.

Odors and sounds assailed his senses in the way he imagined his closest friend, Vander, Second of One Hundred, or one of the other Overwatches might feel as they leapt from mind to mind in battle gathering data and relaying it to their kholster—would his name remain both a verb and a rank, he wondered, now that he was death?—in a cohesive broadcast, allowing him or her to make judgment calls, alter strategy, and . . .

When he collected the soul of the Root Tree Tranduvallu, Kholster sighed, taking only minor solace in the six little Vael lives who had escaped the slaughter. It seemed only right that the young Vael who charged heedless of the flames to clear the wreckage wore a face so similar to his own, the same hard jaw and wolfish expression. Even though Kholburran, like all Vael, had much longer ears almost akin to a donkey's, they were similarly placed: set higher up on the head than a human's or an Eldrennai's, much the same as an Aern's. Kholster's own ears looked more wolfish, with the same shape and motility though without the furry coat.

He lacked the close-cut beard Kholster wore, but despite his head being covered in head petals rather than actual hair, Kholburran kept his in the same style Kholster did, cut short, like a Hulsite mercenary, close to the scalp. Kholster guessed they were of a similar height, roughly eighteen hands tall, though Kholster imagined a male of Kholburran's age would take credit for the length of his ears and claim to be taller.

Kholster resisted the urge to reach out and help Kholburran, feeling further justified and pleasantly surprised when the crystal-twisted woman he had spared and entrusted to the Long Speaker's College reached out to assist. The prince escaped with only minor scorching, and the young female who feared for him seemed on the path to reclaiming her life.

Good for both of you.

There was always some small victory for life to keep his outlook positive. That wasn't the problem, but there most certainly was one. His mind felt empty—alone. The constant thread of other thoughts from other Armored, warsuits, and Overwatches at the edges of his consciousness had died when he had become a deity and been replaced with a near infinity of self. Kholster felt his physicality expand as more than one sentient died at a time. He knelt by dying mothers, drowning seamen, a young knight thrown from his horse, to the sides of the slain in multitudinous battles ranging from bar brawls gone wrong, to domestic horrors in the dark, to a gallows, to two children lost in the mountains, to the bedsides of a scattered handful of the aged and infirm. Any time more than one person lay dying simultaneously, which seemed to be most times, there were more than one of Kholster, his perceptions not split but duplicated. The closest thing he could compare it to was when, as First of the Aern, he'd shared a memory with his people or addressed them all at once. Only this new feeling came with a profoundly impressive headache.

"All know," he muttered. "All recall."

Shall I establish a connection, sir?

Almost alone.

Vander would have been better suited for this, Kholster thought at his warsuit.

Is that a yes or a no, sir? I could easily link you to Bloodmane and through him—

No thank you, Harvester.

At the mention of Bloodmane's name a thought took one of Kholster's many selves to his former warsuit's side. So much history between them. Kholster remembered hammering and shaping every inch of the warsuit, working him into being on the Life Forge. Once joined, they had lived and fought as one for thousands of years, until many had come to think of Kholster as not simply Kholster, but Kholster Bloodmane. They had walked the world together as a force that could be delayed but never truly defeated . . .

Until the Sundering.

When Wylant had shattered the Life Forge in an attempt to win the war against the newly freed Aern, killing all Aern except those who were Armored, her actions, combined with the Vael's desire for peace, had convinced Kholster to accept a treaty forcing the Aern to retreat into exile without their rightful skins, their constant companions, their warsuits . . .

If it had never happened, however, Kholster wondered whether his people ever would have discovered their warsuits' potential. Though their connection remained unbroken, the warsuits, deprived of their occupants, grew apart from their makers, further developing their own sentience . . . and now they fought battles and forged agreements as a separate people, a people led by Bloodmane, armor of Kholster. Kholster could not have been more proud.

Blazing crimson light flashed within the crystalline eyes in the armor's helm. Shaped in the likeness of a roaring Irkanth, a species of horned lion that (before the Sundering and the changes it had wrought to their natural habitat had pushed them in the wood, The Parliament of Ages) had been king of the Eldren Plains, the rich red of the warsuit's namesake flowed behind it in an arc born of velocity.

"Now!" Bloodmane shouted, commanding not only the warsuits but their allies, the Eldrennai Oathbreakers.

On cue, Oathbreaker Geomancers ripped the ceiling of the tunnel open as Pyromancers at the ready superheated rock, letting it fall back as steaming magma. They hadn't been able to save West Watch, but Bloodmane had avenged it thoroughly. If only Kholster's former warsuit realized he was tying up all his resources on feints.

They haven't found the central tunnel yet, Kholster thought. *Or engaged the main force of the Sri'Zaur.*

Skinner was dispatched to check Kevari Pass, he might notice—

He won't. Bloodmane should have sent Scout or Eyes of Vengeance. Kholster stood next to Bloodmane, the magma's orange glow painting his former armor in tones of anger and hate but leaving the bone of which Harvester was composed unmarked. *Skinner was never very good at tracking.*

Maybe he will be lucky this time?

They need reinforcements and they don't even know it.

But surely the warsuits—

It is not the warsuits about whom I am worried. There are almost as many Zaur and Sri'Zaur deployed as there are living Aern in the whole of the Dwarven-Aernese Collective.

I could warn your son?

Which one?

Irka. Harvester thought at him. **He is still your Incarna and there will always be a link there.**

Ignoring the question, Kholster looked down at his white gauntlets, the sight killing his line of thought. "The light doesn't touch me."

Lava's pale glow, Harvester intoned. **No dragon's fire or Ghaiattri flame may reach across the gulf to touch us, but . . .**

The gulf?

Between the realm of gods and mortals. You could cross it if you wished, of course, sir . . .

No. Kholster hated that "no." *Rae'en is First now. She has all of the Armored to advise her. I . . .*

A multitude of Kholster moved along the passageways of Xasti'Kaur and the lands above them collecting the souls of dead and burning Zaur, Vael, humans, and Eldrennai.

No Aern. Yet.

Watching the other versions of himself he couldn't help but picture the Queen of the Issic-Gnoss on her faraway continent with her army of drones that had no thought which was not hers.

Is that what I am now, he mused, *a death spider sitting at the center of my web of life?*

If that was the price for freeing the Aern, for giving them a freeborn kholster no longer bound by the myriad oaths he'd sworn in the past, Kholster considered it a sacrifice well worth making. He just didn't like the hidden costs that came with it.

As one Zaur rolled in agony, clawing at its burning scales and ruined hide, it occurred to Kholster how easy it would be to grant the dying a respite from pain and take them as soon as he felt the pull and knew death was certain.

He did not.

"Every moment of life, each breath, each heartbeat is theirs." The memory of Torgrimm's voice washed over him. "Do not steal it from them. Even at the end, at the last spark of life, the evil can see the error of their ways and the pure and bright can become resplendent in their glory." Kholster turned away from the dying Zaur. The death god smiled to see the warsuits moving unscathed amid the flowing superheated earth . . . a smile that vanished when he felt eyes spying on him in the night.

Aldo?

Aldo, Harvester confirmed.

Kholster growled low and took a single step.

*

Gray and dim, the death god Kholster's destination was little more than a carpeted cube floating in the ether, a single figure at its center. Wreathed in a swirling cloud of ever-shifting lenses, the occupant, a gnome-like being with cavernous eye sockets, twisted to face Kholster. Gold light gleamed from the being's distended ocular orbits. His robes, unlike the ones worn by his statues, were simple and well made but without ornamentation or embroidery. He could assume any form he wanted in a vain attempt to hide his true self from the mortals, but this, Kholster imagined, was the real god of knowledge: a cringing, spying deceiver.

Flinching slightly, as if expecting Kholster to seize him by the neck and lift him into the air, Aldo smiled broadly when the death god stood at arms' length.

"Aldo." Kholster growled.

"Kholster." A full-length mirror appeared in the space to Aldo's right. "Did you wish to see something? Dienox, Torgrimm, and I have spent many a—"

"The eye that spies on me, I shall pluck out." Kholster's voice came as a rough whisper abrading the cloud of lenses nearest him. Convex and concave alike, mirrors of all sizes and shapes, floating circles of various liquids, and even a few made of quicksilver broke and scattered before that voice, shards and silvery droplets drifting in a mass.

"Then it is fortunate," Aldo said amiably, "that I have none of them in at the moment." He reached into his robes and withdrew a lacquered wooden box, holding it open for Kholster's inspection.

He has you there, sir.

I'd noticed.

Kholster glared into the lacquered wooden box at the eyes, one pair for each type of sentient of Barrone, rolling about like marbles within.

"My friend, if pulling a few of my eyes out of their box and shaking them about would mollify you in any way—" Aldo thrust the box at him, further agitating its contents.

"I felt your eyes upon me, Aldo." Kholster reached out, flipping the box closed. "I respect you for the kindnesses done for me when I was mortal, for the knowledge you gave me, the language you gave my people, but—"

"You are everywhere anyone dies, Kholster." Aldo waved away the sparseness of his surroundings as if he were banishing an illusion. The gray cube expanded, filling with light and color to become a fully appointed study with plushly upholstered chairs, a polished oaken desk, and even rows of books and scrolls, along with shelves of massive bookcases upon which the tomes were carefully arrayed. A fire blazed merrily on the lush burgundy carpet a few scant moments before a stone fireplace appeared around it and mystic globes of flame materialized hanging in the air at the corners and center of the room.

Was all this here or . . . ? Kholster thought at Harvester.

He created it despite his gesture's contrary implication. Aldo is

more about appearances than he would have you believe. You might want to kill him.

Kill Aldo? Kholster snorted. *I just came to get him to stop spying on me.*

Killing him would achieve that end rather efficiently, sir.

I think Conwrath is right about you, Harvester. Kholster felt a smile touch his lips despite himself at the thought of Captain Marcus Conwrath and Japesh, the two human souls Torgrimm had assigned to keep him . . . What? Company? Keep him in touch with his mortal way of thinking? Kholster did not know and had not asked, but he was grateful for their presence.

Right, sir? The warsuit intoned. About me?

Yes. He says you're bloodthirsty.

I hardly think so, sir. There need not be any blood. Strangulation, burning, poison, heart attack, stroke . . . a death is a death. I cannot recall ever being thirsty for anything.

You know what I mean.

Actually no, sir, but I am certain Captains Marcus and Japesh would. Shall I summon them?

Not in front of other gods.

As you will, sir.

Kholster thought about correcting that "sir" and insisting on being called "Kholster" or "friend," but even thinking about it sent a spike of anguish through his chest. Harvester wasn't Bloodmane. Could never be Bloodmane.

Perhaps that was good. Kholster was not sure yet. Thinking about his own loss, Kholster wondered what exactly had happened to cause the god of knowledge to become what he was, this being who needed to look through the eyes of others. It occurred to him then, how such a need could be used. He marked it in the same way he'd noted the strengths and weaknesses of the human settlements between his mortal home in South Number Nine and the Guild Cities. He'd relayed them all to his Overwatches, in case the information were ever needed. Then. But now, without Overwatches, if any preparations were to be made, he would have to make them. "All going well in there?" Aldo asked. At some point during Kholster's reverie the god had settled into the high-backed chair, its crimson upholstery covered with embroidered words that flowed and changed beneath the dramatic illumination provided by globes of mystic fire.

A pair of human-looking eyes peeked out from Aldo's ocular orbits behind platinum-rimmed spectacles, and he had grown to more Aernese proportions. Aldo peered up at Kholster over the rim of his glasses, head bent over a volume of forgotten lore, as if Kholster had interrupted him in the midst of reading.

"I—" Kholster began.

Not waiting for an answer Aldo "returned" to the book. It shrank as he read, pages vanishing, as he turned them.

I think I see what you mean, Kholster thought at Harvester.

Him, then Dienox, sir. Just a suggestion.

And then Shidarva, I suppose?

Nomi and Sedvinia. Then Shidarva.

That's quite an itinerary you have plotted out for me.

You are a better god than they are, sir. You understand the mortals more. You are more trustworthy and you care. It is simple logic and expedience.

Let me finish talking to Aldo, first. There was mirth in Kholster's thoughts, and he wondered if that had been Harvester's intention all along.

Of course, sir.

"So you weren't spying on me?" Kholster prompted.

"Hmmm . . . ?" Aldo closed the book and sat back, hands steepled. "Spying?" He rested his chin on the points of his fingers. "Are we still going on about that?"

"Yes, we are."

He's trying to bait me, isn't he?

It is likely. Not to be repetitive, but I refer to you my earlier suggestion, sir. Strictly as a prudential measure.

I'll take that under consideration. And then, not liking himself for doing so, Kholster gave Harvester his plan for dealing with Aldo should the need arise.

I will make the request, sir, Harvester intoned. **An excellent precaution.**

Kholster disagreed, even felt disappointed with himself for taking the precautions, but hard decisions came with the territory and being prepared was rarely as disastrous as failing to be ready to meet undesired eventualities. Hopefully, all he was doing was wasting a few days of Irka's time. And yet . . .

"I'm sorry." Removing his glasses and setting them atop the closed book, Aldo rubbed his eyes. "As we were saying, you are everywhere anyone dies. That is not how Torgrimm did it, he popped the souls out into his little adytum—"

"Adytum?"

"Sanctum, sanctuary, hiding place, foxhole . . ." Aldo sighed. "There are many descriptors from myriad dimensions. That one, in particular, comes from the realm Abyssimus claimed, but I use them all. In this case, I use adytum to refer to the personal dimension Torgrimm had outside of normal time. Souls waited there for him, time only passing—from their perspective—when he was within their proximity. Awfully hard to observe him there. Hear? Yes—at times. See? Not well."

"I don't know of this dimension." Kholster fought the urge to fold his arms over his chest, forced himself to keep his hands hanging neutrally at his sides. Two could play the outward appearances game.

"My theory lays the crux of the problem with the time ratio. There doesn't appear to be much, if any, causal adherence between time within and time without. He could spend an eternity in there without its passage taking place out here, or at least not from his viewpoint or from ours."

Do I have access to this dimension?

After a fashion, Harvester answered. You appear to have internalized it. Multi-presence replacing infinite time for a singular self. I am cognizant of the change, but not how to alter or affect it. Perhaps each death god works according to his or her own skill sets.

Each? Kholster thought. *His or her?*

You have proved that the position of death god is open to seizure. Given that Nomi stole a portion of Dienox's might, it seems reasonable to assume you might at some future date be deposed by a male or female.

True. Kholster laughed. *And what would you do if I were deposed?*

Oh. Harvester's timbre deepened. They would have to destroy me too, of course. I am a part of you, sir. Torgrimm imagined my form, but you made me real . . . forged me into being. You are my maker, my rightful occupant. Anyone who thought otherwise would be in fatal error, as Reaper and I would vigorously demonstrate.

"Am I disturbing the two of you?" Aldo stifled a yawn. "I can leave my sanctum and go read out in the hall. . . ."

"How kind of you to offer." Kholster blinked, not that Aldo could see his face behind Harvester's helm. "We'll only be a moment."

Aldo's jaw dropped open.

Kholster laughed.

"And to think Kilke said you had no sense of humor," Aldo growled. "I have half a mind not to direct your attention to it in advance."

"In advance of what?"

Aldo gestured at the full-length mirror still hanging in the air next to his desk, then withdrew the wooden box of eyes from within his robes and pulled out a pair much heavier than the rest.

"Look and see," Aldo said as he slipped the obsidian eyes with their jade irises and amber pupils into his eye sockets. "I believe you'll recognize the players."

Players. Kholster directed his attention to the mirror as Aldo intended, but he did not like the sound of that word. It embodied the single greatest problem he saw with the divine order of things. The gods should not see mortals as playthings. As he watched, Kholster turned the problem over and over in his mind. He'd already decided to correct that failing of the gods. So far, he liked none of the plans that presented themselves, but that did not stop him from making them.

CHAPTER 6

OLD DRAGON, NEW TRICKS

Dawn broke over a dragon in flight. He roared to greet the light, birds and creatures below him fleeing in panic for miles. It felt good to be in the air despite the chill. A quarter of one black wing, as large as the mainsail on the *AWS* (*Aernese Warship*) *Grudgebearer*, cut through the clouds at a right angle before the dragon's gargantuan head surfaced. Rapid evaporation, brought about by the immense wave of heat given off by his body, cleared the cloud cover more efficiently than the gale-force winds from Coal's flight could have done on their own.

The joints in his mighty wings now worked wondrously, smoothly, with a power and resilience he hadn't felt in millennia. He was not as young as he used to be, but he felt vigorous. Renewed. His scales, once again the near black of his youth, began to glow. Stirred by flight and violent intent, an orange tinge worked outward from the dragon's core, patches of sulfur igniting along his underbelly, burning off to expose the thick, dark armored plates beneath, outlined in flame.

The Parliament of Ages stretched out beneath him. Acre after acre of unspoiled forest. Well, almost. Was that smoke to the distant southeast? He hoped so.

How I long to burn it.

But he was not there to end the life dance of this place. Not that any of his fellow dragons remained on this plane to hold him to such ancient treaties if he chose to break them, yet even so, the life secreted within the Outwork was all that remained of the once canorous and ebullient life song this dimension had birthed. In his mind's eye, he recalled distant days soaring alongside star-quelling flights.

To have been young enough to contain such heat! Casting his gaze northward Coal felt the draw of the Father's Forge Mountains. His short visit had not been enough, but he'd promised his aid to the Aern and they would have it, even if it meant he might never again set claw on the . . . what was it the mortals called them now?

"Sri . . . Sri . . . something." He sounded the words out trying to tease it from his tired synapses. Once, he would have recalled the desired information instantaneously. He still might have managed, if seeing the mountains again hadn't brought back such vivid memories: flights of dragons dotting the mountains, wings spread and soaking in the heat of Jun's new sun as the industrious god worked on the sky.

"Zauran! Sri'Zauran!" He roared in triumph. Elation faded as he considered the words. The Fanged People Mountains. Such nonsense. Father's Forge was a much better name. Coal's memory drifted further back to the sight of Jun in his glittering armor, mirrored helm blazing with light as he . . .

Well, that was long ago. Maybe it was just as well they were named after the infamous new plague of reptiles. He would visit the mountains one last time, if he could, gaze up at a final dawn, and spread his wings accepting its heat. He would never again leave the mountains. Not yet, however. First he had promises to keep. And maybe this time he would succeed in keeping them. Spinning in a series of barrel rolls, he spat fire into the air and roared. "Kholster, but it is a wondrous gift to fly like this again!"

Swearing by his friend's name sent a chortle through the dragon. Swooping low, his body heat drawing wisps of smoke from the treetops below, Coal squinted, narrowing the focus of his blazing eyes to find the armor of his newly deified friend.

Below, a single pass cut through the center of the forest, no smaller than when Kevari had burned it, leaving Coal to marvel at her work.

Kevari? What had happened to Kevari? Had she died before or after the coming of the Junland Bridge? No, he thought, *no, it had been Sulfur that disappeared beneath the waves at Junland Bridge. Kevari had died later, in the Demon War.* A molten tear hissed at the corner of the dragon's onyx eyes, running white-hot along the black.

"How silly," he murmured to himself, "for the Betrayer to have forgotten how he earned the name. Even Kholster is not old enough to have known me by that one—like as not only Hasimak and I could tell that tale— so I suppose it can be explained, if not forgiven."

A rejuvenated body, burning brightly at the end, but my mind is still ancient. I feel young . . . and old . . . at the same time.

Wheeling in the air, Coal flew a series of flips, dives, and recoveries to stretch his muscles. A twinge at the base of his tail reminded him of the time the Ghaiattri had cut into his hide during the Great Demon War, but he did his best to ignore it.

"Work to do and debts to repay." He mumbled the Dwarven phrase and wondered if they still used it nowadays.

His immense shadow stretched over the forest below, his thermal wake igniting tree tops as he descended, searching for a signal, if not for the warsuit itself.

"Bloodmane?" he bellowed. "Dratted armor demands my presence and then doesn't bother to provide an address at which . . . no, I suppose I did fly off before I could be given one." He mulled that over, shifting his jaws. "No, still his fault. Should have mentioned it all in the initial—"

Figures clad in armor careered about the sky shooting gouts of blue, green, and purple flames high into the air to get his attention.

Eldrennai nonsense, he thought dismissively. *Where are the warsuits? I'm not taking orders from some stump-eared haughty elf who thinks . . .*

Flying lower still, flames licking the forest canopy, he spied a lone crevasse of collapsed earth stretching as far as his draconian eyes could see, toward the distant mountains. He landed there in the mass of fallen trees closest to the Eldrennai, fires springing up along his mass and the ground trembling beneath his weight.

"Well?" He clawed the ground. "Where is Bloodmane?"

"Mighty Koa-hul," began a figure clad in bright robes. Coal could not make out his features, the dull haze rising from the fires causing anything further than a few hundred feet away to waver unclearly. "Flame bringer, master of the inner fire, he who is the mighty flow of white hot anger—"

Coal spat a thin stream of lava at the mage, incinerating him in flaming agony.

"Alas," Coal lied, stifling a chuckle. "My aim is off. I only meant to singe him."

Spotting a cluster of surviving figures nearby, Coal narrowed his gaze, shining brighter. "And I am Coal now, not whatever that fool called me." He waited a breath to allow time for a response—well, half a breath. "Did you bring any Pyromancers? I shall not abide shouting back and forth to some tiny pink thing too small to bother seeing. Who dares approach me? Where is Bloodmane?"

One of the mortals, a knight clad in demon armor, flew into the ring of flames spreading rapidly from Coal's body. A flame ward flared brilliantly about his person, smartly cast, by Coal's estimation, not that it would provide any protection at all should the dragon decided to waste breath upon him. But no, he was saving such grand displays for Port Ammond, for surely that was where his true destruction would be most needed, to topple the towers of the Eldrennai that Kholster's daughter and her people might feast upon the tender meat within.

"I am Jolsit of the Eldrennai," the tiny figure shouted. "You do not know me, but I fought at Kholster's side during the Great Demon War, and it was Kholster himself who gave me this armor. I am under Bloodmane's command. Skinner kholsters this particular squad. He and the Armored are still digging their way out."

Jolsit gestured to the dirt-collapsed tunnel by way of explanation.

"Very well, Jolsit," the dragon rumbled. "I am told you need Jun's fire for a lizard roast. Where do you want it?" Only mildly irked by Hydromancers spraying water on the trees around him, Coal paid attention as best he could. It was so much easier to see Aern. Their souls were bigger for one, and, up close, the fields that bound them to one another showed up quite well if he concentrated. Eldrennai were all so . . . small.

"As we speak," Jolsit continued, "Aernese warsuits are driving the Zaur forces back through their tunnels. They will mass near here, and when the warsuits give the signal, my Geomancers will tear open the ground, exposing the central tunnel. That's where you come in."

"You want me to fly into a cave?"

"No, Mighty Coal," Jolsit assured him. "All we want you to do is unleash your breath into the tunnels. Fill them with Jun's wrath."

"I daresay it will be my wrath, not Jun's, despite my occasional poetic license, but what of the warsuits?" Coal raised an eye ridge. "It is hard to melt metal wrought on the Life Forge, but I assure you my inferno is more than equal to the task even at the Third Breath."

"I'm told Bloodmane has taken that into account, Mighty Coal," Jolsit told him.

The knight's demeanor before a dragon continued to impress the ancient wyrm. More water poured onto the nearby flames, as if his holocaust could be extinguished with such meager effort. If it had been any other Eldrennai, Coal might have remained silent, but the mixture of confidence and respect this Jolsit carried reminded the dragon of another . . . mortal.

"Tell your Hydromancers they ought not attempt to quell dragon fire with water. It is insulting! They would need ice, and even then it will not die out so close to me unless I should want to quell it, and such a quelling you would doubtless fail to survive yourself.

"You will lose three dragon lengths in all directions . . . one of your miles, I believe, before their spells will have any effect. Have them fly out half a dragon length farther than that, douse the woods with water, and freeze them. If your Geomancers cut firebreaks into the forest there too, you will stop the conflagration . . . with luck."

"Thank you, Mighty Coal." Jolsit flew clear to deliver the information. Of the assembled Eldrennai, fifteen of them flew off over the forest, the remaining twenty holding ranks in the air. In his youth, Coal would have vomited lava on the ground beneath their formation to put a little fear into them, but after having ignited a mage earlier, he contented himself with resting on the embers beneath him, soaking up the heat to fuel himself for the upcoming exertions. He realized abruptly that he did not actually need the rest, but a youthful body could not so quickly undo the instincts of an elder wyrm.

Lulled into a light doze by the crackle and roar of the forest burning about him, Coal laid his head down amid the embers, blowing black smoke through his nostrils. Spires of ashes billowed into the sky. Wood smoke smelled so much nicer than sulfur. A half-seen figure moved near him in the haze, whispering.

"Burn it," the low voice insisted. "Burn it all! The rage will spur on the Eldrennai and harden the Vael. That is what would be the greatest help to the Aern."

Feigning sleep, Coal listened to the voice, letting his left eye slide open a bit so that he could barely see the armor-clad Eldrennai and its . . . crystal battle-axe? Accompanying the words, a low pressure set up in Coal's sinuses. *Dienox! Who else would try to force his will upon a dragon?*

"If you give me a headache," the dragon whipped its head up and around to face the god of war, "I will burn the skin from your back. No. No. Worse than that, I will pray to Jun."

"You wouldn't!" Dienox threw down his axe.

"I would," Coal snorted. "As I recall, it has been quite a long time since you were banned from influencing dragonkind, bald one."

How that idiot of a war god had let a mortal steal his one redeeming attribute, Coal could not fathom. Then again Nomi was a female and thus so much brighter and more useful than the males of her species . . . Coal caught himself looking around hopefully, but she was nowhere to be seen.

Pity. I should have much preferred to speak to her. She could have told me how Kholster is getting on as a new deity. Ah well.

The dragon turned his attention back to Dienox, who was still prattling on about something.

"—and it's been so long since I saw a dragon," Dienox protested.

"I know." Coal flashed a mouth filled with row after row of jagged obsidian teeth. "Do not think I haven't missed the attention, the incessant begging. It is flattering (in small doses), I assure you, but my tolerance for it has diminished. Soon, I think I shall join my brethren. No more than a century or so. I suppose it would have been sad to leave this place without one last encounter."

"You will join the others?" Dienox asked eagerly, touching the dragon's muzzle with his gauntlet. "Will you tell me where they've gone?"

They? As if they had all gone to the same place or told me where they intended to go. Coal focused his energy, circulating more and more heat through his scales until the god jerked back his hand with a curse. Then the dragon got an idea.

"I will," Coal answered gravely. It was just too easy to get under Dienox's armor.

"Yes?" Dienox still shook his injured hand, blowing at the steam rising from it.

Few mortal beings can harm a deity, little god, unless Shidarva condones it, but you would do well to remember that I am one of them.

"Yes, but you must promise never to tell anyone, not even the other gods, and you must promise to go there directly."

"Of course. You have my word!"

"Very well." Coal's voice was softer than a baby's cry, a whisper for a dragon.

Dienox leaned forward with each word until sweat ran down his face, his cheek reddening with heat and the painful effort of enduring it.

"Well?" Dienox hissed.

"Well what?" the dragon cooed.

"Where did they go?"

"Who?"

"The dragons!" Dienox shouted.

Coal pulled himself up to his full height, stretching out his wings until the god of war was eclipsed in the shade of him. He paused for a long moment, eyes glittering, before he finally answered: "Away."

"Away?!" Dienox stomped his foot. "I know they went away, but where did they go away to? No one will tell me and I cannot see them!"

Coal settled back down, nestling out a more comfortable spot for himself with his nose. "Your promise, Lord Dienox," the dragon reminded him sleepily. "Go away." Chuckling gently, small trails of magma trickling over his teeth and drooling onto the cracked earth, Coal drifted off to sleep and dreamed of planets roasting in an endless sky of fire.

CHAPTER 7

IN THE SHADOW
OF KHOLSTER

Kholster growled. "Did that bald idiot just try to influence Coal?"

Aldo frowned. "Your lack of focus is disrupting my mirror. Who cares what Dienox tries to convince the old wyrm to do? Not even one of *us* can force a dragon's will."

"Then what are you trying to show me?" Kholster eyed Aldo impatiently. "Rivvek has a plan. Coal arrived to help with a plan that won't work, because they have the scale of the invasion wrong. What am I missing?"

"Not the dragon," Aldo answered, "Oot."

"Rivvek was at Oot. So?"

I believe he is making reference to the occasion, sir.

What occasion?

It is the last day of the last Grand Conjunction.

"Rae'en?" Kholster whispered. He had tried so hard to stay out of her way, to avoid looking in on her, thus preempting any temptation to interfere. . . .

"I thought you might be curious," Aldo said. "You have been there for all the others . . . and you were going to have to show up in person at the end of this one in any case."

"She's decided then," Kholster's voice was cold.

"Look and see," Aldo said.

Kholster peered deeper into the mirror, saw the encampment of Aiannai leading back in a ragtag line from Oot. Frustrated with the limited view of Aldo's mirror, the death god took a single step.

*

Two lithe figures flew over an array of statues cast in midnight. They caught a chill wind as it blew in off of the Bay of Balsiph, flowing with the current even as it sent them wending amid the representations of divinity. Arranged in two semicircles, the effigies of the gods faced each other: six on one side and six on the other—opposing pieces in a cosmic game with two gods standing aloof . . . players picking sides.

A seahawk joined the two in flight long enough to take their measure, unleashing a shrill cry of protest when one of the two waggled her ears at it. Clad in formfitting doeskin leathers, the top heavily beaded and exposing the silvery skin-like bark of her midriff, the Vael laughed, letting the air spin her around, casting her long yellow head petals out around her head.

The slightest of frowns touched the edge of her lips. She opened her mouth to speak, exposing unscored dental ridges instead of teeth. With a shake of her head, she banished the thought.

"Careful, Yavi," her flying companion snorted, "wouldn't want you falling out of the sky because your thoughts are too heavy."

"Yours are heavy enough for both of us," Yavi laughed, continuing her spin, arms outstretched. "Thanks for letting me go flying with you, Wylant. I was going crazy down there with those two. Mother should have sent Kholburran in my place. I can't keep Rae'en civil. Far from the usual calming effect my people have on Aern, it's as if my being here makes her even angrier."

Below them, Wylant looked pityingly upon King Grivek, who sat wrapped in furs over his heavy robes, trying to stay warm while the young female Aern across from him wore clothing more appropriate for a summer tryst than for sitting out on a pier at the edge of winter. Long red hair tied back in a ponytail, arms crossed as she loomed over the seated elder elf, Rae'en bared her teeth in thinly veiled contempt, exposing the doubled upper and lower canines that were an Aern's birthright every bit as much as bone-steel and those disturbing jade-rimmed amber-on-black eyes.

Of course you anger her, Yavi, Wylant thought. *To Rae'en you are a Flower Girl. She doesn't know what went on between you and her father . . . only that he obviously made a strong enough impression to strand you in a state of false Spring.* Aloud she said only, "Help me get a new count of them."

The line of refugees, some in ramshackle tents or wooden caravans, others with only bedrolls or the clothes on their backs, was still growing. On the day after Kholster's death—*Was it really death if you became a god?* Wylant mused—they had begun to arrive. First as a trickle, in ones and twos, and then in a flood of tens and dozens, they had come, crowding the forest approach to the Place of Conjunction, not daring to set foot upon the dark marble of . . . Oot itself.

Oot. The name still amused and saddened Wylant in equal measure: glad the artist had succeeded in signing his creation and disappointed her people had forced his hand . . . or talon . . . claw? Would a name like Divine Shadows Wrought in Stone truly have been so bad?

"Won't they be in danger this close to Rae'en when the war breaks out?" Yavi shouted as she met Wylant at the end of the camp.

"Unlikely. What was your count?" Some of the people below waved at Wylant, but she did not wave back.

"Around three hundred."

Wylant counted three hundred and eleven. *I had no idea Kholster had spared so many.* Then again, it wasn't as if she'd checked each of their backs for patrimonial scars. Were they all Aiannai, or had the slow trickle of those who had been spared by the Aern caused an exodus of those who wanted to be anywhere but Port Ammond when the Aern came to destroy the Eldrennai?

"I am sure some of them are Aiannai," Wylant called back. "Dubbed Oathkeepers." *Like me. And Rivvek . . . but no sign of the prince today.* "Those will be fine. Anyone who just followed the tiny exodus, though . . . I wouldn't want to be them. Have you seen Rivvek?"

"The scarred prince?" Yavi dropped a few feet in the air, before resuming her habitual eupeptic mien. "Not since the first day. His tent went up before the rest, but he sure has been coming and going a lot. Maybe he has a girlfriend back at the castle."

"I doubt that very much." Wylant followed her gaze to the spot where Prince Rivvek's tent stood unoccupied at the head of the others. Two royal guards, both Aiannai like their prince, manned the entrance as if Rivvek were still in residence, but where had the prince gone? Perhaps there was no requirement that he be present for the end of the Grand Conjunction, but given what was likely to happen to his father, Wylant had assumed he'd want to . . . say good-bye . . . or bear witness . . . show his king that he . . .

"Then again maybe he doesn't—"

Maybe he couldn't bear it.

"Huh?" Yavi asked, but Wylant ignored her.

Wylant had never known her own father. Kyland had perished in the Second Great Demon War, volunteering to march through a Port Gate with the Lost Command. Did his bones decorate the same macabre resting place as those lost Armored? Did their statues watch over him? Had he thought of her at the end? She and her father had shared the same air for a hundred years, but he had so rarely been granted leave to come home. . . .

Wylant shook her head to clear the thought. It hardly mattered. As a ward of the realm, she'd risen higher in the military than she'd ever have been allowed if her father had lived. There were other women in the Eldrennai military, but few were allowed to fight. She had hoped to change that, in time, but now time had decided to resolve it a different way. Wylant wished she'd been born a Dwarf or an Aern or even a Vael. Each race still had its gender politics, but theirs were so far beyond her people's. Maybe Rivvek would help her to enact that change for those who survived, if there were enough survivors for it to matter.

As the wind rose, a familiar presence fell in beside her, a spirit she felt she knew, better than she knew herself. Death was imminent, not hers, but— she assumed—the king's. Letting herself drift to the ground, she sensed the presence follow her partway down before flowing away toward the pier.

"Are you okay?" Yavi asked, joining her.

"Someone is about to die," Wylant answered.

"Someone is always about to die."

"Here." Wylant stared back at the statues. "There."

"How do you know?" Yavi asked.

"Because Kholster is here," Wylant said.

"And how do you know that?!"

"I was married to him." A sad smile traced Wylant's lips before giving way to a grimace as her fingers clasped the pommel of Vax, the shapeshifting weapon, currently a sword, she'd forged in a blur at the time of the Sundering. She would always carry guilt about Vax's creation due to the source of the bone metal she'd used to forge him. She didn't like to think about it, could not, in fact, clearly remember having done it, though she knew she had. "How could I not?"

"I'd better get over there then," Yavi said. "Fly with you later," the Vael called over her shoulder as she ran toward the deific statuary. Toward Oot.

*

Wylant watched her go, considered following her for a moment, but then headed to her tent. One more witness wouldn't change what was going to happen out on that pier, and as much as she enjoyed the feel of Kholster's presence, Wylant couldn't face him, couldn't stand beneath those jade and amber eyes. And speaking of eyes . . .

Wylant felt the weight of someone's gaze on her.

Caz, clad in Silencer, his warsuit, stood aloof from the non-Aern in the shadow of an ancient blood oak growing at the edge of Oot, its roots waging a losing battle against the black material of which Oot was made.

Silencer's skull-like helm completely obscured the Bone Finder's features, but Wylant knew his attention was on her. Worse, she could sense him focusing on Vax, her . . . Weapon. Each time her hand strayed to the hilt and

Vax responded, the force of Caz's attention caused the small hairs on the back of Wylant's neck to stand up. Running a hand across her scalp, the black stubble of new growth rough against her palm, Wylant frowned.

You'd better not want what I think you want.

She paused en route to her tent, a double handful of feet from Rivvek's, half a moment from walking over to the looming Bone Finder to ask him outright what he wanted.

"This isn't going to go well," Wylant muttered, more to Vax than to anyone.

"Ma'am," the nearest of the guards answered all the same. Wylant did not remember his name, nor did she care to know it. Rae'en's ascension to First of One Hundred had unlocked something in Wylant as well. She knew the young kholster would need help . . . guidance . . . and was pained to know that despite recognized fire in Rae'en's jade-on-black eyes, she was unlikely to accept help from anyone. Given time Rae'en, like her father, would mellow, but time was running out. Wylant couldn't think of yet another way to buy more.

Kholster would have tried to spare the Eldrennai, as many of them as his oaths allowed, by accepting them as Aiannai or letting them flee to new territories where he would be deliberately, but not oathbreakingly, slow to chase them. But Rae'en . . .

Kholster may have become a freshly minted reaper of souls, but it was Rae'en with slaughter in her eyes . . . and an emptiness that would only be filled with blood.

"A blessing from Dienox," the guard continued, "this change in Aernese representatives, wouldn't you say, ma'am? The girl His Majesty can handle."

"That stupidity," Wylant said, jabbing a finger against the guard's crystalline breastplate, all thought of confronting Caz forgotten, "is exactly what killed your race. Not the Aern. Not my ex-husband. Not even the gods. Fools did it." She shook her head, stepping away from the grouping of tents that housed the king and his guards at night. "Fools like you."

CHAPTER 8
SOME ENDINGS ARE BEGINNINGS

The wind howled as it coursed around the statues of the gods, leaving Rae'en wondering whether the wind was magic or mundane. She'd heard Wylant's raised voice and considered the likelihood that she, as a Thunder Speaker, was in any way responsible. Magic or not, the breeze caught a swirling cluster of blood oak seeds, the twirling winglike structures much like a maple seed wrought in crimson on a larger scale.

Why did Gromma give most oaks acorns, but not the blood oak? Rae'en tracked one as it flew, the drill-like tip of the seed so different from that of other trees, a weapon waiting to pierce the ground. At the last possible instant, its vortices would narrow, the speed increasing to strike the soil and find a good purchase. To sink home. Some would wait until the heart of winter to plant themselves in the hardest soil.

No wonder her father liked them so much.

Her father, rendered in obsidian, looked down upon Oot, and Rae'en hoped he did not find her wanting. For several thousand years only thirteen statues had shifted and changed at noon and midnight, revealing to any who bore witness the preferred forms of the gods. Now a fourteenth stood, straddling the pier, his visage hard, fearsome, and full of judgment. On her? On Grivek? On all of them?

Dad.

Seed forgotten, Rae'en smiled up at her father's statue before continuing, wind tussling her hair like the fingers of an unseen hand. Reaching for the leather satchel hanging from her right side, she gritted her teeth before remembering she'd shifted the blade she sought to her left (matching) satchel. Each bag was bound at the bottom corners with bone-steel reinforcements. The left, her father's, was singed but still useable. She reached past the carefully coiled chain with its many charms, forged of the bones of her father's dead children—her slaveborn brothers and sisters who never knew freedom—and found the blade she sought. Gathering her hair in one thick hank with her right hand, she cut it short with a swift flash of the blade.

Long strands of hair landed on her chain shirt, the red shining like fire against the dull pearlescence of the bone metal before the wind caught them up, carrying them away. Stowing the blade back in her saddlebag, she caught the Oathbreaker king sitting across from her, breathing a little easier once the blade was out of sight.

Baring her teeth in a mirthless grin, making sure to give Grivek a good clear look at her doubled upper and lower canines, Rae'en cocked her head to one side, the cold light of early winter reflecting off the amber pupils of her eyes, picking out the jade irises in even greater relief against the black sclera of her eyes.

"I'm going to kill you with my father's warpick, not a grooming aid."

"Of course." Grivek's own pale skin and dark eyes looked so frail in comparison to her youth and vigor, the bronze of her skin. Wrapped in voluminous robes to ward off a cold Rae'en could no longer feel now that her adult integumentary system had things under control, it was hard not to pity him. "All a full-grown Aern needs," her Dwarven uncle Glinfolgo had said once, "are good hobnailed boots, hardwearing pants, a belt to keep the trousers up, a shirt of chain to keep the weapons on the outside, and an enemy to kill."

I'm well-equipped then, Rae'en thought, outfitted in steam-loomed denim jeans dyed black from her uncle's most recent dye lot with an additional blue pair in her rightmost saddlebag. The two warpicks crossing her back, Testament and Grudge, were more than she would ever need to kill the Oathbreaker across the camp table from her.

She remembered a time only a few days ago when the weight of one warpick had made her wince in pain, her muscles beyond exhaustion after the race she and her father had run across Bridgeland. Now that she was Armored, she wondered if they would ever hurt again.

Only if you want them to, Bloodmane thought.

I wasn't thinking to you.

My apologies.

Fine. Shut up then. On some level Rae'en knew the warsuit meant well, but she couldn't stand his hollow metallic voice in her mind. It felt wrong. He shouldn't be joined to her. He shouldn't—

"It looks nice," Grivek said softly.

"What does?"

"The hair."

"I think so, too," Yavi put in.

"No one cares!" Rae'en snapped her teeth at the Flower Girl, half in annoyance at having failed to notice her arrival. Stupid little Flower Girl with her yellow hair petals and Wylant-looking face. What was she trying to prove wearing doeskin leather and flouncing about?

Heartbow or not. Fighter or coward. Rae'en wished the pretty little Vael would take flight with Wylant and stay gone. Her presence was pointless anyway. There would be no peace. She'd failed whether she'd managed to bed Kholster or not. She wasn't pregnant, or Caz would have been able to feel the bone metal growing within and since she wasn't, she'd failed in that mission, too. So what use was she to anyone? Playing dress-up in the woods? Luring male Aern away from female Aern?

"Back to it." Rae'en slapped a hand down on the document that was spread out on a camp table, disturbing one of the chunks of rock that held it in place.

"Of course." Grivek inclined his head in assent, attempting, unsuccessfully, to stifle a shiver.

"What?" Yavi said. "Vael here. Hello? Allies to the Aern." She leaned down between Rae'en and Grivek, breaking their eyelines. "That smell like familiar spoor to you?"

"Yes," Rae'en hissed between gritted teeth. "Of course. Please be sure to keep your head clear when I kill this Oathbreaker. It's a pretty little face and I'm sure someone would be quite upset if I put a warpick through it."

Grivek chuckled softly.

"I'm sorry," he said in response to Yavi's shocked expression, "but here at the end of my life, my sense of humor has become questionable."

"End of your life?" Yavi scoffed. "That hasn't been decided yet."

Rae'en raised an eyebrow at that. What did the Flower Girl think she had to do with that decision?

"I'm afraid it has," Grivek told her.

I hope you aren't planning to kill the Vael, too, Vander thought at Rae'en.

Of course not, Rae'en thought back. *Though maybe if she slipped at just the right moment and fell in front of my warpick . . .*

Vander didn't laugh. Rae'en sighed.

Fine. Back to it then.

"You release all those we accept as Aiannai." Rae'en tapped in the vague area of the clause on the document to which she was referring. "Both in the future and in the past from any oaths they owe the Eldrennai kingdom, the Eldrennai crown, the Eldrennai schools of elemental magic, the Artificer's Guild, and any and all oaths from which you in all your capacities personal, private, and public may free them?"

"Yes," Grivek nodded.

"Really?" Yavi shook her head and stepped toward the statue of Xal-istan, muttering to herself. "That's very generous."

"Sign and seal," Rae'en spat.

The king bent over the camp table, hesitating over the document.

"What now?" Rae'en snarled.

His eyes found the precise cuts still visible as new-forming skin met the edges of the old where Rae'en had sliced away the outer layer in a perfect rectangle, width established by slicing just below her breasts and above her pelvis, the length by extending the incision around her sides and terminating within a finger's breadth of the scars running down her back. She'd seen Aern skilled enough to begin along their spine and work toward the front, leaving the bisected patrimonial scars visible at the edge of the finished parchment as further proof of the document's authenticity and author, but she'd only had to do it twice before (once to create the initial register sheet for the accounting of her bone-steel by the Ossuary and again to document the name, composition, and means of manufacture of her warpick, Testament.

"You saw me cut, stretch, and scrape the skin, Oathbreaker. Cured with my own blood and saliva, it is legal parchment!"

King Grivek coughed, hiding his face. "No. I know. That is . . . of course it is." Their eyes met. "I merely . . . well . . . doesn't it hurt?"

"I'm not tracking what that spoor has to do with this hunt, but yes. On the first day."

"Isn't there anything that—"

"Sign and seal or refuse," Rae'en snapped. Rage bubbled under the surface at the edges of her being. Denied the full legacy of her father's memories, she still had a great wealth of them available to her from her link with Bloodmane and with Vander. When she looked at Grivek, images of every wrong he'd ever committed in the sight of an Aern, each slight, each misstep swam before her mind's eye.

It will fade in time, Vander's voice spoke in her mind. *You will come to summon the memories only when you need them. Most of the time.*

Most?

Have you ever seen you father freeze for a moment at the mention of your mother's name if he wasn't expecting to hear it?

Yes, she thought back.

If the emotions tied to the memory are strong enough . . . There was a pause. *They can still surface unbidden, kholster Rae'en.*

Please, just call me Rae'en in my head, Rae'en asked. *Even Zhan calling me New Bones is better than you calling me kholster.*

Habit, Vander thought back. *I'll work on it.*

King Grivek sat very still, head bowed, eyes searching for . . . what were they searching for? It looked like he was trying get a better look at her through her bone-steel mail.

If he makes another belly button comment or rather lack of belly button comment, I'm going to kill him.

Does that mean you aren't going to kill him otherwise? Bloodmane's echoing voice filled her thoughts.

No one is talking to you, Makerslayer.

My apologies, Daughter of Kholster. I try to filter out when you mean me and when you mean to commune with others, but you still transmit quite broadly.

Shut up!

And, I hate to ask again, but you did say that Coal could assist us, but he has yet to arrive and—

He's a dragon, not a soldier, Bloodmane. The great gray dragon doesn't march where I tell him to march. He went wherever he went and he'll show up when he feels like it!

Ah . . . and Skinner informs me Coal has arrived at West Watch. I apologize again, Daughter of Kholster, I should have been more patient.

Fine. Good. I'm busy!

Not that yelling at Bloodmane accomplished anything, but it did make her feel better. Well . . . not really. Rae'en let her eyes focus on Grivek, then the document itself. He looked old and tired; the look in his eyes reminded her of Parl's when she'd stared into those unnatural eyes and saw such a mixture of emotions, depth she hadn't properly fathomed.

He wanted to live, because living things want that in general, but living was such pain, tinged with such regret with actions and words that could never be undone. Grivek, like Parl, was at her mercy. His future surrendered to her. Make the choices, he seemed to say, I can't make any more, I have chosen poorly so often that I leave everything to your wisdom. You decide.

"Well?" She nodded at document. "Read it."

Grivek read through the document, eyes squinting in the sunlight. He sniffed as he read, the sound reminding her of the cave-in when her mother died, the way her father, nose bleeding, had stared at the pile of rocks covering his dead wife, clutching Rae'en.

"What are we going to do?" Rae'en remembered asking.

"Wait for it to stop. Dig out her body. Avenge her. Then wait for the pain to subside."

"Will it?" Rae'en had choked.

"We'll pretend it does."

Rae'en blinked away an emotion she refused to acknowledge and rubbed her eyes. When her hand came away Grivek was watching her.

"Two things." The old Eldrennai held up one finger on each hand. "Before I sign anything."

"You are in no position to—"

"I am old and about to die." Grivek took in a long deep breath, drawing himself up to his full height. "I am going to sign this document and agree to all of your demands." He let it out again, sagging with the exhalation. "Please let me speak."

Rae'en nodded, wondering in the moment what Parl, the Foresworn, might have said if she'd let him keep talking?

He looked pretty regal there for a moment, Vander thought at her.

If you say it's true . . . Rae'en thought back, begrudging the Oathbreaker even that scant token of admiration or respect.

"One: I will be allowed to choose my successor and you will honor my choice. By which I mean, you will allow him time to perform the Test of Four, be acknowledged, and grant him one audience with you before the Aern attack his people."

"More delays?" Rae'en slammed her fist down on the camp desk cracking the wood. "I have had enough of your—"

"You could at least listen to him," Yavi broke in but seemed not to have the heart to press the issue.

"Just the one request then." Grivek lowered his hands, fingers folding in like dying spiders. "Will you grant it?"

You could have at least—

Shut up, Bloodmane!

"What was the second request?"

Grivek looked away, his eyes lingering at the feet of the statue of Kilke. The massively muscled god with his two extant heads each sporting horns stared down at the pair of them as if bemused by the whole affair, one finger raised to scratch the center stump that had once held a third head before Shidarva had dethroned him and taken his place as ruler of the gods.

"I don't want to be eaten."

Rae'en laughed. "What? Why? You'll be dead. When you're dead you're meat. It hardly matters what happens to it then."

"Even so." Grivek looked at her with rheumy eyes.

If I remember correctly, Vander thought to Rae'en, *the Test of Four takes a few candlemarks. Not more than that. Even if there is to be a funeral first, it's a three- to five-day delay.*

"Five days?" Rae'en asked.

"Two at most." Grivek shook his head. "I will have no funeral. I wish my body to be burned. I will not have my children coming to visit a pit of rotting meat when I am gone."

"Done," Rae'en said.

"I have your oath?" Grivek assessed her warily.

"Yes, but only if the fleet can make port unopposed at Port Ammond."

"They will not attack until after your audience with my successor?" Grivek asked.

"Unless he fails or things take longer than you've specified." Rae'en leaned in. "I won't get caught in some oath trap like—"

"Granted," Grivek interrupted. "This isn't like that. I know you won't believe me. You have every right not to, but I'm not attempting to outmaneuver you."

"Done then." Rae'en drummed her fingers on the document.

"I need to hear the words." Grivek looked into her eyes.

"And I need to see the orders." Rae'en folded her arms across her chest.

Grivek waved over one of his guards and hastily wrote out a set of orders, which he let Rae'en review before he signed, sealed, and dispatched them with the guard to Port Ammond.

"And now the words?" Grivek asked.

What does he expect to happen? Rae'en wondered.

Aldo knows, Vander thought back, *but this agreement will make the landing at Port Ammond a lot less exciting.*

Anything I can do to make sure Uncle Glin doesn't fall overboard and sink to the bottom of the Bay, Rae'en agreed.

"I swear," Rae'en began, "it is my intention to grant up to two days' time, beginning today, to allow your chosen heir a chance to undertake the test you named. Assuming he passes, I will agree to meet with him, also within the same two days, unless he delays or it becomes unreasonable, in my opinion, or in an opinion expressed by my Overwatches, to do so. As for your body, I shall agree to let your people dispose of it and if they keep your wishes or fail to do so . . . that is up to them."

You swear it is your intention? Vander asked.

He's an Oathbreaker, Rae'en thought back at Vander. *He gets what he gets. He won't catch me oathing off until I have my back to a wall.*

"She swears it is her intention." Grivek gave a bitter chuckle. "I suppose it's the best I'm likely to get. Very well."

A blade of violet flame rose from the tip of Grivek's forefinger, and he signed the document with it, the scent of burnt skin rising from the page.

Placing his palm over the signature, the Eldrennai king closed his eyes, lips pulled tight into a severe line of grim concentration. When he pulled his hand away, the symbol of the Royal Bloodline lay emblazoned in its wake.

Rae'en unslung Grudge, her father's warpick, from her back. Grivek held up a hand, imploring her to delay a moment.

He took the thin crystal and silver circlet from his head and whispered fire along it. "Rivvek," he said over the glowing crown. "I name Rivvek my heir. Seek him."

The fire grew. Mystic heat suffused the metal and crystal until it flowed, the molten composite fashioning itself into the likeness of a small bird. The crown flew out over the water where a sea hawk dove, struck, and died in a screeching conflagration.

"In your own time," Grivek said after the crown was out of sight.

"But Rivvek is Aiannai," Rae'en scowled. "Oathkeeper."

"Yes," Grivek agreed. "Your father's scars are on his back. Rivvek is the only Eldrennai other than Wylant he personally accepted."

"This changes nothing."

"He will." Grivek coughed. "He's the only child I've ever had who was brave enough to see what we did to the Aern. Understand it and try to make amends."

"Amends?" Rae'en scoffed, picking up the document, rolling it up, and putting it into her right saddlebag.

"Ask him how he got those scars," Grivek suggested.

"Don't you know?" Rae'en asked.

"It's his tale to tell." Grivek shook his head as he spoke. "And now you have one more reason to grant him an audience."

Did he tell you, Vander?

Only Bloodmane, Vander sent. *Well, and your father. Rivvek asked to share it with them first and afterward Kholster said Rivvek had asked him to keep it to himself. You could always—*

I'll ask Rivvek when I see him.

"Seriously," Yavi said as she walked back over, "can we all just put our weapons away and—"

Sharp and shrill the cry of Grudge, the warpick of her father, her kholster, and now her god rang out as Rae'en struck, ending the final Grand Conjunction the only way Rae'en could ever envision it ending . . . with the death of the Eldrennai king. Blood from King Grivek's punctured throat sprayed across Yavi's face, spattering the statue of Kholster before which a small broken camp table lay.

Yavi drew her heartbow, nocking an arrow even as the king's lifeblood dripped down the silvery expanse of her bark-stripped skin, standing out in sharp contrast to the cheery yellow of her head petals.

"What have you done?" Yavi shouted.

"Killed the king of my enemy." Rae'en eyed the Vael with contempt, the jade irises surrounding the amber pupils of her eyes expanding slightly, banishing a portion of the black sclera so unique to Aern. She bared her doubled canines. "I told him I had a few favors—" she gestured at the signed documents on the table, "—to ask before I killed him. It was not unexpected. Why are you so surprised?"

"But then you killed him!" Yavi shouted. "You really killed him!"

"What else would I do?" Rae'en jerked the hooked beak of Grudge's head free of the dying king's throat as his guards and attendants rushed forward, weapons drawn. "The last Conjunction is ended. Why don't you go home and play with the other flowers, Yavi? Surely they have something or someone useful you could be doing."

CHAPTER 9

PICKING SIDES

Yavi only took two blinks to think before choosing sides. Rolling away from the Aern and the charging guards—cries of outrage on their lips, a wolfish grin set upon hers—Yavi unslung her heartbow.

Was there really any choice at all?

The temptation to shoot Rae'en was there in her core, but next to it burned an understanding of why Rae'en had killed King Grivek. It was all fair hunting to try to change the Aern's mind, but to believe Rae'en might actually choose other than she had didn't track at all. There was no other decision for Rae'en to make: Kholster was dead and Rae'en blamed the Eldrennai for it.

Or Yavi assumed she did. And even if she didn't hold Grivek personally accountable, Rae'en had granted Grivek's last requests, gone so far as agreeing to delay the war even further. True, it might be nice if the Aern weren't so darned stubborn, but when Yavi thought back to Kholster's interactions with the Eldrennai, to the hatred that burned within him tempered by a willingness to reinterpret his oaths as liberally as he could, to grant requests he hadn't been required to even consider. . . . And, again, Rae'en might be less willing to bend than her father, but she'd still done so, still made concessions she had no strategic reason to make.

Aern were willing to be kind when they could be, and Eldrennai, well . . . Yavi squinched her face. She remembered Dolvek's haughtiness, the way he and King Grivek flew about the room at breakfast hurling fire at one another in an argument. She had no trouble recalling the sound of Grivek's sobs when Kholster had retold the story of the Battle of As You Please.

They could feel guilty, but why hadn't they tried to do anything about it in the centuries since the exile, shown any initiative in resolving their differences with the Aern, to the extent they could be resolved, other than by abiding to the terms of the peace treaty the Vael had been forced to negotiate? The Eldrennai had tried to hide their shame so hard that Prince Dolvek had been able to break the truce between their peoples unwittingly.

It was like the Litany.

The Eldrennai who'd lived before the Sundering knew what they had done but preferred to forget what it meant and what it had cost. They had tried to salvage their pride instead of taking ownership of their mistakes and working as hard as they could to make sure each new generation would never repeat them.

In a way Prince Dolvek's sundering of their peace had been an inevitability. At least by making an exhibit of the Aernese weapons and armor, he had been trying to do something good. Sure, he'd utterly failed to realize that the Aern were connected to their warsuits and would know the moment they were moved. He'd misread everything and everyone, trying to do a good thing. He'd failed to listen to any of the many people who'd tried to stop him or explain things. It was like the whole no grabbing thing. Yavi didn't know exactly why her people had such an aversion to being grabbed, but they did. It was almost always unthinkable and intolerable, so when an overprotective guard had grabbed her arm inside the museum exhibit and the warsuits had killed him, Dolvek had thought she'd been in danger and only belatedly realized it had been his own guards who had been in the wrong.

A warsuit would never hurt a Vael.

No, the Eldrennai didn't tend to leave such a favorable impression. There was hope for them, though. While Yavi would have given no credence to any suggestion that Prince Dolvek might talk the Aern out of anything, to find a way for all three races to coexist, his brother . . .

Prince Rivvek had Kholster's scars on his back. He was Aiannai to the Aern, an Oathkeeper. If anyone (other than General Wylant) had a chance at stopping the fighting, it was Rivvek, but if the late king's guard slew Rae'en . . .

All of those thoughts that had been turning round and round in her head since Kholster's death led to a single conclusion: If they killed Rae'en, the Eldrennai were committing suicide.

"There'll be no stopping the war at all, if you Oathbreakers kill her," Yavi shouted.

Rather than engage the guards in melee combat, Yavi called on any nearby wind spirits to lift her into the air. The friendly zephyr who'd helped her soar earlier with Wylant tried to answer, its touch cool and friendly on her bark, but Yavi's anger and frustration with both the Aern and the Eldrennai made her too heavy. Which meant she needed to put herself back in a happy mood, or she needed a different sort of wind spirit. A killing wind.

During the Summer such a wind spirit might have been hard to come by, but the Winter wind was full of anger and death, and though Winter was yet to come, there was always a kiss of it in Autumn. Yavi just had to find it.

Eyes narrowing, vision opening more to the realm of spirits than the physical, Yavi caught sight of a frigid ethereal being twisting around the base of the central obelisk. It was an old being, smelling of bodies in the snow or under the ice. Raw power pushed against her magic, a hatred nursed through the warmer seasons, never dying, merely waxing and waning.

Dangerous, then. Too dangerous to work with? In another two blinks Yavi embraced the risk.

"Let's kill things," she whispered to it with her magic. "Help me fly so we can rage together."

Kill, it thought at her, *freeze and crack. Mmmmmmm.*

Growing opaque enough to reveal cruel blue eyes gazing at her from within a coiled serpentine body of ice and snow, the elemental spirit flowed over her in a wave of frost, chilling Yavi to her heartwood. Icy coils wrapped around her waist, jerking Yavi aloft in the eye of a vortex of frigid wind and hail. Her bark hardening under his rough touch, Yavi drew, aimed, and—

A human male, dressed in traveling clothes and a dark-blue overcoat so expensive she knew she had to be staring at Captain Tyree even though she could only see his back—well, there were clues there, too, but—ran out onto the black marble ground of Oot and blocked her shot.

"Easy, everybody! Easy!" Tyree called. "Here I was coming to say good-bye and every pointy-eared person around is dead-set on killing one another." He laughed. "Guess it must be an odd or even day, right?" His eyes sparkled, under the brim of a wide hat, his voice warm and welcoming.

Yavi felt a flow of . . . something . . . reaching out from him, like his spirit was trying to convince hers to believe what he was saying and follow his instructions. Like her spirit would listen to any old human. Ha! Before she could ponder the feeling too much, the elemental roared: *Kill now!* in her mind.

Wait, Yavi thought back, a little alarmed to be thinking to a spirit rather than speaking to it. *We might not need to hurt anyone.*

Need?! Furious at her failure to deliver the violence she had promised, the spirit hurled her at the obsidian floor of Oot. She caught herself with outstretched hands, bark on smooth marble. Surrendering control of her momentum to the force of the throw, Yavi rolled into one cartwheel then another. Burning off the extra speed in short, quick shifts of heel and palm, she skidded to a halt at the base of Kilke's statue with the two-headed god sneering down at her as if he meant to bend down and charge her with the massive horns of his remaining heads.

"I'm sorry, ishar-ama," Yavi drew her heartbow, notching an arrow of spirit her fellow sentients could not see. "Maybe next time."

Cheat! It roared and charged.

Yavi fired one shot, grunting as she summoned a second arrow of spirit too close to summoning the first and let it fly as well. The first arrow went wild, crashing harmlessly against the central obelisk. Her second shaft struck home, piercing the midsection of the elemental, as it grew more physical.

"And that's why Mom always says to be twice and thrice certain before working with a predatory spirit," Yavi chided herself. "Particularly an old one."

Making as if to pull another spirit arrow from within, Yavi focused on showing no outward display of fear. *I am a confident source of kill kill kill*, she told herself. *Back off.*

We are enemies now, the spirit growled. *I will remember you.* Showering her with a burst of hail, the spirit hissed, retreated to the base of the obelisk, growing insubstantial once more.

"Everyone's staring at me, aren't they?" Yavi asked Kilke's statue over her shoulder. "Yep," she answered her own question. If the human who'd preempted the fighting had had everyone's attention before her spat with the primal wind spirit, all eyes were on Yavi now. "Thanks." She turned around and gave Kilke's leg a pat. "That's what I thought," she told the statue.

She turned back to the center. They were still staring at her.

"What?" She waggled her ears to break the tension. "Some spirits don't like it when the battle plan changes and nobody dies."

"Looks like you got it to calm down," Tyree said with a smile. (How did he keep his teeth so white?) "Which is a great idea for all of us, homely and comely alike. I'm certain," the human winked at Yavi and Rae'en, "you two can guess which category the three of us fall under."

Calm down. Calm down. Calm down.

If Yavi concentrated, she could hear the words, like a voice repeated them over and over again in her mind. It wasn't the spirit. Yavi frowned at the captain (What cute dimples!). He'd helped Rae'en and Wylant escape from the Zaur a few days ago, but Yavi didn't know much more about him than that he'd been well-paid for it and had amazing dental hygiene.

The voice in her head was annoying, but she hadn't needed any help to shift out of shoot-and-stab formation. The Eldrennai guards did seem to need the assistance, though, so maybe it was a good thing Tyree was doing . . . whatever he was doing.

The Eldrennai guards also appeared to be more susceptible than she was to whatever magic the human was using.

Eldrennai never listen to what spirits have to say, so maybe it's a form of Long Speaking? Yavi thought.

One of the Kingsguard looked perplexed, the other guards standing in varying stages of confusion and relief. A few sheathed their weapons.

Neither sparkly teeth nor power of persuasion appeared to work at all on the Aern. Rae'en stood, warpick at the ready, scowl on her face, doubled canines bared, her jade irises expanding to not quite banish the blacks of her eyes.

I can handle her, Tyree's posture seemed to say, with a flash of his perfect grin and yet another wink.

Yep. This totally had to be Long Speaking or some brainacular power or other.

"Tell the stump ears, not me, Randall," Rae'en growled.

"They're backing off." Randall wiped a bead of sweat from his brow.

Back down, guys. Your king's sacrifice. Don't waste it. You've gotta burn the body and make preparations. Get news to the new king. Banquets and things, yeah?

Now that she was listening for it, the words came through even clearer except that they were more emotions than words. The complexity of the emotions made her render them into words to make sense of them, but they were definitely more feelings and impressions than verbal instructions. He had a nice mental voice now that she knew how to pick it out when it was aimed at her.

The guards sheathed their weapons, all save one. He stood, sword drawn, teeth gritted. "Which one of you is doing this?" He spun, cursing. "Is it you?" he leveled his sword at the man. "You're—"

Faster than she could follow, Randall (that was his first name, not Captain, right?) stepped inside the guard's reach, moving around and past in one smooth dance-like motion. A sound of metal on metal snicker-snacked in the unseen exchange, then the guard was falling. Pools of blood gushed from wounds to the guard's neck and inner thigh. Two wounds. Both fatal.

Dark-haired, handsome, and still smiling, Randall Tyree raised his hands in the air in don't-blame-me fashion. His billowy sleeves fell away from his wrists and down to his elbows as if to say "See, no weapons here." Randall let his mouth gape open, feigning utter shock and befuddlement. The guards stared, first at him, then back at the injured guard, and in the space between glances, Yavi caught him flicking the blood from thin twin knives. Lowering his hands to his sides, he casually slapped the weapons over his wrists where they curled into two innocuous-looking bracelets just as the loose cuffs of his shirt fell neatly over them.

"What in Torgrimm's name?" Randall asked in convincing, but (to Yavi) obviously false, shock.

Why kill that guard and not the others? Yavi wondered. Was it that the guard sensed Randall's voice in his head like she had? Also, what other weapons might the human be hiding? Did he have a battle-axe concealed in the black vest and matching trousers he wore? Did his brown leather boots turn into morning stars? Yavi eyed the gold belt buckle with particular distrust.

As she opened her mouth to ask him, a blast of elemental air magic hurled the remaining guards several feet back.

"Enough!" Wylant landed in their midst.

Yavi breathed a sigh of relief.

Crisis averted.

*

"But General," a guard began.

"Stand down!" Wylant felt Vax's hilt in her hand, the weapon unsheathing himself, as his blade stretched and curved. Weight shifted incrementally until—what? Until Vax was sure she would support him—until she held the straight utilitarian sword shape Vax most often preferred.

"We are in the presence of our slain king!" Wylant's heart pounded in her chest, but she controlled her breathing, forcing it to measured pulls of air. "He died so that you might have some hope of ending your lives somewhere other than in the stomach of an Aern. Send a runner to inform Port Ammond."

"You Aern-loving—" He swung; Wylant sidestepped and struck, and he pirouetted headless to the ground.

"Now," she told the other guards. "I will stand vigil over the king."

"You killed one of your own—" Yavi's disbelief was typical for her youth, but Wylant did not have time for it. From what she had overheard, Rae'en had set a strict timetable and there was no room for delay.

"Thank you for your service to the Oathbreakers and the Aern, Princess Yavi," Wylant interrupted. "Please allow me to convey the deep gratitude of the Eldrennai on behalf of our kings old and new to the Vael for their long efforts to maintain the peace. If you would not mind informing Queen Kari that we will not be requiring a Vael representative in one hundred years, that the Grand Conjunctions have ended, I would be most appreciative."

"Of course, but—"

"And you, Captain Tyree," Wylant continued. "Your attempt at calming this down is most appreciated, but you have been well paid and it might be best if you took your leave, as well."

Tyree's eyes flicked to Rae'en, sliding off of her as if he realized there would be no assistance from her.

"Kholster Wylant." Tyree smiled, eyes shooting daggers before the smile took over and reached them as well. Gods, but the man was practiced. He nodded to Rae'en. "Sugar bosom, I guess our marriage will have to wait."

Turning on his heel, he gave a parting wave to the transfixed Yavi, who was mouthing the words "sugar bosom" in mild shock, and was gone.

"You think," Yavi started, pulling her attention away from the departing human and his unarguably pleasant posterior, "I mean. It's really over? I just go home?"

"The Conjunction has ended," Wylant said.

"And there won't be another one," Rae'en spat.

"Then, I guess I'll take my leave as well." Yavi's ears flattened for a few heartbeats before she got them under control. "I'll convey news to Queen Kari about what has happened. Obviously the Aern and the Aiannai are welcome to visit The Parliament of Ages so long as they come in peace and friendship. Long may our peoples know peace."

"Thank you." Wylant wiped the blood staining Vax's blade onto the pants of the dead guard. "Will you be needing an escort back to The Parliament of Ages?"

CHAPTER 10

KINGS DIE . . .

In death Grivek fled. Catching a glimpse of bone armor out of the corner of his eye, Grivek leapt as far and fast as he could, soaring away from Oot, beyond the sky, and into a gulf of never-ending black.

Nothing, he thought, head turning side-to-side seeking light. *Nothing. Has he destroyed everything? Has Kholster——?* Flailing out for anything to grant him purchase and halt his progress into the seeming void, Grivek felt cold creeping into his essence.

Is this the end? Chilled to the core, he wondered. Was this his punishment? A hell of darkness? Had Kholster scarcely paid him any attention at all before hurling him straight into the Bone Queen's clutches? Just a flash of bone before eternity of night and—

"You can't run." A voice broke the silence. Quiet. Hard. Not indifferent, but . . . disappointed? Grivek squinted into the void. "Other way, dead king."

That voice. Kholster.

A hand.

Hard.

Gauntleted. Also Kholster.

"I can let you run that way if you want, but I have no clue why you'd want to wander in the Dragonwaste. There is nothing beyond the Outwork."

"Wh-what?" Grivek stopped, his view spinning as the death god turned him to face a luminous sphere hanging in the yawning dark. Graven images of Jun the builder covered, no—comprised—its gray surface. One statue after another, interlinking seamlessly.

"The Outwork. Nothing living beyond it in this realm. Only me." Kholster glared at him from within a warsuit of pale bone, its helm a skull-like replica of Bloodmane as if the roaring irkanth's head had been stripped of flesh, leaving the skull exposed and angry. "I am pondering it. Why were you running? I've never seen a soul go flying off like that. Where did you think you were going?"

"I—I died."

"You got a warpick through the neck." Kholster laughed. "That's all it takes for most. What of it?"

"Um . . ." Grivek looked into the crystalline eyes of the warsuit. "Can I please see your face?"

"This is my face, dead king," Kholster answered, reaching up to touch Harvester's irkanth skull helm. "But if you mean you wish to see me without my helmet," the death god let out a long breath as if forcing himself to be civil, "I am willing to comply with your request. My daughter did just kill you."

Grivek gazed upon the face of the Harvester.

"You look . . ." Grivek had expected to see something different, a wizened, dried-out husk or some other sickly, transformed being, but Kholster stared at him with unchanged amber pupils, rimmed with jade, in a sea of obsidian. Bronzed healthy skin. Hair and beard the same fiery red, cut close like that of a Hulsite mercenary.

"I look?" Kholster grinned, baring his doubled canines wolfishly.

"Unchanged."

"Why would being a god change my appearance?" Kholster peered down at the sphere, his gaze or some effort of will drawing them closer to its surface. They passed through the stone shell emerging into a sky of lights with another sphere below them, blue and green and . . .

"Barrone!" Grivek gasped. He could just make out the Eldren Plains, but he was surprised to see other continents: the fabled home of the Issic-Gnoss, at the top of the world—a land of ice. He gaped at a massive broken band surrounding the world below. "What? What is that?"

"None of your concern," Kholster answered. "You died. I came. You ran. I followed. Now you wish to talk and I'm willing to do so, but not about things you won't remember in a candlemark. What do you want, Grivek, son of Zillek, ruler of the throne of Villok?"

"Can you . . ." Grivek looked down at Barrone as dawn broke over the surface. Somehow the suns looked smaller than he'd expected. "Can you forgive me?"

"No." Kholster's response came without hesitation, his voice firm and unyielding. Even though something about him gave Grivek the impression that Kholster regretted the answer, the necessity of it. Was that a hint of sadness in the eyes of death? "Anything else?"

His heart, or what felt like his heart given that he knew he no longer possessed a physical one, ached at that denial. His breath caught, but he choked out the next words. "To the hells, then?"

"No." Kholster shook his head, and then it was the death god's turn to sigh. "There will be no afterlife for the Eldrennai. No judgment. No punishment. No reward. I will not allow it. Call it a compromise. If I let you go on to some reward, not all of you would deserve it. If I consigned you all, with the Bone Queen's aid, to the various hells, not all of you will deserve that either."

"But then. What? Will you destroy us utterly? Eat our very souls?"

Grivek blanched at the fierce intensity of the emotion that bloomed in those orbs of jade, amber, and obsidian.

"I would like to, but you all go back," Kholster said after a long moment. "And it has to be all of you or it isn't quite fair."

"Back?"

Kholster nodded, pointing with one bone gauntlet at the world below. "Back."

"But?" Grivek stammered, relieved. "But how?"

"Reincarnation. It works for gnomes. Besides," Kholster's voice broke, and he wiped his eye, "just because I can't forgive this Grivek doesn't mean I can't forgive the next one. All oaths are redeemed in death, and if the new you doesn't remember his crimes and lives in a body, thinks with a brain that never committed them . . . perhaps I could come to forgive that being. Maybe you'll even make me proud. Do better this time, Leash Holder.

"When confronted with something you know to be evil, stand your ground. Speak your mind. Don't just sit there and feel sorry. Act on your beliefs." Kholster pulled the king's soul close, compressing him. "A real king is willing to die for his people. I hope you didn't delay too long to spare yours."

All things fell away, all the old memories, the joys, the sorrows. Nothing left, but a primal understanding of the lessons he had learned. "You chose the right son, by the way. He just might save his people yet."

And then new hands held him, cradled like an infant. A kind god. A loving god. "Shhh," cooed Torgrimm, "he's not as bad as he seems. How about a nice new body? Hmmm? Would you like that? How about a human this time? Or a Cavair? Would you like to fly on leather wings across the sea at night? Live high in seaside caves? Be at peace with the Aern for once?"

He liked that idea very much.

"Very well," Torgrimm told him, "Let's see what we can find."

*

"That was nice." Petite, shapely, and wearing her stolen flaming hair in glorious waist-length locks, Nomi trailed flowing silks as she walked down from the edge of the Outwork, where hung the stars and suns that formed the night sky. Beautiful as she was, she was not Wylant or even Yavi or Helg. Nor did Kholster consider the way he had acted to be nice.

"No," Kholster answered. "Nice would have been for me to hand him over to Minapsis and allow her to deliver him to the White Towers of his ancestors, were they not already empty."

"Empty?" Nomi asked. "I don't pretend to keep track of everything Minapsis does, but when did she decide—?"

"Her husband convinced her, before I took part of his job." Kholster cleared his throat. "As he feared, it did not take me long to decide to seek out Uled, to see if I agreed with the punishment he must surely be receiving, but he was already gone, reincarnated, as were all Eldrennai."

"And you didn't decide to take it out on Grivek?" Nomi pursed her lips. "Impressive restraint."

"Not really. He was a good elf, as Oathbreakers go, and he had learned at the last what he needed to know. This should have been his end, but—"

"Then why send him back?" Nomi steepled her fingers, gazing at him with an inscrutable smile on her face.

"Because I hate him." Kholster shrugged. "I shouldn't, but I do."

"It's okay to hate a few mortals," Nomi said. "A few immortals, too."

"No." Kholster studied the goddess. The way she moved spoke of dances he had never seen and combat stances that had died out years before he'd been created.

"'No' isn't exactly an argument." Nomi winked.

"I wasn't arguing." Kholster closed his eyes and saw through not just the eyes of Harvester but all the other occurrences of Kholster himself. That was shifting as well. The more he thought about how strange it was for there to be more than one of him at any given moment, the harder it became for him to accept it and the more disturbing it became to experience.

Sir? Harvester sent.

I'm fine, Kholster lied. In truth, his head pounded and he felt as if something was missing, but he couldn't get a good hit in to see what color it bled.

Is there anything I can do?

No.

"Maybe it's because you're new to the whole god thing," Nomi said cheerfully. "You'll get used to it. It took me a long time and I still feel a bit out of my depth. Unconnected."

"How so?"

"Well." Nomi took him gently by the elbow, leading them both down to a spot in the center of the ice continent. "I guess . . . you know how the gods tend to have two aspects?"

"Yes," Kholster answered as he joined her on a snow-swept peak of ice.

Beings of a race Kholster did not recognize stood frozen in the snow, halted in the midst of everyday things. They wore garb like Nomi, thin and silky. "You transported me?"

"Gods can move each other around, Kholster." Nomi blasted away a huge swathe of snow, churning it to steam with her might, revealing intricately painted buildings, small, but lovely, made of mud. "We can do all sorts of things to one another if we aren't careful." She ran her fingers through her hair for emphasis. "I know you are the Harvester and everything now, but you need to know how . . . um . . . tricky Aldo is. And Gromma is absolutely frightening. I'm friendly enough, but even I scalped a war god to get where I am."

Maybe you should go ahead and kill her, sir, Harvester suggested. **By her own admission—**

I'll hold off for now, Harvester.

"Does this tie back to the two aspects comment?"

"Indirectly." Nomi sat down against the wall of the newly revealed hut. "Some of them are dual natured, others aren't. People like us, which is one of the reasons I think Torgrimm wanted me to talk to you . . . well, being singular instead of dual, if you claim your role, it can become all-encompassing. To keep myself as myself, I've had to ignore my deific role in many ways. But you've embraced yours."

"And you feel it may change me?" Kholster asked.

"It already has." Nomi leaned her head back against the mud wall. "Just look at Torgrimm. He's already different. Happier, really. Certainly more amorous now that he is the Sower. Take your time. Ease into it."

"Mortals do not stop dying just because I am, in some ways, having a rough adjustment."

"You're the god of death," Nomi laughed. "Reap them on your own schedule. Take things slowly. You need time."

"Perhaps, but if so, it is a luxury," Kholster told her, "I cannot justly afford. Death should not hate the living, nor play games with them, nor make them wait. Torgrimm taught me that.

"I am an ending. Done well, my job is the last line of a bard's tale masterfully sung or the final moments before a smith calls his weapon finished. I will not be idle."

"Yeah." Nomi sat cross-legged in the air. "Torgrimm said you'd feel that way. He thought you might like to have someone to speak with, to, you know, work things out? So . . . if you need someone." Nomi stood.

I like her, but you should still reap her, sir, Harvester thought at him. **She won't expect it. The timing is excellent.**

"I will take that under consideration," Kholster said.

"I think that's wise," both Nomi and Harvester replied: one in his thoughts, the other aloud.

"Thank you." Kholster rubbed his chin, feeling the close-cut well-groomed beard. He peered into Nomi and saw she was not like him. She was sad, really: a mortal soul clinging to divinity via a glorified hairpiece like some of the more affluent humans in the Guild Cities were known to wear, though theirs were made of admittedly inferior material.

She had never fully accepted her role, whatever it was supposed to be, and Kholster wouldn't have lasted three soul reapings if he had refused to take on the whole of his new responsibilities, but it was true that he felt . . . changed . . . thinner . . . stretched. . . .

While one Kholster listened to Harvester and spoke to Nomi, others swept across the world below separating souls like wheat from chaff and sending them where 'ere he would. How to explain to one who obviously did not grasp it, how death: seeing it, partaking of it, could change a person . . . even a god. To have seen the death of millions over the course of six thousand years, and then, within the space of a handful of days, to witness the death of more than a quarter million and to then understand that, by Winter's end, if not its arrival, the deaths would total more than you had ever known . . . and that by the end of a year you will have seen more death and reaped more souls than you had a number to name?

"Well," Nomi said after a long silence. "If there's nothing right now, I'll check back later."

"One question." Kholster realized he was fussing with his beard and stopped. "You rose to godhood after stealing Dienox's flaming hair."

"That's not a question yet." Nomi winked. "But yes."

"You also said you had not fully accepted your role."

"True, but still not a question." Nomi wiped snow off the back of her pants and blouse.

"Of what then are you god?" Kholster asked.

"Excuse me?"

"I took a portion of Torgrimm's might," Kholster said, "creating sower and reaper, but you became . . . ?"

"Resolution," Nomi answered. "In the beginning Dienox was both Conflict and Resolution. War and Peace, I guess, but that's—no. Don't look at me that way. I've never really taken up the mantle . . . I just wanted to live forever."

The cycle of War and Peace was broken then, in the same way life and death had become unjoined when he'd fought Torgrimm. Kholster nodded and muttered a "Thank you" as he moved on to the next dead mortal.

It was so much easier when I imagined myself waging war on the gods and reaping them until the games were done, Kholster thought.

Then why don't you, sir? Harvester asked. **What prevents you?**

My conscience.

Ah, Harvester thought. **It is my considered opinion such things often cause trouble.**

If I am, as Nomi asserted, slowly being changed by my role, you may one day get your wish.

PART TWO

LEGACY OF THE LIFE FORGE

"If only I had understood that my knowledge of the Zaur and Sri'Zaur and their origins was information as uncommon . . . as vital . . . as damning as it was, I would have spread it far and wide, or at least delivered a briefing to the kholster of the Aernese army and the Ossuarian. Despite the scars on my back, through my inaction and lack of foresight, I made myself into my father's unwitting accomplice increasing by one more betrayal (albeit an unwitting one) the debt owed by Uled's blood.

It is, as a direct result of this disastrous oversight, therefore, that I have laid a self-inflicted geas upon myself, my quest to record all that I know of my father's work, the resulting volumes, scrolls, and artifacts to be surrendered completely to the Aern, Vael, and Aiannai leadership that the datum I alone appear to possess may be preserved for their future use, even if I should myself pass into the Harvester's embrace."

From the introduction to *The Reptilian Error* by Sargus

SNAPDRAGON'S FURY

Kholburran smelled Zaur in the forest. Their scent, a mix of reptilian and Eldrennai (amphibian, too, maybe?) spread through the forest in a miasma of odor undiminished even by the billowing smoke from the flames of burning trees that had been following them for a whole day. At night, the northeastern horizon limned orange. The odor rode the smoky taint of the spreading forest fires begun at Tranduvallu. *Is it heavier than the smoke*, Kholburran wondered, *pushed along by it?*

Overhead, the drying leaves of autumn made for a poor bulwark. Lush green forest awaited nearer the other Root Trees, especially near Hashan and Warrune, but getting there was taking too long. "Nature spirits are hard to control during a disaster," Malli had explained to him. As a boy-type person, not very good with spirits, he had to take her word. And so, they ran . . . and ran. . . .

Ahead of him, Arri and Lara moved at a relentless pace. If the loss of Arri's right arm was throwing her off at all, she covered it well, compensating with experience gained from all those formal combat lessons (with sparring and drills, and lots of different weapons, not anything like the private lessons Malli had given him) in which boy-type persons (those with the potential to Take Root, in particular) were unwelcome. Arri had always been talented, the most talented in his Root Guard next to Malli. Thinking her name dredged up all the worry as if it were a new thing. Kholburran risked a quick spot check over his shoulder.

"We're not going to drop her," Faulina hissed, catching the look. "Eyes front, Snapdragon."

Embarrassing or not, it had been enough of a look to verify Malli was still back there safely (or as safe as a Vael with cracked heartwood was likely to be in a forest full of invading Zaur) suspended in the makeshift moss stretcher Faulina and Seizal carried between them, her torso bound as well as they could manage to help her keep from splitting even further.

"Why haven't we seen any other Root Guard?" Kholburran muttered.

"Looking for a rescue party?" Faulina asked. "They'll divide to reinforce the other Root Cities. If we run into anyone, it will be Vael creating a fire break, but Tran picked a spot so far from the others. . . ."

"They've counted us lost," Malli said matter-of-factly.

"I haven't counted any of us as lost yet, Molls," Seizal said with a harrumph.

"Good to know, Say-Say." Malli laughed. "Remind me to hug you when I can do it without cracking in half."

"Don't I get a hug, too?" Faulina asked. "I'm carrying the bulk of the weight."

"If you can't handle the irkanth, don't prick its flank," Seizal murmured.

"Irkanth?!" Malli balked. "Are you saying I'm as heavy as an irkanth?"

"Now that you mention it . . ." Faulina teased.

Kholburran tried to let the banter reassure him, but it didn't. Girl-type persons could joke around and act tough even at the brink of doom. Of some solace, however, was the knowledge that somewhere, a little farther back than Seizal, Mavyn was silently keeping pace up in the trees. None of the other Root Guard could summon up enough air spirit assistance to fly them all home, but Mavyn had no trouble convincing them to give her a little boost when she needed it. He snuck another peek back, but he couldn't spot her.

Maybe I could be doing the same thing if most of my survival training hadn't amounted to "Stay near the girl-type persons so they can keep you safe."

He tamped down the thought with a grunt, and the procession came to a halt so abruptly Kholburran had to do a little jump-skip sideways to keep from bulling into Lara. Arri's left hand was on him next, touching his face. His shoulders.

What in all that was green and growing did she think she was doing? Then it hit him.

"Get off." Kholburran pushed her away. "I'm a little scorched and wilted, but it's nothing."

"That grunt wasn't nothing," Arri said. "Tell me wher—"

She was talking . . .

Then she wasn't . . .

And then she was falling, hands clutched at a crossbow bolt in her throat.

A scaled shadow, the first of the Zaur dropped out of the trees, it membranous flaps flaring wide, catching the air. Lara loosed two arrows from her heartbow. One struck home in its upper thigh. It growled, pain contracting the webbed flaps and dropping the Zaur to the forest floor in a crush of wet grass, Lara's second arrow arcing wide.

Lara never misses, Kholburran thought, eyes shifting from Arri to Malli, then back to the trees for more Zaur. *There should be others. Why don't I see them?* Kholburran reached back, feeling the familiar smoothness of his warpick. Even as he unslung the weapon, he blinked in shock as Seizal and

Faulina dropped Malli. Cushioned a little by the soft moss of the improvised stretcher, Malli still hissed in pain.

"What are you doing?" Kholburran shouted. Faulina drew her sword, darting to the Zaur Lara had wounded. It came up with a Skreel blade, but she thrust past its guard in one smooth motion, dropping into a wary defensive stance even as it flailed behind her in its death throes.

"Watch Molls," Seizal shouted, heartbow now in her hand. "I'm sorry, Snapdragon, but if there are more than a handful of Zau—"

Evasive action cut off her words.

Seizal flipped to the left, narrowly avoiding a crossbow bolt. Halfway through her rotation, she let her heartbow drop. By the time her feet hit the ground her sword was drawn. Swatting one bolt out of the air (by miraculous accident from the look on her face) Seizal swung at a black-scaled Zaur that had lunged from behind the cover of a nearby tree.

Parry.

Riposte.

Appearing to overextend herself, Seizal rolled under the Zaur as it leapt to take advantage and bisected it cleanly.

Two more Gliders vaulted from the trees, both of them loosing bolts at Seizal. The projectiles stuck out of her chest at odd angles. They hadn't hit anything immediately vital, but then it was hard to kill a Vael without doing a certain amount of chopping. A headshot could do it or a shot to the central pump, but that was about it. *We tend to die lingering deaths.*

Triggered by the thought, Kholburran remembered standing with his mother, Queen Kari, at the side of his father Warrune. Hashan had always been the healthier of the two trees, while Warrune tended toward areas that rotted for reasons none of the Arborists could determine or cure.

Kholburran thought Yavi knew more about it than either she or their mother, Queen Kari, would tell him. They'd hid it from him completely for as long they could, but it was hard not to notice something was wrong when occasionally a door came apart when you opened it or a piece of furniture collapsed under its own weight, the once hard wood turned soft.

His father was dying, had been for over a hundred years, with Arborists cutting the rot away and applying poultices, even trying antifungal agents. Whatever they could think of. Every so often he would convince them to let him help tend Warrune, and arborism being something apparently far more acceptable for a young Vael prince to study than warfare, he'd learned more than his mother or sister, even his Root Guards, suspected he did about healing beings and objects of living wood.

Which, in and of itself, was why he was so worried about Malli. It was possible for her to recover all on her own, but the opposite was, without her bonding with him, so much more likely. If they didn't start applying nutrients to her bark soon, given how her wound would have disrupted the natural flow of sap, her outer layers would begin to dry out and die. Once that happened, blight was bound to set in, and if not blight any number of other fungal infections could seize the opportunity and start to take over her air bladder. . . .

Treatable, yes, but for something like fungal infection, the healing ingredients required could be so hard to come by. Blue flower bloomed in veins of copper, but only where the air was dry and it couldn't dissolve away over time. Other types of treatment had to be ordered from the gnomes and imported from Rurnia.

What if she won't marry me and she needs something we can't get for her? What if—"Fight, Prince," Arri croaked as she pulled herself off of the ground. The bolt in her throat made it hard to talk, but she was up and moving to Faulina's defense.

"This isn't fair!" Kholburran shouted. Ashamed of himself for saying it even as the breath passed his dental ridges.

"Of course it isn't fair," growled a voice from the smoke. "Fair is for the god of Hunter and Hunted, but we do not serve him." Kholburran caught a brief glimpse of red scales and the gleam of bright eyes through the billowing gray, but they vanished in a swirl of soot and ash. "I serve His secret purpose. I serve one who is cloaked in shadow."

Four more Zaur charged out of the smoke from the direction of the voice.

"I serve one who thrives in secret."

Another four Zaur appeared from the trees to Kholburran's left.

"I serve one who shall rise once more."

Four additional Zaur burst into view to Kholburran's right. Fanning out, Skreel blades flashing when they caught moonlight, nigh invisible in the dark of night otherwise, two of the four in each group headed for him, coming in low on all fours, tails leaving brief trails in the fallen leaves.

Their susurrant battle cry froze him.

"We have the advantage, noble Vael," the voice called from the smoke. "Surrender. Let us take one of you prisoner and the rest may—"

"We can handle them," Malli assured him, still prone.

"Yes," Arri croaked, stepping over her, sword in hand.

The Zaur kept coming.

"You know how to do this." Trying to keep her heartwood as still as possible, Malli drew the sword free of the sheath at her side, smoke from the approaching clouds stinging her eyes. "I didn't spend all that time training you just because you're pretty and fun to play with."

Fun to play with? Really? Whorls of amber spiraled open in the center of Kholburran's solid red eyes. Kholburran knew that he caused the rot. Had begun to suspect after the times he had to scrape invasive lichen from walls within the Root Tree or treat infection with a mixture of lye and blue flower. He may not have been able to see spirits like girl-type persons, but he could still tell. Warrune was tired of living and growing. Tired of all the little sproutlings running through him. He was ready to go. What Kholburran didn't understand was why.

"I'm not ready." Everything narrowed down to Malli and him. Whether Arri could take care of herself or not didn't figure in to his equations. Two living beings had to leave this place and make it to the Twins. Everyone else could die if needed, because they were not Malli and were therefore expendable.

In his mind, the fear of the Zaur fell away. They were no longer enemies, merely impediments threatening his home, his love. Boy-type person or not, Kholburran could not allow such impediments. Cornered, he felt a rage he'd never before experienced. How dare they threaten Malli?!

"You take the ones on the left." Bark thickened on Kholburran's forearms as he twisted to intercept the two Zaur headed in on his side. Some part of him tracked the others. Two Zaur each on him, Malli, and Arri.

Six.

Faulina and Seizal were dealing with two Gliders, with two more from the left and front peeling off to join in.

Six.

Two of the four on the right held back, readying their crossbows.

Fourteen total.

Just worry about the Zaur closest to you, Kholburran thought. *Don't worry about*—Hildi's pinioned body prostrate in the kitchen at Tranduvallu appeared in his mind, but he blinked it away. Enough bolts or a bolt to the right place and—

"Gah!" he willed the image away. Layers of bark thickened into a layer of rough armor on the rest of his body, coarse and hard along the smooth areas, and thicker than normal—yet still softer and more malleable—formed at his joints.

War drums sounded, their percussive roar inside his head rather than without. He bared his teeth in a wolfish grin, dental thorns exposed. He caught the first Zaur with a downward two-handed swing of his warpick, arm jolted numb, hands hurting at the impact as the wicked point sank into the Zaur's scaly hide, finding bone and breaking it, the tip emerging from the slain Zaur's chest. A killing blow.

Triumph short-lived by the lack of movement when he pulled back on the warpick. Stuck.

Warm air kissed Kholburran's belly in a hot line opened by the blade in the Zaur's right forepaw. A second Skreel knife in his left paw slashed up, stopping short of Kholburran's groin with a clang as Malli's sword thrust out between his legs parrying the blow.

"Not that bit," she joked, dental ridges gritted from the strain of the arm-fully-extended parry. "Takes too long to regrow."

Kholburran used the momentary respite to elbow the Zaur in the muzzle and grab for one of its dead companion's discarded Skreel blades. His fingertips missed the weapon by a space no larger than a hummingbird's kiss. Resisting the urge to turn back and try again, Kholburran stayed fluid as he'd been trained in those private times with Malli, when she'd humored him with a lesson. *Never stay in one place unless it is to your advantage to be rooted there*, Malli repeated in his memory even as she muttered, "Good boy" in the now.

More blades bit into his bark as he charged the Zaur that had been on the left, catching one and sinking his thorns into its arm. He pulled back, dental ridges edged with blood. He caught up a Skreel blade as it fell from the Zaur's numbed claw, its forepaw and arm dropping limp. Killing the Zaur with its own blade, Kholburran turned on the other Zaur as it chopped at the back of his legs.

Pain! Kholburran dropped to one knee as the Zaur cut into the more pliant bark covering the joint.

*

<<Enough,>> General Tsan ordered. <<I wish to address the Vael.>>

<<Sir?>> Kuort tapped on the general's shoulder.

The simple touch set off a muscle spasm so strong, Tsan feared she would scream. Finding out that six little Weeds had escaped had come quickly. Realizing one of them would be a Root Tree had taken far too long. Sleepless nights, forging ahead of the fires had been bad enough, but there had been no time to talk to Brazz. Lurking in the smoke as much as possible had disguised the scent, but the moment they were in a tunnel for any length of time, any Zaur or Sri'Zaur who got a whiff of Tsan's scent would know the gender switch was nearly complete.

I should have grabbed a flask when I had the chance, Tsan cursed inwardly. *Now it is all over but the molting.*

At least when he . . . she . . . shed her skin the pain would stop.

<<What?>> Tsan tapped back.

<<What are we doing?>>

<<The one with the warpick,>> Tsan tapped. <<It's a Root Tree or one of the little Weeds who can grow into one. If we take him hostage I can implement the plan early enough to ensure that negotiations begin before Asvrin's Shades have begun their attack. You will also have an unburnt sample of Vael blood we can send back to Warlord Xastix. Now leave me be.>>

But Kuort was scarcely paying attention to the vibrations of his message, staring instead at the patch of bright crimson where Tsan's ruddy male scales had begun to slough away. Their eyes met in silence, and Kuort wordlessly reached down into the forest floor, clawed up a mass of dirt, drooling saliva into his forepaw before smearing it over the revealing patch of scales.

"Yes, General," Kuort hissed softly, spotting two more patches and obscuring them as well.

<<Mount up.>> Gratitude in her heart, General Tsan mounted her deep walker, riding it clear of the smoke. *I knew there was a reason I didn't let Kuort's brothers eat him.*

*

Kholburran's eyes widened at the sight of the huge headless beast upon which the large Zaur rode. Like an obsidian statue of a headless dragon built on the scale of a great ox, the six-toed beast had dangerous-looking ridges along its chest and the front of its leg joints. The Zaur itself held a long, angled blade, much like the Skreel knives the other Zaur favored, but four feet long with a broader blade. Scales the color of dried blood peeked out from beneath a coat of plates.

"I know," the Zaur said convivially, "you would all die to protect the male." Four black-scaled Zaur with zigzag patterns of electric blue rode out of the smoke on mounts that matched that of the ruddy-scaled Zaur.

"I know this," it continued, "and I promise I am perfectly willing to spare him, to spare all of you. In fact, I would joyfully cease and desist all hostility against the Vael and leave The Parliament of Ages." It leaned forward over its blade, one clawed paw resting on its mount's stony front ridge. "Does that at all interest you?"

"Killing you interests us more," Kholburran shouted.

"This is not the time for games, Snapdragon," Malli told him. "You fight well, but . . ."

"Who speaks for your group?" the Zaur asked.

"I do," Arri croaked. She reached up to fiddle with the crossbow bolt in her throat, and Lara stepped over to help her dig it out, eying warily the Zaur who had been fighting them until the large Zaur had shouted "Enough."

Kholburran had heard the Root Guard gossiping about previous exploits against Zaur. They'd reported several scouts of advance forces getting ready to raid the Eldrennai, but all the ones they had described had been small black-, brown-, or gray-scaled reptiles, slender and quick. He watched as the Gliders, at least a dozen of them, with their mottled camouflaging scales dropped out of the trees.

"You have faced our diminutive cousins in the past," the Zaur spoke. "I believe you call them Zaur?"

"And you aren't Zaur?" Arri asked, shooing Lara away when they'd torn the bolt out quickly.

"I am General Tsan." Its forked gray tongue flicked out to taste the air. "My people dwell in the deep places where the warmbloods do not go, worshipping a god most warmbloods have long abandoned. You know our name, even though you do not know it is ours, because our home bears it. We are the Sri'Zaur and we come in peace."

"Peace?!" Kholburran yelled. "You burned Tranduvallu. Burned him and his protectors without provocation!"

General Tsan began a series of barking coughs. It took a moment for Kholburran to realize it was laughing.

*

"I apologize," General Tsan said once she felt they'd realized she had meant to be laughing. "I do not intend to dismiss your loss, but our ways are different in so many respects other than our physical dissimilarities."

<<Are the Zaurruk handlers in position?>> Tsan tapped with her tail.

<<Ready!>> came the faint reply.

"We attacked your smallest outpost in the ancient tradition of our people," she said aloud, then tapped in Zaurtol, <<Now!>>

"When we deployed the Zaurruk—" On cue one of the mighty serpents burst from the ground directly behind the Weeds. <<Flamefangs!>>

"—and our other soldiers—" Breathing gouts of liquid fire into the air and catching it back in their mouths like twisted fountains in a pyromaniac's Zen garden, Brazz led his Flamefangs out of the tunnel the Zaurruk had opened. "We were only demonstrating our value as allies. We are numerous—" <<Archers!>>

Black-, brown-, and gray-scaled archers charged out of the billowing smoke behind Tsan, crossbows at the ready. Some of them hissed rapidly for air as if they had nearly suffocated in the sooty back. Tsan hoped the Weeds didn't notice.

"And for any alliance to come to fruition in the depths," Tsan trilled, "a show of force—" <<Second Zaurruk!>> it burst from the soil directly behind Tsan and her mounted guard. "—is required before either side will take the other seriously."

"We have shown you some small portion of our military might," General Tsan continued, savoring the looks of awe and dismay on the faces of the five little Weeds, "and we believe you now understand the havoc we could wreak upon your older, more populated Root Trees, just as we now appreciate your bravery and the way you value the lives of your fellow . . . Vael. Your tenacity in the face of a superior force is obvious and we admire it."

"Liar!" the little male shouted.

General Tsan ignored the outburst, waiting patiently while the females shouted the male down.

"Hush, Snapdragon," the one-armed Weed said sternly, "the girl-type persons are talking. What," she asked as she stepped forward, "would be required to establish this peace?"

"Take me," General Tsan dismounted, hip muscles twitching, skin itching like mad. She longed to rip free of the remnants of her male skin, "to Queen . . . Kari. Isn't it? Your young prince will stay behind to ensure my safety."

"And what's to stop us," the one-armed Vael asked, "from coming back with reinforcements and crushing this invasion force of yours?"

Tsan decided she liked humans better. They screamed and got angry, but they usually understood the way of things more quickly than this. Well . . . the Zalizians hadn't, at Na'Shie, but the Holsvenians had been much more pragmatic.

"This, my young Vael," Tsan cooed, "is not Warlord Xastix's invasion force." Her eyes nictated languidly. "What you see here is the meager nego-tiation team I was allowed . . . the right size to ensure our target's destruc-tion. The rest of my army is already in place. Assuming we can come to an accord in the next thirteen days, however, you need never concern yourselves with their locations. What say you?"

Gathering together in a sort of kneeling huddle, the Weeds argued back and forth, the male trying to get a word in, but the females shouting him down until he gave up and sat to the side, listening in dejection.

"Stay here, Snapdragon," Arri told the male. "All right, General." She held out her remaining hand. "It looks like you're with us, but if you hurt the prince—"

"No force on all Barrone will prevent you from avenging yourself?" Tsan flicked her tongue out, tasting the air. "Well, yes, my force would prevent it, but as I have no interest in killing the young male, the point is moot."

Tsan dropped her weapon on the ground and shrugged out of the coat of plates she wore, letting both items drop to the forest floor. "Shall we go?"

CHAPTER 12

. . . AND KINGS LIVE

The mage-formed spires of Castle Ammond shone white in the harsh light of banished summer. On the second-highest balcony of the central spire—below and to the right of the King's Royal Suite—a lone figure stood in a long wool robe, cotton breeches, his feet wrapped in bandages. Salty air from the sea ruffled his garments and mussed his long black hair. Loosely tied with a blue sash, the robe fell open to the waist revealing pale flesh beneath, the training-hardened muscle, but (most strikingly) the trail of scars wending its way around Rivvek's torso.

Everyone saw his facial scars, his ruined ear, the melted wreck that was a third of his face, but few saw the foot-long cicatrix commemorating a Ghaiattri's grip on his left side. Just above the hip: a claw print in wet clay . . .

The matching marks on his right calf . . . the splayed print at his sternum . . . the angry red circle below it where the Ghaiattri's thumb had pierced his chest. When his mind wandered, the scent of his own burnt flesh could still surprise him. Thinking about them brought pain and heat back to the wounds.

"Still alive," he whispered. "But you aren't, are you, Father?"

"Sire," Sargus's quiet voice called behind him.

Rivvek squinted, the sharp features of his face cast in heightened severity. Amid pendulous clouds out at sea, a bright dot in the distance winked at him, catching the sun. Rivvek's long black hair, drawn back in a ponytail, held in place by a brass hair cuff, blew out behind him—a muted halo of black. Goosebumps rose at the increased chill, but he did not step away or draw his robe closer. *I'd rather be back in the tent or at Oot. Anywhere really.* Out over the breakers in the distance, the flaring object caught his eye again.

"Out here, Sargus. Bring my spyglass, would you?"

"Spyglass?" Sargus called from beyond the heavy blue drapes that muted the cold and wind from blowing into the suite behind Rivvek.

"Please?" Rivvek made a loose fist. He held it up, looking through the small dot of clear space. Still flaring, the approaching object came into better focus, but not quite good enough to confirm what Rivvek knew in his heart it would be. "Oh. And watch your step. There's glass."

"Glass?" Sargus stepped out onto the balcony. The leather half cap and accompanying lenses that often covered the haffet of his face were nowhere to be seen. Absent as well was the satchel of supplies he often wore at his back to mimic a hunch. Rivvek considered it a special privilege that Sargus rarely feigned deformity in his presence when it could be avoided. Certainly not when they were alone. Rivvek did not have to ask why Sargus made the gesture, but noticing it brought a half smile to his lips.

"My prince?" Sargus frowned at the scattered shards of glass covering the stone floor of the balcony and the bloodied footprints amongst them.

"Don't baby me, Sargus!" Rivvek spared a glance at his bandaged feet. "I cut my feet and destroyed a priceless antique table and chair set in a fit of . . ." He grasped for the words. ". . . fatalistic rage. Pique. Stupidity. Grief. Take your pick, O he-who-can-sleep-through-anything."

"Did you—?" But Sargus cut himself off, his nostrils widening.

"I treated them," Rivvek interrupted, "and then Bhaeshal insisted on doing it all over again herself. She did a far better job of than I did, though, so I can't fault her for it. I'd have thought you'd smell the laughing salve and cleansing salts."

"Yes, I do now." Sargus was always so amusing when he didn't know what to do. "Should I call a servant—"

"And have Jason or Alice clean it up for me?" Rivvek shook his head. "No. It's my mess. I'll clear it away. Spyglass?" he added, hand held out to receive it.

"Take mine." Sargus held out a telescoping spyglass, its "barrels" over-laid with a richly stained wood Rivvek did not immediately recognize.

"Thank you." Rivvek turned the unfamiliar optic to the sea, raising the eyepiece to his eye. He spied at once the brightly blazing metal construct of silver and crystal that had been his father's crown. It soared through the clouds, a blazing relic of finality. Beautiful and elegant as it was, Rivvek hated the sight of the thing.

"Excellent work." Lowering the spyglass, he closed his eyes and handed it back. "Your craftsmanship?"

Glass crunched under sandal-clad feet as Sargus stepped closer to the balustrade, the soft hiss of the spyglass telescoping outward. A muttered curse as Sargus found the crown in the objective lens.

"I'm sorry, my king."

"Exactly as I forecast. What luck, eh?" Tears streaming down his face, Rivvek let his robe drop. Wind from the bay wove the scent of sea around him, the sun scintillating on the foci that framed his back in the rough outline of wings. Simple circles of brass, steel, gold, or silver at first, the foci ranged into rarer materials as they worked down his side: jade, quartz, even samples of wood and bone-steel . . . anything the Artificers could think of (and justify) to restore and strengthen his connection to the elemental magic that had been his from birth until . . . until it hadn't.

None of it had helped.

Rivvek could still hear Hasimak reporting back to the king. *The damage is quite extensive, Your Majesty, Perhaps given time . . . I'm sorry. No one has ever survived such an assault. . . .*

Rivvek winced at the image of the Ghaiattri looming over him, burning away his skin, his soul, his . . . magic.

He shook away the mental pain, not only to avoid dwelling on past trauma but also because he had no time for it. His father would have been able to bargain for only a few days. Between two and five, if his own math, his version of the great destiny machine, had calculated the Aern's reaction well.

"Closer to five," Rivvek murmured. "Please."

Not much time, but enough time, if Rivvek's other calculations of all known variables on the great destiny machine of probabilities were correct as well. He felt the gentle touch of Sargus's hand on his back where the most important scars of Rivvek or his people's future lay: A diamond pattern at the base of his spine with two lines parallel with and equal in length to each side of diamond. His shoulders were each marked with a right-angled wedge. Along his spine ran a long thumb-width line, essentially a tally mark: the number one.

Getting Kholster's scars on his back had hurt the least but meant the most. Those scars meant hope. The one variable that might let him salvage his brother's mess.

You forgave me, Kholster, Rivvek thought, *even though I failed, you rewarded the effort. The thought counted with you. Why?*

"You never told me how you convinced him to make you Aiannai," Sargus said as if sensing his thoughts. "All save Zhan rejected me, because of my father. But Kholster himself accepted you. He—"

"Simple." Rivvek stepped through the blue drapes, off of the cold balcony, and into the warmth of his modest, if spacious, suite of rooms. A fire blazed in the fireplace beneath a bare mantel. An assortment of rugs covered the stone, but no tapestries or pictures hung on the walls. An array of finely crafted weaponry awaited Rivvek's pleasure on a large wall-mounted weapon rack, but his bedroll and pack (with newly laundered travel clothes within) neatly stored next to the gear were the only signs of sleeping accommodations. A well-worn armchair sat in one corner next to a mountainous stack of books and scrolls beneath a wall sconce. An armor stand bearing a suit of grotesque Ghaiattri hide plate, the ram-like horns of the Ghaiattri itself mounted on the helm, dominated the room. Next to it, a mystic sparring dummy stood at the ready.

"Simple?" Sargus prompted.

"I showed him my other scars, told him how I got them . . ." Rivvek walked to a large wardrobe, opened it, and began rummaging for appropriate attire. White, white, and more white to show the proper respect for the late king. He'd have to wear less traditional clothes for the Test of Four, but he could obey convention in this at least.

"Just that?" Sargus asked.

"The Aern are impressed by scars." Rivvek looked back at him, tears still flowing but already forgotten. "I also told him why." He smiled. "Can you send Jason up to help me with this? I don't want any of the Royal Adjudicators accusing me of deliberately slighting my father's memory just because I prefer to dress myself."

"I could—" Sargus offered.

"No time, Sargus."

"Of course." Sargus nodded, slipping on his pack. He hunkered over preparing to assume his usual disguise. "Do you really think we can . . ." He paused, tapping the side of his leather haffet, letting it meld into an illusion to render to his skull misshapen. "Do you really think we can win?"

"As long as I can pass the Test of Four, it won't matter whether we win or not. The Aern and the Vael will do the rest. The only thing that worries me is whether I've estimated the size of the Zaur force correctly."

"And if you haven't?" Sargus paused at the door.

"If I haven't, there is nothing more I can do to shape the outcome." Rivvek looked into the shadowy realm of the Ghaiattri. He gritted his teeth, forcing the sight away again. Heat filled his scars, and he laughed. "Well, maybe one thing. I wouldn't give myself very good odds, though."

Pain lanced in after the heat, searing the deep muscles beneath each scar as if he'd forced it down into a hot pan. *I'm used to you now*, he thought at the agony. *You can't conquer me. Haven't you seen the scars on my back?*

"You still haven't explained everything you've planned, my prince," Sargus said.

Rivvek frowned, putting a finger to his lips. "The gods might be listening, Sargus. I want to give them as little time to react as possible. Never tell gods your plans."

When Sargus had gone, Rivvek allowed himself another hundred count of grief.

"You deserved more, Father." He clenched his fists. "I would mourn for a year and a day, had we the time. . . ."

But I don't, he thought, *so we move on.*

His mother's funeral had been a grand thing. The heavens and earth shook to see her pass. Father's elemancers had seen to it. He and Dolvek had worn the white of mourning for two years. The king had grieved for decades.

Rivvek reached out to the elements trying to touch the planes of air, water, fire, and earth—the magic that had been his birthright—and felt from only one of them even the slightest glimmer of contact. A hint of flame. From the others, he sensed nothing at all.

"Oh, how the mighty Flamewing has dimmed," he mocked himself. Rivvek resisted the urge to draw on the flame, forced himself to let sensation of connection be enough. "Barely a wisp of fire now, but even the tiniest spark . . ." He caught himself speaking aloud and stopped his words. One never knew who might be listening. First he must attend his father's cremation and then the Test of Four.

No, blast me, I've left something out. Cursing to himself, he strode to the door and opened it to find Bhaeshal exactly where he'd instructed her not to be.

"Good, you disobeyed and kept watch anyway." He smiled, knocking on her pauldron. It was amazing how you could tell the intelligent guards from the morons. No one had had to tell Bash to start wearing metal armor. She'd started showing up in the demi-cuirass and brigandine she'd worn back when she was a Lancer the hour they'd received news about the Zaur at Oot. "I need to send someone intelligent and deadly down to the docks to make blasted sure they are prepared for the Aern to arrive today. The roof is unlikely to collapse on me even without you here to hold the wall up, so perhaps you'd like to go . . . and if not then please send someone."

Bhaeshal blinked at that, the slight click as her steel eyelids tapped against each other, proof, if any need it, that the silver domino mask she wore was an elemental foci and not a mask at all. In the light, the Vael-like uniformity of her white crystalline eyes was even more striking.

"You think they'll be early?" she asked, pinning him with those blank orbs.

"I think they will be early and I think they will try to provoke anyone they can." He leaned against the doorframe and lowered his voice into a conspiratorial whisper. "They would love an excuse to kill us all, so make certain you assign someone unflappable . . . if you decide not to go yourself."

"They won't get a rise out of me, Your Highness." She smiled. "I will send Olivan around to hold the wall up, though, just to be on the safe side."

"Thank you." Rivvek watched her go. What was it about female Eldrennai that made them so reliable? Muttering to himself, he let the door close and ran over the plan for the Test of Four again, thankful he'd been able to delegate one more item. He smirked, surprised at the flash of good humor. Bash could handle the Aern and the dockworkers. *If only I had more like her.*

CHAPTER 13
DOCKING MANEUVERS

Vander laughed, the sea breeze nearly stealing the hat from his bald head, and his soldiers laughed with him. Oathbreaker vessels moved across the waves in frantic panic, butting against one another, cutting to and fro, blocking each others' passage in a unanimous, yet useless, attempt to flee from the mighty Aernese warships the Overwatch kholstered. Two three-masted merchant ships moved past each other with only scant feet separating the two hulls, the crews shouting at each other and the serving Aeromancers and Hydromancers working desperate magicks to avert a collision.

"If you don't start following orders, I will sink your ships myself!" shouted an Oathbreaker female whose elemental foci looked like a silver mask. "I am sending squads to man your vessels. You will cooperate with these soldiers. There is no other option!"

"Squad one," she boomed, giving out assignments and marking ships with coruscating blasts of electricity that arced harmlessly around ship and crew alike.

Are you watching this, Khol . . . Rae'en?

Did they think they were under attack? Rae'en thought.

They didn't know what to think, Vander sent back, *until she showed up.*

Do you know her?

She looks different with the elemental focus, but I'm pretty sure that if it isn't Bhaeshal, it's her daughter.

Arriving as if the act of thinking her name had summoned her, the Aeromancer flew directly toward him, arms folding across her breastplate, pale white eyes crackling with lightning.

"Could you please stop firing those cannons, Overwatch Vander?" Her eyes narrowed. "We know you are here and you will be clear to dock shortly."

"What if I refuse?" He glared up at her from beneath the hat he wore to keep the suns from burning his bald pate.

"Then we'll have your path clear a little more slowly," Bhaeshal answered in an even tone, cordial but unamused.

"No threats?" Vander stifled a laugh as two more cannons boomed. "You aren't afraid of our artillery?"

A look of mild bemusement touched the Oathbreaker's lips, if only for a heartbeat.

That's enough, he thought to his Aern.

"I've given the order," Vander said. "Anything else, Oathbreaker?"

"If you could keep brawls to a minimum, it would be most appreciated."

"You're Bhaeshal, aren't you," he asked, "Wylant's grandniece?"

"That's my name, but I'm not related to Wylant. That's just an assumption made by people who think the only way a woman can be worth anything in the military is if she has Wylant's blood." She dropped low, still not boarding the ship but hovering a hand's breadth from the rail.

"That's what I get for overhearing conversations on the training grounds." Vander doffed his canvas hat. "They called you Lieutenant Bash back then."

"And I've risen as high as lieutenant general," she answered, "but it's Brigadier Bash now."

Vander watched the map in the corner of his field of vision, where other Overwatches fed him data. He admired the way Bash's squads took their positions and began clearing up the mess without the need for further instructions. Well trained.

"Why the demotion?"

"Once for losing my temper. A second time because it was the only way they would let me stay in direct command of Prince Rivvek's security."

"He means that much to you?" Vander breathed deeply, trying to pick up her scent. Wylant often smelled of *jallek* root, leather, and sweat. Bash smelled of royal hedge roses, sweat, and sea air. *That's a scent I could get used to*, he thought, hoping none of the others overheard. From the way rose-covered vines began to flow up the edges of his map, it was clear at least one of them had.

"And to you, I imagine," Bhaeshal retorted, "given the scars on his back."

"I don't see the hate in your eyes that I see when I look at other . . . Eldrennai." Vander stepped closer, leaning on the rail. He'd expected her to fly back and give him space. Instead, she floated lower, until they were eye to eye. "You didn't give any orders at As You Please, and I can't recall you abusing your authority over us. Why haven't you asked to be Aiannai yet?"

"Do you want to put your scars on my back," Bash dropped a fraction of a hand closer, "or did you hope to get me out of my armor for some other reason?"

Vander's mouth dropped open. The lack of proper ocular anatomy made her hard to read. No veins to watch. No pupils to dilate or contract, but that sounded like flirting to him.

"Because my prince asked me to wait," she continued, mercifully ending the awkward pause in conversation.

"And why is that?" Vander frowned.

Are you going to propose? Rae'en taunted.

She's intriguing, Vander thought back. *I can't remember her ever holding the leash. Wasn't she married to an Aern at one point?*

To Abrax. So because she never gave orders to an Aern and has a certain fondness for them, you want to rescue her?

Abrax? Vander could think of more than one Abrax.

By Zabrax, out of some Flower Girl or other, Rae'en answered. *Why does it matter?*

It doesn't, Vander thought back. But it did. Abrax hadn't been one of the Armored, so the Sundering had probably slain him and sent his soul to become one with the group. He wondered how that made Bash feel, both about Aern and about Wylant.

"I didn't ask." Bhaeshal drifted farther away from the ship and Vander. Her scent was muddied by the wind.

"I'm sorry about Abrax," Vander blurted.

"As am I." Bash's voice went quiet. "But there was nothing else I could do. He was after then-Prince Grivek." She shook it off, her voice more normal in the next sentence. "And, for the next time it happens, Overwatch Vander: When you meet a female you fancy? The husband she had to kill is not a good choice for conversational gambits. Even asking me what my focus was made of would have been more delicate."

Yep, Rae'en thought, *you kicked that irkanth right in the nose.*

I can't be perfect all the time, Vander sent back. *Still . . .*

"I'm sorry, Brigadier Bhaeshal." Vander pursed his lips. "Steel, isn't it?"

"Don't be sorry," Bash told him, a hint of humor creeping back into her tone. "You're an Aern. That means to be fair I have to give you another chance or two to do it right. Try and keep it down with the cannons, though, yes? You're scaring the mice, and they won't be any fun to play with later if they've already drowned. Can you do that for me, Overwatch Vander?"

"*Va vari ka,*" Vander shouted over his shoulder to the crew, drawing in a huge lungful of air and letting it all blast out of his chest in those three words: an Aernese shout meaning "See it so." His crew and the crew of the other vessels, the fifty-eight troop transports, the frigates, every Aern echoed his cry simultaneously. Even the thin-lipped human Long Speakers were caught up in the moment, cackling like old men.

"That's better than the cannon blasts, I suppose," Bhaeshal shouted over the din. "You have my thanks."

Vander wondered what they all thought it meant: the shouting. A show of force. Was it a show of force? Was it not? Was he showing off? It was unusual for an Aern to marry an Eldrennai. Vander didn't think it could have happened more than four or five dozen times in six thousand years.

"I acted like an idiot," he muttered to himself, "Ah, well. I won't do it next time."

Can you show me that memory again? Rae'en asked. *Before your next-betrothed showed up and started flirting?*

Vander did so gladly, only feeling a little strange at the teasing. It was exactly the sort of thing Kholster might have said, and that was a good sign. It showed Rae'en was getting more comfortable with him and finding her own path as First, but it still felt so strange to be kholster'd by someone (anyone) other than his lifelong friend.

I'd wager . . . , Rae'en sent, *well, not naming rights, but something interesting, they heard those booms from the royal apartments.*

Why not naming rights? Vander asked.

I never wager naming rights, Rae'en shot back.

Vander smirked at that.

Just what your father would have told me, he sent back.

Good.

Any special instructions?

I don't think they're likely to, Rae'en answered, *but if they break their word, attack last.*

It was a quote Kholster had used in the early days, and the reference brought a smile revealing all eight canines to Vander's lips. "Let the enemy strike as hard as they can. Let them show us what they're made of, and once they've given what they have in the first attack . . . we attack last."

Let them start it, but you finish it.

"Torgrimm's name, I miss him," Vander breathed.

There was no need to acknowledge Rae'en's command. Instead, Vander drew his warpick, Scorn, the weapon's serrated head glinting savagely in the sun, and stood at the bow of the ship, both hands on the head of his weapon, its burnished bone-steel haft resting flat against the deck. His men followed suit, lining up along the sides of their ships, showing themselves to the enemy. Attack us, they seemed to say. Attack us, please, that you may be arvashed.

Vander felt the presence of Scorn's spirit at his shoulder, its insubstantial claws clicking next to his ear. When he had forged the weapon and sent a piece of his soul into it, he had seen the thing skitter down his sweat-soaked chest as a bright-red mountain scorpion, poison dripping from its triple tail. It wanted to kill the Leash Holders as much as he did. It longed for revenge.

Sun beating down upon his bald head, hat lost to the waves, neither Vander nor his men moved a muscle until the harbor was clear three hours later. Without a word, the Armored moved, going about their jobs with precision and care. Unlike human sailors, once the ships had docked, the Aern lined the docks in perfect rows, weapons ready, automatons of doom.

Vander walked proudly past his warriors, along the central dock, stepping over a precious upturned crate of out-of-season strawberries abandoned by the merchants in their hasty departure. Before him, Port Ammond rose above the docks, the central high-stepped stair leading up to the covered walkway that served as a secure route to and from a royal estate no longer the pristine white he remembered from before the Sundering. Without the Vael to tend them, the once beautiful marble was now off-white at best. High on either side of the stair wooden posts rose from the marble, red-brown rust stains marking where iron had once stood. Each post supported a brass lantern in the shape of a mighty irkanth, but where once the mouths of those irkanths would have been filled with mystic blue flames, they now held lamp oil and lit wicks.

Two sloping cobblestone roads curved wide around the bluff upon which the royal tower stood, the wall that wrapped itself around the city broken by two wide reinforced doors. Both of the doors were shut tight and barred. The tower itself seemed to stare imperiously down at Vander. He fancied the enormous edifice little more than a tremendous finger thrusting up from the ground wishing nothing more than to shake itself at the Aern disapprovingly. Or was he just in a mood because Brigadier Bash and her squads had left when their mission was accomplished without saying good-bye?

I'm in position, he thought to Rae'en.

*

Want to trade? Rae'en sent back to her uncle from her place in King Grivek's death procession. *I could have beaten you there if not for these Oathbreakers. It's only five jun! How can they not run five jun in their sleep in under an hour?*

Ahead of her the long line of grieving Oathbreakers clad in white cloaks trod at a solemn pace. They sang songs of gratitude to Torgrimm, the lyrics hastily altered to allow them to apply to the new death god, but not by name. Kholster was merely referred to as "The Harvester" by the Eldrennai clergy. Wylant walked at the head of the procession, hand on her sword hilt, while four of the seven Sidearms who had survived the fight in Xasti'Kaur carried the king with their magic.

Kam's elemental held the late king's body aloft on a miniature thundercloud, its tiny lightning strikes leaving scorch marks on the path. Globes of earth, water, and fire orbited the corpse (which was itself draped in white) in a precise pattern that Rae'en assumed had some meaning.

Vander, do you know what that is?

Only because I've seen the same sort of thing at other Oathbreaker funerals.

He wasn't providing much of a map in her head because of the distance between them, just an estimated time of arrival at Port Ammond and a direction arrow, but he drew the same pattern the Sidearms were making with their magic across the upper right quadrant of her vision. Seen from the top-down perspective Vander had used and letting the lines stay in place even after the fire, earth, and water symbols he had chosen moved on to the next point in the pattern, it was simple to see the three castles' outlines formed by the ever-moving globes.

Reserved mainly for elemental lords, ladies, or royalty, I think, Vander thought at her.

And the cloud represents the backdrop?

I think so, Vander thought back. *But it isn't like they gave us a class on it. The Leash Holders only wanted us to stand there and look impressive.*

I bet they wish we were a little less impressive now. Rae'en grinned.

I'd wager naming rights on it.

Which is why, Rae'en sent, *one of us has a son named VanZhander and the other one . . .*

Has made her point, Vander replied, clearing the design from her field of vision.

Walking slowly enough to keep from bumping into the Oathbreaker in front of her—one of the surviving three Kingsguard—made her feel like she was doing muscle control exercises back home in South Number Nine with Quana or Malmung. And while the temperature didn't bother her, the scent of the Oathbreakers around her sweating through their underclothes did.

She tried to occupy herself by admiring the colors of changing leaves, the crisp crunch underfoot as she walked over them, but that could only keep an Aern occupied so long. Maybe Irka would have been able to spend hours enjoying Gromma's "gifts of nature" all around, but really all Rae'en wanted to do was bury Grudge or Testament in another Oathbreaker's skull.

She could always check in with Bloodmane, but the fact of the matter was, she didn't want to talk to him at all, much less look through his eyes. She caught glimpses when she closed her own, but until she had to do otherwise, she'd decided to let Vander do the seeing for her.

Any news? she almost asked him. Almost because she'd just had an update. It was too soon to ask for another.

Zhan, she thought to the First Ossuarian. *Any update on my ring?* Her father's final gift to her had been a ring of silvered bone-steel made from his own bone metal. Inside, he'd inscribed the words: "Daughter, of you I am proud." On the outer ring, he'd wrought a stylized representation of his scars. She lost it in the blasted Zaur tunnels when she'd gone into the Arvash'ae far too early and was still kicking herself over it. Two Bone Finders had been sent to find her back when she'd been captured and feared dead, but she'd already escaped with the help of Wylant and Captain Tyree. They had meant to go back for the ring immediately, but when Kholster had gone missing, it had interrupted everyone's plans.

Teru and Whaar are working on it, New Bones. Zhan's thoughts, tinged with gentle teasing, touched her mind. *I'll admit, it does seem to be taking them overlong. Would you like me to have Alysaundra speed them up?*

Would you mind?

Would it matter if I did? Zhan asked.

Of course it would, Rae'en thought back.

Good. Then I don't mind. Zhan paused, composing his thoughts, which felt strange to Rae'en, as if he were broadcasting silence. *It is merely that I seem to recall quite recently when the Firsts of One Hundred, both previous and current, were screaming at me to find bones. In one case they were the bones of a living being and therefore outside my Oathbound purview, and in the second case they were unattainable for less mundane reasons.*

My father had just died, Zhan.

I know. His thoughts were warm but firm. *I understand you were both under great duress. But you must understand that I am sworn to seek the bones of the dead or items made from bone metal. I am not to knowingly seek, as Ossuarian, the bones of the living. I must protect myself from being Foresworn as well, New Bones. As much as I may wish Uled had not encumbered me with such an oath, he did, and by it I am still bound.*

Rae'en had not understood that, not at all.

And Grivek's release didn't—?

I did not swear the oath to Grivek, Zillek, or the crown. Uled took it upon himself to work it into me, in much the same way keeping oaths is worked into all Aern.

Why? Rae'en asked.

I have my suspicions, Zhan thought back, *but dwelling on them does nothing but stir up old feelings I would prefer not to awaken.*

Didn't Uled's death free you from it?

No, nor did Kholster's. He sounded impatient with the line of questioning there, but Rae'en kept asking.

Why not?

I have asked the same thing of myself many times, Zhan told her. *I did not have the answer then either.*

"Fine," Rae'en whispered into cupped hands. Letting out a long breath, she went back to watching the Sidearms. "I wish I could see better, though."

After a moment, she felt the touch of Bloodmane's mind connecting her wordlessly to another of the warsuits.

It may be wise to speak a little more quietly, Silencer (Caz's warsuit) intoned. **However, having heard your request . . .**

A second view of the procession, this time from the front, appeared in the leftmost corner of her field of vision.

Can he get me a better view of the Sidearms?

One moment.

Rae'en had met them all briefly at Oot. Mazik, the only one of them with hair short enough that her father would have approved, was the one with the bandana tied around his neck pulled up to his nose to conceal the way his elemental foci had taken over his throat and lower jaw, converting them to brass. He was the one who'd stayed behind to try and help Wylant fight the Zaurruk in the tunnel.

As far as Rae'en could tell, he was Wylant's second-in-command, even though he walked at the back of the group of Sidearms. Number one in the front and number two in the back? Yes, that had to be it. With Rae'en at the very back of the procession, they didn't need to cover it, so they'd bracketed the king's corpse between them.

Frip and Frindo walked on either side of the corpse, Frindo on the left with his right hand slightly upraised to control the whirling globe of flame, inset crystals in his palm and (in place of) his left eye, the metal around them a polished brass.

His twin brother Frip took the right side, his left hand with its steel plate and blue crystal angled in extremely similar fashion to his brother's. Just as Frip was his brother's opposite in so many things, he controlled an orb of ice, letting it dance in an orbit counter to Frindo's flames, the steel plate over his right eye with its inset crystal sparking with the cold blue in defiant opposition to his brother's red crystal.

She skipped curly-headed Roc with his metal feet (the lone Geomancer and therefore obviously the elemancer responsible for the twirling hunk of granite that completed the globe pattern) and watched Ponnod. She couldn't see it through his breastplate, but he was supposed to have lost his entire upper torso to his elemental foci, becoming, at least externally, a being of brass and steel. Rae'en could hear his breathing even from back where she walked. It sounded more like a bellows than any set of lungs she'd heard before.

When Mazik, Roc, Kam, and Hira had gone back to try to retrieve the bodies of their fallen comrades, they'd found Ponnod dragging Frip and Frindo behind him on an improvised Zaurruk-hide sledge. The three of them had been terribly injured but were not quite dead.

Wylant charged down a dark Zaur tunnel, ran right into one of those giant serpents, and only lost four men, Silencer commented. **Impressive.**

Griv, Tomas, Dodan, and Bakt had all died. Rae'en would have remembered their names even if she'd only heard them once, not only because she, like her father, was incapable of forgetting anything, but because they'd been drilled home by the series of toasts Wylant and her Sidearms had made back in the camp near Oot on the night they'd retrieved their lost companions.

Silencer was right. They impressed her then as she pieced together the battle that had led to Wylant's capture, eavesdropping, albeit unintentionally, while she sat at the base of her father's statue and Grivek and Yavi slept.

They impressed her now, too. She knew that, like her, they could have made the trip to Port Ammond much more quickly. Flying in tandem, they could have made the trip faster than she could, but they kept a pace their fellows could match. Wylant's Sidearms were the only Oathbreakers Rae'en had met that she actually liked. Of course, she was open to at least the idea of liking any Oathbreaker her father's First Wife found acceptable to serve under her. Rae'en was tempted to make them all Aiannai, but she wasn't completely sure whether she could or not. Was it that simple? Wylant had been a Leash Holder, but Kholster had made her Aiannai because she had kept her oath in grand fashion at the breaking of the Life Forge and because he loved her.

Did liking and respecting them make them fit to be Aiannai, too?

Hours later, with Port Ammond looming in the distance, cast in shades of red by the sunset, Rae'en still didn't have her answer.

CHAPTER 14
BONE FINDERS

Teru and Whaar, one of fifty-two pair of Ossuarians who had been reunited with their warsuits, moved through the tunnels of the Zaur, giving more thought to the construction of passages through which they traveled and the quarry they sought than to the combats raging in the surrounding areas. The warsuits Bloodmane kholstered seemed in little danger, and now that Rae'en was safe and appointed the new First of One Hundred, the item they sought had little to do with the living.

Some stinking Zaur has it, Teru thought.

So it would seem.

What? You think something else has it? Snagged on an animal?

It would not be unheard of . . .

No, Teru shook his head, *there was no meat on the bones this time. It has to have been something of Kholster's that New Bones had with her.*

You could always ask her.

The day I need to bother the First of One Hundred with—Teru rounded a sharp turn, surprising a squad of reptiles. Twelve Zaur, bellies low to the ground, Skreel blades in their forepaws, drew up short. Their Sri'Zaur squad leader hissed a challenge.

<<We come for the bones,>> Whaar pounded in Zaurtol with No Surrender's pommel against the wall of the tunnel as he drew up next to Teru.

No Escape's crystalline eyes sparked red in the dark, punctuating his occupant's message with a threat of his own. Crimson light painted the unsullied portions of his pearlescent bone-metal surface the shade of spilt human blood. The axe-like blade that ran from the crown of No Escape's knobby brow to the base of his helm cast even darker shadows on the wall.

<<We. Come. For. The. Bones.>> Teru tapped with Last Kiss, creating the sounds with alternating slaps of the double-bladed axe's cheeks on the stone.

Teru's warsuit, Bonestripper, bore a thick layer of congealed blackish Zaur blood from the base of his heels to the tips of the small sharp horns mounted over the vertical eye slits of his skull-inspired helm.

The leader, the Sri'Zaur, tapped something back in Zaurtol, but Teru didn't quite follow it.

What are they going on about? he thought at his armor.

They say they will steal your bone metal and—

"Engaging the idiots," Teru shouted, smiling as Whaar charged in only a beat behind him. Working in tandem, the two Bone Finders cut through three of the twelve, stopped, turned, and tapped out their message again.

<<We come for the bones.>>

The Sri'Zaur charged.

His soldiers did not.

*

Less than a candlemark later, the two Bone Finders turned down yet another side tunnel. The closer they got, the more clearly Teru could see the missing bone metal in his mind. Something small. Round. A circle.

A ring?

We could ask kholster Rae'en if she knows exactly what we're looking for, Bonestripper suggested.

Teru did not dignify that with a response.

They moved past an area that still smelled of jun powder.

"Why did First Bones make a ring?" Whaar wondered aloud.

"A gift for New Bones?" Teru answered. "A more interesting question is why she left it behind."

"She knew we'd come get it back for her?"

Teru laughed. "I hope not." He jerked his head to the west following a sudden change of direction made by his quarry—it was certainly being carried. "Zhan was upset enough when Kholster sent us seeking New Bones without knowing whether or not her bones truly needed collecting yet. You saw her at Oot after First Bones went into the water. She was dismissive of the Ossuary then, but we were all pretty shaken so—"

Zhan requests an update, Bonestripper said in Teru's mind.

First Bones is still in the wind, Teru shot back. *We're following it, but the relic is on the move.*

And you want me to tell him that?

Tell him to come find it himself if he wants it faster. He may have noticed there is a war on. We keep getting interrupted.

End Song is connecting him now.

I don't want the Ossuarian in my blasted head—

I enjoy it no more than you, came Zhan's voice, his words echoing as if he called to Teru from a hundred feet or so farther down the tunnel, *and yet here I am.*

Teru knew the other Aern, the soldiers of the Aernese army who were not Bone Finders of the Ossuary, were in each others' heads from dusk til dawn and all through the night. They seemed to like it well enough, not having a moment's privacy even in their own skulls, but to Teru, the increased level of communication was the single largest drawback to being Armored.

"Are you sending what we're seeing and hearing?" Teru snapped.

"No, Maker," Bonestripper intoned. "Never without express permission—"

"Good."

"I should warn you, however, that Whaar is having No Escape transmit everything."

No Escape, covered in a similar gore, waggled its helm at him, the axe-like blade that ran from the crown of its knobby brow to the base of its helm catching the light of Bonestripper's eyes as it did so.

"What the hells, Whaar?"

"He asked." Whaar shrugged, the movement matched by No Escape to make sure the other Aern caught it. "Dark or white, it's all meat to me whether he wants to look through my eyes and hear with my ears. It's his headache."

Yes, it is, Zhan thought at Teru. *So . . . no progress to report?*

Don't dull your blade, Zhan, Teru thought back. *We have this dinner skinned.*

Teru walked on as they conversed, trying to track the best route to follow the ring.

That is exactly what she said you would say. Teru felt more than heard the sigh that Zhan broadcast following those words.

She? Teru cursed. Zhan, the Bone Harvest doesn't need to—

She is kholstering this recovery now, Teru. Zhan's voice trailed off, as he ended both sentence and connection at once.

"He's sending Alysaundra?" Whaar asked.

Teru nodded, and it was Whaar's turn to curse.

"He didn't have to bother her with this." Whaar punched the wall.

The Bone Harvest is requesting a link, Bonestripper whispered softly in Teru's mind.

Now you ask permission first?

Nope, laughed a sultry feminine voice in his head. *He put me right through. Same old Bonestripper.*

"Bone," Teru hissed at his warsuit. "When we get done with this mission, you and I are going to have a very long talk about—"

She is your kholster, Teru. Bonestripper gave him a mental shrug.

Stop worrying that gristle and pay attention to the spoor on your boots, sweetmeat, Alysaundra thought. *You need to quit messing about and get after the ring.*

You know it's a ring?

Of course, Alysaundra thought. *A ring of bone-steel silver alloy. The exterior of the band bears a stylized representation of Kholster's scars. On the band's interior, there is an inscription which reads: Daughter, of you I am proud. And before you ask, I know that because I asked kholster Rae'en if she would send me an image of her father's missing bone metal. She was quite happy to do so and to point out (as if I hadn't noticed) that it was the final piece ever forged by Kholster.*

Oh. Teru blanched.

So what is your plan? And it had better be something other than running through the tunnels like Kilke's own Armored scarecrows waiting until you come upon a group of Zaur so you can feel like the Lord of the Tunnels when you tap <<We come for the bones>> at them.

We haven't—

Please remember to whom you are lying, sweetmeat. Alysaundra's laughter rang out in his mind. *I've been married to both of you. You are playing around.*

I track you there, she continued. *It's fun. I'm just as much an Aern as you two, and I know you haven't gotten to play with Zaur for centuries. But now you have had your happy time, and the last work of First Bones is in the wind. Get aboveground. Run through the forest until you find the spot where the blasted Zaur is and then get the ring even if it means you have to follow it for a hundred jun to find an air vent.*

"I think we passed an air vent a little ways back," Whaar offered.

Sighing deeply, Teru turned and ran for the vent. He remembered it, too. He tried to pretend that somewhere Alysaundra wasn't shaking her head in disgust at both of them.

*

Lurching through the lightless tunnels in a four-legged lope, his shadow-black belly scales a kiss from the stone, Lieutenant Kreej heard the bragging stomp of the Armored Bone Finders behind him and hissed at the sound. Such arrogance to tread so loudly without purpose, without message and to do so along His passageways, Xasti'Kaur—the Shadow Road. . . .

Cursed scarbacks!

It warmed the blood with rage and hate. Resisting the urge to hiss, Kreej found himself having to double back all the way to the area where Captain Dryga had insisted they hold the prisoners. The air was still burnt and stinking like an alchemist's crèche from the jun powder blast the human, Tyree, had unleashed. Kreej clawed over the mass of charred and cut bodies.

Keep going, a voice seemed to hiss in his mind, *you're almost there.*

A few more turns took him back to the supply storage where the prisoner's equipment—what of it they hadn't reclaimed—lay interred beneath the bodies of another dead Zaur. He pulled the bloated stinking body of the dead guard out of the way and looked through the detritus.

The guard's Skreel blade was better than his own, so Kreej stopped to swap it out. As he ate the remainder of the guard's lunch, dried bugs that didn't exactly go stale with any sense of urgency, he pawed through the equipment. Not much of use. The Eldrennai's armor was no help. It wouldn't make much of a prize even if he managed to haul it all the way back to the warlord.

He took a canteen but tossed it away after a sniff. The mouth of the thing smelled like *jallek* root, its acrid scent stinging his nostrils.

Finding the ring seemed an afterthought. He snagged the tunnel rat who'd become entangled in the broken silver chain to which it was attached, silencing it with an envenomed bite and stowed it (ring, chain, and all) in a pouch for later.

How dare Captain Dryga abandon him this way. General Tsan's forces had already blocked off every direct route with which Kreej was familiar. It felt like he was going around in circles.

Now, the voice seemed to whisper, *this way to the air vent and cut over to one of the main transport tunnels.*

And then the cloud was lifted, and he know how to get out. There was an air vent. Yes, close by. Maybe the one the prisoners themselves had used to—

Two scarback warsuits dropped through the air vent as he approached it, like nightmares come to life, covered in Zaur blood and death scent.

<<We come for the bones,>> they declared in heavily accented Zaurtol.

It doesn't matter, the voice whispered. *You're useless to me now. Die well. Unless you don't. Now, if you survive . . .*

"What bones?" Kreej coughed in the Trade Tongue. He backed away from them, trying to think up another escape route.

"It's a ring," one of them said. "Give it to us and you can go."

"Whaar?" the other shouted. "Just kill it and get the ring."

"We aren't here to kill Zaur, Teru," the one called Whaar answered. "Or do we want another visit from the Bone Harvest?"

"True." The other scarback threw its hands up in some strange gesture the other understood, but Kreej didn't.

"This?" Kreej reached into his pouch and pulled out the rat, letting the whole mass of dead vermin, chain, and ring fall to the tunnel floor. He scrambled back from the items as if they might explode or strike him dead at any moment. "Take it. I just want to go home."

"Thank you." Whaar reached down and reverently unwrapped the chain and ring, depositing both of them gently in one of the satchels he had strapped to his thighs. "Do you want your rat back?"

"Yes?" Kreej stood perfectly still. He barely had the presence of mind to catch the rat when the scarback tossed it to him.

"So," Teru cleared his throat. "Have fun with your rat. We're going now. Attack us and die . . . all that."

"Um . . . yes." Whaar coughed. "Good luck with the rat."

Kreej said nothing, watching them closely, ready for the deathblow he felt sure was coming. *We're staring at one another,* he thought, *because no one knows how to handle this. Should I say something?*

"Thank you for returning my dinner," Kreej started. The scarbacks were still standing there. "I am not going to attack you . . . you head to where you were going and I'll wait here and go a different way. Yes?"

"You aren't going to try to follow us or anything crazy?" Teru asked.

"You are heading to where there are more scarbacks?" Kreej dropped down on his haunches, scratching at his shoulder with his hind paws.

"Yes." Whaar's gauntleted hand dropped back to his sword hilt.

"Then I am headed away from there."

"Good," one of the scarbacks said.

"Are you Named?" The one with the axe-bladed helm studied him, eyes glowing in the dark.

"Lieutenant Kreej," he answered evenly. "You are Whaar . . . ?" He let the name trail on, not wanting to show disrespect by lacking the scarback's other name. All the ones in armor had two names at least: Kholster Bloodmane, Vander Eyes of Vengeance . . . Kreej did not understand how one with four names could report to one with only two, but he assumed the scarbacks could keep track of their own confusing system.

"You want my name as well as my occupant's?" a voice intoned deeply from within the axe-bladed helm. "I am No Escape."

Three names? Kreej discounted the talking armor's foolishness, of course. He could not see what the scarbacks gained by such strange lies, but armor, even that as fine as the armor worn by the scarbacks, could not talk. But if it made the thrice-named happy to taunt him . . .

"Whaar No Escape." Kreej nodded. "How many of those names did you pick? I can't tell from your scent." He flinched away despite his attempt at bravery.

"The 'No Escape' part," Whaar answered in a less echoing tone.

"A great honor," Kreej muttered, exposing his throat.

"Thanks," Whaar said. "If you don't kill any scarbacks on your way home, I hope you make it. The Zaur could use more soldiers smart enough to negotiate."

Kreej's eyes widened in shock as the two scarbacks abandoned him. Their shapes vanished into the black and then their heat faded, and he could only hear the rhythmic metal on stone of their footfalls. Then they were gone.

Alone in the dark, Kreej shook with fear, expecting the scarbacks to return. His forked gray tongue licked the air, tasting for vibrations. Nothing. When they didn't come back after a five hundred count, Kreej stuffed his lucky rat back into his pouch and scampered away.

You thought to ask which bones and surrender them? the voice whispered. *I don't think I've ever seen a Zaur do that before. Maybe I have a use for you after all.*

*

Rae'en stood next to Vander and Caz in the Hall of Elements. As the core of the Tower of Elementals, the circular room encompassed six floors of white marble walls ringed with viewing boxes and hovering platforms of ice, stone, and crystal-wrapped flames. The highest and mightiest of Oathbreaker nobility took up the viewing boxes and floating platforms in a hierarchy Rae'en didn't follow beyond obvious divisions.

Okay, show me the seating chart. Rae'en nudged Vander.

What chart would that be? Vander replied in feigned ignorance.

The one you and the other Overwatches have been hoping I'd ask for, Rae'en thought, adding a very real elbow to the ribs for emphasis.

Well, if you think you need something, I suppose we could arrange a rough map of sorts. Even as the words hit her mind, names and titles started popping into existence, overlaying her vision. *Until your Overwatches get here.*

Uncle! Was he still upset about that? *I just want them to get used to it. You are still Second, Third, Fourth, Fifth, and Sixth of One Hundred. I just want . . .*

She didn't know how to explain it.

There was nothing wrong with Vander, Feagus, Amber, or Varvost. They were giants among Aern and Overwatches. Amber, by Gho'arn out of Unknown Vael, was the youngest, having taken her father's place among the One Hundred upon his death, much like Rae'en, but even she was ninety times Rae'en's age. Rae'en hadn't even built up the courage to ask her how she'd wound up being named such a . . . human-sounding name . . . and

Vander wondered why she wanted her own familiar, safe, comfortable . . . younger . . . Overwatches around?

Glayne, though, he was pretty scary, but that could hardly be news to anyone. Scars were attractive, but he'd lost his eyes in the Demon Wars, burned away by Ghaiattri fire and . . . gah!

I know, Vander thought at her.

Rae'en doubted that, but she lost herself in the sea of data before her, noting the way the Stone Lord and offspring stood on matching platforms, Lady Flame and hers on crystal-wrapped fire, Lady Air and her ilk hovered where platforms of air would have been, completing a circular pattern that would have been broken without them. The Sea Lord's family on their ice oval served as a demarcation line, behind which other less noble attendees appeared.

Vander, Rae'en started to asked, *have you noticed the children of the high elemental guys are all Aiannai?* Then she felt Zhan reaching out to her, not interrupting but wanting her attention.

She waited, watching as down at the very bottom of the hall, below them, Prince Dolvek stepped out in his white robes, nodding to Wylant and her Sidearms. Hasimak, the Elderly High Elementalist, stepped forward and without any speeches or warning beyond his prince's nod, reached out a hand and engulfed the corpse of King Grivek in flame.

Go ahead, Zhan. Rae'en watched the old king burn as she listened to Zhan's news. If the short yip of glee she made was out of place, Rae'en did not care. They'd found the ring!

A Zaur? she thought at Zhan.

Yes. His tone gave the impression he found the turn of events as confounding as she did. *I can't recall a civil conversation ever having taken place between a Zaur and an Ossuarian. Even the humans rarely surrender the bones when we demand them.*

What did it look like? Rae'en caught the eye of an Oathbreaker, his lips pursed as if he'd disapproved of her outburst. Folding the little finger of her right hand against her palm, she waggled the other digits at him. To an Aern, it would have been gentle teasing or a mild insult, the equivalent of calling the Oathbreaker a baby or telling him to act his rank—well, probably age rather than rank would make more sense to an Oathbreaker.

A moment. Rae'en felt a shifting of contacts as her connection to Zhan through End Song and Bloodmane shifted. No Escape touched her mind, bringing with him an image of the Zaur.

How good of a look did you get at it? Rae'en asked, all thoughts of the offended Oathbreaker dropping away.

It left quite an impression. Smoke from Grivek's burning remains spiraled up in twin lines controlled by Wylant at the base of the tower, her usual black leather doublet and pants augmented by a white cloak that obscured the crown and double bar insignia on the upper arm of her top and the pattern of scars embroidered onto the back, but the same design had been stitched in red on the back of the cloak. At the top, Prince Rivvek's Aeromancer Brigadier Bash maintained other complex patterns worked in smoke.

The most complex portion of the pattern, in the center of the room, seemed to be worked by Lady Air, the lines shifting to form a three-dimensional likeness of the late king, clouding, shifting to become the royal seal with its three towers.

The Zaur, Rae'en prompted End Song.

My apologies, I thought you were watching the—

It just makes me feel strange, Rae'en thought at him. *It's off-putting to kill someone who won't fight back. I had to, but . . . well, and to not eat him after felt wrong. I was, I don't know, relieved that I was Oathbound to let them burn his body instead. Glad, really. Is it odd to feel so happy I didn't eat my enemy?*

End Song withheld any comments he might have, filling her vision instead with an image of the Zaur named Kreej. He was of the black scaled rather than the brown or mottled scale variety, but other than that, he seemed unremarkable.

Do all Zaur have copper-colored eyes? The lines of smoke twined through and behind the image of the curious Zaur as she rotated it in her mind's eye. *No, never mind*, she sent. *I saw Zaur with yellow, green, brown, black, blue, red, and silver when I was a prisoner.*

Rae'en pulled the view in closer. Kreej had keeled scales. A raised ridge ran down the center of each scale. They would be rough rather than smooth to the touch. A lack of gloss meant they would scatter light differently, too, not reflecting it like most of the Zaur she'd seen.

If Zaur are all the same species—she ran through the others in her head— *why do they come in so many different colors and scale patterns?*

Humans are the same way, End Song thought back. **Different shades. Multiple hair and eye colors.**

So you don't think it's something about his breed of Zaur that makes him smarter?

It could be, Vander butted in, *but I think he's just a clever reptile with a stronger sense of self-preservation than most of them possess.*

Maybe, Rae'en thought.

Looks like they're wrapping up, Amber thought, wiping the Zaur out of Rae'en's field of vision. Rae'en's mental map lit with gold around the edges to show it had been updated. A red line flared and dimmed, depicting the projected path Rae'en would be expected to take from the ceremony to the castle proper. Acknowledging the intel with a green check, the map's opacity shifted, letting her see through it easily. Even the name tags labeling the Oathbreakers faded out of existence unless she concentrated on bringing them back up.

Kazan and the others aren't this skilled, she thought at Vander.

Amber and Varvost are showing off, he thought back. *Kholster didn't care about the showy stuff, but they're pulling out the stops for you to see what kind of information you want to receive.*

Good work, she sent to her Overwatches. *I appreciate it.*

And don't imagine your other Overwatches haven't learned a thing or two, Vander sent. *They got high praise from Malmung, and he still complains about my lack of presentational style.*

I wish they'd hurry up and get here, Rae'en groused. *It's taking them forever.*

CHAPTER 15

ROADSIDE HAZARDS

Forest to the left of them, ridge-line to the right, Rae'en's young set of Overwatches ran for their lives feeling more than a little confused. True, they *had* all been a little overexuberant when Kholster had defeated Torgrimm and became the new god of death. Kazan, even now, found it hard not to smile at the remembered thrill and the sound of his fellows chanting with him: Kholster! Khol-ster!

And, yes, the humans had seemed upset, but he couldn't understand the level of irrationality with which the knights of Castleguard had responded. Hoofbeats, from one of those responses, pounded behind the four of them on the rough dirt road that, Kazan hoped, ran from Castleguard to The Parliament of Ages or, at the very least, up to a defensible point on the ridge overhang along which the road ran.

Arbokk held Charming, his soul-bonded mace, in his uninjured hand. His right arm, paralyzed by an arrow to the shoulder, flapped uselessly at his side, the offending arrow waggling as he ran. Pulling it out carefully would take too much time, and jerking it free on the run was too risky.

We aren't Armored, Kazan thought to himself. *We heal fast, yes, but to heal a gaping shoulder wound? On the run? Without stopping for meat to speed the healing process along?*

At the back of the group, Kazan took turns swapping off with Joose trying to soak up the arrows and keep track of their pursuers.

What did you say to those knights?! M'jynn sent to Kazan.

You were there! Kazan glanced back, catching an arrow in the cheek for his trouble, which he ripped out, broke in half, and tossed to the side. *They were out for blood. Anything would have set them off.*

I think, Joose interrupted, *it was part of that poem you were making up about whether Torgrimm tasted like chicken or beef. I guess Knights of the Order of the Harvest have a short temper when it comes to jokes about eating their god.*

I guess I can see them finding it a little gloating, Kazan thought, *but their god lost, and I really did wonder what he tasted like—*

Are anyone else's feet bleeding? Arbokk asked. All the others' tokens lit up on their respective mind maps. *So long as it's all of us. I hate to bring this up, but how much longer do you think you guys can keep this up?*

What other choice is there? M'jynn sent. He, like the others, tried his best to keep his pain, the burning in his muscles from seeping into the mental exchange, but the greater the discomfort, the less effective they all were at keeping it to themselves. *The last time Mister Head Overwatch sent us off the trail, we got bogged down in the mud. If these guys could fire more accurately from horseback they'd have had us.*

Anyone have any idea how we get up on that overhang? Kazan asked. From the dirt road, he could just make out a tent and a low fire. Information from Arbokk's view filled in a seated figure, hand shielding her eyes from the suns as she watched their plight.

At least we're entertaining someone, M'jynn sent.

Let's turn and fight, Joose offered. *I know there are thirty of them, but they won't kill all of us. The survivors can haul our bones to kholster Rae'en, let her build something useful out of them. She doesn't need us. She's got the Second through the Sixth. Armored Overwatches! What good are we?*

She doesn't know them, M'jynn thought. *Not the way she knows us.*

And it's not up to us to decide whether or not she needs us, Kazan snapped. *She ordered us to come and we do our best to obey, right?*

Arrows rained down, as the tokens in his mind's eye lit up in agreement, catching Kazan in the thigh and lower back. He hopped on one foot for three steps before regaining full control. Even then, he felt the muscle tear when he put the injured leg down. Joose dropped back to rotate out with him, but Kazan couldn't speed up enough to take Joose's forward position.

I'm done, Kazan sent. *Another hundred steps or so and I won't be able to get this leg to do anything. Muscle's torn.*

They can't have many more arrows, Prime, Arbokk replied.

Actually, I think that's why it took them so long to come after us, M'jynn sent. *I don't think any of them have had less than four quivers and an extra horse.*

Behind the Aern, hoofbeats hammered ceaselessly, and the cries of the knights grew louder. Each exuberant whoop of delight reminded Kazan of the sounds his own squad of Elevens had made at their first deployment. Ahead, Kazan saw the figure—a woman—stand. She rose straight from the ground without using her hands, and it made him smile to see a non-Aern who did such things. Sunlight picked out odd colors in her hair, reminiscent of the unnatural hues they'd seen on people back in Midian.

I think I like the other side of the battle better, Kazan thought. *Think they'd let us swap up?*

Orange iron-deficient blood ran from their various wounds, wetness making their jeans cling to the skin. Kazan had never had a rash before, but he felt like he was getting one from the rub of denim on skin.

I'm turning to fight on a hundred count, Arbokk sent. *Sorry. You guys keep running. Whatever I can do to slow them down I'll do. Got to stop.*

Me, too, Joose thought.

I'll die under the gaze of a beautiful female, M'jynn sent along with an image of the lady watching them from the overhang. *I've never wanted anything more.*

Okay, Kazan agreed. *Me as well. Survivors take our bones to Rae'en?*

Four gold tokens lit up in unanimous consent.

*

Why the Aern had chosen the low road rather than the ridge path which was more defensible, Cadence Vindalius could not say, any more than she could explain why her premonition had been accurate about the point at which they would finally turn and fight, but not about how many knights would be chasing them, or about how many allies they would have fighting on their side. In the most recent version of events, she'd seen a man join in at the last possible opportunity. Breathing in deeply through her nose and out through her mouth, Cadence focused on the Long Flame, red and orange streaks in her black hair glowing as heat rushed in and became a part of her. Once the flame was hers and ready, the purple tones at the ends of her long hair took on an inner luminance, too.

"You might want to knock the first few knights off of their horses," Sedric suggested. "Or try to shield the young Aern from the initial volley of arrows. Your Long Flame is one of your greatest strengths, but you are a Long Arm as well."

Sedric's familiar robed figure stooped next to her in muted shades of gray. Her campfire, clearly visible through the bulk of his form, told Cadence he wasn't physically present, but—"What kind of Long Speaking do you call this?" Cadence asked.

"Myriam the Ever-present who developed and refined the ability called it 'The Seventh Transmission of Self.'" Sedric scratched at his nose. "Who am I to disagree?"

"You here to make sure I come back to the school?" Cadence asked.

"No," Sedric shook his head, gray particulates swirling within his shape in response to the motion. Peering around him at the smoke from her fire, she saw a branch split off from the main column, composing, at least partially, his form. "Kholster asked me to educate you. I did not promise I would do so in the school, though I would prefer it—oh." He nodded toward the Aern on the road below as they stopped, turned, and charged. "We can talk later. Your pet Aern there seem to need you."

Less than a mile away, a depressed-looking human sat astride his horse, traveling at a walk. Head bowed low under a wide-brimmed hat he'd purchased from the same merchant who'd sold him his stylish new garb and from whose cousin he'd purchased horses—a snowflake-dappled gypsy vanner for whom he'd paid a princely sum and an obstinate mud-brown pack horse for whom he'd paid considerably less. The horses, new clothes, gear, and a few extra items from the right sort of merchant had cost him a full two-thirds of the reward he'd received for his part in assisting the Aern, the Eldrennai, and, unbeknownst to both of them, the Zaur.

All total, it still wasn't enough to buy a new ship outright, but he knew a lady who knew a lady who could convince a certain shipwright to accept what he had as down payment on one of her ships. Cold crept in, mist rising from the forest off to the west. With The Parliament of Ages behind him, the trees in Castleguard—a mixture of conifers and hardwoods—seemed far less beautiful or varied in their shading. Here, the leaves were brown and sodden, their trees skeletal and bare rather than—

A wave of mental strength hit him in the chest so hard it stole his breath away.

"Ow?" It hadn't been aimed at him, but the strength of it was massive. He let out a long whistle, feeling the thrum of the power still out there ahead of him on the road.

"A wise man would turn back and take the ridge road, Alberta," he whispered to his horse. "Are we wise men, do you think?"

Alberta neighed in response, shaking her glorious mane.

"I know you're not a man," Captain Tyree told his horse, patting her shoulder. "I was only being clever."

Alberta whinnied at that.

"Okay," Tyree agreed. "Okay. You're the clever one. What do you think we should—"

Alberta burst into a gallop heading toward the sound of other horses, screams, and death.

*

Less than a mile farther down the road, a Castleguard knight on a lathered horse—its tongue lolling as it struggled for breath—burst smoking around a turn. Empty quivers hung from his back, though Tyree saw no sign of a bow.

His eye was swollen, and his forehead dimpled around a nasty wound. Tyree wondered if the knight knew he was already dead.

"Aern," the man shouted, his mail armor jangling as he rode, open-faced helm askew, "and a crystal twist! Turn back!"

"Now this, Alberta," Randall Tyree said, smiling as he let go the reins, flicking out his wrists in just the right manner to cause the bracelets on either wrist to uncurl into daggers, "is one of those times when my dear old late Uncle Japesh would have told me to mind my own business and go find a tavern or a brothel."

With a dagger in either eye, the knight didn't ride much farther.

"Then again," Tyree told the horse, "Uncle Japesh got drunk and fell off a brothel's balcony, so in some matters it may be wisest not to take his advice." With another flick of his wrists, the enchantments he'd paid an Eldrennai artificer to put on his two favorite weapons (and his most versatile lockpick) took effect, and the bracelets were back on his wrist as if they'd never been gone—without even bringing the blood along for the ride. "And that, Alberta, is where a full half of the money I spent went."

*

When the first three riders caught fire, rocketing into their comrades, Kazan thought he had died and that Rae'en's father had decided to let her Overwatches have a little fun before he added their spirits back to the whole of the Aern. When Joose shouted, "Kholster's name! Did you all see that, too?" Kazan was too stunned to remember to turn his token gold in acknowledgment.

"Fight them, scarbacks," yelled a voice from the ridge, "I can't kill all of them!"

A wave of arrows hit an invisible wall, splintering and twanging off in directions that were not toward Kazan's body. Blood spewed from the noses of two different horsemen who appeared to have caught the edge of the unseen barrier. Red streaks splotched like ink along the bottom of the field, before falling out of the air as the woman on the ridge cried out.

I think that took a lot out of her. Arbokk sent an image of her dropping to one knee.

She's kholstering this engagement at the moment, M'jynn thought loudly, *so let's do what the nice crystal twist said and fight the bad humans on horseback.*

Kazan rolled out of a riderless horse's way only to have to jump clear of a second. Leg going out from under him as the injured muscle ripped free of some important ligaments, he felt the Arvash'ae come over him and did not fight it.

*

Killing one more horseman before he got to the battle proper, Tyree reined Alberta in when he saw three rampaging Aern with eyes of amber and jade.

"Amber and jade; be dismayed," he quoted the old rhyme. "I guess those knights skipped over the whole 'Talk 'em back' part of the lesson. Huh, Alberta?"

Several riders fled back along the path to Castleguard while the bulk of the rest lay dead, burning, or both. A few were still fighting on the ground with the Aern. A one-armed man ran screaming past Alberta, head engulfed in flames, the fat visibly sizzling off his jowls. Tyree put a knife in him half out of pity and half out of a desire to stop the man's high-pitched keening wail.

Waves of power turned his head to a female crystal twist with admirable curves Tyree might not have minded learning to navigate under other circumstances. Always a little sensitive to what type of Long Speaker he encountered (usually getting a mental image of fire for Long Flames, a shouting mouth for a Long Speaker, et cetera) Tyree shuddered at the mass of floating, shouting, and flaming eyes, mouths, and fists that filled his mind's eye when he considered her.

"It would probably be wisest to run from that one, Alberta," Tyree whispered to his steed. "Let's go say hello."

None of the Aern looked interested in chasing down the fleeing knights. Doing a quick run through of the surrounding area in his mind, Tyree tried to pinpoint exactly how far it was to the nearest Castleguard watch station and whether its knights were a mixed order or on a rotation. He couldn't recall, but he could identify these knights. Clad in chain and brigandine, the fallen wore a circle of wheat symbol on their belts and around their necks.

Why were the Order of the Harvest attacking Aern? Torgrimm's followers believed in the need for all mortal beings to work together toward the mutual goal of achieving their full potential. Aern used to fall under that umbrella . . .

"Kholster." Tyree lowered his head in disgust at having taken so long to spot the obvious. "Yeah, I bet the Harvest Knights were all smiles and free soup until your guy killed their guy."

Alberta whinnied nervously, backstepping with loud jittery clops. Growls. Tyree laughed even before he saw the Aern limping toward him with a broken spear jabbed under one arm to use for a crutch.

"You might want to back away from them until they calm down!" the crystal twist shouted.

"Don't worry about me." Tyree looked the approaching Aern in the eyes, trying not to be disturbed by the blood trailing from his mouth. "I'm fine." He held empty hands palms up and clearly visible before placing them behind his head. "Me and the Aern are great friends. I helped rescue their new beauty-in-command: Rae'en." He thought *friend, friend, friend* at the four Aern as hard as he could. "By Kholster, out of Helg, from the Zaur. She lets me call her Sugar Bosom."

The Aern drew closer, sniffing the air, teeth bared, before turning around and sinking his teeth into the exposed throat of a bearded knight with no arms.

Better him than me, Tyree thought, sitting as still as he could while coaxing Alberta to continue backing up slowly. *Better him than me.*

*

Cadence Vindalius looked at the four Aern and the man, and bit back the urge to mention what she saw. Handsome and charming even without the touch of Long Speaking he had, the human moved from one Aern to the other, making friends and getting them chatting with him as if he were a part of their unit or, rather, an old human friend of the family.

It would have been warmer near the fire the one with the mace (Arbokk) had helped Tyree build, but she didn't want to be so close to the Aern, who gnawed casually on parts of the slain knights. How did this "Captain" Tyree manage to keep smiling while the Aern next to him ate corpses? With a shudder, she drew her cloak around herself more tightly, starting only briefly at the hazing image of Sedric as he coalesced next to her.

"I was meditating," he groaned peevishly, "but your distress was enough to wake this old Long Speaker even from the deepest of meditations. And while it is true that a Bearer of the Seventh Eye can go for days without sleep, we must still meditate to refresh ourselves for an hour or so at minimum."

Birds Cadence had never heard before called in the distance, drawing her gaze away from the group at the fire, even away from her teacher.

"How is Caius?" she asked.

"I checked on him," Cedric said, waving his hands in exasperation, "just as I told you I would. It seems the rift created within the Castleguard sect of Torgrimm's worshippers by Kholster's ascendance has generated little obvious strife, but I have relocated him to the school just to be on the safe side."

He'll kill you. Cadence saw the old man's death, not soon but certain. Caius was a young man in the vision, full-grown but still a child in that way men are before they have families, with great leathery wings spread out behind him, red eyes peering coldly at an elderly Sedric. As Caius struck, his face changed, showing different variations of the same event. He wore a bone-steel mask in the shape of a skull, a golden mask with no face, even a thick red scarf carefully wrapped to conceal his face below the eyes. He struck out with twin long knives in one version, firing strange Dwarven pistols in another, but in all of them there was blood and anguish.

Seeing that made it easier to look away and stare back at the camp where those she looked upon were shifting too. Injuries came and went, but when she look at one happy figure at the fire, she knew they would be attacked again on the road and that one of them was going to die.

"One of them dies," Cadence muttered, fiddling absently with the purple ends of her tricolored hair. "It's why I had trouble pinpointing the attack. There's more than one attack along the road. One of the knights that fled must have made it to an outpost."

"Did you see if it can be avoided?" Sedric asked.

"The death? No, not by mortal means." Cadence let her head rest against the bark of a tree. "Yours can't either."

"Don't tell me about mine," Sedric laughed. "I'm old and I want it to be a surprise."

"It will be," Cadence whispered.

"Good." Sedric smiled, his voice gravelly as he spoke, nodding all the while as if agreeing with himself. "Can you save the rest of them?"

"All but the one."

"Then save those you can." Sedric's hazy form began to dissipate. "No one can ask more of you than that. Have you been pulled into any more Long Seeing sessions involving the young Vael and the attacking Zaur?"

"No." Cadence shook her head. "I guess he and his Root Guard made it clear of the attack force."

"Let's hope so." Sedric yawned. "I'm going back to my meditation. You might consider getting a little rest yourself."

"I will," she assured him as his smoky form came undone and he was gone. But instead of settling down to rest, she gazed into the fire and then . . . beyond it.

CHAPTER 16
DROPS OF BLOOD

The low reverberation of Zaurtol rang like music to the mechanoreceptors of the reptilian warlord. Subtle vibrations of his many servants, relayed to him via the pounding of their tails upon the stone, carried news both from the war front and about domestic issues. His agents could have spoken directly to him had the warlord not gone into sequestration while awaiting the arrival of the blood. Sensing a distinctive drumming in the mix he silenced the advisers directly outside his bathing chamber with three sharp slap-scrapes of his tail.

Zaurtol contained few common unaccentuated poundings akin to the rhythms used to control the mighty Zaurruk; Tail Tongue's elegance lay in its resounding subtlety and nuance: the essence of deep thoughts conveyed by the simple variation of pressure and stroke, force and precision. Xastix closed his eyes in rapture at the distinctive cadence of Captain Dryga's unusual percussive flare. A curve touched the corner of his muzzle then fell away, despite the soothing heat of the hot springs in which he sought brief respite from the constant itching between his shoulder blades.

<<Only two, Dryga?>> he tapped out on the wet stone rim of his private bathing pool.

Reaching back to scratch the spot where a pearl-sized shard of the world crystal had been lodged, Xastix winced, fangs gritting tightly when his foreclaw touched the open wound. Long furrows of injured scales raked his back around the small splinter . . . a blessing . . . true, but a painful one. Its presence had brought him insight, strength, and an edge when it came to matters of chance. Combined with the secret voice he'd heard since hatching, the gifts it granted had been essential in his rise to power, but now the sword had proven to be double-edged.

Xastix had been assured the discomfort would abate once he bestowed a sample of all three races of the Grand Conjunction, Eldrennai, Aern, and Vael, to Kilke's decapitated head as a sign of his faith and obedience, but the waiting . . .

<<Yes. We have obtained the blood of an Eldrennai and an Aern.>> Dryga paused over the next bit as if, based on the nervous scuffing of his tail, he didn't want to elaborate.

<<And the third?>> Xastix tapped.

<<I am informed General Tsan has dispatched a runner with a sample,>> Dryga tapped peevishly.

So that was it. Dryga wanted all of the glory for himself. It doesn't matter who gets it here, whispered the voice in the warlord's mind. *If only matter could be transported as quickly as sound . . . without a Port Gate, of course.*

The voice muttered to itself angrily. Not one of the rare and precious communications from Kilke that he so desperately craved, but from the other voice: cruel, arrogant, and heartless, a constant companion to be loved and hated, even feared.

That voice.

In his youth, Xastix learned quickly that other Sri'Zaur did not possess such a gift, and he wondered if it was tied to the shard slot he possessed. Regardless of the source, it was always right, even if it was not respectful or loving. *We need all three! Ask him how long before it arrives.*

Sniffing at the blood in his bathwater, Xastix rolled his neck, scratching his chin with bloodied claws. He breathed deeply, unable to do anything but successfully not scratch his back, for several long minutes.

<<How much longer until it arrives?>> Xastix tapped finally.

<<Nine to ten days, Warlord.>>

Too long! Stifling his rage and impatience, Warlord Xastix submerged himself beneath the now-pinkish surface of the pool. He stayed down for an hour, feeling the vibrations of his people going about their duties, sending reports, redirecting troops. All things Xastix wished he could concentrate on.

We'll be fine when the last sample of blood gets here, the voice told him. Xastix found comfort in that thought. Once he had a sample of all three types of blood, he could present it to Kilke's head and the itching would finally stop.

That's not what we'll be doing with the blood, the voice berated, its tone scornful, outraged. *Give it to that decapitated failure?! He doesn't intend to help you. He senses my presence but doesn't know what to make of it. He'll never love you or make you better. We have other plans for the four types of blood.*

"Four?" Xastix whispered.

Who?! the voice thought. *How dare she?!*

"I don't understand," Xastix told the voice, waiting for an explanation, but the voice did not answer him. It rarely bothered unless it felt the need to correct him.

*

Blinking at the image of the warlord bleeding in the natural hot spring, Cadence tried to pull away from the vision, to move on to some other site or even to stand and go check on the young Aern and the human, Captain Tyree. It was easy enough to recognize the warlord as what had become of the same reptile she'd seen hatch, the one who had killed his siblings. That something could seem so strong and yet so pitiable twisted her stomach, bringing to mind the image she'd seen of her son, Caius, as he was now, and the deadly being he could (would? might?) become.

This once-small being, this Xastix, could have become many things, but it had walked the path of conquerors and been dreadfully altered.

Dreadfully? hissed a voice in her mind. *You stare upon my second self with disdain? You weak, pathetic cow!*

Cadence had known fear many times. She had stared into the face of Kholster, white muscle exposed beneath melted skin, as he looked upon her with painful recognition. She had felt the ache, the need for crystal as the last of it left her body. Being beaten and worse had been a regular occurrence of her early life, but even in the depths of Hap's depredations, she had never felt a sensation as distasteful as the touch of the mind to which that voice belonged.

I . . .

No! But it shut down her response with a slap of its thoughts. Intangible claws sank into her chest, clawing at her heart. She gasped once, twice, trying to fight, to push it away, but . . .

Powerful, the voice sneered. *I suppose you are powerful, but compared to me you are nothing! You, a mere female, a human waste of potential! You do not get to mock, to judge me, and live!*

Breath stopped.

Heart stopped.

Thought . . .

And then there were lips on her lips. Her face flushed with warmth, her thoughts were bombarded with salacious images of herself and the man with the whitest smile she'd ever seen. His breath was clean. His kiss tasted of fresh-cut mint. Hands moved over her body and then . . .

"Better?" Captain Tyree asked.

Cadence's eyes snapped open to find Tyree leaning over her. Reaching up to cover herself, she found her clothes still in place, though her head lay among the dry leaves. Other than falling backward, none of what she had felt appeared to have taken place in the real world.

"Wha-what?" Cadence bolted upright, seizing Tyree with her Long Fist and lifting him into the air until his feet dangled over the fire. Despite the shock, it was such a relief to feel the external presence gone. She still had an impression in her mind of an angry thing lurking within a fanged skull, but it was gone.

"Not that I mind a little rough stuff," Tyree said, his grin broad though strained, "but these are new boots. Leather scorches, and we're a long way away from anywhere I can buy a new pair, so . . ." The smile touched his eyes, but behind it, she felt a motion in potential. Raised arms and a flick of the wrists.

Calm down, pretty lady. His thoughts, a form of untrained Long Speaking, bounced off her mental defense. *The bad things are gone and while I'm not always a gentleman, I'm definitely better than whatever that was inside your head.*

"So." She kept him in the air but shifted him away from the fire. "You felt my distress and responded with groping, kisses, and erotic imagery?"

"In my defense," Tyree's smile became more genuine, mischievous, but real, "you didn't respond to a slap. I confused whatever that mind thing was enough to let you break free. Didn't I?"

"So." Cadence let him drop to the ground, suddenly aware of the watchful gazes of the young Aern. "You think you rescued me?"

Tyree's laugh was a magical thing, so enticing and genuine. *Have I ever felt that free?* she wondered.

"Not likely, sister." Tyree sat on the ground, checking his boots to ensure they were undamaged. "I'm no match for whatever that thing was, but you were. I felt its power, but also its distance. That far away, you could shove it off, but only if you could stop being scared long enough."

"She's your sister and you kissed her like that?" Joose asked.

"Not my literal sister," Tyree groused. "It's an expression. Oh, and it's okay now, Alberta." Cadence saw past the implied threat of the weapons on Tyree's wrists to the true danger she'd been in as the man's horse clopped around from behind her. The second layer of threat bloomed in her mind, a horse's hoof to the head.

"You would've had your horse—?" Cadence asked.

"Call Alberta my backup plan." Tyree's eyes went hard. "There was always the chance I would have to break your link to the mind monster in a less elegant manner. Not that you aren't elegant, Alberta," he spoke past her to the horse. "You know you're my best girl."

"Thanks," Cadence muttered.

"That was like no Long Speaking I've ever sensed." Tyree poured water from a battered-looking canteen into a shiny copper pot. The smell of mint awakened her senses as he placed crushed leaves into the pot along with a few cubes of brown sugar.

"I like it sweet," Tyree explained. "And when I make it everyone drinks it the same. . . . Just to be—" he laughed. "Sorry, old habit."

"Habit?" Cadence pondered that. The man had the canny wariness of a thief but the charm of a much different breed.

"I've been a captain," Tyree told her as he set the teapot atop a three-legged collapsing frame. "The Zaur destroyed the *Verdant Passage* and killed my crew."

"And you escaped?" Joose, the brashest of the Aern, joined them, his eyes once again normal for an Aern's. All sign of blood had been washed away from his face and hands.

"No." Tyree shook his head. "Not as such. I cut a deal that should have spared my crew and my ship, but it only spared me. If you ever make a deal with General Tsan, understand that he considers it flexible. Oh, he said he was going to pay me for the crew and the ship, but you can't put a price on a lost life. An amount to end one or another to spare one, but that's as far as it goes."

He offered Cadence a slice of smoked and dried beef, but she waved it off. She didn't trust her stomach to hold it down. It still felt tight and twisting.

"Anyway." Tyree chewed at his jerky. "They took me prisoner at Na'Shie and brought me to an underground camp where they intended I should wait out the war and then leave with my money, but I escaped with an Eldrennai named Wylant and an Aern named Rae'en."

Joose looked at one of the other Aern, Arbokk, as he approached and settled near the flames. Tyree waited expectantly for one of them to say something, but when they didn't he smirked and spoke on. "They paid me for my knowledge of the Zaur tunnel systems. I resupplied at Port Ammond and headed for Midian. Hopefully I can secure funds for a new ship there and—"

"A new *Verdant Passage?*" Arbokk asked.

"*Serpent's Promise.*" Tyree's eyes narrowed. "You know about me now. I'm Captain Randall Tyree, Maker of Bad Deals. Now how about you?" He poured out a measure of steaming tea into a lacquered wooden bowl and offered it to Cadence.

"I'm Cadence Vindalius," she managed. "And the power you felt, it's called Long Sight."

"What did you see?" Tyree asked.

She told him. By the time she'd finished, Tyree was refilling the teapot from the same canteen he'd used to fill it in the first place, which gave her pause until she remembered that the two Aern who had rescued her from Hap, Kholster and Rae'en, had possessed Dwarven canteens as well.

The water that poured out of them was cool, clear, and pure, and if the Dwarves understood how they worked, then that meant at least someone did. She took a sip from her second cup of tea and then another, the warmth of the lacquered wooden cup in which he'd served the aromatic beverage sinking into her fingers, chasing the cold from them. One by one, the injured Overwatches had gathered around. She'd feared she'd need to repeat sections of her story as each Aern roused and came to sit by her fire, but Joose, Arbokk, M'jynn, and Kazan each asked only clarifying questions, never needing her to repeat a point. Best of all, they believed her. Never once did they doubt the veracity of her fantastical story or abilities. Was it that they could smell whether or not she was lying?

"There's one other thing." Cadence set her tea bowl aside, the fire picking out the purple hues in her tricolored hair. "I saw something else. No. Saw isn't the right word. Because it was black as pitch there, but the blood Warlord Xastix mentioned. The third sample. When it gets there . . ."

"Bad things?" Kazan asked.

"Very bad."

"For us or for the Zaur?" M'jynn asked.

"For everyone."

*

Kuort galloped through the deepest pathways of Xasti'Kaur, a flask of the male Weed's sap-like blood strapped to his chest beneath the splint mail armor and a second on his back. Not that the annoying little Weed hadn't complained, but who cared? They had agreed not to chop his legs off unless he tried to escape a second time. They'd even bandaged the shallow wound from collecting the blood.

Kuort chuffed at the thought. *Silly Weeds.*

The ribbed walls of the tunnel flashed by as the Sri'Zaur ran. He enjoyed the dark and the closeness of the half-sized tunnel. All quiet except for the slap of scale on rock. Few had walked this tunnel. Kuort's chest swelled to recall General Tsan's trust in him not only to oversee the tunnel's construction but also to kill the Zaurruk handlers who'd commanded the juvenile Zaurruk that dug it in accordance with the general's labyrinthian design.

Glands aching from failure to express his musk, the Sri'Zaur heeded his general's orders despite the discomfort, racing past turnbacks and dead ends along one of the two paths that led to the Sri'Zauran Mountains, leaving no scent trail to mark his passing.

Thoughts of home often flung his mind along familiar corridors to the crèche caves where he had roamed with his brothers under his Matron's watchful eye, learning at her claws how to hunt. How to fight. Stealth and trickery. The wonderful art of the ambush and even the headlong charge. His brood brothers seemed not to care for her anymore when her gender shift happened and she became a male again, a fellow soldier and therefore a competitor, and took a new name, but Kuort could never fail to recognize her. Maybe that made him defective . . . maybe it had slowed his elevation through the ranks and cost him a few names, but if so, he was glad to be miscast.

He had never risen high enough in the ranks for his first gender switch to occur. Kuort thought perhaps it would make sense to him then. There were many Sri'Zaur who, having once risen to great heights, achieved such heights again . . . Sri'Zaur like his mother. Once the gender-switching process had begun a single time, it would always recur. Many resented their fellow reptiles so much that their personalities began to change. Even so, to watch members of her other broods, to see the way Asvrin and Dryga treated Tsan as a threat, disgusted Kuort. How strategically foolish to allow competitive drive to weaken the whole in exchange for personal glory and rank.

He hoped the general was wrong about the extent of their willingness to put their own aims above those of the warlord, but he trusted Tsan enough to follow his . . . (now her again) instructions no matter what gender Tsan was when she had given them.

<<I like to think they will not interfere,>> Tsan had tapped upon his muzzle. <<But if they do, you know what course to take, yes?>>

<<Of course, General,>> he'd answered.

Like all of Tsan's bodyguards, Kuort's black scales with their striped zigzag pattern revealed a common biology. Their venom was a coagulant, turning blood into a thickened gel-like substance. It wasn't that Tsan hoped for the rewards herself, but she knew giving Asvrin or Dryga too much power might tempt them to rebel against the warlord and that—

Kuort hissed.

That sort of thinking was exactly what Warlord Xastix had managed to overcome when uniting the Zaur and Sri'Zaur. Did it matter that there were whispers the warlord was mad? Of course, he seemed that way. His ideas were so new. So bold. So . . .

Vibrations from above disrupted Kuort's train of thought. Up ahead.

Rhythmic, but meaningless in Zaurtol, the feel of the sound stopped him, claws still on the stone. No. Not meaningless but imprecise, like an injured Sri'Zaur tapping out a call for help as best he could. Nostrils quivering, forked tongue flicking out into the black, Kuort lowered his belly to the ground light as a cobweb's kiss.

All his senses told him to go forward.

The training his Matron had given him hissed a single word: Trap.

Belly scales stretched out across the tunnel floor, Kuort's sensitivity to vibration increased sufficiently enough for him to gut the first of his attackers as they sprang. Whether the assassins had been sent by Dryga, Asvrin, or another commander, Kuort did not know. But as the first stab caught his thigh, he knew he could not escape or outfight them in such a close space.

"Give it to us," hissed a voice. "And we might—"

"I will surrender it to you." Kuort tried to make his voice sound shaky, as if death were a thing to fear and life precious. Drawing the canteen of blood from his back, he unscrewed the top and spat his venom inside. Screwing the cap back into place, he began to shake it even as the fangs and knives found his vitals and cut him down.

But it was too late! He slumped to the ground, chortling, a sound like dry leaves stirring. He could feel the lumps thunking against the sides of his canteen. The blood was useless, as now was he. Tail writhing wildly as his nervous system died, Kuort blinked at two pinpoints of light. A glow that would have been unnoticeable in the light of day blazed a bright amber in the dark of the tunnel.

"I'm impressed," the death god said, pulling him to his hind legs. As he rose, pain vanished.

"You are Torgrimm?" Kuort asked the being. "I had expected Kilke perhaps, or—"

<<Bloodmane is coming.>> The death god bared its canines in a threatening grin.

"A scarback?" Kuort dropped to all fours, padding closer, tasting the air. "How?"

"The scarback," Kholster said. "I am Kholster, and you did not run from me or curse at me or even spit your venom in my eyes."

"What purpose would any of that have served?" Kuort lowered his arrow-shaped head in acknowledgment of a more powerful warrior. "I am equal to many, better than some, but I know my limits, and fighting you is beyond them." Kuort spared his corpse a backward glance. "What next?"

"I think you're the first Sri'Zaur I've met who might need to go on to

Minapsis." Kholster held out a hand. "Walk with me. I want to know what you see in this General Tsan of whom you are so fond."

To meet the sister to the Master of Secrets and Shadow, to have completed his mission, and to have impressed the god of death? Kuort glowed, and in that light he saw two human spirits watching him.

"Marcus Conwrath and Japesh," Kholster explained. "They have never seen a Sri'Zaur impress me either."

"Some spirits walk with you forever?" Kuort asked.

"Just these two," Kholster said, "and not forever. They are here now to remind me."

"Of what?" Kuort asked.

"I don't remember."

*

"Torgrimm looks better in farmer's clothes." Marcus Conwrath leaned against the wall of the foyer to the home of the Horned Queen and the Sower. Sharing bites of an apple with the soul standing next to him, Marcus watched Sower, Reaper, and the supposedly impressive Sri'Zaur spirit. Could Japesh and he have each had their own apple? Marcus had no doubt they could ask and Kholster would provide, but he couldn't count the number of meals the two old campaigners had shared over the brief span of years the two of their lives had intersected even if he tried.

When there was only one of something, they split it unless one or the other of them didn't want it, and even then there had been more than one time one or the other had had to force the other to eat his share anyway. You kept your friends alive in battle as best you could before, during, and after.

"When's sa last time you saw the hunnert smile like 'at?" Japesh asked around a mouthful of the sweet, crunchy fruit, juice spilling down his chin.

"A better question is where that warsuit of his got off to." Marcus gestured with the remains of the apple (mostly core) at the empty space Harvester had occupied a few breaths previous. He sniffed at the apple, bit it in half at the core, and chewed, the bitter taste of the seeds something to be relished, in his eyes, just as much as the sweet meat. He held the other half of the core out to Japesh, who waved it away.

"I ain't looking for him this time," Japesh snorted. "I get lost."

Marcus's laughter brought a frown to Japesh's lips.

"I don't know what you think you're laughing after," the scowling spirit pouted. "The last time he had to come and find me."

"That's—" Marcus polished off the apple in two more bites, talking between mouthfuls "—because you kept leaping around from Kholster to Kholster. There's plenty of him, but only one real Harvester."

"Well, maybe." Japesh sniffed, jutting his chin out at the conversing deities. "If he'd killed me with his bare hands I'd be more of an expert."

Marcus blanched, but he'd had that coming and knew it.

"Fair enough." He wiped the sticky sweetness of the apple off on his pants. "I'll go. You'd know where he was if you thought about it much instead of being so worried about getting lost."

"How would I know that?" Japesh asked.

"Well." Marcus looked down his nose at his friend, counting the options off on one hand. "We already know he's watching Vander, Rae'en, Wylant, Vax—"

"And them Overwatches his girl's so fond of." Japesh jabbed his finger at his former captain as if pinning the point to his chest.

"And the Overwatches. They're all up to their cheeks in this war business."

"And?"

"And if Kholster's watching the ones at war . . ." Marcus winked, ". . . then, given how protective warsuits feel . . . which one is Harvester likely to keep checking up on?"

He vanished before Japesh could answer, feeling for the armor like a boat for its anchor. It was true enough that the Bone Queen had taken Conwrath and Japesh from their spiritual rewards to stop Kholster from completely arvashing her husband, and it was further true that she'd left them to keep the new god company, but she'd tied them to Harvester . . . not to Kholster himself.

Swirling like mist through a world of gray cold, Marcus materialized on a warm ocean-view veranda built of polished stone.

A female Cavair, one of the bat-like race common to the seaside mountain of southern Barrone stood very still while an Aern, the spitting image of Kholster save for the colorful facial tattoos and the bleached and braided hair, carved its likeness into a block of stone.

Clean-shaven and clad only in a pair of loose-fitting silk pants, the Aern, obviously Kholster's Incarna—one of those who were born identical to a member of the First One Hundred forged by Uled—laughed loudly at the warsuit standing next to him.

Marcus knew at once such a laugh had rarely escaped Kholster's own lips but came frequently to this Aern's. He was well muscled, his body as honed as Kholster's, but his chest and arms were covered in the pigmented dye used by the Hulsites at weddings or on holy days, but where the dye was the same, the patterns were not. His looked whimsical, at first, then one caught the design and found depth and beauty in it.

"Why are you laughing at me, Irka?" Harvester asked.

"Because you know all the answers to your own question, silly bucket." Irka kissed the bat-like female on the cheek and told her to go get something to eat and rest her arms.

Marcus's eyes bulged when she nuzzled his neck in return and flew off of the balcony and out into the salty air.

"Please explain." Harvester held out his gauntlets, pleading.

"Don't beg, bucket." Irka patted the warsuit's chest. "I'll lay out the hunt for you." He walked to the veranda, warsuit following close behind. Irka sat on the edge of the marble railing, leaning back at a treacherous angle. "He is acting strangely because he's been strangely altered."

"Who has?" Harvester asked.

"Well, I, for one—" Irka winked, "—thought we were talking about my father."

"But he hasn't been altered."

"Was he a god last month?" Irka asked.

"No," Harvester said.

"The month before?"

"No."

"Was he a god of any kind in the past six-thousand-odd years since his creation until quite recently?" Irka closed his eyes, leaning back farther as the wind picked up and blew his hair about wildly.

"I think I understand," Harvester said.

"I don't think you do." Irka pushed himself away from the rail and put his forehead on the armor's breastplate. "I heard my sister in my head. And I'm glad she is First. Kholster knows I had no interest. But you say Kholster left Bloodmane behind?"

"He did."

"Exactly how?" Irka did not wait for an answer. "Because I'll tell you how Amber's father did it. She used to come visit me out here in the summers and go air dancing." His eyes twinkled. "We'd have a few of my Cavair friends fly us out to Ripped Wing Point and fish up as much as we could eat. Diving for mussels, trapping coastal lobsters, and crabbing. We'd mate and sleep out under the stars. You'd be amazed the things you talk about lying on a beach with a full stomach, utterly sated and staring up at the stars."

That all sounded good to Marcus. He'd always wondered what it must be like to live as strong and free as the Aern were capable. He'd even met an Aernese female who took a liking to him once, but as he was already married, Marcus had been forced to leave that curiosity unsatisfied. Nothing was worth hurting his wife like that.

"It sounds decadent," Harvest intoned.

"Maybe a little." Irka laughed. "Anyway the point is, she told me when Scale Fist joined with her, it was like moving into a berth in a new squad. There were signs someone had slept there before, memories they'd left behind, but the person was gone. It took over a year before there really was a Scale Fist again, with its own distinct personality, because it held a sliver of her soul now. Her father's memories and knowledge were there, but her father's spirit was not. Do you see?"

If Harvester didn't, Marcus did. Kholster's soul had burned when it touched Bloodmane, and he hadn't taken it with him into the afterworld but had left Bloodmane behind—a piece of his soul. But which piece?

"But isn't that what Kholster did?" Harvester asked.

"If it was . . ." Irka looked up into the bone-steel armor's crystalline eyes. ". . . would I be talking to you, my father's new warsuit, or to Bloodmane transplanted into a brand-new suit of armor?"

"I had not considered that," Harvester said. "Perhaps I should go."

"Before you do . . ." Casually, as if it were nothing, Irka walked over to a work bench and grabbed a small bag. Its contents rolled together and clicked like two big rocks or marbles. "Give this to Father, won't you? But don't look inside." Irka waggled a finger at the warsuit. "It's a surprise."

"Of course."

They didn't stay much longer, but when Harvester rejoined Kholster, Marcus Conwrath followed, his mind ablaze with questions. What exactly had Kholster left behind when he had severed his connection with his original warsuit? What piece of him was he now functioning without? What was in the bag? The last question the warsuit resolved easily enough by peeking in the bag after he had given it to Kholster. What did Kholster want with a pair of fake Aern eyes?

CHAPTER 17

A PANOPLY OF SCARS

Wylant shrugged out of the ceremonial cloak, instinctively catching it with a burst of air magic wrapped in a sigh of relief. Relief at being back in her room. Relief that she'd managed to make it through the king's funeral without staining her robe. Relief Grivek had made the decision to appoint Rivvek as his heir.

Bitter and acrid, the scent of *jallek* root clung to her quarters as if it had leeched into the stone. Cold air pushed aside the heavy curtain between her bedroom and the balcony, sweeping away the odor in compliance with her will. Gooseflesh raised on Wylant's skin, responding to the brisk decrease in temperature. A little chill was such an insignificant price to pay for ridding herself, even momentarily, of that scent. Eyes closed, breathing deeply without a hint of congestion or sinus drainage, she smiled—a flash of good humor that faded when she reopened her eyes on the newest additions to her bedchamber.

Her room felt cluttered to her even though the only new pieces of furniture, temporary at that, were an armor stand (occupied) and a cloak stand (unoccupied). Wylant studied the cloak stand, gaining a little extra time before she faced the armor stand.

Why white for mourning? Gray or brown would be so much easier to—

Pondering mourning and the king's cremation held its own mental trapdoors. Thoughts of white gave way to recollections of brass and steel flowing over flesh and bones, replacing it, converting it . . . Wylant's head swam with images of her Sidearms' elemental foci. Grivek would have never wanted them to show him the respect they had at the costs they had incurred.

What on Barrone had possessed them to keep up the elemental display over Grivek's corpse throughout the entire procession? Frip and Frindo's foci, by the end of things, had spread over their entire respective hands and up past the elbow on their affected sides. She hadn't seen Griv's legs yet, but she hoped his foci hadn't quite made it to the knee yet, not with war coming.

Coming? Wylant curled her lip. *Isn't it already here, but in disguise?* At best it was a conflict in suspension, as fragile as the surface tension on a pond that allowed water spiders to dance across the thin skin, which could be so easily pierced.

She released the wind holding up the white funeral robe, catching and hanging it neatly, in one motion, from the stand the Royal Clothier had provided. Kholster's scars in embroidered lines of crimson blazed at her from the back of the garment. Why hadn't Kholster put his scars on her back properly? Everyone knew she was an Aiannai, and burning Kholster's scars onto her own back as she had centuries ago had gone a long way to making sure no one ever forgot that, but they weren't the same as his exactly, just a good facsimile. Would that ever be enough?

The embroidery thread, smooth under her fingertips, had no answers to give, and as much as she wanted to hide from those thoughts, Wylant hid from nothing long.

Beside the cloak stand stood a blood oak armor stand, its braces and helm rest lined with blue velvet, the eyes, bolts, and other fittings appointed in polished brass.

Just like it must have been in the blasted museum. I wonder how much willpower it took for the docents and the curator to give it back?

Vax stirred in his sheath, sensing Wylant's mood.

"I'm fine." Wylant drew him and laid him softly on her bed. "I wonder what the plaque says. You know there has to be one."

Was it cowardly that she'd never gone to see the display? She'd been invited but couldn't see the point in that sort of morose navel gazing.

On the bed, Vax shifted into a chain whip: seven metal rods, joined by lengths of chain, with his hilt shrinking to match his new form, his metal rasping against the coverlet. At the other end of him, the terminating rod twisted and tapered until it was a stylized dart with a serpent-like head. Wylant watched him, a parent dutifully paying attention to her child's new trick, until he coiled himself with the snake-head in her direction.

"I don't know how to fight with that, Vax. Where did you even see its like?"

He couldn't answer.

She wished he could.

Eyes wet, Wylant turned back to her bride's gift.

It hung from the armor stand, a functional masterpiece: bone-steel half-breastplate and chain with layered black brigandine to protect the abdomen and lower back. Kholster had designed the hybrid armor, long before the creation of the first warsuit, for fighting the Zaur more comfortably. It granted increased flexibility without too much compromise in the toughness of the armor. The breastplate provided an adequate glancing profile. Bone-steel pauldrons, arm plates, leg plates, and boots granted protection against striking Zaur and Skreel blades. Brigandine gauntlets gave her better hand protection than hardened leather gloves. Not much would punch through the bone-steel plates shielding the back of the hand and each knuckle joint, but the grip (made of irkanth leather, like all of the leather in the suit) granted better digital flexibility than any heavy armor she'd ever worn. It didn't interfere with casting either, like some heavy armor did.

Its visorless war helm with a Y-shaped opening for the eyes and mouth seemed to glare at her from the helm rest. The chain collar, stiffened but comfortable as such things went, hung beneath it. Lines of detail beneath a hard layer of enamel, precursor to the technique Kholster had later used on Bloodmane, lent the helm a leonine cast while keeping the surface smooth to the touch. She was alternately pleased and disappointed he hadn't given it an actual mane. He'd left it out because giving an enemy something extra to grab hold of made no sense if one wasn't a nigh-unstoppable Aern. Even so.

She placed a hand on the breastplate, tracing the lines of enameling, letting her fingers glide along its surface as she walked around to the back. And on the back, in the same way, Kholster had (of course) inscribed his scars.

This set had been his gift to her on their wedding day. All the metal was bone metal, and every bit of the bone-steel had been his and worked by him. She hadn't worn it into battle against the Aern at the Sundering because full-plate made more sense against Aern and using bone-steel against Aern was moronic. And also—well—Wylant knew he would have been flattered, thrilled to see her charge into battle, keeping her oath to defend her people, while wearing his gift . . .

She hadn't worn it again.

Never intended to wear it again.

Smiling despite herself, she found the cunning little panels on the cuirass that flipped back to reveal tiny anchors to which a cloak could be tied without the need of it being fastened around the wearer's neck. He'd had a cloak made for her, too, all black except, of course, for his scars embroidered on the back in gold thread. All hand-stitched, his own work for everything, even though he'd had to learn how to sew before he could begin. A short, snorting laugh escaped her then.

"Kholster," she said, "you put your scars everywhere except actually on my back."

"The rendition you burned into your back is accurate," a deep voice spoke, "but not quite the same as if I put it there. Would you like me to?"

*

Are you sure this is all right? Kholster thought at Harvester.

I don't see why it would not be, the echoing voice sent back. **She prayed to you. Called you by name. It is the very definition of inviting you. And if you are worried about how much like yourself you are being, she would know, of all mortals.**

Good.

Wylant hadn't been the first person to pray to Kholster. He'd felt multitudinous mortals say his name in fear or desperation. But to hear his wife's (or ex-wife—he still wasn't clear on how that hunt was going) words in his mind . . . he could have done nothing less than come in person.

A scant growth of raven black adorned her head now that Dienox had finally taken the hint and realized she no longer revered him. Kholster wondered why Dienox had chosen blonde hair as a sign of his favor. It had been beautiful. She was still stunning without it . . . and would have been regardless, but even so, he found it hard not to picture her with red hair like his if she was going to give up the blonde.

All those thoughts rushed through his head in a single blink, while Wylant was still caught flatfooted by his appearance. He wanted nothing more than to snatch her up in his arms and . . . but Wylant had said exhusband thirteen years ago when she had confronted Prince Dolvek and when the idiotic Oathbreaker had still had time to stay within the technical boundaries of the treaty between the Aern and Dolvek's people.

No, if she initiated a kiss, then perhaps, but otherwise . . .

"How did you," Wylant began, but even as she spoke, Kholster could see her dawning comprehension. He treasured the way her brows furrowed as she thought, lifting a touch as she puzzled it out. "Deity . . . right." She took her hand off her armor as if it had stung her. "Kholster, you cannot just appear—"

"I can." He remained still, his voice soft and even. "If, however, you would rather I did not do so in the future, I could . . . not—"

"No." She closed her eyes. Pausing. Processing. When she opened them again, Wylant was in motion, crossing the room to reach him. "Warsuit," she prompted. The word an implied preference, explicitly not a command. Not quite a request, but something an Oathbound slave could either honor or ignore. She wanted the armor off, and Kholster realized he did, as well.

Harvester, Kholster thought, realizing as he sent the command that he hadn't removed Harvester normally since remaking him. Harvester had teleported away, but Kholster did not want that now. He was here with Wylant. And if he had to try not to blink so he could see her instead of dying multitudes, it was a perfunctory cost, easily paid.

Where Bloodmane opened at the back, plates flaring open like the petals of a blooming flower, Harvester split at the breastplate, the first crack appearing at Kholster's sternum—or the Aernese equivalent. Humans and most mammals had ribs, whereas Aern had flexible plating beneath the skin.

Flowing up and down, the seam split into six lines of separating bone as it approached his neck. Two central lines converged in a V-shape at his throat, unified into a single line as his helm split open into two equal halves. Other lines worked similar magic at his shoulders, hips, and groin.

A cacophony of snapping bones accompanied the widening of each seam, more pronounced as large sections of plate folded away, revealing the Aern underneath. A muslin shirt, soft, white, and sheer had replaced Kholster's chain mail, but it was cut in roughly the same style, hanging loose with ragged edges where the sleeves hit mid-bicep. He stepped forward in black steam-loomed jeans, bare feet slapping the stone. The jeans were new, too, but the corded bone-steel belt at his waist was the same one he'd worn for as long as most mortals (Oathbreakers included) would have been able to recall.

What happened to my boots?

I have them, Harvester intoned. **Footwear is awkward to remove in the heat of passion.**

Is there likely to be . . . passion?

If there isn't, sir, I submit to you that you are doing it wrong.

Doing what wrong?

Things.

Kholster stepped forward to meet Wylant, gaze fixed, deliberately not looking at Vax, pretending not to notice him at all. Harvester resealed himself with a sound akin to that of wooden wind chimes clattering together, stirred by a sudden breeze.

Wylant met him halfway, closing with him as if it had not been centuries since last they touched. Her arms slipped around him. He enfolded her, and it felt like home and hearth and family in a way South Number Nine never had or could. Tears ran down his cheeks. He smiled under them, knowing there would be no matching tears from Wylant's eyes. She had always been made of some material more fantastic and resilient than bone metal.

Her head nestled against him, the short stubble of her newly black hair brushing his clean-shaven chin.

You shaved me?

It IS how she prefers you, sir.

This close Kholster missed the smell of *jallek* root he'd come to think of as part of Wylant's scent. Still, the intoxicating fragrance of her skin, her hair, even her sweat sent him crushing back to intimate moments and to their marriage vows: the first ones sworn in secret on the battlefield, the second set at Fort Sunder before the Aern, and the official ones (under Oathbreaker law) before King Zillek years later with Uled's scowling face looking down and disapproving of them.

Amber light reflected in her eyes as she pulled away from him, the illumination from his memory-trapped pupils shining in Wylant's when she gazed up at him.

"Me, too," she whispered as if she were sharing the same memories. Wylant kissed his cheek, her lips sending him deeper into more erotic exchanges they had shared as husband and wife. She blushed and so did he. His eyes dimmed. With so many people, even lovers, an Aern had to explain about the power of memories, how an Aern could be chained by the past, trapped in thought, still capable of physical defense, but cognitively dissonant. Wylant needed no such explanations.

His heart sank when she stepped back, ending their embrace, but Kholster could not allow himself to chase her. If Wylant wanted him, he was hers, but too many years as First of One Hundred had conditioned him to lead in all respects except romance. Years of courting Vael with stillness held him back. The fear of unintentional force through implied command, the thing that kept him from pursuing Aernese females for fear that, as First, they would feel obligated to return his affections, kept him now, as a deity, from picking Wylant up and never letting her go again. Wylant's own careful pursuit of him while he was still enslaved and Oathbound had become his moral compass when physical intimacy came into play.

He'd slipped with Yavi when he'd kissed her through her samir, but Wylant was more important than any Vael. Kholster owed her the same careful restraint she'd employed at the start when setting out to woo him. He was careful to offer and be still, avoiding even the appearance of demand or insistence. Her assiduousness in that regard had played a significant part in what had led Kholster to open his heart to her in the first place, to be capable of truly loving and trusting any mortal who was not under his command. Their love had defined all his romantic dealings since the Sundering. It was why Helg had had such a hard time convincing him to be her husband and beyond that, to have Rae'en and be father to a second freeborn child.

Sir, Harvester transmitted, *if I might recommend—*

No, Kholster thought, *but thank you. I believe Wylant and I can kholster this battlefield.*

Of course, sir.

Kholster was doing the thing.

Wylant found it at once insufferable and endearing to watch him stand there, so obviously filled with emotion but showing such restraint.

Stubborn, she thought, *but then that is part of his charm. That and those shoulders. A translucent shirt?* She wondered briefly whose idea that had been and smirked. Vander was her first suspect, but Kholster wasn't connected to his Prime Overwatch, his literal number two, in the same way he had once been. Or was he? No. There was a loneliness in those eyes. He was adrift and trying to hold things together as best he could, but he needed help. And he wasn't going to ask for it. Maybe he would open up afterward.

"Are you honestly not planning to kiss me?" she asked.

"I wasn't certain you wanted—"

"I want." She wet her lips, and it became evident Kholster wanted, too. As kisses became more intense, Wylant noticed Harvester beckon to Vax, looking first to her for silent approval. Wylant nodded and the warsuit lifted Vax from the bed, carrying him out into the hall. *So the warsuit was responsible for the clothing*, Wylant mused, before her thoughts became more primal.

She let herself relax and be one.

*

Wylant expected Kholster to be gone when she woke up. Did gods stay the night, even when one had once been married to them? Always one to rip the bandage off rather than delay inevitable pain, Wylant resisted the urge to lay in bed feeling the empty space next to her, the still cooling mark where Kholster had lain. His scent lingered there, a tailor-made combination of . . .

I will not say his name, she thought. *I will not call out for him and make a fool of mys*—Other scents made her nostrils flare, nose pulling eyes open like a sleeping hound catching the scent of a hare. *Fresh roses . . . and tea?*

"K—" she caught the word in her teeth, clamping them together to stop her tongue.

"I'm spending time with Vax." His voice, rich and strong, and masculine, yet still so tender and—

VAX?! Eyes popping open, Wylant jolted up, sheet falling away, cool air from the open balcony curtains wreathing her skin in tiny gooseflesh bumps. Her nose crinkled at a change in scents even as her eyes widened at the casual manner in which Kholster had said Vax's name.

What am I missing? she asked herself, trying keep her attention on the smells of the room rather than the way the light from the balcony painted her husband in warm natural tones emphasizing the bronze of his skin, picking out the lighter reds scattered through his close-cropped hair. Aern don't gray, but Kholster's hair had lightened over the centuries—the only physical sign of his age beyond the knowledge (sagacity?) of his gaze and the still assurance of his presence. Wylant knew her own aura of command was impressive, but Kholster had commanded for so many years that his name had become his race's verb for it. He turned, smiling, his wolfish doubled canines bared— such a small leap from a smile to a threat, but he wasn't angry. She had rarely seen him happier. The sunlight picked out his muscles, the flat washboard of his stomach plainly visible through the gauzy material of his shirt.

He'd found or conjured—gods could do that sort of thing, couldn't they?—a pair of hobnailed boots from somewhere, scuffed and broken in as she knew he liked them. His belt, corded bone-steel chain, didn't look like his own work—she'd never asked who made it, but he wore it like it was part of him, just like the black steam-loomed denim jeans.

Vax glinted joyously in Kholster's arms, holding the shape of a warpick. Kholster wielded Vax two-handed, testing his weight, his balance, and finding no flaw. He reversed his grip and twisted, rotating Vax in an arc as he would have done Grudge or Hunger. In Kholster's hands Vax's surface sported intricate detailing, whorls and curves of sapphire blue glistening against the matte black lacquered metal, with only a hint of bone-steel peeking through in crafted waves as Vax shifted in the light. His hilt, which had always been wrapped in a mottled blue leather when Wylant wielded him, was the color of old bones.

"If you like." Eyes flicking from Wylant to Vax, Kholster shrugged, answering a question Wylant could not hear. "No, I won't give you my preference. I'm sorry."

He paused, nodding at Wylant with that one-moment-if-you-do-not-mind-I-have-to-handle-this-first look he'd perfected a thousand years before she'd been born. She noted she still ranked an apologetic bob of the head and reassuring wink when he did it—something only accorded, as far as Wylant could recall, to Vander, Kholster's children, and Wylant herself.

"Because." His attention was back on Vax. "My opinion can become someone else's opinion far too easily when given before a person has had time for thoughtful consideration."

To whom was he talking? Wylant's eyes widened. Vax? He could talk to Vax?

"Yes." Kholster laughed. "I'm told I can be exceedingly annoying." His brow furrowed, his eyes pained. "No." He swallowed and took a deep breath. When he let it out, Kholster found Wylant's gaze and held it. "I am not angry with her." Another pause. "That would be up to you and your mother."

Wylant had never fainted when she wasn't injured or ill, but she would have been lying if she claimed the room hadn't spun just then and that the gorge had not risen in her throat.

He knows, she thought, willing her stomach to calm. She searched for a god's name to use in vain, but the only god she trusted was already in the room. *Vax!*

Vax coiled into a chain, dropping to the floor and pulling free of Kholster's grip. Puzzled, but without further comment, Kholster changed his stance to a reserved neutral and let Vax slither off along the stone.

"Sorry about that. He had many questions." Kholster crossed the room and kissed her rather chastely given the state of her clothing—or lack thereof. "He seemed to be building up to the big one and I wanted him to have a chance to get it out."

He could hear Vax's thoughts?! Of course he could . . .

Wylant pulled free of her husband. How long had he known? What had Vax and Kholster said? Why hadn't Kholster FIXED him? Could he not . . . make him right?

I have to think about this. I have to . . . to . . . get some clothes on.

Her husband's eyes tracked her every movement, taking it all in, memorizing her as she moved to the washbasin (filled with rose petals) and cleaned up, interrupting her ablutions long enough to sip at the tea waiting in a metal cup beside the basin. The strong black honey-sweetened brew had a hint of . . . had he bled in her tea? It was something he'd always done before battle to help in case she got bitten by a Zaur in rut.

Can he hear my thoughts, too? She closed her eyes and waited. Nothing. No, then. Either that or he knew enough not to do so. Kholster had scant patience when it came to his enemies, but his reserve appeared inexhaustible for those he loved. The towels had been swapped for clean, fluffy ones exactly like those he always used to bring her. Apparently his supplier was still alive, or maybe he'd conjured it with deific might. She wiped away moisture, drying her skin, feeling more ordered, clean, but it did nothing to clarify her mind or calm her racing thoughts.

How long had Kholster known about Vax? She couldn't let go of that one. *Could he help him? Was that why he'd come? Had he truly not been angered about . . . what . . . what she'd done? Am I forgiven*, she wondered, *or was he never mad?*

Clothes.

Dried, but still shivering, Wylant looked at her husband and scoffed. *I am not having this conversation with no clothes on.*

Taking a clean set of small clothes from her wardrobe, she suppressed the urge to glance around for the ones she'd worn the night before. *Look for them later*, she told herself. *There is no need to feel so flustered. He's still my husband. Or thinks he is. Do I want him to be? Yes, but—*Except things were so much more complicated than that. Once she was clad in her doublet and leathers she could breathe easier. Her mind clearer, equilibrium restored, she turned her attention back to Kholster and found him folding her things from the previous night. He smiled at her, eyes twinkling as he placed them in her wardrobe.

"This is one of the self-cleaning ones the Artificer made?" Kholster wrinkled his nose at the wardrobe.

"Yes." Wylant held in a laugh. Of course, he would rather hand wash everything. "He gave it to me when you told him he could only discuss being Aiannai with other Aiannai."

"Sargus?" He pushed the wardrobe door firmly closed. "Yes, well. I imagine he was grateful to have a compatriot with whom to speak." Kholster's hobnailed boots hammered the stone as he stepped away from the device, studying the lightly stained mahogany. Tutting at some minor defect in the workmanship Wylant couldn't see, he rapped the side with his knuckles. "I prefer doing laundry the old way—"

"You have to admit, it is much more convenient this way."

"Of that I have no doubt." Kholster put his ear to the wardrobe. "But this way, when do you get to hang it out to dry?"

"But there's no need." This was the Kholster few people got to see. Inquisitive. Open. At ease. *What had he and Vax discussed? Ask him*, she told herself, *he'll tell you.* Instead, she settled for "How do the Dwarves do it?"

"Even the Dwarves prefer their shortcuts." Kholster opened the wardrobe and checked the clothes. "They're still—"

"It takes a few candlemarks." Wylant stepped over and closed the wardrobe door. So unreal to talk about trivialities like laundry with a being who was not only her husband, but—*Kholster, are you really a god, now? Can you read my thoughts?*

"Yes and yes, but I only do so when you address me directly or think about death or what comes after. Those thoughts I hear automatically when I'm outside of Harvester or filtered through him when we are united."

That was not the whole truth. Wylant pursed her lips briefly. A lie of omission. But why? With beings Kholster's age, and her own, once she turned her thoughts in that direction, it could be so hard to tell if, when you suspected someone of holding back the fullness of the truth, they were doing it because they were hiding or erring on the side of brevity. Ask Kholster about warpicks or smithing, for example, and if he told all he knew, you'd die of old age before he finished.

"Do all of the other gods like to do laundry?" Wylant asked, deliberately letting it go.

"No." Kholster laughed. "They cloak themselves in god stuff and shape it to their will."

"And you don't?" Wylant touched the smooth muslin of his shirt. It felt real, smooth under her fingers, but solid. Material.

"Not if I can help it." He covered her hand with his own. She'd once expected them to feel rough with skin that didn't need a gambeson between it and mail, but Uled had given the Aern an appealing softness that—she pulled free and punched him playfully in the center of his chest, trying to break the mood. "You and laundry . . . do you still do that?"

"Do laundry when I need to think? That and other chores." A breeze blew in from the balcony bringing with it scents of . . . and that's when she realized what was different about the room.

No jallek *root.*

"You got rid of the *jallek* root smell?!"

"Well. Yes." Kholster looked at Vax to keep from meeting her eyes. "I like the scent, but we had time after we got back from Fort Sunder, and Vax said you hated it so I—"

"Magicked it away?"

"I did no such thing." Kholster recoiled as if struck. "I used soap and lye."

"Last night?"

"After you fell asleep. I—gods don't need sleep." Another partial truth. Hmmm . . .

"How did you do all of that without waking me?"

"You slept like the grave." Well, Kholster was right on that point; she always slept soundly when they were together. Kholster grinned, baring his doubled canines and moved to kiss her but stopped himself. Her lips found his all the same.

"Why do you keep doing that?" Wylant stayed close, each of them breathing the other's breath. "Holding back. Kiss me if you want to kiss me. If I need you to stay at arm's length for a bit, I'll tell you."

"As you please," he answered.

"No." This close she could see the minuscule veins in his black sclera. They did not appear to pump blood, but some dark fluid composed of Uled only knew what. "You can't push me away by 'As-You-Please'-ing me, you old irkanth. That was before my time, and my father refused to shout an order to the Aern."

"Kyland." Kholster closed his eyes, and Wylant knew he was remembering her father, wished he could share with her that image of an elf she'd barely known. "He was a good soldier. I would have named him . . . Vhoulk (Redeemed) or Tesset (Forgiven) if he had lived to see my vengeance. Some name to spare him."

"Not Aiannai?" Wylant asked.

"He was an Oathbreaker," Kholster said, "but it was not the Aern to which he broke those oaths. He would not have liked to see us married, but perhaps he would have come around."

Kholster pulled away.

Wylant wanted to ask him so many questions in that moment, she couldn't even list them all. Conversations could be like that when you were married to a being more than ten times your own age. She'd long since adopted a habit of picking one and going with it. Otherwise any discussion had the risk of becoming an interrogation.

"See?" She waved her hands through the space between them. "What is this?"

"I want to make certain I don't overstep my boundaries."

"What boundaries?" Wylant closed with him again. "I'm your wife. You're my husband. I stayed away because I thought you'd hate me if . . ." She looked at Vax and hoped he understood.

"I don't hate you." He touched her leather doublet, tracing the crown-shaped stitching at her shoulder before letting his hand drop to his side. "I love you. And I think you know that, but as for boundaries, you called me ex-husband not too long ago. I am pleased that appears to have been a misunderstanding, but . . . you did not used to require armor in order to have a conversation with me."

"I—" She wanted to say it wasn't armor, just clothing, but it was every bit the armor he claimed it was.

"You never answered my question," Kholster interrupted. Even as her eyes narrowed, eyebrows furrowed, he clarified. "Do you want them? Do you want my scars on your back? I can replace the ones you have. . . ."

She took two steps back without meaning to, and Vax found her hand before she'd consciously known she wanted to hold him. His markings maintained the new level of detail they'd had in Kholster's hands—stylized scars. His father's scars. Flowing like molten metal Vax became a warpick, and she knew that would have been the weapon Vax would have forged if he'd been properly awakened. She blinked away a tear as he morphed again, this time into a sword—her sword . . . the sword with which she'd sundered the Life Forge.

"What would it mean, Kholster?" Wylant sheathed Vax, her hand trembling until she forced it to stop. She didn't remember forging him, but she knew she had done so. She had forged Kholster's son, her son . . . their son . . . into a weapon and had used him to destroy most of his father's people. Eyes closed against whatever answer Kholster had to give, she wished she could remember why.

CHAPTER 18
WYLANT'S MEMORIES

Wylant's eyes widened, lost to recollection.

Standing close by, Kholster waited for her answer to what he must have assumed to be a very simple question. She knew her husband was there, but she was lost in memories for the moment. Just talking to him brought things back from a deep place where she had not realized she had buried them.

"Do you want my scars on your back?" Kholster had asked her the same question early that morning so many centuries ago . . . and she'd said no, not because she hadn't wanted his scars on her body, but because she couldn't spare the time to recuperate from the wounds.

Winter had come, but no cold had come with it. Fire burned in the skies, a pale purple light pulsing and roiling as thousands of elementalists combined their might to hold the Ghaiattri within the Eldren Plains. She had stood on the battlements of Fort Sunder, the eldritch luminescence of the defensive barrier flaring momentarily brighter each time one of the Eldrennai powering it died and fell from the sky.

Wylant waved Mazik away as he worked with her right pauldron, trying to get it to fit even though it was badly dented. The rest of the Sidearms stood nearby. No joking, laughing, or conversation amongst them. Every eye stared either up at the sky or out over the plains at the sea of yowling horned demons, the screeching musical wail of their language so loud, it was hard to be heard over the din.

"What are we going to do, General?" Jolsit, then one of the new batch of Lancers pressed into service, asked. He'd been a glassblower by trade, but he had shown potential in the two exchanges in which he'd already partaken. And he'd survived—unlike half the soldiers at Kevari Pass. "This is the end, isn't it?"

"No," Kholster had barked, walking out to join them. That she remembered. The image of him strutting, clad in Bloodmane, helm under his arm so the troops could see the grin on his face. It was one of the last times Wylant would feel safe for months, staring at the way his doubled canines caught the light and the single upper left canine, looking out of place without its partner, which Kholster had lost. If she looked closely, she could the replacement tooth growing in, but until it did, he would have a certain rakish (if snaggletoothed) air. "There is a limit to their numbers. That means we can

167

win. Anything finite can eventually be reduced to zero. Any foe bound by mortality can be defeated."

Like a painting viewed through guttering torchlight, the memory faded and rushed forward. The war had lasted twenty years, but Kholster had been proven right, even if the population of the Eldren Plains had been halved in the process. Vax had been conceived on the eve of victory and had been born . . .

She shied away from that memory, focusing instead on the ceaseless cravings for red meat she'd had while carrying Vax. Aern only gestate for three to sixth months, the length of the pregnancy depending on the iron content of the mother's diet. Abandoning that line of thought, too, she remembered herself standing in formation with her troops at the victory celebration.

King Zillek had managed to look regal, clad in his crystalline breastplate and purple robes, signs of the four elements blazing on his crown—despite the loss of his right arm. Cheers from the crowd went up despite the sour looks on the faces of the loved ones of those who did not have the luxury of being regenerated over and over again within a blood-filled warsuit. Kholster himself had been stripped and dipped, as they called it, a dozen times or more, but the resilience of the Aern and the monstrous death toll incurred by elemancers had successfully warded the Ghaiattri after the wild gates had begun to open, trapping them in Eldrennai territory lest they spread to the rest of Barrone.

She'd watched Kholster ascend the dais to be commended by his master. For centuries Wylant's only memory of those events had been seeing Kholster swing the warpick and kill the king. There had been nothing she could do. She had been forced to retreat and regroup, there had been no way to stop it, but she saw with clear eyes now, as if the key to a box had been finally inserted in the lock of her mind, turned and opened.

Married for as long as she and Kholster had been, she had seen the set of his shoulders change, spotted the crux of decision.

"No," she'd meant to shout, calling the wind to amplify her voice even as it carried her to her husband's side. "You're free, Kholster! Rejoice and forget Zillek. You can go anywhere now with no one to command you. We can go, and Vax will be born free somewhere far from here."

No, a brutish voice had whispered in her mind, as an insubstantial hand closed around her mind, *this is too interesting to interrupt. A civil war to follow the Demon War? I can't risk your stopping that.*

And so she'd been trapped there, watching helplessly. If only King Zillek had been less proud and had haggled with Kholster once he'd made his disastrous yet wonderful mistake. He could have secured an alliance with the newly freed warriors without the warpick through the skull he had received. Kholster would have growled and raged and been insulting, but he would have given Zillek peace, Wylant was certain of it.

She had a hazy memory of telling the Sidearms to spread the word about the death of the king and then flying to Fort Sunder where she'd found . . . Uled. The parade of thoughts came into hyper-clarity on Uled.

Cruel eyes set in kind face, whenever anyone pictured the ancient sorcerer, they always seemed to mention that dichotomy of images. His left side, after millennia of mystical experimentation, had become subject to an uncontrollable twitch. Robes that had once been white, cleaned and maintained on a regular basis by myriad fungible acolytes back in the days before Zillek had banished him to Fort Sunder, were spotted with blood and grime.

Tasked with stopping the Aern, there had been only one threat she thought might work, but when dealing with the Life Forge what better expert was there than Uled?

"Destroy the Life Forge?" He hurled a vial of ichor to the pitted stone floor of his lab where it hissed and bubbled on its way to the huge central drain. "My Life Forge?!"

"Would it kill or weaken the Aern?" Wylant waved the fumes away with a touch of elemental power.

"Kill them?" Uled had growled. "Destroy MY Life Forge? Why would I want to do that?"

"We're at war with them, Uled." Wylant, hands out, low and open, calming gestures, despite the connection with elemental air she was keeping open just in case. "The Aern are killing Eldrennai as fast as they can."

"Good. More corpses could be useful." Uled rubbed his hands on his chest. "Fresher might be better, too. War, eh?" His eyes narrowed, glittering as he pinned her with his glare. "Are you going to seize the throne, harlot? I knew you would! I prepared for this years ago when I found out Zillek let you marry my beast. And now you've come to kill me. Well, I'm ready for that, too. I—"

"Kill you?" Was he too insane to assist her? "I came to you for help, you mad old Artificer. We need to save our people!"

A whirring of gears sounded all around her. Nothing visible, but twisting flashes of reflected crystal flickered in the air.

Had it been a mistake to visit him in his laboratory? Perhaps, but no more so than visiting Fort Sunder itself. Normally an Armored would have been stationed here, but Zillek had ordered all of them to attend him at Port Ammond. Even then, Kholster should have announced the offensive with an

All Know or by sharing the moment with an All Recall. That he hadn't done so Wylant took as a sign of just how shocked her husband was at being free after all those millennia of slavery. His people were truly running mad in their release. Or maybe he had done all of that, and since she was alone, and his wife, the Aern had all been ordered not to attack her.

Stop it. She took herself strongly to task. *If you hunt down that trail you'll never come out the end of it with whatever advantage you have left. The insane Artificer or his son are the only options here.*

Sargus. The misshapen male's name rose in her mind. He might have been helping Uled conceal his madness. If he had, he might have the knowledge she needed. With that chain of thought, Uled moved from essential to expendable. Which made dealing with him exponentially simpler.

"Listen, Uled," Wylant cooed, giving the peaceful approach one last attempt. "Consider this carefully. Use that magnificent mind of yours. Kholster is on the warpath. The Aern, even those in this very fortress, are free. I need to stop him. You need to stop him." She watched his face for any sign he understood her, but all his tells were lost in the trembling twitches of his left side. Were those scars on his face? Close up a spiderweb of pale white lines covered his face, vanishing under his hair line. What had he done to himself? "All Eldrennai need to stop him. We lost more elemancers, Artificers, and soldiers than the Aern because they heal more effectively that we do. Our military might without the Aern is less than fifty thousand, and only a few thousand of those are elemancers of any significant ability. He has over two million troops at his disposal."

She swallowed hard.

"You think I want the throne?" Wylant took a careful step closer. "There won't be a throne if we don't find a way to stop them. I don't care who rules. I'm trying to save our people, not rule them."

"Help?" Uled's grin carried with it a pale green pulse of light below the faint scarring on his head. His eyes twinkled, and in their depths Wylant fancied she saw rot and decay. "You want my assistance? Can't solve your puzzle without Uled's inestimable intelligence? Yes. Of course. How can Uled save our people this time? Does he have a plan?" He coughed, gagging, in what Wylant realized was some sick approximation of a laugh. Steadying himself the sorcerer wiped black phlegm from his mouth and onto his robes.

"I always have an idea, a masterwork of thought and foresight." His fingers writhed like the paws of a raccoon washing its food as if he were fondling the notion in his crazed head. "Not a new race this time. Three was too many. But—" he raised one shaking finger, "—if we could lure him here . . ."

"Kholster?" Wylant asked.

"Useless harpy!" Uled raged, dark spittle flying from his chapped lips. "Torgrimm. We lure Torgrimm here. What would my beast have to do with any of this?!"

Outside Wylant heard the pounding beat of Aern marching in the pattern they used when Kholster was with them. A phrase in Zaurtol: <<Bloodmane is coming.>>

"So that was why," she muttered. "He wanted to make sure Uled stayed here. He wanted to kill you himself."

Uled's upper lip curled into a sneer, revealing pearlescent teeth that had once belonged to Kholster . . . right down to the doubled canines, which looked so out of place in an Eldrennai's mouth. Wylant spotted more scarring on Uled's gums. Nothing on his neck or hands. Just his skull, then? What had he done? She squinted. Was he wearing a wig?

"We can lure Torgrimm here and once we have him, we need only to syphon from him a portion of his—"

"Uled!" Wylant snapped the word, amplifying it with a hint of her Thunder Speaker addressing-the-troops voice. "You are out of time. The Aern are at the gates. Hells, they man this fortress. Will destroying the Life Forge stop the Aern or not?"

"The Aern? Yes." Uled yawned. "I'm unsure about the warsuits." He chewed his lower lip, tearing off a small chunk without noticing. "The beast was quite clever there. I've often wondered how he derived the process and tricked Zillek into allowing their creation. I made him too clever, I suppose. It's hard to quantify a reasonable level of intelligence when everyone is so inferior to me. But would King Zillek allow me to vivisect him and find out? No!" Uled threw out his hand, the rank smell of him hitting her full blast.

"He was too pleased with my second race, and Kholster in particular, to allow anything to happen." Uled leered. "I'm astonished he let you share the beast's bed when it was so clear he wanted that . . . privilege . . . for himself. But I am smarter than the beast, smarter than all of you. I have found a way to—"

"Uled!" Wylant's heart pounded in her chest as if it were trying to match the beat of the Aern outside. "How do I destroy the Life Forge?"

"You?" Uled looked down his nose at her, erupting into another burst of choking laughter. "You?! Destroy my Life Forge? You can destroy nothing! We, perhaps, or I, but you? Ha! My bones and blood would be needed . . . plus my beast's bone metal." Uled's eyes unfocused, peering far away as if he kept an unseen list hovering in the air for easy reference. "Perhaps one of his offspring would work . . . not a grandchild . . . an unawakened spawn would work reliably, but a femur from the beast himself would be best. I would forge it into a weapon on the Life Forge itself, slake it with a quenchant oil composed of my own blood, powdered bone, and fats."

"Not something I could do quickly and survive. Give me . . ." Uled clucked his tongue, running it frantically across his teeth, each tooth previously belonging to Kholster. His head bobbed from side to side as if he were weighing options and, watching him, Wylant wanted to tear her husband's teeth out of the old elf's gums, even though Kholster did not miss them, had long since grown them back and shed and regrown thousands to replace them. "Give me three years *and* return my assistants . . . then I—"

"We don't have that much time!" Wylant grabbed the wretched Eldrennai's shoulders and shook him. Arcs of mystic blue flowed up her arms like minute lighting strikes. *A ward?* Each strike stung like a wasp had struck her, but she didn't see how Uled thought such a ward would stop anyone. Light flared from the crown patch on her shoulder. "What?"

Mouth falling open, eyes wide with fear, Uled struggled to pull free of her.

"No," he screeched. "No! No! No! Zillek chose you? A female?! I gave him immunity to my wards and he transferred it to a female!"

"I suppose he did." Wylant peered down at her shoulder. When Zillek had promoted her to General, established her as subordinate only to him, he had pressed a token against her shoulder. She remembered the burning warmth as it had seemed to dissolve on her skin. . . .

"Krio'Khan!" Uled screamed. "Defend!" Launching from the shadows, a crystalline golem two kholsters tall charged Wylant's position. "Malkarnius, attack!"

Buzzing madly, a cloud of prismatic wasps made of translucent jade erupted from the ornate floor tiles. Putting Uled between herself and her enemies, Wylant summoned as much elemental air as she could—

"Sargus override," said a small quavering voice. "All guardians, suspend attack. Return to your positions and be still."

Hunched and cloaked in brown robes etched in silver-threaded symbols, the figure stepped not from the shadows but forward from a spot near a scarred and acid-etched worktop. Color seeped in like drops of ink into a glass of water, filling in first the base color then the shading in finer details. His face filled in only after the robes were fully rendered—and what a face! Grotesquely distorted around the orbit of his right eye and the top quarter of that quadrant of his skull, the overlarge orb glinted with an incarnadine light.

Wylant thought one arm of the robe had been slow in appearing, only to realize as the arm itself was shading into full detail that the sleeve of the robe had been hacked away, exposing a ragged gash running the length of his forearm. Clamped to the severed artery a thin tube ran to a fountain pen with a bone-steel and gold alloy nib. Holding the pen in his left hand, a wicked-looking Ghaiattri horn dagger in his right, blood still wet on its edge, Sargus trailed blood from the narrow hooked beak nib of the pen, each drop forming arcane symbols on the tile in thick, precise, italic strokes. A pattern formed in his wake and all around him, growing with each step.

"Sargus!" Uled growled. "What do you think you are doing?!"

"Aiding and abetting in your death, sir." With more context, Wylant recognized that the trembling in the young artificer's voice had been—not fear—but barely reined-in rage.

"How?" Uled gasped.

Not "why," Wylant noted. Obviously Uled knew quite well why his son would want him dead.

"I am my father's son." It came as whisper, the words echoed in blood on the tiles. "And a subtler monster.

"Your supposition that I can assist you is quite correct, General Wylant." Sargus straightened as the cloud of jade wasps named Malkarnius sank back into the tiles and the golem Krio'Khan returned to his cleverly concealed closet within the shadowed corner of the laboratory. A pack of leather and brass took shape, revealing his hunch to be illusion.

"But I broke you," Uled breathed.

"And what you broke I repaired." Sargus's lips quivered into a sneer. His facial deformity washed away to reveal a leather cap with various lenses ready to be dropped into the brass loupe covering his right eye. "Everything you have done, I will cleanse. Your every misdeed I shall expose and ameliorate. You tried to ensure my passivity. Instead, you have wrought in me the eventual absolution for your misdeeds. I am not so smart as you, sir, but nor am I so lost to madness."

"You're certain you can help me destroy the Life Forge?" Wylant asked.

"Yes." Sargus lowered his left hand, and the flow of blood stopped. Spiderlike metallic limbs of various shapes and alloys reached out of his pack and carefully put away his dagger and pen, while other arms tended his wound with flesh knitters and laughing salve. "I lacked the tools, but I found Father's secret journals and broke his private decryptions long ago. I would kill him for you, but I lack your immunity to his wards. I believe I have constructed a workaround, but I would rather not test it needlessly."

"A moment," Uled said. As he spoke, it was as if he summoned sanity from some scant reserve, tick lessening, voice steady, eyes clear. "Grant me one concession and I will assist you willingly even unto my own death."

"Grant him nothing," Sargus cautioned, pale from the loss of the blood drying into a ruddy brown behind him on the floor. "Kill him before he even tells you what he wants."

"Surely you can grant me a final request." Uled smiled at his son. "It's something you can do after you destroy the Life Forge. It won't delay you."

"What is it?" Wylant understood Uled's reputation but refused to be intimidated by an addled male who had been effectively neutered by his own son.

"No," Sargus begged. "There is no limit to the evil of which my father is capable. There has never been another mind like his, and we have his full attention now."

"You think he has a plan that involves his own death?" Wylant gave Sargus an incredulous look.

"No," Sargus answered, the strength going out of him a bit as he spoke. "Not involving. I think he has no less than a dozen plans in the event of his physical death. At least one of which involves Torgrimm becoming lessened or altered in some way."

Uled frowned, sucking in his cheeks.

"What is the favor?" Wylant asked.

Sargus sighed, settling down on a collapsible stool that emerged from his pack and was set in place by the brass armature.

"Keep my skull intact. Don't let the Aern crush it into powder or break it. Throw it into Kevari Pass or somewhere remote. I wish at least the part of me that housed my brain to be safe from my creations."

"Sargus?" Wylant looked at him questioningly.

"Do what you will." Sargus closed his eyes, breathing in deep, even pulls of air. "I have no idea want he really wants, but we'll most likely do it now. His mind is nothing but gears within gears. Either he wants us to smash his skull or he wants it preserved, or maybe there is some event he knows will take place if it lies undisturbed." He gave his father a look of bitterly grudging admiration. "Uled may have contingencies involving all three. My default would have been to ask your opinion. Barring that, I would have asked Kholster's advice." He peered at the entryway. The door swung open on an empty hallway, but he watched it warily. "He, however, might be disinclined to assist us in our current endeavor. You know best, General."

"Me?" Wylant was not used to males not in her direct line of command giving her opinions the credence they deserved.

"Well, you *are* General Wylant."

"And?"

"I'll put it to you this way." Sargus stood, color coming back into his cheeks. "King Zillek was given two tokens that would grant the bearer immunity to my father's wards. The king came to me and I told him I couldn't duplicate them without my father's knowledge, and that it would actually take both tokens to grant full immunity." He shook his head to clear it.

"The king came back to me two days later to ask if I could alter the tokens so they would bond with the individual upon whom he bestowed them. Permanently. Once I completed the work, he obviously instilled that immunity in you."

"Brat!" Uled scowled. "Without your meddling—"

"She'd be dead," Sargus agreed. "Yes, which is why I am pleased beyond measure that the king recognized—" His eyes widened. "You might want to kill him now to set off the lab's contingencies."

Gods. Wylant followed his gaze and saw Bloodmane striding down the corridor. *These males would tear the world in two if I wasn't here to stop them.*

"I will shatter the Life Forge, Kholster!" Wylant shouted to her husband. "If you do not stand down. I will do it." She waited for a reply, but she heard nothing. "You'll all die!" Why couldn't he do something, come up with some loophole to stop this?

Why can't I? But she knew why. Kholster could not stop his people and remain true to them. Couldn't swallow all that abuse. He had to be stopped or he betrayed the Aern.

"We will merely most of us die."

"Kholster!" Pain wrenched through her abdomen, and she resisted the urge to place her hand on her belly. "Don't make me do this!"

"Do it." Kholster halted his advance ten paces from the door. "It's within your power—your only chance to win."

Sharp and jagged the pain grew. Vax was coming. Too early.

"But I don't want to win; not like this." She hadn't known it before she spoke the words, but she knew it to be true. She would just as soon let all the Eldrennai die than kill her husband's people. They deserved to be free. Revenge was their right. *The annihilation of the Eldrennai is just.*

"Then you understand, in your darkest hour, what it is like to be me in mine." On the last syllable, he charged. Wylant snapped Uled's neck. The door slammed shut, and then there was no door. A color shift toward the blue spectrum of light cast everything into altered tones. Even the air tasted stale and strange.

"That was kind," Sargus told her.

"No." She let the frail corpse slip from her gasp. "There was no time and I wasn't sure how much blood we would need." She grunted as the contractions began in earnest. A normal Aernese birth was painless, but when the unawakened Aern came too early . . . it meant the Aern would be fine. More blood in the bucket, more time soaking, but the mother, unless she too was Aern, would have no other children.

I know it hurts, said the dark, brutal voice, *but you need the bone metal to destroy the Life Forge. A victory over the Aern. Think of the glory!*

"No!" she screamed, but the voice would have his way. She remembered then. Dienox's hand on hers, his will supplanting her own. Dienox had forced her to forge Vax into the weapon that shattered the Life Forge. Fury and relief in equal measure tore at her heart. And with those emotions, guilt that she had not been strong enough to stop him . . . and worse, the nagging possibility that she could have stopped him if she wanted but had chosen, in some deep part of herself, to do whatever she needed to do to win.

CHAPTER 19

NEW SCARS

"I've never seen anyone but an Aern do that." Kholster's voice snapped Wylant back to reality. She was still standing near her husband, her hand on Vax's hilt, but it seemed, for the first few seconds, as if she were in the wrong place at the wrong time. She'd been standing over the Life Forge melting down her unawakened child. Her right hand closed around Kholster's forearm, nails digging in; her left gripped Vax tighter, knuckles white.

"I remembered things." Wylant checked the corners of her room. Wardrobe. Washbasin. Bed. Balcony. Armor stands. The armor she planned to give Rae'en. . . . "Lost history I could not recall at all before . . . even when it was happening, it was veiled from me."

Kholster nodded, his lips drawn into a tight line of grim control.

"A nod?" She released his forearm and swatted him in the chest.

"I already told you I had never seen a non-Aern get trapped by memory that way." Kholster sat down on the edge of her bed, concern on his face. "I imagine it has its explanations, but none upon which I feel comfortable commenting further." His eyes found her, whatever he'd been feeling gone. "Did the newly recovered information help you decide?"

"Dienox," Wylant said under her breath, "he controlled me. More than once."

Kholster's nostrils flared at the name before she got the rest of the sentence out, jade irises growing larger, eclipsing the black, but not all of it. *So he knew, then. Is it because he's a god that he can't act? Or is this one more matter he trusts me to handle? What if I don't want to handle it alone, Kholster?*

"I will always help you." Kholster touched her face. "*If* you ask me."

"Why should I have to ask?" Wylant pulled his hand away.

"Because otherwise I would be meddling in the affairs of a mortal who very rarely needs anyone's help . . . much less unwanted divine intervention, and because I trust you far too much to butt into your affairs when you do not explicitly request it."

"What do you know about being mortal?" she asked with more venom than she'd intended.

"More than you." Kholster folded his arms over his chest. "Of the two of us, which one died and was collected by the Harvester?"

"And tore his throat out."

"I hope you don't have the same plans for me when your time comes." Kholster shrugged.

You think I could beat you, too, you old irkanth, she thought.

"You are still the Aiannai I married." Kholster smiled. "There is very little I think you could not do and nothing with which I would not trust you."

"Yes." Wylant began to strip out of her doublet. "I want your scars on my back, if you still claim me."

"You are never mine to claim." Kholster twirled his finger in the air, and Wylant turned around obediently. "You are always your own to give. The same is true of me."

"You're so stubborn," Wylant tossed over her shoulder as he stood and gently pushed her down onto the bed.

"For the last six hundred years or so the only thing keeping my people free was that obstinance," Kholster said.

Wylant felt his weight on her back, sighed contentedly and smiled even bigger when Kholster's hand didn't go for Vax. His new warpick, its surface white and pearlescent, the haft wrapped in black leather, appeared in the air when he reached for it.

"What did you name this one?"

"Reaper," he whispered.

"Harvester and Reaper," she started, "how—" she hissed in a lungful of air as Kholster ran his hands along her back, her version of his scars melting away. The skin left in its wake was new and tender. Wylant gritted her teeth when the warpick broke the skin on her shoulder. "—appropriate." Outlining the markings at the shoulder and neck, he cut two parallel lines down her spine in long, fluid strokes. The diamond at the base of her spine came next followed by the parallel lines opposite each facet.

"Do you want laughing salve for the next part?"

"How bad is it?"

"I peel the skin off in strips and rub my blood into the wound to kill the little animals that will try to grow there. My blood should also promote scarring."

"Little animals?" Wylant asked doubtfully.

"Too small for the eye to see." Kholster reached back for something from his saddlebags. "The Dwarves say the beasts are what make wounds go rotten or hot and red."

Little animals? she thought again. *Well, if the Dwarves said so they were probably right. . . .*

"Did Rivvek get laughing salve?"

"No."

"Did Sargus?"

"No, but I'm not married to either of them and Bloodmane didn't have any on hand at the time." She heard him uncapping a bottle as he spoke. "It wasn't exactly part of the exhibit."

"No salve for me." Wylant gritted her teeth.

"As you please," Kholster told her, putting the cap back on the bottle. "It makes the skin taste bad."

"You're going to eat it?"

"You would rather I throw part of your body out with the offal?"

Of course, he wouldn't want to waste the skin. It was like throwing away food and, given that it was her flesh, likely a special honor for him. It could have been nothing more than Aernese practicality, too. Wylant decided it was the former whether it was or not.

"Go ahead."

Kholster used two tools for the second part, a pair of tweezers to hold the skin and a sharp razor to cut it away. There was pain, but a rush of adrenaline, too. To surrender that way, to trust him as he cut and claimed her (whether he admitted the latter part or not) brought a smile to her lips. No one else would have deserved such trust, but there was nothing with which she couldn't trust him . . . or it felt that way.

When it was done there was a pause.

He's about to eat my skin. It sent a shiver of revulsion through her so strong bile rose in her throat, burning the back like acid, but she forced it back down. *What good was it going to do me, all cut into strips?*

His weight shifted, hands on her bare skin as he checked his work, rubbing his own blood in the wounds. Heat from his breath touched her back, punctuated by a soft cloth wiping away excess blood. Bursts of heat and tightness followed each swipe of cloth accompanied by noises of artisanal approval from the artist.

Finally, after retouching the diamond at the base of her spine, he climbed off of her and she rolled onto her side. *I'm already half-naked, maybe we should*—wherever that thought had been headed, it was derailed by the sight of her shirtless husband, his chest and hands wet with a mixture of red and orange blood, his mouth marked with flecks of her from devouring the cut-away flesh.

His breath came faster than normal, the hunger in his eyes told her what he wanted to do next, she wanted to as well . . . or had a second ago, but her head was too full of the image of him chewing her skin and swallowing it for her to be that intimate with him just now.

"Maybe after you've cleaned up a bit?" Wincing, eyes closed against the sight, when she opened them again the moment had passed. Kholster stood before her in his warsuit, looking every bit the grim impassive gatherer of souls, which stood so at odds with Torgrimm's welcoming appearance.

"Now who has their armor on?" She scooped up her doublet. "How long do I have to let this—" Reaching back, she felt scars on her back. Not wounds, but scars already formed. "You healed them?"

"Sorry," Kholster said, his voice echoing behind the horned skull helm. "I should have asked. Vax can reopen them if you like."

"Kholster. Wait." The tone, the awkward stance, the way his gaze fixed on a point right above her head, not actually at her. Wylant recognized them all as signs of what she called a Kholsterian dismissal. He did it whenever he wanted to brood—pondering, he called it—only now, she couldn't walk into the hall after him; he could vanish to wherever it was gods went, conveniently sidestepping all attempts at pursuit. "We have to talk about Vax."

"Yes." His saddlebags snapped into place on his armor, his warpick already clinging to the warsuit's back. "The two of you have much to discuss. If you still intend to pass your bridal gift on to Rae'en, I've made adjustments so that it will fit her properly."

"Excellent." She was halfway through buttoning her doublet. "Thank you, but, Kholster, I can't talk to Vax. I think he hears me, yes, but—"

"Whose scars are on your back?"

"Yours, but—"

"Then hold your soul-bonded weapon and he will hear you. My scars are on his back as well. My blood ingested and now inscribed should have completed the faulty connection between the two of you."

"Vax?" Wylant tentatively allowed her skin to touch his leather hilt.

Yes, Master Mother?

Master Mother? If she had ever received a greater injury than the one inflicted by that title, Wylant could not recall it at that moment. *Please*—she caught the order, changing it to an opinion Vax could either address or ignore. *I prefer Mother, but you can call me whatever you like. Even Wylant, if that is amenable.*

"Khol—" She looked up, but he was gone.

You want him to come back, Mother? Vax thought at her. *He is there whenever mortals die. So we could kill someone or . . . he also told me whenever you call his name, he can hear you. He will come when you call, if it is within his power . . . and appropriate.*

Too much information.

Dienox.

Vax.

Kholster and his scars.

Returning memories.

She walked out on the balcony, Port Ammond unfolding below her, to find Silencer looking up at her from the street. She'd felt like he'd been giving her strange looks back at Oot, lingering on her like an irkanth stalking a deer.

"I do not have time to worry about what the Bone Finders want," she told no one.

Can we give my sister her armor now, Mother? Vax thought. *I want to see how you like your new armor as well.*

"What new armor?" A chill breeze blew across the balcony, stinging her cheeks. Below, in the market, a child laughed and dogs barked.

It awaits you at Fort Sunder, Mother, Vax told her. *Father and I made it.*

Which means there is something at or on the way to Fort Sunder he wants me to see. What did we miss? Her mind turned to Zaur tunnels and warsuits. *If he didn't hope to reveal intelligence to me, he would have presented me with the armor here. Wouldn't he? Unless there was something about the armor itself that required it be viewed at Fort Sunder. . . .*

"Come along, then, Vax," she told her son. "Let's go see your sister."

A NUMBER OF NEEDLES

Personal appearance had never meant much to Rae'en. Back in South Number Nine, she hadn't even owned a mirror. Looking into the full-length mirror featured so prominently in her palace guest room brought on a frown. It irked her, the way this silver-backed glass was meant to fill a role her own unit should have handled. If an Aern needed to be dressed and styled in a specific way, they helped each other. Why use a mirror when you could look through the eyes of your Overwatches? Or was that only a kholster and Overwatch thing? Even so, clad in her new armor, she couldn't stop looking at the fierce young warrior in the looking glass.

I think it's a privacy thing, Vander sent her. *The armor looks nice on you. When did Kholster make the alterations?*

Kholster? Rae'en squinted, studying the half breastplate for whatever Vander had seen.

He's gotten better at rolling edges over the centuries. In several spots, the alterations to the armor glowed gold as Vander highlighted the changes. *If you look at some of the detail-work, he's retouched it, smoothing out lines and sharpening the definition.* An image of the original ensemble floated, rotating on the right side of her field of vision.

All the leather is new, too, Rae'en added. *Isn't it?*

I think so, Vander thought back, *but I wonder how he broke it in so quickly.*

Maybe one of the museum docents? Rae'en thought.

Smell it. Vander transmitted a scent. *Leather on which Kholster has worked and taken time attains a distinctive aroma. Sharp and rich, an undertone of his blood.*

Rae'en took a deep breath. Vander was right. It smelled like Kholster.

That's not why I interrupted, though, Vander sent. *Prince Rivvek is requesting that you partake in the Test of Four.*

In what way? Rae'en rolled her eyes and let loose a low growl. Rivvek was slowing everything down.

Let me show you?

Go ahead. Her current surroundings dropped away, subsumed by a view of the throne room. Platforms (once floating, based on memories Kholster had shared in his All Knows) hung at varying levels supported by crystalline lattices. Delicate tile-work on each platform showed stylized representations of Aeromancy, Geomancy, Hydromancy, Pyromancy, and the gears-within-gears symbol of the Artificers.

Reminiscent of the Tower of Elementals she'd viewed at Grivek's funeral, the throne room centered on a ragged-edged square of unknown metal alloy. Partially melted on one side, the gray square looked as though it had been torn free from some larger object. Upon its surface, four bowls, one filled with water, one with soil, one with kindling, and a final empty bowl were arranged around a single massive carnelian-colored candle.

Dragon tallow candle, Vander thought at her. *I wonder how many of those they have left.*

Four steps, each emblazoned with an elemental symbol, led up to a throne carved of a massive slab of granite, the Throne of Villok. Behind it, an open, uncurtained veranda overlooked the docks and the Bay of Balsiph. Vander moved past Eldrennai going about various preparation, dusting and polishing, to stand in the middle of the room where he spun in a slow circle so she could see the tiered seating on either side of the room, not lower than the king but on an equal level.

Don't most kings loom over their subjects? Rae'en asked.

It's said Villok felt anyone who had to look down on his subjects to rule them was unfit to hold the throne. Vander zoomed in on the open space behind the throne and then back at the entryway, which was also open, without a door. *He felt the same way about being able to seal off the throne room.*

He wants you to sit on the throne, he said as he jumped up the steps and rested his hands on the stone, *as its ceremonial guardian until Rivvek passes, fails, or abandons the Test of Four.*

Why not Wylant? Rae'en's view returned to normal.

She informed the prince she would be unable to attend the ceremony shortly after she delivered your new armor. I couldn't hear what was said, but Amber was close enough to catch some of it. Wylant mentioned Fort Sunder and flew off without her Sidearms.

Kholster Rae'en, Bloodmane's echoing voice intoned.

Wait your turn, she thought at Bloodmane. To Vander, she thought, *Did any of the Armored see her leave?*

Two Bone Finders, Vander shot back. *Why?*

Ask Zhan if he minds having one of them follow her—

He says, Vander replied, *Alysaundra already is and that the Ossuary will be happy to share this information with the Aernese army.*

Thanks. She sat down on the floor, not wanting to muss up a bed one of the maids had taken such pains to make. Stone felt better against her, more reliable than the soft mattresses Oathbreakers preferred. *Tell Rivvek I'll defend his throne ceremonially, as long as that's all there is to it.*

Scooting clear of the wall, Rae'en lay down, eyes closed. Willing her heart to slow down, her breath to come in a slow controlled rhythm, only then did she look through Bloodmane's eyes.

Fire flowed around him as he and his warsuits slew Zaur after Zaur. His helm tilted up, giving a signal to Oathbreaker elemancers. Behind his team, the stone tunnel collapsed, forcing a wave of flames explosively forward. Oathbreaker lancers dived down on any Zaur foolish enough to believe there was anywhere to flee. Dark-scaled reptilian bodies burned as they screamed and died.

What do you want?

We are killing many Zaur, but I have a concern. Bloodmane swung Hunger one-handed, piercing a brown-scaled Zaur's chest. With a gurgling hiss another Zaur leapt at him, Skreel blades sparking on his helm with little effect. Catching it by the throat, Bloodmane crushed its windpipe and spine. Tossing it aside he moved on to the next batch of attackers.

It's a slaughter. Rae'en thought. *What's so concerning about that?*

Everywhere we suspect we will find a tunnel, we do. Bloodmane dropped Hunger, letting the warpick cling to his leg plate. Hands free, he tore an attacker in half, gore covering him.

That doesn't sound like a problem to me, Makerslayer, Rae'en sent the warsuit.

Each tunnel also holds an identical complement of Zaur. Molten rock hissed under Bloodmane's boots, the dead he cast aside steaming and splitting open as the rock pushed them along with its flow.

Identical how?

Bloodmane pulled himself free of the rock, trudging out of the tunnel when the Oathbreakers and warsuits joined him. Shouts of victory went up from the Oathbreakers, but the warsuits kept their silence, steam rising off of them as they cooled.

There are one hundred and thirteen Zaur, Bloodmane told her, transmitting highlights from each of the seven engagements that he had led. **Even in the central tunnel.**

It's a prime number? Rae'en thought churlishly. *So? What?*

Exactly one hundred and thirteen Zaur in each engagement.

Vander? Rae'en sent.

Eyes of Vengeance says it has been the same for his engagements, Vander answered. *Look at this.*

Point of view shifting, Rae'en watched as Eyes of Vengeance charged to the back of a line of Zaur where slightly larger Zaur with scales in different patterns waited to die when the Geomancers collapsed the tunnels.

In the beginning, Eyes of Vengeance told her, **I thought these were the Sri'Zaur Wylant and you described—**

No. Rae'en sent back an image of the Zaur she had seen. *They look like this.*

"I didn't share the information because I was mad at Bloodmane," Rae'en whispered. "Idiot. Vander didn't ask me much about them because he has more experience with Zaur than I do and since I couldn't show him a Zaurruk. . . . Blast!"

Ah. Eyes of Vengeance seized one by the back of the neck and hoisted him aloft. With a swipe of his gauntlets, the zigzag lines of electric blue smeared across its scales. **And may I assume—**

No, Rae'en sent, *the patterns I saw don't rub off. They're real, like a snake's or a lizard's.*

I fear we are doing, Bloodmane cut in, **exactly what this Warlord Xastix wants us to do, destroying only the decoy emplacements he intended us to find.**

What did Skinner find at Kevari Pass? Rae'en asked.

Nothing unusual, Bloodmane, Eyes of Vengeance, and Vander answered all at once.

And he is our best scout?

No, Vander answered. *Those would be Eyes of Vengeance, Scout, Hunter, Scale Fist—*

Why did you send someone to Kevari Pass? Rae'en sent the thought to Bloodmane, but Eyes of Vengeance answered.

General Bloodmane did not choose to send Skinner. I did.

General? Rae'en asked. *Why General Bloodmane, not kholster Bloodmane?*

Because, though I did not mean for my maker to die, I do not deserve to bear his name . . . even as a rank, Bloodmane answered.

Rae'en had never felt anything like the waves of grief that flowed with those thoughts, not from anywhere outside herself.

Even though that is what he called me. The Eldrennai dubbed me General Bloodmane and . . . it feels less abominable to answer to that name. I mean no disrespect. Quite the opposite—

Shut up, Rae'en ordered. Taking a moment to look through no one's eyes but her own, she examined the red that showed through the lids of her eyes from the light outside her window.

Look. I'm going to forgive you. . . . Rae'en sent to Bloodmane. *Just give me time. Know that I'm going to be rude, even when you don't deserve it. I miss him and I blame you even though I know . . . I really do know that it wasn't your fault, that he saw an opportunity and took it for reasons I don't fully understand. But I can't be mad at him, so I'm mad at you.*

Thank you. Bloodmane's voice echoed. **Take as much time as you need.**

Where is Skinner now?

I . . . Bloodmane's voice dipped low. **I cannot find him. Eyes of Vengeance, can you—?**

No, Eyes of Vengeance answered. **I have a bad feeling about this.**

Who is Skinner's Aern?

Miryndal, Bloodmane told her.

I don't recall that name, Rae'en sent. *Is she an Overwatch? A kholster?*

She's a grunt, Vander thought at her, *in Mokk's kholstering.*

Mokk is Ambush's maker, Bloodmane added.

Where is she? Rae'en got up off the floor, pacing to the side of the bed where Testament and Grudge were propped. Slinging her warpick over her right shoulder and her father's over her left she took a deep breath. She brought to mind her interactions with her father, when he was happy and when he was sad or upset. He always kept an even temper with her and with his troops. The enemy could go to any of the Bone Queen's hells they like, but to be Aern was to be family.

Mokk is checking, Vander cut in.

Why doesn't he know? Rae'en asked with thoughts like clear water on calm seas.

Everyone who wanted to has been restoring the barracks to habitable levels. Vander sent with the thoughts images of plans underway and sites already completed. *Opening up our old berths—where they still exist. There were plenty of volunteers, so many of the grunts are drilling or reading. Catching up on extra sleep. We're all Armored, so with every soldier only a thought away . . .*

Not every soldier. Rae'en opened the door to her room, surprised to find no guards there. Was that blood? She sniffed the air and brought both warpicks to the ready before she noticed the dead Oathbreaker. One needle-thin dagger clanged off of Testament, the other caught her in the side of the knee.

Pushing away the pain, she whirled on the injured leg, knowing the knee would give, not caring.

Bloodmane howled in agony as her attacker struck home again, sliding the weapon up to the hilt into her side.

It hurts, Bloodmane, Rae'en thought. *But not that badly.*

No reply.

Colors bled together on the wall, rippling mirage-like in the same way the air did over the Guild Commerce Highway when the suns were high. She struck at the discoloration, Testament rending flesh and scale, the near-black, iron-saturated blood of the Zaur coating her weapon. With the strike, the Zaur's—no, the Sri'Zaur's, she self-corrected—scales pulsed gray then black as if trying to adapt to its surroundings and blend in despite the wound.

It tapped something in Zaurtol with its tail and hurled its weapons. Rae'en took one of the slender blades to the palm in order to catch it, but the other was snatched from the air by another camouflaged Sri'Zaur.

She reached out for Vander, then for Bloodmane, and found nothing but mindquiet in their places.

Hoping it would help, Rae'en shifted her vision to thermal imaging, the back of her eyeballs growing cold. She cursed under her breath. It wasn't much better that way either, as if her attackers were the same temperature as the walls and floor. *How many of them are there?* Hearing the scrape of claws on stone, Rae'en rolled back into the guest room. She snatched Grudge from her back, catching the weapon with the side of her hand and holding it there with the attraction that Aern exploited over all bone-steel items.

—an you hear me? Bloodmane's voice snapped back into her mind. **Oh, thank Kholster you're back. What happened?**

I'm not sure, but— Rae'en began to think back.

Kholster Rae'en! Vander shouted in her mind. *I'm nearly there. I—*

"Bird squirt!" He vanished from her mind. Rae'en roared, *"ALL KNOW!"* transmitting the last few seconds to any Aern who could hear her . . . no longer certain that it reached all of her people.

Incoming, Amber's voice filled Rae'en's mind as she took the lead in Vander's absence. *I see Vander, ma'am.* She sent a snap image: Vander on blue carpet, warding off unseen blows with Spite, his warpick. *He's hurt, but I think the two of—*

And then Amber was gone, too.

Bloodmane, what is happening?!, Rae'en thought angrily. Then, *Never mind.*

Where are Vander and Amber? Rae'en ran back through the snippet she'd gotten from both of them. Blue Carpet. Okay, so where did that put them? Was that the sea corridor or the corridor of breeze? Remembering her way quickly back through the short walk-through after the Oathbreaker king's funeral, she'd seen several different patterns.

Think, Rae'en, she berated herself. The corridor of breezes was a diamond pattern of white, gray, and turquoise. Rae'en was about to charge back into the hall when Feagus painted his visuals across the whole of her field of vision. Losing her balance, Rae'en crashed into the doorframe with the muffled metallic sound of bone-steel on wood. The wood lost.

Feagus! Rae'en shouted in his mind. *I need to see what's around me, not—*

Sorry, kholster, Feagus gulped, instantly drawing his visual back to the upper-left corner of her view. He stood in the Corridor of Flames making calming gestures to frightened guardsmen as a multitude of Aern rushed past shouting Rae'en's name. *Things are a little out of control.*

Visuals from Varvost and Glayne appeared in the lower left and portions of her vision while a rough map of her location occupied the upper right, leaving an addition-sign-shaped window for her own surroundings. Varvost, engaged in a heated exchange with Bhaeshal, Prince Rivvek's personal Aeromancer, gesturing with his battle-axe, Assault II.

Glayne's window displayed a collage of perspectives from the exterior hallway of her own room. Blinded by Ghaiattri flame in the first Demon War, Glayne had learned to see exclusively through Hunter, his warsuit. After the Sundering, he had learned to see through one of his soul-bonded weapons and then, with practice, through all of them.

Chips of stone skipped from the walls, cut loose by the whirling blade at the end of a thin chain that he spun at a pace so fiercely alacritous the chain itself couldn't be seen. With each step, he shifted Long Fang's rotation, covering different arcs: front, back, left, and right following no set pattern Rae'en could discern, each clear from one angle or another of his clustered visuals.

Moments away, kholster. Glayne's thoughts were icy smooth.

Could you cut it down to one viewpoint? Rae'en asked. *You're making me dizzy.*

Obediently, the view from Lookout, the punch dagger that hung from a chain around Glayne's neck, supplanted the others . . . shifting every few seconds with the view from Hindsight, the garrote he wore along the back of his belt. Rae'en tried to recall everything she knew about Glayne, but all she could remember was his disability and that, of all the One Hundred, he had made the most soul-bonded weapons after the Sundering . . . and that none of them was a warpick.

Are you certain none of them got into your room? One of the needle-thin daggers spanged off of Long Fang's chain, disrupting its steady circle. Viewpoint spinning with Glayne as he jumped, letting Long Fang's chain wrap around his torso and simultaneously reversing the direction of the weapon's spin. Rae'en had no idea how he had the presence of mind or the dexterity to have done so, but mid-turn he'd thrown one of his soul-bound throwing daggers (either Plan, Backup, Hush Now, or My Love—she couldn't tell which), pinning one of the Sri'Zaur assailants to the wall, the dagger's flat, ringed hilt protruding from the Sri'Zaur's eye. Glayne fanned the other three blades.

I'm fine. I—

An alarm went off in the strategist part of her brain. *Always know what your enemy wants from you*, she could hear Kholster saying. Lessons she'd heard even before she was an Eleven. *Analyze their attacks. Learn to know which are feints and which are serious. Do that, and you can guess not only where they will strike next, but why. It is more important to know—not where the current attack originates—but where the next one will be.*

"They stopped attacking me once I was back in my room," Rae'en said under her breath. "They didn't want to kill me. They would have, had I given them opportunity, but—"

Bloodmane, she started, then stopped herself.

Kholster Rae'en?

How many kholsters are currently under attack?

Checking, Bloodmane intoned, thoughts still pained. **I have no contact with three kholsters.**

How many Overwatches?

I-It's a lot of them. Twenty at least.

"All Know," Rae'en thought and spoke the words. "I'm not sure what the Sri'Zaur think will come of this, or even how they are doing it, but they are after the Overwatches. The Zaur are trying to blind us!"

*

Standing over her Prime Overwatch in the Hall of Healing, Rae'en could not help but smell fear. It clung to the Oathbreaker followers of Sedvinia who attended the single patient, to the human errand runners who ran back and forth to gather herbs and other medicines from the Apothecary or into the marketplace or nearby groves for whatever might be needed. Worst of all, it came from Vander, lying in the utilitarian cot, sweating and shaking.

The ninety-three less specialized soldiers of the One Hundred lined the halls standing two abreast, parting only for those Rae'en or one of her Overwatches warned them might be coming, eyeing even those Oathbreakers and humans with open distrust. Glayne, backed by one thousand fighting Aern, manned the entrance to the building itself, having locked and barred the other three ground-floor entrances.

The blind Overwatch, Glayne, held Long Fang at the ready, twirling the blade and chain in threatening arcs whenever any non-Aern approached. He had only agreed to go that far from Rae'en and Vander when she had allowed him to jam Hush Now and My Love into opposite ends of the hallway outside Vander's room. Back Up let him keep watch from the door post of the room itself as if Amber and Feagus standing back-to-back in the doorway were insufficient.

It ought to be me out there, Rae'en thought at Glayne.

No, kholster, he answered. *You are First and given what happened to your father we cannot be sure we could strip and dip you if an assassin's needle slew you. Without you, there can be no All Know or All Recall. Subtract the First and we are only one step from Foresworn.*

Four gold tokens lit in Rae'en's view signifying assent. The fifth token was not there at all.

Prince Rivvek, Varvost sent from his post in the throne room with Bhaeshal, ten Aern, and the assembled elemancer guard of those who had come to observe the Test of Four, *wishes to know if Vander has made any improvement.*

Rae'en began to tell him no (yet again) when Vander moaned, his unbandaged right eye flipping open. Wide orange streaks ran through the black sclera, the jade irises narrow bands around wide amber pupils.

Has anyone ever seen an Aern's eyes look like that? She asked the four Overwatches and Bloodmane. Gray tokens were her answer.

Vander? She sent at her uncle. *Vander?* Nothing.

"Hello, lazy." Rae'en knelt over him, putting a hand on his chest just in case he tried to sit up despite the aged priest of Sedvinia working on the wound half a hand below the center of his chest where one of the assassins had managed to jam one of the long, needle-thin daggers through Vander's inner rib plates. Left eye bandaged, various lacerations dotting his bald head, arms, and chest, Vander had definitely looked better.

He reached up, feeling the edges of the bandage over his eyes, then tried to sit up just as she'd feared he would. Holding him down with less effort than Rae'en had expected it would take, she cooed a series of hushes and said, "It's okay" more than once before settling for sharply shouting his name.

"Vander!"

He froze, his unbandaged right eye seeming to see her for the first time since he'd opened it.

"I can't feel Eyes!" Vander said in a quivering panicked voice.

"It's bandaged for your own good," the aged healer working on his chest wound began.

"That's not what he meant," Rae'en growled at the old Oathbreaker. "Bloodmane and the Armored are escorting Eyes of Vengeance to Port Ammond." Rae'en touched his cheek with her free hand. "He is just as worried about you."

Vander sagged, relief as palpably evident physically as it was alarming, since Rae'en could not feel it in her head and his token did not reappear in her field of vision.

"Amber?" Vander asked urgently. "She was in the corridor, too. Did they—?"

"Right over here, Prime." She waved from the doorway. "Scale Fist is good, too." Amber tapped her temple. "Still connected."

"Varvost, Glayne, and Feagus are all okay," Rae'en told him. "You were the only one of the One Hundred who got his scars marred."

"And you're sure Eyes of Vengeance is all right." Vander clutched her hand. "You're certain?"

"He has a few wounds on him," Rae'en answered, "but he can walk and talk. He is cut off from everyone like you are, but you took the worst of the beating. He'll be here as soon as the warsuits can get him here."

Vander closed his eyes, then his face went slack. Rae'en watched the rise and fall of his chest to be sure he was still breathing before stepping away.

I wish I could reassure him, Bloodmane thought. None of us can reach either of them.

Maybe when we get them close enough to each other, Rae'en offered. She thought about Kazan, Joose, Arbokk, and M'jynn out there on the road. Probably somewhere between Castleguard and Oot by now.

I'm sure they are fine, Rae'en, Bloodmane told her.

I still wish they'd get their butts up here a little faster, she thought back, just so I could keep an eye on them.

They don't have your father setting the pace, Rae'en, Bloodmane said. Should I send a contingent to get them?

No. Rae'en pictured the look of indignation on their faces if she sent a crew to escort them to her like they couldn't handle themselves.

Kholster Rae'en, Varvost sent. Prince Rivvek says he understands completely if you would like him to postpone the Test of Four.

What? Rae'en hadn't given it any thought at all since the attack, even though she was still wearing the amour Wylant had given her. Tiny blood-crusted holes marked her injuries from the fight, but she hoped she could repair them eventually. He is asking about that now?

He says he is willing to delay as long as you like, Varvost transmitted, but we have only given him a certain amount of time in which to complete it before we—

No. Rae'en began relaying orders to various kholsters and their Over-watches. I understand. He's right about the timetable. I'm heading there now.

Do we still need to kill them? Bloodmane thought at her. I am not refusing, but I wanted to know if Rivvek's coronation—

Leave it alone, Bloodmane, Rae'en snapped. I don't plan to actually declare war on a king with my father's scars on his back unless I have no other choice.

PART THREE

A KING ARISES

"Eldrennai, it is said, do not die; they are killed. Not as resilient as the Aern or the Vael, the Eldrennai live on, untouched (or mostly untouched—for more on this, see my ruminations about Hasimak in volume 11) by the ravages of time to which the majority of Barrone's inhabitants are subject. Maturing rapidly, all Eldrennai are born without physical defect. We may be maimed in life, of course, and we do not regenerate, as do Uled's creations, under our own power.

Time, however, and the appropriate application of healing magic granted us by Sedvinia allow a remarkable range of recovery possibilities for injured or dying Eldrennai. Artificers, like myself, can construct new limbs or organs where divine magicks fail or are withheld. Yet I have never seen a common Eldrennai, one of those who share my race but not my magical affinity, granted full access to the Halls of Healing. It was noticing this at the age of three while touring the halls with my father for likely subjects who possessed magic, but not nobility—and would not, therefore, be missed should he require their assistance—in whole or in part, that I realized the true depths of my father's evil and began plotting to kill him.

I once wondered if that patricidal desire made me evil, too.

It didn't, for I have known love, and true evil can know only desire. As a result, when I first understood what I was feeling for my beloved, where others might have felt unbridled joy, I experienced a profound sense of relief."

From the preface to *Eldrennai or Aiannai:
An Examination of the Greatest Fallen Empire* by Sargus

CHAPTER 21
WYLANT'S NEW ARMOR

Cracked and upturned, the terrain of the Broken Table, the mesa at the center of which stood Fort Sunder, made travel on horseback problematic for most. Vax had sensed a few urgent transmissions from Rae'en, but, as an unawakened Aern of unique status, he could only say that it seemed to have been related to the Zaur and if the Aern couldn't handle a few Zaur there was little even she could do to assist them.

Leaving her Sidearms back at Port Ammond meant she could make much better speed. Not having to worry about limiting flight time to minimize elemental foci growth cut the journey in half, even if it did cause the occasional pangs of grief when she remembered how much Mazik had loved that feeling, soaring through even the coldest air at the highest altitudes with an exultant expression he never wore with his feet on the ground.

The ground. Once, before the last Demon War, this had been some of the most beautiful land in the Eldren Plains. Dotted not only with the ever-resilient myr grass but also with blood oak groves where now only dwarf varieties and shrubland remained amidst artificial plateaus, ravines, buttes, cliff ranges, and wide expanses of glass left behind by the combination of elemental bombardment and geomantic attacks. What few rivers remained were shallow, the life within them changed. Fish were still edible perhaps, but with tougher scales, sharper teeth, and the occasional extra eye or spider-like legs.

Natural elemental energies flowed in twisted ribbons and jagged spikes, unpredictable for most Eldrennai (and Aiannai, for that matter), causing elemantic control to become unstable, unpredictable, or fail completely. It worked for Wylant because she had been at the epicenter of the blast that warped the magic here, and it functioned properly for the descendants of Uled and the royal family for reasons Sargus understood far better than she. Few were the Eldrennai who had been spared.

"We should be seeing the crystalline shield soon," Wylant shouted to Vax over the wind.

You can think to me, Mother.

"I know," she told him, "but I'm more comfortable this way. Does it bother you?"

No, Vax thought, *but I'm told my emotions are blunted because I have yet to be properly awakened, so very little bothers me.*

"The shield can be beautiful from the air." Wylant flew higher. "When the suns are both shining through at the right angle, it creates multicolored flashes and circular rainbows. You get the same sort of imagery off of the guardian golems at times, but it's more dramatic off the shield itself."

Where was the shield? Gliding in lower and lower in case a trick of the light or atmospheric effect obscured the shield from view, Wylant saw Fort Sunder, but no shield.

"What have they done to it?" Wylant muttered.

The shield or Fort Sunder? Vax asked.

"Both?" The massive edifice of stone had cast a wary watch over the plains for thousands of years, its blue-gray walls made from rocks mined from the quarry at the end of Kevari Pass by the Aern long after Eldrennai has ceased to dig there for fear of the Zaur. Before the shield had gone up, at certain distances, the whole of Fort Sunder had taken on a blue sheen as if it contained no gray at all. Gone now was that azure shade, and in its place she saw walls, battlements, the same buildings and, up the rise, a keep comprised entirely of pearlescent white loomed vast and unknown despite its familiar profile.

Naught remained of the crystal shield or the insectoid golems who had patrolled the site since the warning signs had gone up shortly after the Aern had gone into exile. Still as statues, a mix of Bone Finders and warsuits from—it felt so alien to say general rather than kholster—General Bloodmane's command dotted the walls and grounds, keeping vigil. Moving in closer, she spotted the ground around the fortress, once thick with myr grass, lined now with blue-gray stone spreading out in all directions in a perfect circle of open ground an invader would have to cover.

Up close, Wylant saw the details of the fort and cringed. Skulls, leg, and arm bones, even the plate-like ribs of the Aern had been merged together, as if the entire fortress had been rebuilt with the bone metal of the dead Aern who had been slain when she shattered the Life Forge. How many millions did this represent? She knew the number, had tallied it up once, but after the first million the sum lost its meaning. Endless murder. Attempted genocide. There was no pleasant name for it. And now Fort Sunder, the place she had once called home during the best parts of her pre-exile marriage, was a monument to her greatest glory and deepest shame.

Was this what Kholster had wanted her to see?

No. Kholster was cold when he needed to be, yes, but never cruel. He—

It is amazing, isn't it, Mother? Vax thought to her. *No one could tear that down!*

"Tell me what it means to you, Vax, please. If you don't mind." Wylant added the last sentence quickly to rephrase everything as a request, not an order. She had performed the same verbal gymnastics during her entire courtship and marriage with Kholster, but she'd gotten rusty.

Wylant landed on the battlements, the bone metal cool rather than blindingly hot as it would have been if it were any other metal. Looking out from that vantage point, she could begin to see what it might have meant to the Aern. A gesture, maybe? A way of saying to the rest of Barrone, "This is ours. Anything of ours you destroy we can rebuild and make stronger. Whatever you take, we can reclaim."

It means the Aern have returned, Vax said. *My father's people abandoned their homeland once, but now they are back. Their bones no longer lie unused in silly useless piles. "Even when we die," Fort Sunder tells the world, "the rest of us grow stronger. Nothing can long defeat the Aern."*

"Setbacks only," Kholster had once told her, "never real defeat."

"You truly aren't angry with me?" Wylant asked. "Even after what I did?"

Of course not, Vax replied cheerily. *You are my mother and we have had many victories together. I love you. My father loves you. I told him I wanted to be with you, as your weapon, until he harvests you . . . and then one of my brother or sister Aern will awaken me fully. No child has ever been as lucky as me. I get to be with you all the time.*

Tears flowing freely, Wylant patted Vax's hilt and floated down to the inner courtyard. It was so easy to forget how differently the Aern saw things, to accurately register the magnificent and terrifying diversity of their alien thought processes.

Father said you might prefer for me to be awakened sooner than that, Vax sent as Wylant's feet touched the bone-steel cobbles. Were those kneecaps? Phalanges? An instinct sent Wylant soaring back up to the wall, curiosity about the exact construction of Fort Sunder abandoned. She felt . . . stalked. Peering out along broken plains, she spotted two Bone Finders. One was out past the ridge-like demarcation separating gnarled shrubland from myr grass. It was the same one Wylant had spotted diverting its path to follow her a few miles from Port Ammond. The flared crested helm of the warsuit narrowed the Bone Finder's identity down to either Alysaundra or Ravil. Its tapered waist gave her the final clue. The warsuit was Bone Harvest, which meant the Bone Finder within was Alysaundra.

"If you'd have asked me where I was going," Wylant muttered, "I would have told you, kholster Rae'en."

Wylant had no trouble understanding why kholster Rae'en (or perhaps

Zhan) might want to keep track of her movements. Beloved as she seemed to be by the Aern, she had defeated them—given them serious . . . setbacks— once, and she had offered no oath she would not do so again. So . . . that explained Alysaundra's watchful presence.

Skull-helmed and with an unhurried, even gait, the second Bone Finder's presence sent a shiver up her spine. Caz, twin long knives hanging from Silencer's back, stared—even accounting for distance—directly at Wylant. First Oot, then Port Ammond, and now here at Fort Sunder. If Alysaundra was following her movements, then what was Caz doing?

Was Caz's observation related to what Kholster wanted her to see . . . or merely a sign that Caz was under different orders than Alysaundra? Whatever Kholster wanted her to discover, she was certain of one thing. . . .

"He's cheating." Wylant smirked.

Who is cheating? Vax asked.

"Your father," Wylant answered. "Whatever he wants me to discover by sending me here is something he knows and we haven't figured out yet. That would be just like him."

No. Vax's thoughts, the sound of them, made Wylant wonder if that's how he would sound if he were a living, breathing Aern, instead of what she and Dienox had made him. *He would be cheating if he told you what he thought you needed to know directly. But giving you a gift in celebration of your acceptance of his scars and placing it somewhere that he thought might lead to the knowledge . . . there's no rule against that. He checked with Aldo, and Aldo said a precedent was set by Dienox when he courted Nomi. Physical gifts to love interests are allowed.*

"Vax," Wylant asked, "do you know what he wants me to find out?"

As they talked, Caz kept on walking closer, eyes still on her. She didn't like it or the protective feelings that watchful gaze stirred within her. Right now, there was only one bone-steel item on her person, and if, in some misguided, ill-timed Bone Finder madness, Caz had decided to come for those bones, he'd be stripped and dipped repeatedly until Kholster harvested Barrone itself at the end of things before he'd take Vax from her.

"Vax?" Wylant prodded.

Ye-es, Vax answered, voice muted. *Was he not supposed to?*

"I assume he made you promise not to tell me?"

He didn't make me promise, Vax said. *I offered to promise in exchange for the information, but I am permitted to confirm it when you discover it for yourself.*

"Please don't do anything to break your oath," Wylant whispered. "I'll puzzle it out on my own."

Warsuits returned warsuit salutes as she approached the main keep. An occasional clang of metal on metal, her own footsteps, and the creaking of leather were all that broke the silence. Guardians who moved only if they were needed elsewhere watched all approaches, the only outward sign of their actual natures the flickering of light within their red eyes or visor slits as they communed with their makers and each other.

Unchallenged, she reached the keep.

"Where from here?" she asked Vax.

Down deep, Vax answered, *where the Life Forge stood.*

"Of course it is." Hugging her arms, Wylant stepped into the main hall only to hug the wall to avoid being trampled.

"Excuse us, kholster Wylant." Scales, Cadimeer's warsuit, one of Bloodmane's command, ran past her followed by two dozen of his fellows. One of the warsuits, Scout—if she recalled the leafy pattern of his armor correctly—near the edge of the troop in a traditional Overwatch position, went limp and fell, clattering down the steps up which Wylant had just climbed. Bone Finder warsuits stepped in to collect the fallen warsuit as Scales's group kept moving.

"Is he okay . . ." The name escaped her . . . something that rhymed with Bricklayer, and his warsuit was . . . some kind of poem? Requiem! That was the warsuit! And the Aern was . . . Alton? No! ". . . Kaulton?" Where had she gotten the Bricklayer thing from? Oh well.

"He is ended," another Aern answered. "But surely you know this."

"How would I know it?" Wylant gasped. "What do you mean dead? You can't kill a warsuit."

"You are correct." Kaulton and the Bone Finder she didn't recognize looked at one another. The unknown warsuit was skull-helmed like most Bone Finders, but in this warsuit's case a skull lacking eyes, the red crystal with which the warsuit appeared to see located in the open jaws of the skull. "*I* cannot kill a warsuit."

"And you think I am responsible for Scout's end?" Wylant shoved the armor, grateful that it yielded enough her hand was unharmed. "I'll make this simple. On my oath, if I've had anything to do with the death of any Aern or warsuit since the Sundering, it is unwitting. I destroyed the Life Forge. This Fortress is built with the bones of my victims. I have no idea what happened to Scout and I am sad to see him fall."

"Truly?" The eyeless-skulled Bone Finder asked.

"Whose scars are on my back?" Her own heartbeat pounding in her ears, Wylant turned away from Scout and the two Bone Finders, heading quickly down for the area that had served as Uled's lab and the home for the Life Forge.

"We get the new armor and then get out of here as fast as the wind will carry us." Vax didn't answer, but it hadn't been a question, and she cursed herself for the misstep. "Okay, Vax?"

Okay, Mother.

Oil, blood, and metallic scents choked the air, growing more potent as she started down a stair of skulls. Absent the ever-present smell of *jallek* root, each new odor hit Wylant harder than before, possessing a depth and nuance she'd missed without knowing.

Stairs gave way to corridor, hers the only footsteps.

Storage rooms that had once been filled to bursting with shelves of books and various alchemical solutions or artificer contraptions sat empty now. Clear glass plate lined the hallway at canted angles, making use of mirrors and exterior sunlight to illuminate the cold passageway. Where once glowing orbs had floated to fight off the night when the suns set or the sky was overcast, Dwarven rune lights, square and mounted the walls with sturdy brackets, now sat ready.

"How much farther?" Her heart pounded. There were no pleasant memories farther down this way.

You know the answer to that, Vax sent.

Marshaling will, courage having never been something she lacked, Wylant walked toward the epicenter of her crime.

Victory, Vax corrected.

"One and the same," she whispered.

Her first look at the door to Uled's lab lit a fire in her mind.

"Bird squirt," was all she managed to get out as the flashback took her. Eyes burning like she'd hurled a lightning bolt at point-blank range, Wylant screamed as she hurled Uled's skull down into the snow atop the Sri'Zauran Mountains. She'd wanted to smash it to pieces, but Sargus had been able, once Uled's tissues had been cleaned away, to point out web-thin lines of arcane symbols on the interior of his skull.

"I don't know what they do," he had told her, "but I guarantee you it is part of a contingency plan. I don't know what sets it off, but we should probably put it far away."

Mother?

Vax's voice sent her back further, to his forging. She'd never been able to recall it fully before, but now that whatever had blocked her mind's journals of the past had done its work, she could relive it all: Heating Vax's bone metal. Hammering him. Honing his blade there in the Smithy, which in its totality comprised the Life Forge.

Don't fear, girl. Dienox's voice had played in her head when Vax was close to completion. *It will be a weapon worthy of my champion. Warpicks and warsuits! Ha! No Aern ever had a weapon as fine as this. Nor the other god's champions or justicars.*

Kilke will be so jealous! She felt the burning of his hand on the back of her head, his other on her wrist and connected that memory with the last time she'd seen Queen Kari in The Parliament of Ages.

"So, kholster Wylant," Queen Kari had said, "How long do you suppose it will be before Dienox deigns to lift his fog of war to allow you to discern the location of your ancient foes?"

Kari's words echoed in Wylant's thoughts. "The shroud of the god hangs over your spirit so that it pains me to see it and not be able to help. Your soul struggles so valiantly to keep you free of him that he only manages to blur the edges. He does not control you, but he has in the past."

"Control me?" Wylant had told her then. "The gods cannot control the living unless the living are willing. I'm not some foolish God Speaker."

"But you have opened yourself to war, to the thrill of victory. The times Dienox has reached in and pushed you in one direction or the other have left his burning handprints on your living spirit, marks your soul cannot scour away in this life. I see a conflagration engulfing your right wrist . . . and one trailing fire from the back of your head as if he'd grasped your skull one-handed, forcing you to change direction . . . and . . ."

"Kari knew," Wylant panted back in the present. "She tried to tell me and I discounted it as foolishness from some silly Flower Girl."

With eyes opened to the depth of the war god's tampering, other times he had controlled her became clear. Heart pounding like a trip hammer, Wylant's lips and face went numb, left arm dropping to her side.

"Vax," she tried to say his name, but something . . .

It's better this way, said the familiar voice of Dienox in her mind. *We had such good times together, you and I. You can be with your husband. Won't that be nice? And Vax can be my new champion. Aern are forbidden, but after what we did to him, he isn't strictly an Aern*—Wylant dropped to her knees, and the god of war bent over her. She couldn't remember his name, but she didn't need to. All she needed to do was fight, and her muscles knew how to do that almost entirely on their own. Left side unresponsive, Wylant drew Vax with her right and stabbed the war god through his shining breastplate.

Screeching, the war god vanished, and, even as she thought his name,

Kholster was there, helping her up. At his side, Aldo and Shidarva stood in flowing robes, their presence so luminous Wylant could no longer see the walls of the corridor.

"Dideye kilm?" Wylant leaned on Kholster, her words slurring unintelligibly. "Warged. Eversnam is."

"Aldo . . . Shidarva," Kholster said calmly, "I demand an amercement."

"Where have we heard those words before?" Aldo looked knowingly at the queen of the gods.

"Very well, Kholster," Shidarva answered, eyes blazing blue. "He tried to make her forget everything all over again and murder her in the process. What penalty do you suggest? I suppose you want permission to harvest him?"

"No," Kholster answered. "The Harvester requires permission to reap no soul human or divine. This is about Wylant. She is the wronged party. I want her granted immunity. I want her healed. And then, I'd like you to grant *her* permission to kill him."

"I'll start on the second part." A third goddess, Shidarva's twin, Sedvinia, goddess of sadness and joy, emerged from Uled's old laboratory. She looked down on Wylant with open eyes glistening with one extreme of her emotional responsibility or the other. "With your permission?"

"G'hd," Wylant answered.

"Kholster," Sedvinia called as her glow suffused Wylant. "Given time it seems as though she would have made a full recovery of her own. She has deific essence flowing through her body. Do you know anything about that?"

"All I did was put my scars on her back," Kholster said evenly, "as requested. It is possible a little of my blood may have been absorbed as part of the traditional scarification method."

"Traditional method?" Shidarva asked. "She's the only person you've scarred yourself, the rest were done by your warsuits."

"Who," Kholster asked, baring his doubled canines, "would know more about Aernese tradition than me? And given that I was First Forged, however I choose to perform an Aernese ritual . . . well, that is the traditional method, by definition. If you want a default, Shidarva, I am the traditional method."

"He has you there," Aldo clucked.

"Sleep now," Sedvinia whispered, her refreshing presence flowing around and through Wylant's body, mind, and soul. "You'll feel much better soon."

None of that was the thing he wanted you to find out, Mother, Vax thought at Wylant as she drifted into slumber. *Just so you know.*

The general tried to laugh, but all she got out was a snore.

CHAPTER 22

EVERYONE HAS A PLAN

The Chamber of Four, the throne room of the Eldrennai, was an open room without doors. Rae'en, flanked by Glayne on her left and Varvost on her right, felt her eyes drawn to the accents of various crystalline devices representing the gods inlaid into four steps that led up to the throne. Large, but not cavernous, the white marble room showed a simpler aesthetic than she'd expected. No banners or tapestries hung here, and even the royal emblem appeared worked in stone on the granite throne itself rather than the walls.

At the center of the chamber, serving as the focal point of a widening circular pattern of variegated tiles, stood a large table wrought of a metal Rae'en did not recognize. Ragged along one quarter, the rest was smooth and unlined as if it had been ripped free of some larger construction. A candle sat atop without a candle holder, just a plain off-white cylinder of wax with a new wick jutting from the top.

Four metal bowls sat arranged at the ordinal points around the candle. One bowl held water, another sand, one held kindling, and the fourth bowl was empty.

Have you ever seen this done? Rae'en asked Kazan first by default. *In a memory or—*

She caught herself before she tried Vander next, then sent the question to Glayne. Even though he was Sixth, the others seemed to have decided he should be Prime until the current emergency was resolved and Rae'en picked a new Prime . . . *if* she had to.

New to me, Glayne thought back. *Grivek took the throne after the Sundering, and Aern were not high on the Oathbreaker guest list.*

Rows of benches composed, via some Artificer manipulation Rae'en did not fully understand, of the same platforms she had seen suspended from the ceiling earlier lined either side of the room, populated by elderly Oathbreakers in varying outfits. Some, the Elementalists—Glayne provided— wore robes, others wore armor or tunics. Yet another delegation, mostly younger, wore scant tops leaving their backs and the scars (in some cases wounds) Bloodmane had carved there clear for all to see.

In Rae'en's mind's eye a map of the room unfolded with those individuals Glayne or her other Overwatches could identify plainly labeled, the others noted by presumed role, magical ability, and threat rating.

"The Overwatches will be granted full access," Rae'en bellowed, stepping out from behind Glayne. The shouted phrase sent four guards who had shown no sign of moving to intercept her Overwatches back farther out of positions cowed and frowning. "Sorry about that." Rae'en gave Glayne a brief nod as three Overwatches she'd borrowed from Mokk's kholstering moved into position at the corners of the room.

And you're sure this is all I need do to let him know I don't hold him responsible for alerting us sooner? She thought at Bloodmane.

He'll take it as an honor and know you still trust him.

Good. With the loss of nine Overwatches and their warsuits, the last thing Rae'en wanted was anyone feeling worse than they already felt and running off to try and prove themselves before they had some idea how the Zaur had done this. *Do we have any clue what is taking my uh . . . personal . . . Overwatches so long? I know my father set an impressive pace, but how long does it take?*

If they sleep when they are tired and maintain a reasonable pace, Bloodmane thought back, **it may take them up to twice as long. If you have changed your mind about a patrol . . .**

No, Rae'en thought back. She wanted to say yes, but the pride of her Overwatches aside, how would it look under the current state of uncertainty? Officially, she guessed it didn't matter how it looked. The First could just order it done, but she couldn't picture Kholster handling things the same way. He would have trusted his troops, given them time to carry out their mission unless he had firm intelligence suggesting a needed change of plans. *We'll give them another few . . . days?*

No more than another week would be my projection, Bloodmane sent. **I took the liberty of having End Song check and he said, "The bulk of the bone metal of Joose, M'jynn, Arbokk, and Kazan is all in one place and moving in the appropriate direction for them to be en route to their kholster. Soul tokens of those individuals entrusted to the Ossuary are, of course, still in the Ossuary back home in North Number Two."**

Thanks. Rae'en felt relieved and silly at the same time. *And please convey the First of One Hundred's thanks to the Ossuarian as well.*

That doesn't sound lofty at all, she thought sarcastically. In her mind's eye, the numbers Five and Six (looking very strange in the positions normally occupied by Vander and Amber's token) as well as Square tokens from the borrowed Overwatches flashed golden to let her know they were in position.

So weird to have Overwatches who were so old their numbers were their symbols send data to her mind. Stranger still to have gotten used to them enough that not having Amber and Feagus covering her had become awkward. Did her core Overwatches feel the same about her age? Of course, Amber had replaced her father when he'd died and chosen to be merged with the souls of all Aern. Rae'en wondered if it annoyed Amber to no longer be the highest-ranking Aernese female now that Rae'en had become First.

No, kholster Rae'en, Amber replied. *That's a younger Aern's concern.*

Sorry, Rae'en thought back. *I didn't mean to send that.*

You didn't send anything, Amber thought, *I just felt the edge of it and I can read you well. You think a lot like your father.*

That's high praise, Rae'en thought.

Yes, it often is. Amber paused a moment. *And praise is how I meant it in this instance, but you could do with a little more of your brother's viewpoint, too. Oh, and Vander's still fine by the way. Sleeping soundly.*

Thanks for watching him, Rae'en thought. *I know others could have done it, but we'll both rest easier having you and Feagus right there with him.*

I think they are about to start, Glayne interrupted. *On your right.*

Rae'en inclined her head toward a hunchbacked figure with a deformed skull shambling forward, flanked by Crystal Knights and Elementalists on either side.

The guardian of the throne thing, Varvost prompted.

Right, she thought back. It had slipped her mind completely in all the rush and chaos. *Thanks.*

"I apologize, kholster Rae'en," the elf purred. "Prince Rivvek has asked if you wouldn't mind observing the proceedings from the throne."

The name Sargus scrolled under the Aiannai's image in her mind's eye in Bloodmane's elegant script. An image of the Aiannai as he truly was without his false hunch and haffet disguise and of Bloodmane etching Zhan's scars into his back flashed through Rae'en head.

He's an Oathkeeper, Glayne thought at her. *Safe to trust him, like as not.*

"There will be no objections?" Rae'en asked.

"No further objections." Sargus bowed. "It is a statement of acknowledged authority Prince Rivvek feels imperative. Not necessarily for today's audience, but—"

"I have no objections."

Kholster Rae'en, I'm sorry, but you should know that Prince Dolvek is on his way to the capital to interrupt the ceremony.

It was on the tip of her mind to tease Bloodmane, call him something mean, but she couldn't do it. In the rush of things, she was glad to have him in her head. His steady calm was balm to her mind, his advice, his presence reassuring.

What does that idiot think he's going to do about it? Isn't he supposed to be at South Watch?

He slipped away from the group. I apologize. I—

Don't worry about it, Bloodmane, Rae'en thought. *If he shows his stumpy little ears here, I'll kill him just like I killed his father.* Rae'en growled. *Wait. I have a better idea.*

"Hey." Pausing at the top of the steps to the throne, Rae'en tapped Sargus's fake hump. "Prince Dimwit has abandoned his post and I am reliably informed it is his intent to disrupt the Test of Four. What happens if he does that, Sargus?"

Sargus blinked. "Under the old law, an acknowledged sibling in good standing may challenge his brother's right to rule and demand a trial by elements, but—"

"Good standing?" Rae'en nodded. *You said he left without leave?*

Yes.

You were officially kholstering him?

I was.

"I am further informed that he left his post without permission from his kholster . . . General Bloodmane." Rae'en showed her doubled canines in a wolfish grin. "Does that leave him in good standing?"

"No, it does not." Sargus bowed.

"Fantastic. Then as kholster of your realm's defense by virtue of command having been given to my warsuit, I declare Prince Dolvek a traitor and order that he be killed on sight."

Glayne? Bloodmane? If you don't mind sending the word around?

*

How dare they?!

Dolvek rocketed across the Eldren Plains, propelled by a roaring column of elemental air. Salt trails of anger and grief dotted cheeks flushed red with rage. Sorrow felt bitter and wasteful to him, but fury could be wed to action. He could recall times when he would have charged into battle wearing a breastplate of conjured crystal, but no more. The sun heated the steel of his new armor.

They could call him stupid, but it had only taken him one encounter with the Zaur to understand the foolishness of the "crystal" plate employed by the knights of his order. Summoned crystal made marvelous armor for fighting humans or other Eldrennai, but against Zaur or Aern . . . something non-magical as a base became necessity.

Even then, the armorers at the watch city had looked at him like he was a fool when he patiently described what he wanted made for his personal use. Jolsit and the others could wear full plate all they wanted, but Dolvek needed to maneuver. He did have to give the armorers credit though; once he'd explained what he wanted, they'd done an excellent job with it: a steel demi-cuirass, spaulders, and vambraces over blue brigandine, reinforced with mail. The armorer hadn't had time to finish the legs, so he wore black high boots to protect his legs below the cuisses.

He hoped it would still give him some protection from Skreel blade slashes, which would serve, but the next time one of those cursed reptiles tried to sink its fangs into him, Dolvek wanted them to break. Flexing his brigandine gloves, he smiled. They still weren't exactly right, but they would be easy to cast in.

The only nod he allowed to his former attire was a cloak of dark blue with the royal seal, three intertwined castles, embroidered in silver thread across the back. He wore the hood high, buttoned into place over his three-quarter helm with a handy snap attached to the leather of his flying goggles. Dolvek had thought the goggles a stupid and ugly affectation of lazy Aeromancers until he'd gone flying in battle amid the dust and debris raised by the Geomancers and Pyromancers under Bloodmane's command. As it was, he had come to regret his own refusal to wear a scarf or mask to cover his mouth and nose.

He accomplished the same thing with a touch of Aeromancy, but it was yet one more spell of which he had to keep track. Reaching back to touch the hilt of his sword, actually one of Jolsit's spares, he pictured his father's face. Past arguments flowed through him as his shadow stretched out on the plains beneath.

They had never agreed about anything: not the Aern, the Vaelsilyn . . . not even elemancy. All of those clashes of word and magic lay on his heart, and he wanted to feel bad about them, to sense some form of regret, but rather than regretting the fights, rage that they would never have another one drove him on. So the Eldrennai had done terrible things to the beings they had created. Once they were freed, once as much amends as seemed reasonable had been made, what gave the Aern the right to come marching in and destroy everything? Some promise? And even if they were Oathbound to keep it, with Kholster dead and the oath nullified, how dare his daughter choose such barbarism.

To extract promises from the king and then to murder him . . .

A new surge of wrath pushed him on.

And Rivvek.

Flames curled round the edge of Dolvek's gauntlets. To invite their father's killer to attend his Test of Four? Dolvek had been prepared to accept his brother as his father's chosen successor, had expected the choice for decades, despite his older brother's . . . disability, but this . . . this . . . outrage. It could not stand. Dolvek refused to let it.

*

Sitting on the side of the Big Road, eating a bit of raw hare, wind blowing through her head petals, Yavi spotted a figure flying in the distance, trailing fire in his wake, a wounded heart streaking through the sky.

Looking at him through spirit eyes, she knew him at once. Rage, pride, hurt, and vengeance in such quantities, combined with the working of multiple elements at once, meant it had to be a member of the royal family, and the only member she could think of who would be headed from the outskirts toward Port Ammond with revenge in his heart . . . well, it didn't take a very clever daisy to forecast that weather.

"Dolvek!" she shouted, flinging the remnants of her meal far from the road so the scavengers could eat it more safely. "Prince Dolvek!"

*

Dry scales had all but flaked away from Tsan's body as they traveled toward the twin trees of Hashan and Warrune. She plucked the last stubborn remnant of her male skin away from the back of her neck with an absent flick of her hind paws. Surely it would be more appropriate to meet with Queen Kari with her new scales unblemished by the detritus of her former self. By the time they'd reached the outskirts of the twin trees, her Root Guard escorts were gawking openly.

"My gender switch," Tsan explained to the one-armed one. *Arri?* Tsan noted the location of various guard posts overhead in the branches, but only out of habit.

Hardwoods grew larger toward the center of The Parliament of Ages, but she recognized on the macro scale what she had destroyed in miniature at Tranduvallu. Each outpost grew at the optimum distance from each adjacent outpost and the twin trees at their center. She assumed the Vael, of all races, knew why that happened, but even if they didn't, it confirmed a suspicion Tsan had held for hundreds of years. The Vael did not arrange their cities themselves. Not exactly. The Root Trees followed a growth pattern similar to that of leaves on a plant. Each leaf or sprout at the perfect angle needed to maximize access to resources and minimize duplicated effort.

"Sooo," Arri asked. "You're a boy-type person now?"

"The reverse," Tsan answered, not sparing the conversation much thought and focusing on her observations. So the trees were arranged the same, but were the numbers identical as well? Would Tsan need the information? She doubted it, but it was useful to know how to tear things down and break them apart. Would the Weeds be disturbed by her natural examination of their defenses?

Most certainly. But if they thought the Aern failed to do the same, the charming little plant people were fooling no one but themselves. As if Kholster had not spent a portion of his centennial trips to and from Oot making the exact same observations.

Rising from all fours, Tsan spared herself a moment to bask in the delight her more flexible form allowed. How wonderful for bipedal motion to feel stable and strong.

Outposts, General Tsan reminded herself.

Tranduvallu had possessed six outposts, but—though it was harder to spot here—she observed the same basic arrangements now that she knew what to look for. Based on the spacing, she guessed twelve outposts for the twin trees. Moss and hanging vines acted as natural camouflage netting to obfuscate overhead walkways, where limbs of one tree literally fused with its neighbor's, and guard stations.

"Reverse how?" Arri asked.

"How am I a girl-type person?" Tsan flexed her foreclaws before dropping back to all fours, sighing in relief at the continued lack of pain in her joints. An urge to test herself against the nettlesome Root Guard in single combat rose and died quickly. *I already proved them inferior. Why give them a second taste of poison?*

"Now that I have brighter scales?" Tsan continued the thought, watching the one-armed Weed for a reaction.

"Yes," Arri asked.

"Your reasoning isn't flawed," Tsan purred, cherishing the sensuous way her tongue moved in her mouth. Even the sound of her voice was more pleasant: confident, strong. "Unlike birds, who possess the color variation you seem to have expected . . . brighter for males and less colorful for females

. . . more blending in for ease of hiding . . . our maker wanted to be able to tell at a glance when we changed from male to female."

"Your maker?" Arri scratched at the stub of her arm. She shooed away a curious sproutling who peeked out at them from a walkway overhead. "Kilke?"

"No," Tsan laughed, amused by the way her susurrant trills made the Weed recoil. "Our mutual maker."

"What do you mean?"

Tsan tasted the scent of the Weed's confusion with her forked tongue, but offered no explanation. *If I'm going to explain this once*, Tsan thought, *I'd better wait until the important Weeds arrive.*

CHAPTER 23

THE TEST OF FOUR

Rivvek entered from behind the throne on which Rae'en sat. She felt his presence, looming behind her, waiting for the room's attention and for all scattered conversations to cease. Rae'en couldn't imagine why instead of quieting down the conversation spiked until Feagus sent her the view from his vantage point.

Darkly handsome once, by an Oathbreaker's skewed sense of aesthetics, Rivvek was the single most attractive non-Aern Rae'en had ever seen. She'd heard he was disfigured, but no one had mentioned that the so-called disfigurements were actually battle scars. Shirtless, the prince stopped next to her, smiling regally with black eyes rather like his father's, only where Grivek's had been guilt-haunted and pitiable, Rivvek's gaze was confident and friendly.

Now, him I might not mind mating with, Amber thought, and Rae'en came close to choking.

"Thank you for agreeing to this, kholster Rae'en." Prince Rivvek gave her the barest nod, granting her a spectacular view of his melted ear, the mottled pink, brown, and white at the side of his head where the hair, instead of grown long to cover the scarring, had been shaved short in a revealing arc.

Foot-long trails of what had to have been a Ghaiattri's grip on his left side, just above the hip, like a claw print in wet clay, disappeared below the waistband of his dark-blue trousers. Rae'en realized she was staring openly at his bare chest, turned her downward gaze into a matching nod, and switched back to Feagus's view.

The leather belt at his waist was corded in an approximation of the style Kholster had preferred, the buckle a brass gear. He carried a thin golden crown in his right hand, but if Rae'en's breath had been taken by the scars on his front, she was mesmerized by the scars on his back.

My father's scars, she thought as the prince moved past the throne and down the four steps toward the testing table. She hadn't been expecting the prince to be so well-muscled, either. Eldrennai tended to have a certain softness to them. *Well, Wylant didn't. Maybe that was part of being Aiannai? Maybe her father only took the hard ones, the battle-ready?*

No, she thought better of that. It wasn't a fitness test. Being Aiannai meant you could be trusted to keep your word. It meant that you understood slavery was wrong. It meant—did it really mean all of that?

I've seen Aern who made it through the Demon Wars with less impressive scars, Rae'en thought at Glayne. *How did he survive——?*

It's not as bad as all that, her temporary Prime Overwatch answered. *Well, maybe for an elf, but my eyes——while unpleasant——aren't the most painful injury I've ever felt.*

Really? Rae'en asked, embarrassed she'd brought that up with Glayne of all Aern.

This was the worst of it, he sent the memory to her. She didn't scream, but only because Glayne cut it short.

And that's why everyone is afraid of you, Rae'en growled back. *What in Kholster's name are you thinking you——*

I'm thinking there's a reason your father put his scars on the boy's back, Rae'en. Glayne sent her the image, not just of her father's scars but of the winged outline of what had to be the most varied collection of elemental foci material she'd ever seen. *You can ask the king about it after, but I suggest you remember that as impressive as his battle scars are, and as much of an honor it was that Kholster put his scars on the elf's back, Grivek named him heir because he thought Rivvek could stop your army.*

Point made, but don't—— She caught herself, quickly rephrasing the order as her father might have. *I mean to say, I would appreciate a little more warning before you send that type of transmission again, please.*

Pay attention, Feagus broke in, *they're shouting about something.*

"This is unseemly, Prince Rivvek," one of the oldest Oathbreakers in the room, Hasimak——according to her mental map——said as he stood. "There is a dress code to be maintained . . . a certain sense of decorum that——"

"No," Rivvek said without turning to face the old Elementalist. "There is a suggested mode of dress set out by Hurrek the Third and further amended by several other kings, queens, and even yourself, High Elementalist. I counted two concordances dealing with trousers alone, but none of that is law."

"It is——" he paused to meet the eyes of Hasimak, and a succession of other important dignitaries, before finally settling on Rae'en herself, "——merely custom. And customs are going to change."

Rae'en flushed to meet his eyes again. Her father had once described the eyes of the royals as rat droppings stuck in bird squirt, but Rivvek's had gone from convivial confidence to smoldering: controlled emotions, passion reined in and kept on a tight leash filled those eyes.

Try not to pant, Amber's voice gently chided.

Amber! Rae'en admonished.

Or drool, Amber continued.

What are we drooling about? Feagus asked.

No one is drooling! Rae'en thought.

I was, Amber thought back, *but only a little bit. Tell me you don't want to see what kind of scars he's hiding under those pants. I mean, was all that one Ghaiattri, or did two get their hands on him? And how did he get away? If he actually killed one, I think I'll marry him.*

Rae'en watched as a sketch of Prince Rivvek loomed off center of her visual of the prince himself. Each of her Overwatches save Glayne began annotating his scars, theories about how he had gotten them. Had he stopped one of the extra-dimensional beings on this side of a port gate or in their home plane beyond?

Enough. Glayne's thoughts cut in. *Take this talk to a sideboard. You're distracting kholster Rae'en!*

You're the one who sent her memories from one of Uled's torture sessions, Amber countered.

Hush! Rae'en sent. *What did I miss?*

Rivvek and Hasimak argued politely, Glayne sent. *General Treyk joined in, too. Then the Stone Lord and Lady Flame sent Sargus to retrieve the necessary volumes to prove the prince's case.*

Rivvek stood before the testing table, right hand resting on its edge, waiting as Sargus rushed into the room trailed by two acolytes in brown robes carrying massive leather-bound tomes.

*

Patience, Rivvek reminded himself. *If I rush him, he will ask for a recess and that sort of delay . . .*

"This may take a candlemark longer, Prince Rivvek." Hasimak's voice quavered with concentration. "Perhaps you would prefer to—"

"In your own time," Prince Rivvek interrupted. "Please call on any additional resources you may require. I am certain the Aern will not begrudge a brief span to ensure everything here is done in accordance with the law of our fathers, but their patience is not endless."

Rivvek saw the spark of the idea form in Hasimak's eyes and resisted cutting an amused glance to Sargus. The Test of Four had been addressed by the late King Grivek as well, but Rivvek had no intention of pointing that out.

"Let Hasimak find the proof upon which your argument hinges," Sargus had told him last night in the prince's quarters. "Point it out to him and he will argue earlier precedent. Let him find the new information himself and he will latch onto it and make your case as if it were his own."

"Where—" Hasimak licked his dry lips, "—are the late king's compiled rulings, judgments, and proclamations? I do not see them here."

"I'm sure his rulings would not be of any greater weight than the combined wisdom before you, High Elementalist," Rivvek said, looking away.

"Has your father commented on the Test of Four, my prince?"

"That's an excellent question. I . . . ah." Rivvek frowned, not liking the charade but glad to be able to avoid an actual lie. "Sargus?"

*

One retrieved document and some arguing later, Rae'en's eyes had long since glazed over. A wind she could not identify as cold or hot blew across her back smelling not of the docks but of the sea. Did they manage that with magic, too? Probably. Rae'en would have been fine with the fish scent of blood, offal, and death that might normally have blown in from this close to a major harbor, but she liked the sea smell, too.

Not drumming her fingers on the throne in an outward display of impatience took an extreme effort.

Are the others still discussing something? Rae'en thought at Glayne.

Yes, they're trying to decide whether the winglike pattern of implants on the prince's back are decorative or if it was supposed to serve some mystical agenda.

Oh. Rae'en wished she could hear them, but she felt strange asking to be included when Glayne had been so clear about the others needing not to distract her. *What are the Oathbreakers arguing about?*

Grivek's opinion on the Test of Four. After Rivvek lost most of his magic, the king ruled that it was his opinion no magic should be required at all. Hasimak is defending that, but he's largely arguing against himself at this point. I'm not sure he realizes he was led to the slaughterhouse on this one.

Huh?

I didn't follow all of it, Glayne thought. *This is the sort of thing in which Aern were never included before the Sundering, but the prince and Zhan's Aiannai clearly arranged this debate.*

So this is all artifice, then? Rae'en asked.

To be honest, I think Hasimak is playing a part, too. At its core—

When there are stealthy Zaur Overwatch hunters on the loose with weapons that can mind-blind an Aern or kill a warsuit?! I'm—

"—putting an end to this." Rae'en stood. "Does the prince get to take the test or not?"

"Excuse me?" Hasimak stammered. "This is an important point for future generations of Eldrennai and—"

"I have yet to decide—" Rae'en bared her doubled canines in an expression more threat than smile, "—whether or not future generations of Oathbreakers will be allowed to exist, Leash Holder. So perhaps—"

He actually wasn't, you know, Glayne thought back.

What? Rae'en asked.

A Leash Holder.

Never mind that. Get ready to kill everyone in the room who isn't an Aiannai or an Aern, Rae'en ordered. *Maybe these Oathbreakers don't realize that in the course of defending ourselves, we have essentially already seized their capital.*

Multiple voices started up at once as, around the room, guards moved their hands to their sword hilts, a handful of new Elementalists whispered preparatory phrases to their familiars, and many a visible elemental focus began to softly glow. Aern with warpicks ready filed into the back of the chambers, those already present drew theirs.

At a subtle nod from the prince, Brigadier Bhaeshal's voice cracked like thunder. "ENOUGH!"

Everyone hold, Rae'en broadcasted. *I think we just made the prince's point for him.*

"Have none of you noticed that the Aern hold Port Ammond?" Rivvek gestured to Rae'en. "Have you failed to understand that the most intelligent of your sons and daughters do not stand at your sides because they have been accepted by the Aern as Aiannai—as Oathkeepers? We debate and kholster Rae'en sits calmly and admirably by when she has injured who need to be tended. She grants us courtesy we have not earned."

He stepped toward the center of room, foci on his back catching the light, twinkled as muscles rippled, arms spread wide. "To whom amongst you have the Aern granted such boons?"

He practiced that, Varvost sent.

The speech? Rae'en asked.

Most of it, Amber thought to her. *He's tricky.*

Rae'en could not see it as easily as her Overwatches, but then again they were all centuries old. Wait. She tracked his eyeline. *He's waiting for a specific person to speak up, isn't he?*

Look at their eyes, Varvost sent. *The key lords and ladies are in on it. They know what he's doing and have already been purchased.*

He's waiting for the old guy, Rae'en sent.

Hasimak chewed over the prince's words visibly. He didn't like it, but they'd all watched him talk himself into agreeing with the prince's right to take the Test of Four and therefore the legitimacy of his reign should Rivvek pass the test. Hands trembling with age or emotion, the old Oathbreaker sighed . . . which had obviously been the capitulation for which Rivvek had been waiting, an internal, but vital swing vote. Rae'en could read that much into what was happening even if she didn't know why or how.

"I do have a plan to save the people of this land." Rivvek approached the testing table, resting both hands on the nonreflective surface. "Not everyone can be saved. We have done too much, to too many, for too long, to expect these former slaves to forgive."

"The Test of Four requires magic to be used." Rivvek held out a finger to the dragon tallow candle and lit it with fire from the tip, his scars turning pink, then red. "Magic has been used. Pyromancy. Fire."

Glayne took a step back from the edge of the throne room, unnoticed by most who weren't Aern.

Glayne? Rae'en sent.

A moment, kholster Rae'en. Cold and sure, Glayne's thoughts were suffused with fading fear. *I will adjust.*

"Command of water." Prince Dolvek quenched the flame with water from the bowl.

He relit the candle with his finger.

"Command of earth." He snuffed the flame with dirt from the bowl, cupped in his hands.

He lit the candle again.

"Command of air." Rivvek blew out the candle.

"And the candle . . ." Taking a stick of wood from the final bowl, he set it alight with his finger, then used the branch to light the candle. ". . . is lit a fourth time."

"Am I king?" Rivvek folded his arms across his chest and walked up the four steps to stand by the throne. Rae'en reached for the crown to put it on him, but the look in his eyes told her to wait.

Hasimak bowed low and the others followed.

"Excellent." King Rivvek took the crown and placed it upon his own head. "My first act as king is to sentence all Eldrennai the Aern will not accept as Aiannai, or some other acceptable name, to death."

CHAPTER 24

DWARVEN KNOW-HOW

While one embodiment of Kholster stood in the throne room admiring King Rivvek's ingenuity, another waited by Vander's side. A third Kholster kept an ear on Sedvinia as she helped heal Wylant's wounds. But a fifth Kholster paced a warehouse at the docks where Glinfolgo supervised the storing of what Coal, the great gray dragon, had referred to as Kholster's equalizer.

Junpowder barrels lined sections of the walls with cannon, cannonballs, rifles, and stores of ammunition arranged in a pattern Kholster knew made perfect sense to Glinfolgo, even if the Aern around him hadn't quite assembled it yet. On either side of the massive stone doors, torches and crystal glow lamps lay scattered next to piles of broken crates containing mercantile goods for shipping. Dwarven replacements cast an even white light from the corners and ceiling.

Four Aern stepped through the open doors carrying a disassembled bed, which made Kholster chuckle. Why the hard-hided Dwarves slept on such cushioned contraptions he would never understand.

The spirits of Marcus Conwrath and Japesh materialized nearby, watching the assembly.

Conwrath wore the same embroidered sash and poncho he'd had on when Kholster had snapped his neck to free him of Shidarva's control thirteen years earlier. His ear was notched to show his rank, and his clothes were still dusty from the road between Bridge 37 and Darvan. Japesh's brown skin had grown wrinkled, only a few straggling hairs clinging to his bald pate, his tunic wine-stained.

"What're they going to make out of all that nonsense?" Marcus inclined his head in the vague direction of Aern carrying a metallic frame and wooden headboard.

"It's a bed." Japesh laughed at the recognition on his captain's face as more Aern carried in a mattress, pillows, and bed linens. "Some of the girls up to the brothel in Midian had beds like that. All extra soft and stuffed with feathers."

How did he know to unload the junpowder and weapons from the ships? Harvester asked.

"He did not know." Kholster smiled broadly as he paced the chalk outlines Glinfolgo had drawn on the floor of the warehouse. "But no one is better at guarding their secrets and treasures than Dwarves."

I don't understand.

"Glin doesn't think there is going to be a war with the Oathbreakers," Kholster said. "He's afraid someone will steal them."

"If them elves are planning to fight you," Japesh said, scratching his chin, "they picked a funny way of doing it. Your girl already has Port Ammond."

You think Rivvek has a plan?

Whose scars are on his back?

Yours, but I'm growing concerned, sir.

Concerned how?

You did not reap Dienox when he attacked your wife. A simple penalty is not—

He's not mine to kill. Only to reap.

Sir?

Did he wrong me or did he wrong Wylant?

Wylant, sir. Even so—

Let me share a memory with you, Harvester, Kholster thought.

Reaching back to Helg's death, Kholster shared it with his warsuit. Pain at not just the loss of a wife, but also the exponential sorrow of knowing that Rae'en had lost her mother and, in so doing, had been injured in a special sense with which Kholster could not identify. The investigation, discovering Helg had died in a senseless quest for political power . . . all over a Dwarven Foreman election.

Rage. Harvester quivered with it, but Kholster kept sharing that intimate and terrible time. Sense memory washed over both of them. Harvester grunted, a sound Kholster had never heard Bloodmane make, when the warsuit experienced Midio's skin tearing, her bones breaking in his grip. She screamed until her voice was gone and blood gushed from her throat.

Kholster showed Harvester the varied looks of horror on the faces of the male and female Dwarves of the voting committee. The sigh of relief when Midio died for the cave-in she had rigged. They thought it was over.

And then Varvost and Glayne had dragged Polimbol, the architect of the plot, out between them with Feagus, Amber, and Vander positioned so Kholster could miss nothing.

"You ordered the mine collapse that killed my wife," Kholster seethed, spittle hitting the light gray cheeks of the conniving thing that had stolen his wife with his lust for power, for control.

All the proof was there, but Kholster had wanted to hear it from Polimbol's lips.

"Confess." Kholster's voice cut the air, low and harsh. "And on my oath I will not kill you."

"It's true," Polimbol said. "I did everything you say I did, but Helg wasn't supposed to die. I meant to—"

Kholster bared his doubled canines and snapped at the air, slightly embarrassed by the lack of control even as he surrendered to it. He didn't like to think about it, but revisiting the memory this time, he understood it was one of the closest times he'd ever come to becoming Foresworn.

His Overwatches pulled him back from the edge of disaster, just as they'd been ordered to do.

He's to be Glinfolgo's kill . . . Vander and the others shouted in his mind, *not yours. Stop.*

And stop he had . . . and stood there watching while Glinfolgo pounded the Dwarf to death with the bone-steel mattock Kholster had forged for him.

Kholster let the memory end, but Harvester still trembled.

I understand, sir, but I don't see how, even with the penalties you have requested in her favor . . . she can't kill Dienox alone.

Your failure of imagination, Kholster teased, remembering when Coal, the great gray dragon, had said the same to him back at South Number Nine, *not mine.*

Given that you forged me, sir, I believe any failure of imagination on my part to be at least partially yours.

Kholster let loose with a barking laugh but explained no further. One never knew exactly how much Aldo or Two-Headed Kilke could overhear.

Across the room, Conwrath and Japesh sat on the newly assembled bed watching Glinfolgo address the Aern. He looked so young with his beard shaven close to the skin, but sea sickness had encouraged the change. It had been that or smell sour beard the whole journey. Not that Vander hadn't teased Glin anyway, but . . .

Vander.

"I know you're all concerned about your Prime Overwatch," Glinfolgo shouted, "but we'll handle this first and then I'll go check on him."

Fifty Aern hoisted barrels of junpowder and rolled (or carried) cannons from the warships at the docks.

"But, High Foreman . . ." An agreeable, but slow—if the Dwarf judged him charitably—Aernese soldier stood in the center of the warehouse they'd commandeered (next to the bed), while his soldiers moved around him, following Glinfolgo's plans. "Why are we—?"

"I'm busy!" Glinfolgo shouted, adding a furious stomp to the floor and a growl for emphasis. "We're three-quarters done. If you need another explanation when we're finishe—no!" Glin bellowed at one of the Aern stacking junpowder barrels. "None should be stacked atop another. Look around! Do you see any other barrels double-stacked?"

"No," the Aern grumbled, "but usually an Overwatch is showing us exactly where—"

"Chalk!" the gray-skinned Dwarf bellowed. Hand outstretched, expectant, he growled when no chalk appeared. "Fine. I have some, but if you want me to mark the floor for you the least you could do . . ." Thick fingers fumbling at the various pouches on his belt, Glinfolgo pulled out a long stick of chalk. Rows of perfect circles appeared in his wake as he crawled across the stone floor. Behind him Aern unloaded one barrel, lined up perfectly within each circle until they were all in place. He paced back through the rows of barrels, checking each one, muttering the tally. He did the same with the rifles, cannons, and ammo, before rolling four cannons in front of the bed, mouths aimed at the door.

"Now." The Dwarf turned to the fifty Aern standing guard. "I will calm down." Rifles and cannons lined the walls and floor with the barrels of junpowder stored along the back wall with a second row surrounding the side and rear of the bed. "You can tell the Oathbreakers, if they come looking for me, I'm sleeping in the warehouse until this is all over or until you need to use these weapons again."

"I want no less than twenty of you guarding this warehouse at all times," he shouted behind him as he strode for the doors.

"And where will you be?" One of the Aern asked.

"Checking on Vander," Glin snapped. "Where did I tell you I was going when we finished up here?!"

*

Glinfolgo pushed his way past lines of Aern shouting, shoving, and berating the uncooperative soldiers as he went. Vander couldn't see any of that through the eyes of his fellow Overwatches, couldn't see anything at all beyond the confines of his own limited point of view, but the picture painted by the Dwarf's outrage out in the hallway beyond his room was unmistakable.

"You listen to me, you bone-clad wheelbarrow." Glin's rumbling displeasure echoed through the Hall of Healing. "I know you heard me explain, with sufficient clarity that even a useless rock carrier like yourself could not have failed to understand, to the last dung-brained idiot why you will let me pass."

Vander chuckled, pain lancing through his chest where bandages stained orange from his anemic blood bound him tight. *What did that assassin stab me with?* he wondered. A knife wound should have been long healed; no Aern should be laid low like a human or a stump ear. If the Aern at whom Glin was shouting had a reply, Vander had missed it.

"That's my friend in there." Glinfolgo's voice got louder, one shade from shouting. "And these Oathbreaker buffoons don't understand any more about your eclectic innards than they know about proper mineral food prep. For all I know they've bandaged up his chest without double-checking the primary magnetoreceptor and what on Jun's Outwork is still stuck in it."

"Magnetoreceptor?" Vander rolled his head to the side, the world threatening to toss him top over tail until he stopped moving. When the room stabilized again, he saw Amber standing by the room's single entrance and exit, her back pressed to Feagus's back. "Rae'en must be worried beyond reason to have you two playing mother bear over me. How many Aern are out there in the hallway?"

"Ninety-six of the One Hundred." Amber's hair, cut short as Kholster's own Hulsite militia buzz, was shot through with dried patches of umber-colored blood around wounds that also should have been healed by now.

"Rae'en had some meeting." Vander puzzled it out aloud. "Zhan is off being Ossuarian. I'm in here. Who's the fourth we're missing?"

"No one's missing." Amber's eyes had dark bruising under the lower lid, what humans called having circles under one's eyes. "I didn't count myself because I'm in the room, not in the hall."

In the hall, Glinfolgo sounded as if he'd made it past that Aern and was now browbeating the next in line.

"Let him in." Vander licked his lips, finding them dry and cracked as if he'd fallen asleep in a desert and slept in full suns all day. An aged Oathbreaker in robes imprinted with the wavy joined smile and frown of Sedvinia offered him a pewter cup filled with what smelled and looked like water. "Get away from me." Vander pushed the cup away, surprised when the gesture meant to knock the cup from the Oathbreaker's hands resulted in a kitteny nudge instead. "I don't trust you."

Snapping his teeth at the flummoxed old healer, Vander closed his eyes against another effort-induced bout of vertigo only to snap them open again in fear. There was no one else with him in the darkness behind his eyelids, and he couldn't stand it. How could other races bear that fundamental sense of singularity?

"Ha! Ha!" Glinfolgo boomed out in the corridor as the sounds of hobnailed boots on stone signaled the parting of the remaining Aern that stood between him and the room in which Vander lay. "Finally see reason, aye?"

"Why did you keep him out in the first place?" Vander asked.

"Rae'en is busy." Amber stepped clear of the door. "Things got complicated after the Test of Four, and Glayne told us not to disturb her unless it was an emergency. Since you'd already given orders to let the Dwarf go anywhere he wanted if he was persistent enough, it seemed to be working itself out. . . ."

"Why didn't you ask Glayne?" Vander's voice came harsh and strained. "And why is he acting as Prime Overwatch instead of you? I only had him stepped up into the core four because I thought Rae'en might need some extra attention." He wished he could feel Amber's mind. Having to rely on words and physical expression to relay nuance was so tiresome and inefficient.

"He's in the right spot," Amber answered, the sound of grumbling, stomping Dwarf fast approaching. "We all ceded position to him." Amber closed her left hand as if grasping for words. "He made it to Rae'en, Vander. When the rest of us couldn't get to her, he found a way. Glayne grabbed a Geomancer and made him rip out a section of wall so he could get to Rae'en quickly enough. When you can, you have to see what he was like. The assassins didn't lay a claw on him." She shook her head. "He scares the yarp out of me at times, but until you're better . . ."

"If his instincts are more effective in the current crisis . . ." Vander could recall many situations like that in battle where being Prime didn't matter because Amber, Feagus, or Varvost grasped how to respond to an enemy battle plan in their bone metal, and not letting them take the lead would have been stupid and reckless. He nodded, regretting the motion instantaneously, yarping up what remained of his last meal, jagged spikes of agony searing through his chest and behind his eyes. Breathing shallowly, he reached up to wipe his mouth but was too exhausted to do it.

"Just temporary?" Vander asked as the Eldrennai healer lifted the slick pellet of yarp from Vander's chest and wiped the remnants from his lips with a cool washcloth.

"That's up to—" Amber started.

"Get away from that Aern, you stump-eared butcher!" Glinfolgo burst into the room, waving a bone-steel mattock over his head. He clanked across the room in his scale mail, a junpowder and machine-oil stink flowing with him like a cloud. A large steel toolbox hung from his left hand, wrenches and other less familiar implements dangled from loops between multiple pouches on his belt. A pair of green-tinted goggles hung round his neck— so-called Dwarven "Reading Glasses." Dropping his mattock on the aged Oathbreaker's foot and his toolbox on the floor next to Vander's cot, Glinfolgo unslung a heavy pack from his back, knocking the Oathbreaker both away from Vander and onto the floor. "I said out of the way!"

Scowling, the healer scrambled to his feet, limping from the room without a word.

"I have a feeling there will be complaints about that." Vander smiled weakly.

"Jun's name, Vander." Glinfolgo said brusquely, as if Vander couldn't see the wetness rimming the Dwarf's eyes. "Were you trying to make the lizard feel good about itself, or did you decide you wanted to see Kholster again real quick?"

"I—" Vander felt the urge to reach out to Eyes of Vengeance and found nothing there. He knew his warsuit was fine, but he couldn't resist the compulsion to ask. "Amber, are you sure—?"

"He asks about you even more often than you ask about him, Vander." Amber smiled, but Vander wished he couldn't see the pity behind it. "Scale Fist says Eyes of Vengeance is no more injured than the last time you asked."

"You can't sense your warsuit," Glinfolgo said. "Can you sense any of the others at all?"

"I can't sense anyone, Glin!" Vander growled, wincing as his body informed him he wasn't allowed to shout right now. "If you didn't know that already, why did you say all that in the hall?"

Glinfolgo held up a hand in the classic "halt" gesture then knelt on the ground, with a wet sound that let Vander know exactly what Glinfolgo had knelt down in, and rummaged through his pack. After several minutes, the Dwarf pulled out a handful of coin-sized runestones, clicking them together until he had constructed a small pyramid. Inspecting it carefully, once with the green goggles over his eyes and once without, he threw the assembled structure into the air where it flashed with a bright burst of blue light that began dimming to tolerable levels and hovered as it emitted the low hum so synonymous with many Dwarven rune magic contraptions.

"Some things show up better in rune light," Glin said. He pulled a Dwarven canteen from his pack and held it out toward Amber. "Help him with this. He'll down that before he'll even bathe in an Oathbreaker's water."

Amber stepped forward and helped Vander take small sips, which made his stomach object noisily, but he kept it down.

Blue light from the floating pyramid picked out reflective bits of mineral deposits in Glinfolgo's gray hide. The pyramid floated slowly around the room until it settled into a stationary position over Vander's chest.

Amber tipped more water over Vander's lips, but he sputtered, not ready for it. *What*, Vander wondered, *distracted her?* She looked back at the door, and questions exploded in his mind. Did the way she checked the doorway mean she was concerned she needed to resume her post? Was she doing a physical check on Feagus? Were they talking about something happening outside the room? Reviewing images from somewhere else? Listening to orders from Glayne or kholster Rae'en? Not knowing tore at him.

"He'll need fresh meat and blood," Glinfolgo called out to the air.

"I'll have some procured," Feagus blurted.

Glinfolgo gave a low, bitter chuckle.

"And one of you better start talking to him." Glin reached down and came up with a pair of scissors, which he sat on the edge of Vander's cot along with a pair of forceps, a long-handled blade, and an opaque bottle. "And hold this." He thrust a frosted glass vial at Amber.

"Right." She took the vial, but the Dwarf still stared at her expectantly.

"I took it," Amber said.

"I meant it when I told you to talk to him." He bent down, pulling out more equipment: towels, thread, a needle . . .

"Well?"

"What are you talking about?" Feagus asked from the doorway.

"Oh." Recognition sparked in Amber's eyes. "Tell him what's happening in the army, with the army, what we're thinking. Kind of like we do with an All Know when we're standing next to Dwarves."

"I hope you're a very gifted fighter," Glinfolgo snorted over his shoulder at Feagus, "because she's the smart one."

CHAPTER 25
THE REPTILIAN
NEGOTIATION

Kholburran chewed on the dry-roasted beetles his captors had given him and tried to pretend they tasted worse than they did. Crispy, with a nutty flavor. The young prince caught himself wishing he knew how to prepare them. There was a spice that gave them a heat that did not appear in Vael cooking.

"Want more?" a brown-scaled diminutive Zaur asked.

"Are you going to have more?" Kholburran asked.

"No," the Zaur answered. "Why would that matter?"

"No, thank you." Kholburran shook his head, thinking he would first refuse and then accept the second offer, but a second offer did not come. He'd expected, even if the Zaur did not press its offer, for it to react with some outward show of emotion, or to show pleasure at an abundance of food for itself. It turned without comment, heading back to the camp (was chef the right word?) food preparer, who accepted the bag, dumping its contents out onto a broad cloth where it began to crush the uneaten portions into a dry, powdery meal.

Kholburran had expected the Zaur to be cruel, but aside from the ropes binding his legs together, mostly they were just boring. When not actively on guard duty or performing other functions, the reptiles slept for amazing portions of the day in nigh motionless dozes. One of his guards (he really couldn't keep their names straight any more than he could tell most of them apart) had cut him deeply enough to draw proper blood and not sap shortly after Arri and the others had left, but the Zaur had bandaged the wound afterward and apologized for the discomfort.

When that Zaur (or were the bigger ones Sri'Zaur?) left, another one of the black-scaled ones with the blue stripes took his place. Picking a bit of brittle insect leg out from between his lips and dental ridge, Kholburran watched the Sri'Zaur across from him, its mouth hanging open. They did not do that at night when it was colder, so was the thing regulating its temperature somehow?

While the bigger ones tended toward stillness, the littler ones seemed constantly on the move. Were they nervous around the big ones? They seemed to be, though the big ones didn't appear to bully them in any way. Kholburran found himself becoming more and more interested in them and

225

the way they interacted. Small Zaur tended the strange headless-dragon-looking mounts. A mixture of Zaur and Sri'Zaur cared for the gigantic serpents, the ones they called Zaurruk, stopping to wash away and repaint the differing patterns of concentric rings on their scales when they had to swap off and change which Zaurruk they were handling.

Twice they hauled whole forest elk out of various tunnels to feed to the massive beasts. It was during one such feeding when a yellow-scaled Sri'Zaur with orange stripes wearing a vest covered in flasks approached his current guard.

"What is it, Brazz?" the black-scaled reptile asked.

"The young prince's blood should now be well out of the big wood." Brazz's voice, a grating hiss, enunciated the words clearly enough that even Kholburran could follow them.

"Fine." The guard drew its long, angled Skreel knife and slashed the ropes binding Kholburran's legs with thoughtless precision. "Go home. Tell your queen we've released you as a gesture of trust."

"Really?" Kholburran frowned at the lines the ropes had left on his thin skinlike outer bark. He rubbed his legs vigorously, hoping to force sap back into them without bruising.

"You can stay if you want, little Root," Brazz cackled, "but—"

"No." The guard pulled Kholburran forcibly to his feet and thrust Resolute, Kholburran's lacquered wooden warpick, at him. "No staying. Go home." The guard leaned low. "Do you need an escort?"

An escort? In The Parliament of Ages?! No matter how helpless the girl-type persons thought him to be, the realization that these lizards shared the same opinion was enough to make his head petals quiver in anger.

"I know the way." Kholburran took a few steps away, expecting it all to be some sort of trick or odd reptilian joke. "I can handle this hunt alone."

"Then do it." The guard turned away and settled back down.

"And don't forget," Brazz hissed, its breath like brimstone, "Your release is a gesture of trust. We've shown you what we can do, how powerful the coldbloods are. Now we want you to understand we can be trusted, too."

First moving at a walk, then at run, Kholburran headed for Hashan and Warrune.

*

Once the princely Weed was out of earshot, Brazz watched the Gliders and Shades head off after him, an unseen escort. *In His secret service*, he thought after them. It wouldn't do to have the weak little thing get eaten on the way home. Though it was a shame that it didn't seem like he and his fellow Flamefangs would get to burn any more Root Trees. Ah, well. Some pleasures only happen once, leaving just memories to savor. So long as things went according to the general's plan, there would be plenty of burning left to do back out on the Eldren Plains.

*

Tsan lounged semi-coiled on a sun-drenched rock within the grand arboretum. Stripped of her weapons and armor upon arrival, she imagined how confident the Weeds must feel, could smell it, a patchwork of pheromones hitting Eldrennai and Aern notes intermixed with floral accents. Too bad not much of them was suitable for eating. Still, at least they were predictable in their way. Made for peace, they craved it. Therefore, if one offered peace, removed from the Aern's sterner resolve and burning desire to kill . . .

Breathing deeply, she peered up at the dome overhead, her eye membranes nictating. A masterwork of crystalized sap, Arri had proudly told her, formed by the combined effort of Hashan and Warrune. Beams of sunlight shone down on an unchanging portion of the seasonal cycle, a garden locked in a perfect blending of spring and summer.

How do the flowers bloom and grow? Tsan wondered. *Do the Weeds coax the floral spirits to bend to their desires or is this more male Root Tree magic?*

Lurking amid the tree limbs and vines that formed the structural support for the dome, one of the Weeds—Seizal, if Tsan had their names straight now—glared hatred at her.

Don't kill me yet, Tsan mused. *Once I've accomplished my mission you can do whatever you like with the serpent in your garden.*

<<Anyone speak, Zaurtol?>> Tsan clicked on her limestone perch.

"You just stay silent and wait, murderer!" Arri snapped.

"Feel free to strike with that sword." Tsan declined to grace the one-armed Weed with a backward glance despite the sound of Arri's blade coming free of its sheath yet again. "There are at least thirty of your Root Guard concealed amongst the branches, hedges, and flowers. Surely that should be more than sufficient to slay one lone Sri'Zaur?"

"You're right." Arri walked into view from the left, so Tsan peered farther left, fixing her gaze on a clutch of blue and lavender snapdragons. "There are plenty of us here to slay our enemies!"

How old was this one? Tsan wondered. *Ten years? Twenty?* Arri's passion was intoxicating in its way, due, Tsan was certain, in part to the effect, blunted but unmistakable just the same, of the calming royal hedge rose aroma emitted by each and every Root Guard within the Arboretum. Despite the anger, the disrespect, Tsan was reminded of the human captain who had delivered the Eldrennai census data. Like him, Arri stepped right up to the edge of too far, but not over . . . drawing her sword but doing nothing with it.

"Enemies?" Tsan purred. "Do you have enemies here?"

"You are our enemy!" Seizal shouted from her perch, all but the shadowy smear of her shape lost in the amber glare.

"No." A languid roll of Tsan's red-scaled neck brought her impassive eyes to bear, the first of her nictating membranes dropping down to shield them from the glare. "Unless I am mistaken, I am to be a boon companion to the Vael."

"You murdered my—" Seizal began, only to be cut off by a barking laugh from Tsan.

"There is no murder in a proper attack . . . only killing." Straightening her forelegs, Tsan rose to her haunches after a long stretch. "Some deaths will have served a purpose." She shifted her eyes to Arri. "And some will prove to have been an unfortunate waste." In the light of the warm sun, Arri's eyes took on an amber hue matching the rich, clear shade of Tsan's irises, as her slit pupils narrowed. "I sincerely hope the loss of your fellows, the fall of your Tranduvallu, will have not been for naught."

"Don't you say his name!" At the edge of her perception, Tsan noticed Seizal draw her heartbow and notch an arrow. *If you were a real warrior*, Tsan chided inwardly, *you'd have already loosed that arrow, little Weed. But if you were going to do that, you would have done it long before you brought me here.*

"Seizal!" Arri snapped.

"It was senseless." Seizal dropped from the intermingled branches, landing noiselessly upon the rich green grass.

Giggles, like children traipsing through dry leaves, escaped the edges of Tsan's ruby maw. It was enough to rekindle her belief that Kilke did have a secret purpose and that this mission and her own pleasant, yet ill-timed, lapse into the feminine gender might not result in her own death.

Perhaps His secret purpose was served by even this.

"If you kill me," Tsan said, angling her neck up to present an excellent shot at heart or throat, "if I die, my second-in-command will be convinced you either have no interest in peace or that the Sri'Zauran army has failed to demonstrate sufficient aggression and destructive capacity to impress you."

"He'd kill Kholburran, too, I suppose," Seizal growled. "Why not threaten your hostage, isn't that what—"

"Hostage?" Tsan shook her muzzle. "Oh, that? Your Root Tree, the young prince, is already on his way home by now. We only took him prisoner as long as we did to convince you to bring me here. He's quite safe."

"That doesn't undo the deaths you've caused," Seizal pressed as Arri summoned a few Root Guard and sent them off. *Going to fetch the weed prince and test my veracity*, Tsan thought. *Why would I lie now? There is nothing to be gained, silly Weeds. If I betray you, you won't see it coming. That is, after all, the key.*

"Either way . . ." Tsan let her eyes shift, following a merrily buzzing green bee as it flitted from flower to flower. "Either way, many coldbloods will die, as, in the end, will all of your people who continue to actively oppose us on the field of battle. And the Root Trees that would burn . . ." Tsan shuddered. "I don't like to think of it."

Because thinking it makes me yearn to do it. She focused on Seizal.

"Such needless loss of life and . . . limb." Tsan's lips twitched up at the corners.

Seizal loosed her arrow.

More fight that I thought, Tsan crowed. *Well done!*

The chock as arrow struck wood forced Tsan to lower her wedge-shaped head sharply to conceal a smile.

"Seizal!" Arri snapped from her place, interposed between the two of them, arrow sticking out of her abdomen.

"Let her." Tsan settled back onto the rock, tail curled around the edge, head stretched out low. She knew there had to be greater pleasures in life than a warm rock but couldn't think of one at the moment. "Would you know what happens if you let me live?"

<<We many curious to know,>> tapped a voice in heavily accented Zaurtol. <<You tell I?>>

Queen Kari swept into the Arboretum. Where the Eldrennai loved finery, elaborate gowns and jewelry, the Queen of the Vael wore a flimsy gown that matched the pale white of her head petals over her smooth silver bark. What struck Tsan most were her eyes: two orbs of unmarred crimson only a hue or two off from Tsan's own beautiful female scales. Tsan could recall when her own eyes had been a similar shade, so long ago she couldn't recall whether she'd been male or female then . . . had that been back when she was dark gray or pale blue? She missed having eyes that unrepentant shade.

<<Your Sri'Zaur is . . .>> Tsan eschewed the use of her intended lie at the last moment. <<. . . less than perfect, but better than I expected.>>

"While you speak Eldrennaic and Vaelish like a native." Queen Kari banished Arri and Seizal with a subtle wave of her hand.

Better, actually. Why wouldn't I? Tsan tried not to hold the Weed's ignorance against her. Not everyone served the lord of secrets and shadow. Even so, one would think Aldo would have at least given the Flower Girls a hint. General Tsan waited a beat for the Weed Queen to realize she wasn't going to acknowledge the compliment.

"Would you care for some refreshment before we begin?" Kari asked.

"It hardly matters." Tsan rose on her hind legs, a practiced toss of her head to suggest arrogance. Weeds actually responded quite well to a precise level of conceitedness.

Conditioning from the Maker? Oh, yes. How else could the Vael be expected to serve the Eldrennai with a smile on their lips and a glint in their eyes?

"As you please." Kari approached Tsan carefully until the two of them could taste each other's breath. "I see our favorite spot in the garden is mutual."

"Shall we share?" Tsan gestured with a sweeping forepaw, the back of her paw and the claws at the end of it brushing with butterfly lightness across the queen's abdomen. Completing the gesture with a turn, Tsan's arm rested under Kari's, palm side of her paw facing down. A look Tsan interpreted as pleasant surprise crossed the queen's face as she accepted the gesture as intended, resting her weight on the offered arm as she took her seat.

"I'm unused to any but the Aern and other Vael knowing how to do that." Queen Kari narrowed her eyes slightly.

Checking my spirit for motive, Queen of Weeds? Tsan couldn't know for sure, but she imagined she could feel the queen peering into her soul.

"Would you like to sniff my hindquarters, too?" Tsan slid down next, her hip and the base of her tail touching the Vael, tail curved carefully away so as to not enfold or entrap. A pretty lie. Tsan imagined how easy it would be to kill the weaker creature; a pleasant inborn aggression.

"Perhaps," Kari laughed, "you would feel more comfortable if I allowed you to sniff mine?"

"Why?" Tsan matched the laugh. "You have nothing interesting there, you don't defecate any more than the scarbacks do. I trust you saw what you need to see, however?"

"More than I expected." Kari's eyes narrowed further. "Exactly how old are you, General Tsan?"

"General Tsan was only a handful of centuries in age when his career ended with an untimely change of possessive pronoun." Tsan scratched her chin absently with a claw, eyes meeting Kari's. "It's just Tsan now, but I have had many other skins, careers, and names. Truth be told, I can't keep them all in order anymore. This, however, is my last one, so let us concern ourselves with it only, yes?"

"Why the last?" Kari leaned forward.

"What do you think will happen if you let me live?" Tsan ignored the slight flirtation. She knew enough about the courting rituals of the warm-bloods to recognize it for the unconscious gesture it was, a simple fact about the Weeds . . . one they could scarcely resist if it might result in peace.

Reproduction for recreation was a concept foreign to Zaur and Sri'Zaur. Mating for Tsan could not have been less "romantic" (whatever that really meant). Perhaps if the process necessitated even being in the same cave at the same time . . .

"I'm not certain I have the training to track that quarry." Kari closed her eyes, thinking. "If I had to take a wild shot, I would have said you get an extra name, additional rations . . . a promotion? Given your statement, I presume I would be mistaken?"

"Oh, Warlord Xastix would thank me." Tsan couldn't keep the venom out of her voice, biting the "thank me." "He would then formally strip me of my rank and relegate me to a breeding crèche until I agreed to lay eggs and let some idiot fertilize them, and then they would add Matron to my name."

"I'm a mother myself," Kari offered. "Together with the pollen of Hashan and Warrune, I have—" Something in Tsan's expression silenced the queen, and Tsan frowned to have lost control to such a noticeable degree. "But it is different for the Sri'Zaur, I presume?"

"When the offspring hatched," Tsan continued, "I would be expected to raise and train them, culling the weak and encouraging the strong. By the time the last one was ready to serve, the war with the Eldrennai would be long over.

"Some idiot—" Tsan tried to stop her tail from twitching, but the tip still jumped, punctuating each word, "—like Dryga will have squandered an advantage it took the Warlord and me over three centuries to establish."

"Are you saying," Kari asked incredulously, "that they will not let you fight because you are a . . . girl-type person?"

"Given my rank and the lengths to which I have gone in the past to stave off my transformation to a non-combat gender . . . and the infertility that will have almost certainly resulted from those efforts . . . not being allowed to fight is the least of my problems. I have committed heresy. Even if the Warlord chose not to notice my predicament, Dryga or Asvrin would, I presume, ensure he discovered it."

"Why go back?" Kari asked. "You aren't spellsworn. Stay here and advise my people."

"No." Tsan closed her eyes, taken aback by the sudden temptation to seize Kari's offer. "I want to kill Eldrennai. Aern, too, if they stand in our way."

Kari placed the back of her knuckles against Tsan's scales, a gentle entreaty. "But surely it would be of greater advantage to your people to make peace with the Aern."

Peace . . . Tsan weighed that mention and wondered briefly whether to bring up the treaty immediately or delay? Let the rest of her sympathetic narrative unfurl or not . . .

"They treat my race as if we were their favorite food . . . which, admittedly, we are." Tsan shifted, crimson hind claw digging into the soft grass. "Besides, the Aern are incapable of a lasting peace. They always find an excuse to—" she brandished her claws in a mock slash, "—attack."

"But you can't win against the Aern. The warsuits—"

"Are not as immortal as they once presumed." Tsan shook her muzzle violently.

"I'd like you explain that last statement." Kari stiffened.

Scales slid with silken smoothness across the rock as Tsan rose, tail lingering, soaking up one last measure of decadent heat. Flexing her claws into the grass, feeling the layers of dirt and moss below, the Sri'Zaur general yawned, drops of poison glistening at the tips of her upper fangs. Acid joined the flavor of her saliva as she closed her mouth.

Am I truly that nervous? Tsan pondered. Unlike Zaur, Sri'Zaur were immune to their own venom, a definite benefit given that Tsan's poison— also unlike the Zaur's—was effective whether injected or consumed. *To have my venom sacs tensing like a hatchling's?*

"They, even the so-called Armored, are killable," Tsan answered, eyes half-closed, reaching out for the calmness of her surroundings, attempting to feed on it, like the heat she so loved. "By now Asvrin's Shades should have killed seven of the Overwatches." Swaying softly with an improbably present breeze, she peered back at the queen. "But Asvrin, unlike Dryga, is one of my *overachieving* offspring . . . he will have slain no less than a dozen."

"You truly believe that?" Kari frowned but made no move to rise.

"That he is one of my offspring?" Tsan said, deliberately misunderstanding the queen. "While it is true that the clutches do blend together from switch to switch, the memory fading, I still recall the last few."

"May I assume you know that is not what I meant?" Queen Kari asked.

"Of course. And yes, I believe it. Why do you think I was so happy to be taken directly to the Arboretum of Hashan and Warrune?" Tsan dropped low again, forked gray tongue flicking out to taste an unfamiliar vibration. "I presume that, despite my impressive, if imperfect resistance to magic, you've had ample . . ."

No, not unfamiliar, just out of place. Tsan fought the urge to rush, trying to match the cadence of her words to the arrival of an Eldrennai with a princely gait.

". . . ample time to read my spirit in its most relaxed state." Easing herself down onto the grass, Tsan sprawled out on her side. Lying flat out, tongue flicking, would have given her a better feel for the approach of the Eldrennai, but Tsan wanted to avoid being obvious about it, settling for a combination between comfort, surveillance, and submissive display. "Everything," Tsan said as she let her head touch the grass, "I've told you has been true."

"You haven't mentioned the treaty." Kari shifted nervously, then stopped herself.

Awkward to talk down to me this way, Weed? Give it time. Things are about to get even worse.

"My people want a treaty with the Vael." Tsan rolled onto her back. "I presumed your Root Guard brought me here because you were already open to the possibility of an alliance or, alternately, because you wanted to execute me for my role in the fall of Tranduvallu."

"Execute you?!" Royal hedge rose and anger assailed Tsan's nostrils as Kari's eyes bore holes in her, the queen's wide and impenetrable orbs of crimson revealing nothing of her thoughts. The anger was unexpected, coming on the utterance of the words "execute me" rather than "fall of Tranduvallu."

Was it the reference to the killing of a prisoner Queen Kari found so shocking? Why was life so important to the Weeds when it came so easily and could be spent so lavishly to achieve one's military aims? Had Uled worked the trait into his floral creations so they would endure the hardships of slavery and breed with the Aern more readily?

"Your name will have a litany, to be certain, General Tsan." Queen Kari's voice was hard and clipped. "Once we have come to an accord and you leave, you will never again be welcome within The Parliament of Ages except for those times when on official business, but to think that we would execute any being who seeks peace with us, no matter how misguided or distorted that being's overtures have been—"

Beyond the amber dome, Tsan sensed the vibrations of the Root Guard shifting positions. And *there* were the footsteps. Tsan thrilled at the timing.

"Remember that when your next guest arrives." Tsan rolled to her belly, paws beneath her, ready for anything.

"What?" Kari asked.

"Footsteps," Tsan hissed, "hard, arrogant, and without message or meaning. An Eldrennai. And . . ." Shifting to a sitting position, Tsan eyed the doors of living wood. ". . . as they are about to let the visitor interrupt, I will call him royalty." Cocking her head to one side, Tsan's tongue flicked out and wavered in the air. "Ah . . ." The scent of Eldrennai, tinged with a sweet dangerous hint of Aern, colored by touch of Zaur . . . "The brave idiot who was poisoned at Oot and then saved by a Vael."

Two Root Guards, Seizal and Arri, entered alongside a yellow-petalled young Vael clad in doeskin leathers with a heartbow on her back who fit the description one of Asvrin's Shades had relayed after the feint at Dark Gods Standing, a place other races called Oot. Despite her dislike for him, Dryga had been correct about that one. It hadn't started the war that Warlord Xastix had hoped it would, but the Shade had reported back with valuable news: the Aern were planning to kill the Eldrennai all on their own because of something the prince had done that still made little sense to Tsan.

But, if the intelligence about this idiot prince were to be believed, then why was he here? Some Aern in a warsuit, Tsan had half-expected, but an Eldrennai . . .

*

Susurrant laughter greeted Prince Dolvek, even more unwelcome than the noxious humidity unescapable this deep within The Parliament of Ages. And this, this Arboretum was even worse. He reached out to the plane of elemental water and air in an attempt to chill the sweat running down his back only to find a warm barrier blocking him.

Not unlike the wards some Artificers had at their disposal, this spell block walled off elemental planes from the physical world. Gentle heat flowed over him, far less abrupt than the jarring spike of pain Artificers tended to use, a discouraging nudge rather than a slap on the wrist.

Yavi elbowed the prince gently. "Hashan and Warrune don't let strange magic work this close to the center. I told you that."

"What exactly is strange about elemancy?" Dolvek whispered, flushing with embarrassment. Would he be turning so red if Yavi and the other Vael had been wearing their samirs, those horrid veils they wore for the express purpose of helping Eldrennai control their urges? Possibly, but it was hardly rational to expect all these Vael to accommodate for a single Eldrennai.

Spotting the red-scaled Zaur chortling near a magnificent Vael in white who could only be Queen Kari, Dolvek's ill humor transmuted to anger. "And what is that thing doing here?!"

"Sunning itself?" Yavi squinted, her ears twitching. "Oops. No. Herself. And behave yourself, Gloomy, if you want Mom to help you."

"Of course." Clearing his throat, Dolvek knelt before the queen, head bowed. "I beg your pardon, Queen Kari. The presence of a Zaur . . ."

"Sri'Zaur, Prince Dolvek," the creature purred, offering him an open paw, as if he might actually touch such a foul thing. "No?" It withdrew the paw. "I am Tsan, and you, I see, have taken to wearing armor based on the design Kholster Bloodmane dreamed up early in our people's little conflict. Before the advent of the warsuits, it was quite popular among the Aern. I smell more Zaur blood on it than Eldrennai, so I trust it has served you well?"

"It has." Dolvek straightened, forgetting the queen. "How do you know my name?"

"Spies," the reptilian thing answered merrily. "We find them useful for finding out things our opponents would prefer we didn't. I highly recommend them."

"How dare you sp—?"

"I'm Yavi." Another elbow from Yavi, this one strong enough to steal his breath, was slipped in with a smooth motion as if Yavi's abrupt curtsy to the reptile had been ill-considered and clumsy. "Could you forgive Dolvek and then formally introduce us, Mom?"

"Tsan, envoy of peace from the Zaur." Queen Kari gestured with an open palm to the creature. "My daughter is forward, yet I remain pleased to present to you Princess Yavi."

"A pleasure." Tsan, the so-called envoy of peace, held out a paw, this time at an angle appropriate for Yavi to slide her own hand against the hideous thing's scales, back of her hand against the back of its paw. "And I suspect any exuberance on her part was perpetrated in a valiant effort at mitigating the prince's surprise at my presence. Rather than being at all insulted, may I say that I find your tact and your gentle reproach refreshing and impressive. I wish to express my condolences for the horrible loss we have inflicted in our overture of peace. It simply did not occur to us that you would approach the matter in as nonconfrontational a manner as I now suspect would have been more culturally appropriate."

Yavi looked at her mother.

"I will explain that later," Queen Kari said firmly. "Envoy Tsan has been sent to us with an offer of peaceful alliance from Warlord Xastix."

"That's fabtacular!" Yavi grinned, and it melted Dolvek's heart so much he almost forgot the nonsense the Sri'Zaur had just spouted. "May I introduce you both to Prince Dolvek of the . . ." She avoided saying "Oathbreakers." Dolvek heard it in the broken cadence of her speech and the momentary pained expression that graced her gorgeous face, but she changed it to "Eldren Plains" at the last instant. "He's probably not the best choice for what may become a formal negotiation of alliance between our—"

"Alliance?!" Dolvek shrieked, unable to hold it in any longer. "You would even consider such with something so . . ." Dolvek clenched his fists and stemmed the tide of outrage. He took in a single deep breath and held it for a ten count. "I again owe all present my apologies. To come to The Parliament of Ages seeking assistance and to judge others harshly when I am little more than a beggar at the gate . . . it is unforgivable. Within the last few days, I have had reason to question everything I ever thought I knew about the Aern and the . . . Oathbreakers. Perhaps, I must now adjust my understanding of the Za—the Sri'Zaur as well. If there could be peace between all of our peoples? Well, I could ask for nothing more."

*

"Oh," Tsan sniffed. He was far too composed, this pitiful example of Uled's race. Tsan had intended to save the knowledge until later, to let the Weeds pry it out of her after a series of dropped hints, but she had to knock this prince out of control, to cue that marvelous self-destructive instinct all Dolvek's people possessed. "There can be no peace between the Sri'Zaur and the Maker's race."

*

"Uled created my people then tried to destroy them once we'd served our purpose. He took a peaceful race of thinkers and twisted our bodies to his alchemical will, then deliberately used us as an external threat against which to unite the Eldrennai under one king.

"No, we would happily make peace with our fellow creations. We would even consider peace with the Aern, *if* the noble Vael say such is possible, but not with Uled's cursed breed. We know what you do to those who show weakness . . . but now we are strong. Every stump-eared arrogant one of you must die."

Yavi's mouth dropped open, revealing her unpruned dental ridges.

"Oh dear." Tsan touched her forepaw to her chest in a very human gesture, much as Dolvek could recall Emma doing time after time back home whenever someone said something scandalous in the kitchens. "I'm sounding more like the Aern every moment." She blinked at Queen Kari. "Won't this be fun?"

CHAPTER 26
LEAVE THE BONES

Mom!

A tug at Wylant's scabbard combined with Vax's voice in her head brought the prone Aiannai to instant wakefulness. She came up swinging: a downward strike with her right hand to dislodge the gauntleted hand on Vax's scabbard. Eyes blurry, her opponent seemed a mass of white and black.

Armor?

A warsuit!

Dienox had attacked her and she'd fought him off . . . then Kholster had been there with other gods.

"Sleep," Sedvinia had said. But what then?

"He comes for the bones," Silencer intoned. Deep and resonant, the warsuit's voice echoed off the walls as it caught Wylant's hand.

"Don't make me hurt you, Caz." Wylant rose slowly, eyes locked on the crimson crystalline eyes inset within the skull helm of the Bone Finder's warsuit.

Silencer is worried, Vax thought.

Why? Wylant did not want Silencer's statement to mean what she feared it meant, but she knew she was right even before Vax confirmed her suspicions.

Caz is upset that you haven't made me a normal Aern yet, Vax thought.

Can he talk to you? Wylant shifted her wrist to see if Silencer would ease his grip. He didn't. *Even though you aren't fully awakened yet? But your father kept answering you out loud.*

That's because he wanted you to overhear his side of the conversation, Vax sent.

"I tried, Caz." Wylant walked through the steps in her mind, tracing, even as she spoke, a possible route to victory against the warsuit and the Aern sheathed within. "He doesn't want to be awakened yet. You talk to him. Have Silencer talk to him. If you can convince Vax, I'll wake him now. I'll do whatever it takes to do it. Give me a birthing bucket and I'll use my own blood!"

Warmth lit her up from the inside out. Compassion, joy, and love enfolded her, a warm comforter on a frozen night. Emotions familiar and yet alien in their primal simplicity cascaded over her.

Vax? Her breath caught in her throat.

Yes. Trembling with feeling, his thoughts quavered in her mind. *I was hoping you felt that way. Father said you did, but I've never been sure.*

Of course I do. Overcome with the desire to hug him to her chest, Wylant pictured it in her head and thought it at Vax as hard as she could. *What I did to you, even though I wasn't entirely me . . . perhaps I would have done it in the end, even if I hadn't been forced . . . but that thought, that I would sacrifice my own child, even to save my race—*

If you hadn't, Vax sent back, *you would have broken your oath.* Which explained everything to him. The fundamental difference between the Aern and all other races. They would justify anything in the service of keeping an oath . . . no matter how monstrous.

"I would rather I had been Foresworn than hurt you," Wylant gasped. "Do you—" She swapped back to mental communication. *Do you understand that, Vax?*

Vax went silent. Whether he was offended at the idea his mother would rather have been an Oathbreaker or if he thought no comment was needed, she could not guess. Wylant blinked at Silencer still standing there, her wrist in his bone-steel grip. Her lips drew into a thin grim line.

"Why now, Caz?" Wylant asked. "Why confront me in Fort Sunder? Why didn't you attack me at Oot?"

"He did not know Armored could be slain when we watched you at Oot," Silencer answered. "Now that they fall, he worries he may die with his oath to Kholster unfulfilled."

"What oath?"

"His was sworn to secrecy," Silencer answered.

"Kholster made him promise to see that Vax was awakened," Wylant said, answering her own question. "But if he died before that happened, or in the attempt . . . death redeems all oaths."

"Caz does not wish death to redeem his." Silencer tightened his grip. "Now . . . we come for the bones."

"Vax will be awakened when Vax is ready to be awakened, Caz." Wylant closed her eyes, summoning her connection to planes of elemental ice and air. "He told you that himself."

"I'm afraid Caz remains insistent." Silencer squeezed even harder. Wylant felt the pressure break her skin.

"I don't want to hurt you, Caz." A truth that was rapidly becoming a lie . . .

"Caz wishes to remind you that he is Armored and you, despite your elevated status, are merely—"

"Wylant," she boomed with the maximum volume she, as a Thunder Speaker, could achieve, her voice a cannon blast. Seizing Silencer's free gauntlet with her left hand, Wylant froze not the floor itself, because it was bone-steel, but the layer of air above it, a slick glazing of ice flowing along the floor and into the room that had once contained the smithy whose components had comprised the Life Forge.

Hurling herself backward in flight, Wylant felt Silencer struggle to retain his balance. He lost it, but not his grip. She judged this to be fair enough because her wrist broke, but her concentration did not. The two of them rocketed toward the door at the end of the hall. Such a common mistake, Wylant mused, to feel invulnerable because of a warsuit, to think just because you have a hand on me or land one blow that you've won. Kholster himself had made the same error in multitudinous sparring matches over the years. Sure, she'd lost every match at first, but eventually, it was Kholster who tended to lose more than he won.

The Armored could treat death like a game, because for them it was an option, not an inevitability. They called her the Destroyer, or they had in the past, because she had brought her son, her soul-forged weapon, down upon the overlong anvil of amber-hued metal that was the core of the Life Forge, rivaled in power and importance only by the mystic forge of Jun itself in which fires burned that could shape souls and melt reality.

She had cracked open the forge and split the anvil in twain without result. The Life Forge was of a piece: forge, anvil, and tools. All had to be sundered. All had to be rent and broken. When she slammed Vax down upon the final tool, something Sargus called an aetheric hook, the walls had begun to shake, the anvil blazed from within in violent purple. Only then had the Life Forge surrendered, exploding, every piece of it as one, with such force Wylant had been sure she was going to die, but the debris had flown through them, leaving Sargus, and her, untouched. The explosion had left both of them in an empty room with no sign the Life Forge had ever been there . . . except for Vax, who had been so recently forged with it, and for its creator, dead and bloodless on the floor.

Wylant had never wanted to go back into that room, but she flew on all the same, toward whatever armor Vax and Kholster wanted her to see, toward a clash with Caz in Silencer. Wylant waited for the fear to come, but it didn't. She might not beat Caz, but even if she lost, then Vax would be awakened, which would be a victory itself. A rising tide of desire to just awaken him anyway rose in her heart, but she stemmed that tide.

No. His choice.

Soaring past the threshold, Wylant scraped Silencer off on the door jamb with a thunderous clang that would have signaled his occupant's death if he weren't one of the Armored. Vax flowed up along her forearm, holding her wrist in place as a spiked gauntlet. When Wylant touched the floor she heard whispers. Names and lineages at the edges of her thoughts. In the entryway, Caz struggled to his feet. Wylant backed away from him, each step bringing with it another whisper.

"It's the bones." Wylant looked down at the bone-metal flooring. They had not done this before. What had caused the change? The scars on her back alone, or had Sedvinia, Shidarva, Kholster . . . or even Dienox done this when she slept? Or was it simply Vax serving as her intermediary translating whatever broadcast emanated from the Aernese bones?

"Silencer," Wylant began, "I'm almost positive Caz was deafened by my shout, but . . ."

Her words fell away as, taking in her surroundings for tactical value, she realized the changes that had been wrought upon the room that had once housed the Life Forge. All around her the smithy had been remade in hues of pearlescent white rather than whatever alloy Uled had used for the original. All remade, but without the exotic tools for crafting souls. The tools which hung from these new walls were the mundane sort used by any smith. The only specialized pieces were items of Aernese dental equipment.

Most shocking of all was the warsuit standing near the center of the space, next to the elongated anvil. Heat poured into the room from the open forge, but it could not suppress the chill Wylant got from the amber-tinted hue of the warsuit itself, which exactly matched that of the Life Forge.

Do you like her, mother? Vax asked.

A new warsuit? Wylant studied the thing, noting the way even Silencer appeared shocked by its presence. Where other warsuits tended to have heads inspired by nature or weaponry, this warsuit's helm was a mass of intricate crystalline lines. The rest of . . . her . . . was without adornment other than the lacquered chatoyance so common to Aernese artwork, but it was made more stunning by the lack of detail in contrast to the helm.

Yes, Vax thought at her, *but she isn't quite finished yet. I did the helm myself, so you can see out of her, but—*

"But the Life Forge was destroyed." Silencer stood in the doorway, blocking all exit.

Yes, Vax thought. *That's true.*

So how could you forge a new warsuit? Wylant asked.

I killed the Life Forge, Vax thought with a laugh. *Father says I absorbed enough of its power to complete at least one warsuit, perhaps more.*

But why would you— Wylant started to ask.

Want to be Armored? Vax's surprise hit her in a wave. *Why wouldn't I? I'll be the last one to ever manage it!*

"Do you mind explaining that to Silencer?" Wylant asked.

I tried. Caz is scared by all the new stuff. Vax's voice was tinged with sadness. *He is feeling his mortality for the first time and, well, he's not handling it gracefully.*

New stuff? He said the Armored could be slain? Wylant asked. *How is that even possible?*

I can think of two ways, Vax thought back. *I'm one of them. The other is—*

*

"A shard of the Life Forge." The minuscule sliver of metal held aloft in Glinfolgo's bloodied tweezers flared amber in the blue light of the floating pyramid. The Dwarf twisted and turned it in the air, blinking gravely through the green-tinted goggles, his so-called Dwarven Reading Glasses. A frustrated sigh escaped Glinfolgo's lips, his breath hot on Vander's cool skin.

"How is that possible?" Vander asked. He made as if to lean up, only to have Glin hold him easily in place with his off hand.

"Stay put, you stubborn idiot." Glinfolgo dropped the shard of metal into a nearby basin and set the tweezers down on a towel he'd lain across Vander's legs. Setting aside his goggles and rubbing his eyes, Glinfolgo shook his head. "When you shatter a window, do all the pieces cease to exist?"

"No." Vander tried to keep his breath even, to remain calm, but not being able to sense other Aern or . . . especially his warsuit . . . preyed on him. It had been enough of a challenge getting used to having Rae'en in his mind instead of Kholster, but this . . . every moment felt like what he might imagine a blind and deaf human endured, stumbling through a world of smell and touch or warmth and cold, but all else dark and silent.

"But . . ."

"But?" Glinfolgo sniffed. "But what? When Wylant smashed the cursed thing it exploded. The debris was cast into another dimension if our sourc— if what I've been told about it is accurate."

"But if it was lost in another dimension," Amber got the words out before Vander could speak them, "then how—?"

"How? How what?" Glin snatched the floating pyramid out of the air and held it low over the open incision he'd made in Vander's chest. White muscle exposed. Orange blood seeping slowly. Two sections of the bone plates that protected an Aern's vitals lay atop the towel next to the twee-zers, their edges warped and rounded where the Dwarf had used yet another Dwarven gizmo, this one a tiny handheld flaming device to cut through and reach the depth of the wound.

"Does anything look off to you?" Reaching into his box, Glinfolgo pulled out a polished steel mirror and held it at an angle so Vander could see down.

Other than the fact that all of the stuff at which he was looking ought to be covered up with a nice strong layer of bronze skin, Vander did not see anything particularly strange. Not that he'd taken to cutting open his chest and prying loose the plates. . . .

"Wait," Vander said. "What is that mass of black stringy things?"

"That," Glinfolgo answered, "is a bundle of dead nerves, specifically from one of the main nerve clusters that house your magnetoreceptors."

"You said that before," Vander said. "I still have no idea what it is."

"You know how some animals know how to fly toward warmer climates in the cold part of the year and then back when it is hot?"

"Yes, but—"

"They do it by reading the," he searched for a word, "unseen language of Barrone. It's the same language that lets a compass point north. Your Over-watches can use it to leave messages in bone metal."

"Like the mountain steps back home?" Vander asked. "Is that what you mean?"

"Yes. Bone Finders sense along the lines of it that wrap around Barrone to feel the presence of Aernese bones. It's what connects you all."

"And now that you have the metal out," Feagus asked from his spot near the door, "he'll heal?"

Teeth that could break rock ground together: the telltale rumble of Dwarven indecision. Vander's chest rose painfully. So silly, he thought, to feel afraid to know the answer to a question.

Curious beyond words, Vander waited for the Dwarf to answer with a resounding yes and gesture with confidence at flesh knitting beneath his gaze. Then he recognized the scent of the wound. He had caught its sweet, rank bouquet from Ghaiattri wounds in the Demon Wars, where injuries on otherwise resilient bodies had to be cut away layer by layer until they found the healthy meat that could heal and scar.

Caz's throat.

Glayne's eyes.

Other less debilitating injuries and some worse. Kholster had insisted that he see each wound that would not heal, as if staring at the horror of a world gone wrong would help him understand why some could heal from the sizzling bite of a Ghaiattri's fire without a mark and others could not. Even the same Aern might heal some wounds but not others or initial wounds but not subsequent injuries.

Maybe he doesn't want to heal, Kholster had thought to Vander as the two had stood over the prone form of Alfan, who had once been Armored. It had taken far too long for them to realize that none of Alfan's limbs would heal below the knee or elbow. *Could that be it?*

I don't think he lacks a will to heal, Vander remembered thinking back. *If Uled is correct and a Ghaiattri's flame can burn the soul . . . perhaps his spirit, thus injured, lacks the strength to support his whole body.*

When stripping and dipping did not grant improvement, some Armored had learned to live with their disabilities, and others, both among the Armored and the Armorless, had chosen to die and strengthen the army with what remained of their souls.

"Vander, there are other things we can try." As if reading his thoughts, Glinfolgo gave Vander's knee a reassuring pat. "When Eyes of Vengeance gets here we can see if proximity restores your link. If it does, then we'll do a simple strip and dip and—"

"And if it doesn't?" Vander grabbed the Dwarf's shoulder.

"That would be up to you," Glinfolgo said softly. "Now be still and let me make sure I haven't missed any fragments."

*

"Caz," Wylant growled at the advancing Bone Finder, "Vax is fine. He doesn't want to be awakened yet, and as much as I would rather Vax be flesh and blood, I owe it to him to let the choice be his. Don't make me hurt you any more than I already have."

"We come for the bones," the warsuit, Silencer, intoned.

"I will protect you," the unfinished warsuit said softly, the front of its unsettling amber alloy folding outward as if to encase her.

"You back off, too," Wylant snapped. "I'm not sure what to think about you yet and when I need help, I'll ask."

"Of course, Vax's Mother." The warsuit turned on its heel, its metal snapping shut as it walked from the center of the room to stand next to the forge. Looking at the anvil gave Wylant all the battle plan she needed and the terrain to help make it work.

"Vax, by Kholster, out of Wylant." Silencer walked slowly toward Wylant, reaching behind its back, long bone-steel knives dropping into the warsuit's waiting gauntlet. "Must be awakened. Caz has sworn an oath to see it done."

"He can see it done when I'm dead, according to Vax," Wylant growled. "And not before."

"As you please." Silencer sped into a run even as Vax morphed into the familiar utilitarian sword Wylant preferred, though its mottled-blue blade was now inset with fuller renditions of his father's scars along the center.

Silencer's skull-like helm lowered into a charge, its flashing crystalline eyes locked on her, immovable, impenetrable, inescapable—or so they seemed. Wylant readied herself to receive the attack, wondering what kind of conversation was going on behind those eyes. Was Silencer trying to reason with his maker, or had the armor already surrendered wholly to this wrongheaded endeavor?

Long knives clashed with sword in a flurry of strikes, rapid but controlled. Too controlled. Wylant prepared to make one final appeal and then . . . didn't. It was all too much. Too much recalled history. Too many emotions. Too much control and lack thereof. Wylant wanted to think her reaction was considered, measured. . . .

It was not.

Going on the offensive, she pressed the attack, forcing Silencer to parry Vax, fighting defensively, to block without time for strong counters or time for any reasonable follow-through. There were many ways to fight an Armored Aern, but the most reliable hinged on waiting for a kill shot. All other injuries were merely feints in service of that single strike to decapitate or lance through the eye and into the brain.

Caz's movements were more powerful inside Silencer, but he lost a fraction of his speed, and Wylant's feet and blade were more fleet than those of most of the One Hundred, much less the rest of the army.

Thrust. Feint. Slash. Thrust.

Even the warsuits had weak points . . . fewer at the joints and more at the helm, but Wylant struck for the back of the knee, the crook of the elbow, strike after strike landing on target as she maneuvered them to the anvil. Refusing to look or even think about where she needed Caz, slowly letting him gain some appearance of momentum, as if she were tiring steadily, which she was, but not as rapidly as she led her opponent to believe.

"I'm sorry," Silencer said as it moved in for the kill.

Vax, Wylant thought. *This is it. You know the maneuver?*

Yes, Mother, the weapon sent back, *but do you want him truly dead or just disabled so that a strip and dip will work?*

Unless we have to, we will never kill Aern, Wylant thought. *Agreed?*

Agreed, Mother.

Sparks spat from the tile when Wylant's foot shot through Caz's guard, sending his warsuit leaning backward. As expected, he latched onto the bone metal floor to maintain his balance, much as he held the knives to his back, shifting his right hand back to steady himself.

Rolling not past but up and over Silencer, Wylant brought her heel down hard onto Caz's left hand and the long knife clutched in it. Vax went long and thin, hanging in a loop from a handle in her uninjured hand and from the gauntlet containing her other.

At a width so thin and tenuous as to be rendered nigh invisible to the naked eye, Vax caught Silencer under the chin of its helm. Though, like most warsuits, Silencer was completely sealed when worn in battle, Vax worked himself into a minuscule seam.

Pulling with both hands, Wylant delivered an additional boot to Silencer's back, thrusting herself away from him even as she brought her hands together. Vax merged the handle with the gauntlet protecting his mother's hand, letting it encompass the other hand too, to increase the strength with a combined grip.

Caz swung his free blade up toward the thin cord, grunting in confusion when it stuck fast, refusing to cut.

"Using bone-steel against an Aern," Wylant forced between gritted teeth. There was only so much even Vax could do to keep her injured wrist protected—all the jarring blows had left it aching, pulsing in time with her heartbeat.

"You are not Aern," Silencer intoned.

"No, I am merely Aiannai . . . but my—" Wylant found the trail of elemental air, felt the way it warped near the remaining Port Gate at Fort Sunder, the tug and twist of aetheric echoes from the Life Forge's destruction. Inhaling the magic deeply after she spoke the next word, "—son—" letting its elemental essence rewind itself in her lungs, recognizing its proper shape within . . . loosing it on a final word, "—is!" She hurled herself backward with the resulting vortex of air.

There was no sound as Vax pulled tight then cut, weight vanishing, unspent momentum slamming Wylant backward, the wall forcing even the mundane breath from her lungs. Writhing, snakelike, Vax thickened and drew in, further reinforcing the gauntlet protecting her injured wrist.

Silencer's helm and the head within dropped free, rolling off of the elongated anvil to land at Wylant's boots, orange blood pooling at her heels.

I didn't kill them, Mother, Vax whispered in her mind, his thoughts unsure. *Though I still can, if you . . .*

"No." Wylant dragged herself up, back twinging from the impact with the wall. "We had to stop them. We had to defend ourselves against them, but we're still allies."

Wylant stripped the decapitated head out of the helm even as the wobbling remainder of the warsuit crashed to the floor. Two Bone Finders rushed into the room, and Wylant tossed them Caz's head.

"You come for the bones," she growled. "I know. Take them, but Vax stays with me . . . and by the way, here's a new warsuit. It's ours. Tell those two, once you've put them back together, that we could have ended them but chose not to do it. If they come for Vax again before he is willing to be awakened, I might not be so lenient."

Crystalline crimson eyes flickered in the helms of both Bone Finders' warsuits, communing, she assumed, first with each other, then with Zhan.

"Understood, kholster Wylant." The one on the right reached down to lift Silencer by the arms while the other Bone Finder reunited head and helm. "The Ossuarian thanks you for your mercy."

"It helped that Silencer didn't continue the fight once Caz was down."

"Both Caz and Silencer saw reason at that point."

Once they had gone, Wylant addressed the unfinished warsuit.

"Well?" she asked it.

"Well, kholster Wylant?" The warsuit approached her, head at a quizzical angle.

"That bought us the better part of a day." She sat down on the anvil, spared a brief bit of curiosity at the blazing heat of the forge. Was it this hot all of the time? She pushed the thought aside, rubbed a gloved hand across her forehead. "They won't be back until they've done a strip and dip for Caz to ensure he'll be fine. Who knows what will happen after that."

I'm sure we've made our point, Mother, Vax sent.

"I hope you're right." Wylant closed her eyes, resisting the urge to unleash a torrent of rapidly barked questions. She settled on one. "Does your warsuit have a name, Vax?"

Our warsuit, Vax thought, *for as long as we both live. And yes, she does.*

A pleasure to make your acquaintance, the armor spoke in her mind. **I am Clemency. I look forward to protecting you. You will, I fear, only be truly Armored when you are inside me. If it is amenable to you, I would like you to don me so that I might better speed your recovery.**

"Oh, Kholster," Wylant sighed, "what the hells have you gotten us into?"

Mother? Vax asked.

"Yes?"

None of that was what Father wanted you to find out.

Wylant took a deep breath and, biting back a caustic reply to her son's teasing, stepped toward the waiting warsuit, not surprised when Clemency split at the breastplate, seams appearing, then growing increasingly pronounced until they split apart and folded outward. Instead of the sound of cracking bones made by Harvester, who opened in a similar manner, Clemency had a soft scrape of metal on metal.

Wylant paused for another deep breath, looking at the velvet lining inside the armor and knowing Vax had put it there for her comfort and not his own. Once he was awakened and was one with his warsuit, he would be one of the Armored, a true Aern. The warsuit waited, split open to receive her, looking both vulnerable and threatening despite the contradiction in terms . . . and then, before Vax had time to tease her again, she stepped forward and let Clemency enfold her.

*

"Kholster," Torgrimm said, standing next to the god of death as he smiled unseen by mortals at his wife, son, and the warsuit they now shared, "if that doesn't count as cheating, I do not know how a deity could come closer without—"

"No rules were broken," Kholster laughed. "You asked Nomi to give me the talk and she did. I also spoke with Aldo, Two-Headed Kilke, and Shidarva. Or one of me did."

"Kilke?" Torgrimm scoffed. "Kholster, if I had known you would take advice from that destructive—"

"Two-Headed Kilke is not the god trying to undo the web of destiny." Kholster stepped free of Harvester, facing Torgrimm in the same clothes Kholster had favored in life: jeans, a belt of corded bone-steel chain, matching chain shirt, and hobnailed boots. The only thing different was the warpick. Reaper was more jagged than Grudge and slimmer than Hunger, a refined warpick made by a death god with a lot of experience.

"What?" Torgrimm's jaw gaped open. "You've been there? You've seen the web? If not him, then which god? Who?"

"It's not a god at all." Kholster favored Torgrimm with one of those uniquely wolfish smiles for which he was well known. "He merely wanted you to think he was."

CHAPTER 27

THE BLOODY THRONE

Rivvek's nostrils flared at the stench of blood. Many of the dead lay in pools of water, charred and sizzling. Some still hung in the air, while others lay battered and broken with signs their deaths had been more personal.

At the open balcony overlooking the port, Hollis, the Sea Lord, stood wreathed in an undulating mass of seawater. Blood kissed the air in drifting droplets suspended by virtue of the hydromantic might of the warm-eyed Eldrennai. Hollis had cast aside his formal robes early on in the battle, revealing a coat of plates and seafaring garb beneath. His navy waistcoat, complete with ivory buttons, covered a long-sleeved sea-green shirt with ruffled sleeves. A dark-olive sash hung at his waist, more for decoration (Rivvek assumed) than anything else. Hollis's laced leather pants tucked into matching boots with ivory-trimmed straps, wide sculpted cuffs, and bone-steel buckles. Hollis breathed a heavy sigh and rubbed his eyes.

One wouldn't have known it to look at him, but Hollis was a veteran of the Demon Wars and the Zaur conflicts before. Rivvek had been worried that the ancient Eldrennai, one of the few who could recall a time before Villok had united the elemantic bloodlines, would be hard to convince, but Hollis had been the one to approach Rivvek.

"You know there is a way the Aern might spare some of us," Hollis had said. Rivvek had smiled and let Hollis explain it all before agreeing to *go along with* the idea Sargus and Rivvek had been hatching for the last thirteen years.

Hollis and his guard had struck hard and fast, freezing unsuspecting nobility who either lacked family young enough to be accepted as Aiannai or whom Rivvek had already decided the Aern would find unacceptable.

Even though they had gridded it off ahead of time, establishing who would attack whom and when and how, Rivvek had worried something would go awry at the last moment. Several things had, but nothing Sargus or the Aern couldn't handle. As the Sea Lord struck so, too, had Lady Flame and Lady Air, Zerris and Klerris by name. The two were twins (minor nobles by birth, but great in elemental ability) who had married into their respective clans in exchange for rulership.

Both still wore their elegantly embroidered robes as they whirled in concentric circles at opposite orbits. Their targets burned, were deafened, suffocated, were struck by lightning . . . or some combination of all of the above. Rivvek felt chilled. He hated to see the deaths, necessary though they had been, of so many loyal subjects. And this would not be the end of them. Not by half.

Klerris dropped to the ground next to the testing stone, the hem of her robe catching on the edge of the single rough quarter of the square hunk of metal. Rather than pull it free with her hand, her familiar, a winged hand composed of clouds, darted across the distance and slipped it free without a creating a snag. Klerris bowed low before Rivvek. Her sister, landing on one of the testing table's smooth sides, bowed identically.

Powerful females among the Eldrennai were used to dealing with chauvinistic males who valued them for their looks and intimidating talents alone, mistaking them for tools rather than people. Winning them over had been simple enough. He had admitted their wisdom. He had acknowledged their talent and political machinations of the past and then asked for help. It had taken time, but once they understood he was genuine, he had done the next most important thing: He valued their opinions, treated them as the superior elemancers and experienced leaders they were.

He could remember seeing the two female elves dueling in the tournaments King Grivek had held when Rivvek had been a toddler, back before the Eldrennai had realized the full cost of Wylant's destruction of the Life Forge upon Eldrennai magic.

They were two of the only old-school elemancers Rivvek knew who had managed to adapt to the new familiar-focused form many of the younger Eldrennai tended toward now. Both bore foci disguised as pendulous gems hanging from platinum necklaces. It was an excellent illusion, even when one noted the way the "necklaces" never swung from side to side, the chains delicately taut.

Despite the rumors Sargus had relayed to him about their courtly intrigues since those days, Rivvek had been surprised when they had attempted to seduce him, separately, and then together, but he'd passed that test as well. He attributed it to their many years of experience dealing with a different sort of male. Declining without giving insult was a skill he'd mastered quite well over the hundred-plus years since his own Grand Conjunction.

"Ladies," he and Sargus had finally settled on the wording, "you offer me delights of which I may not in good conscience partake. Perhaps one day, when I have grown closer to your equal in wisdom. . . . Until then, however, I assure you I have nothing to offer in that area, and I am not so loathsome as to deal so unequally with those I consider my allies."

At the back of the room and with a sound like a hammer encountering and defeating a melon, Lord Stone dispatched his final opponent, letting the second skin of granite he'd summoned fall away.

Fully half of the Eldrennai witnesses to his coronation lay dead. Rivvek fought back a cough, unable to trust it not to devolve into an insane cackle.

It's working, Rivvek wanted to shout.

Yes, of course it's working, he rebuked himself inwardly. *It has to work.*

All of those he'd considered to be the most likely to unseat him, to create uncontainable civil strife had been invited to attend. It was a smaller list than he'd expected, but a lot of that had to do with the successful inclusion of the four Elemental Nobles on his side of the battle, because without them he could not be sure Hasimak would go along with things, and though he'd never understood exactly why they held him in such esteem, he valued their opinions. If all of them agreed he must have Hasimak on his side, that Hasimak must view him as the rightful king, then he'd have Hasimak as well, even if it meant jumping through all those legalistic hurdles he'd tackled earlier.

But the apparent success of the first phase of his post-coronation plan, devised to save as many of his subjects as possible, did not mean he had failed to realize that his rule would be looked upon as the bloodiest reign of all time.

"Majesty?" Sargus hovered over his single target, the limp form of Hasimak, the High Elementalist, still breathing, but heavily sedated with some concoction of Sargus's. Sargus touched a thin dagger to Hasimak's throat, a question in his eyes.

"No." Rivvek felt like an overtightened lute string that might snap at any moment, but he kept his voice even, his breathing measured, his expression revealing only what he wanted it to show: confidence. "I'll want him with me in the second phase, if he will agree."

It was only after he'd given the order to spare the ancient Elementalist that Rivvek noticed the ebbing of a latent strike in the air around them. An air shield to protect Hasimak, earth and water to strike Rivvek down, and fire for Sargus.

The nobles would kill their friends and fellows but would commit regicide to protect their teacher. All four of them, without even the need for debate. Why? There was no time to question it now, but he would need to know before much time had passed. If they planned to overthrow him and put Hasimak in his place, Rivvek did not actually care as long as he made it to the final phase of his plan. Whatever happened after that would happen.

The likelihood that he would still be alive to see what came next was the thinnest of hopes and the least of his worries.

*

"Second phase?" Rae'en asked. When the Oathbreakers had started killing each other Rae'en had stayed put. Even if guarding the throne had been meant to be ceremonial, it was her assignment, and by Kholster, if by none of the other gods, she intended to carry it out. Glayne had suggested a withdrawal, but she'd overruled him and was now glad she had.

"Ah." Rivvek acknowledged his bowing Oathbreakers, walking down the four steps to where they stood and bidding them to rise with a hand upon each shoulder. By the time he'd finished with the first three, the other one—

The Sea Lord, Glayne provided.

Had joined them and bowed in time to receive the king's (blessing?) touch as well.

"Thank you," Rivvek told them each in turn, before mounting the steps again without any sign of fear that the four behind him, the ones who had done most of the killing, were any threat to him at all. As Rivvek approached Rae'en, his steps, his measured gait—not quite regal, but not far from it— were those of a conqueror.

"My apologies, kholster Rae'en," Rivvek said, giving her a half bow before offering her his hand.

"It's fine." Rae'en took his hand and stood. "The after-coronation slaughter wasn't on my event schedule, but I'm not complaining. I like to see Leash Holders die."

Had he flinched at that?

"Of course." Rivvek's smile was charming, even more so given the slickness of his bare chest, scars glistening with a thin sheen of sweat. "I know you were looking forward to a war with the Eldrennai, but once you have sorted through those you will accept and those you won't, I do not expect for there to be any further need for conflict unless it is one in which the Aern, the Aiannai, and the Vael fight together against the Zaur."

CHAPTER 28

DOOM IF BY SEA

<<What are they doing?>> Dryga clung to the seabed, tapping commands in Zaurtol directly on the forehead of a Sri'Zaur whose scales ran to tones of light gray. Green bands, like seaweed or kelp, wended their way along the second hatchling of the third brood of Astur, flexing as he relayed Dryga's question in Zaurqal, the loud clicking booms from his chest and throat carrying to the other Lurkers.

How they made any sense of all that percussive sound underwater, Dryga did not know, but as Lurkers were one of the first specialized breeds of Sri'Zaur Uled had created, he did not insult them by doubting. Dryga caught a word, perhaps one in seven, but enough to guess how much the meaning of his message was altered . . . it sounded like the same sort of question, but . . .

It does not matter, Dryga told himself.

Behind him, five thousand Lurkers lay in wait, spread across the seabed, with another five thousand Zaur making their way to their places. Dryga heard the response clicking in the distance but couldn't follow it through the underwater distortion.

<<Well?>> Dryga tapped impatiently.

<<Shades,>> the Lurker tapped carefully on the side of Dryga's head, <<say they have reinforced the gates. Doubled guards. Eldrennai gather in the streets presenting themselves to the new king and to hear his words. Scarbacks are with them and the Elemental Nobles.>>

Outer lids nictated in doubt, obscuring the pale glow of the Lurker's eyes as it asked something, waited incredulously for the response, head rearing back when it heard the same message as before.

<<They seem to be dividing the Eldrennai.>>

<<Dividing how?>> Dryga interrupted.

<<Into those the Aern will scar and those they want to eat.>>

Wasting breath with a burst of laughter, Dryga held his own muzzle closed with both forepaws in embarrassment as his air bubbles floated rapidly to the surface.

Could that be true? Dryga wondered. Asvrin's Shades were the best and most deadly of the few Skin Tinters Warlord Xastix commanded. Always in small numbers and great demand, the Skin Tinters, like Flamefangs, could not breed true. The alchemical process creating them halted the reproduction cycle permanently, leaving them all sterile neuters.

Too many of them had died in clan wars Xastix had waged to unite all the coldbloods, Zaur and Sri'Zaur alike, under one Warlord.

<<How many of Asvrin's Shades made it through the attack?>> Dryga asked. He waited long seconds for a reply.

<<Asvrin asks why you want to know,>> the Lurker tapped, relaying the reply.

<<Very well.>> Dryga ignored the question. <<Is there anything else he thinks we ought to know before attacking?>>

<<He says,>> the Lurker tapped, <<that he is surprised you asked. But since you did, he can tell you the Dwarf unloaded a large quantity of junpowder and metal spitters—both the large and small ones. They are in a dockside warehouse.>>

Dryga managed to hold the laugh in that time, remembering what the human, Tyree, had accomplished with a sack full of junpowder. . . . Who knew what havoc his forces might be able to unleash with a larger supply? The warlord's alchemists had long ago solved the puzzle of the black powder, had even found ways to alter its color to match the Dwarven version, but producing the powder in any significant quantities resulted in Dwarven retaliation so swift and complete, they'd actually lost the formula the first few times they'd discovered it.

Could they prove it had been the Dwarves? Had they ever seen a single hair of their scheming little beards? No, but He Who Ruled in Secret and in Shadow had revealed the information to them, accompanied by instructions to stop development of the black powder and to beware any direct conflict with Jun's chosen people.

But if he could seize the existing supply and deploy it here, winning the war without the need for a protracted siege at Fort Sunder, what reward might not be his? A second chosen name would be his at the least!

<<Get a breath count.>> A crab scuttled by on the seafloor, and Dryga resisted the urge to crack it open and feast. He could feel his air supply diminishing faster than he liked, gazing with naked jealousy at the rudimentary gills, so hard to see aboveground, possessed by common Zaur, flaring open as they breathed in the depths. Something even the Lurkers with their massive air capacity and specialized communications couldn't manage.

<<A few candlemarks,>> the second hatchling of the third brood of Astur tapped after an exchange with the other Lurker officers, <<for the surface Sri'Zaur. Hours yet for my biters. But the Zaur—>>

<<I know how the Zaur are!>> Dryga drew blood with the last tap of his claw and stifled a wince at the thin, dark trail rising up from the Lurker's forehead. Shifting higher and to the side of the wound, he finished his orders. <<Tell the borers to get into position then make sure everyone else is in position. We go soon or we will have to swim back through the sea tunnels to fill our air bladders.>>

*

A cold wind stirred early fallen leaves along the corners of the storefronts and other buildings facing the Lane of Review. King Rivvek stood, the figurative jewel at the apex of the assembled mass of Eldrennai, clad now in decorated plate armor of Sargus's design, ready to address his subjects. Smoothed by an alchemical process Rivvek had not been able to follow, the plates were forged of folded tempered Ghaiattri hide, the leather lining crafted of the tender skin found beneath the demon's outer layer, carefully scraped and treated. Flexing his gauntlet, the king watched thin bone-steel cat claws slide out with a quiet click—a deadly display of razor sharpness.

Sargus expects me to survive all of this, he thought. Pale gems embedded in the first knuckle of each finger on the gauntlet and its mates concealed a control mechanism, but that bit of artifice eluded him as well.

In a different world, if this had all happened sooner, when there were more of us . . . but now . . .

Sunlight caught the claw tips, picking out the color of the metal without glare or reflection. Pearlescent bone-steel had been worked in whorls across surface of the armor, smooth to the touch, beneath a layer of enameled chatoyance reminiscent of the technique Kholster had perfected millennia before. Decorations unlike those on an Aern's armor included the royal seal of Rivvek's house over his heart and a duplication of Kholster's scars on his back.

Standing to his left, a human child, one of Emma's ubiquitous sons, held Rivvek's helm on a pillow of blue velvet. The demonic cast to all Ghaiattri armor had proved harder to obfuscate there, leaving it with a striking resemblance to the skull-like helms that seemed ever the fashion with Zhan's Ossuarians.

Jagged edges had been smoothed and the brown color transmuted to steel with a muted amber hue where it caught the light, the fangs of the beast embellished with more bone-steel, upper and lower jaws meeting perfectly when the visor was closed. He had asked Sargus what the translucent crystal substance was that sat in the wide eye sockets of the helm, only to be informed it was probably best if the king did not know and have to think about it.

"Truly?" he'd asked as the two of them talked late at night in his own private chambers.

"You have your plan, my prince." Sargus had rested his hand on Rivvek's silk-draped shoulder. "It is a good one and if any has a chance of working, it does. But please, allow me my own plot to ensure your safe return."

"Highness?" A mystic whisper from Bhaeshal cast the thought away, the Sargus of his mind's eye replaced by his people, frightened but hopeful as he delivered his message to another hundred of them. As he called up his people, a hundred at a time, he wondered how many of them had ever seen his father, King Grivek, let alone the four Elemental Nobles who stood with Rivvek now: the Stone Lord and Lady Air on his left with the Sea Lord and Lady Flame on his right. Several steps back and to the side, but unmistakable presences.

Surrounded by a sea of soldiers, knights, and elemancers (not to mention an array of Aern and their warsuits), Rivvek remained astonished by the small number of Port Ammond's citizenry who had attempted to attack him once he'd explained the decision they faced.

Hollis, the Sea Lord, cleared his throat.

Resisting all urges to straighten the slender crown upon his brow, Rivvek started again.

"There will be no war with the Aern." Rivvek's voice, amplified by Bhaeshal's elemancy, echoed as his words bounced off of the buildings behind the crowd. He waited, but this group did not cheer. Either they knew what he was going to say or word had gotten around that not all who attended the new king's series of intimate addresses came back again.

"I am your king: Rivvek, son of Grivek, heir to the throne of Villok and I have passed the Test of Four."

Out in the city, his knights and Elementalists, along with Aern and warsuits, were rounding up the people of Port Ammond to be sorted and brought, in an orderly fashion, before their king. He could have tried to ignore the import of that, but he could not bring himself to do it.

They will think me . . .

Words failed him. Let them think whatever they liked so long as they lived to think it.

"He is king," the four Elemental Nobles recited as one.

"I am also Aiannai." Rivvek looked over his left shoulder for Bloodmane, those assembled gasping when the living armor, looming taller than

258 **OATHKEEPER**

all present, stepped up behind the king to rest a gauntlet on either of the king's shoulders. "Oathkeeper."

"He is Aiannai," Bloodmane boomed, "an Oathkeeper with my maker's own scars upon his back."

"Each of you will present yourself to Bloodmane." Rivvek stumbled over the end of the name but pressed on. "Or one of the other warsuits present. If you are acceptable as Aiannai and are willing to bear the scars of the Aern who finds you acceptable upon your back, you may leave here in peace."

A rumbling rose from the crowd. They did not like the sound of that. No Eldrennai yet had, but with such a show of force—

"Go to hells!"

Alas, he thought, *I have already been there.*

"Walked right into the hunter's trap," yelled another person in the crowd. "You're no king. You—"

A handful of others shouted. Well, it had to happen eventually. One of the groups was bound to know what he was going to say and have their hearts hardened to his words before he spoke them.

One threw a rock. Then another.

Those who did . . . died.

Is it merciless to kill those one cannot save to spare others one can? Rivvek's stomach burned and his bowels churned, but he did not look away as the ones who had thrown rocks were killed with them, either by the Stone Lord or one of the Geomancers present. Hasimak's presence would have helped, but after countless repeat performances, the old Eldrennai has grown too fatigued to continue and retired to the Tower of Elementals.

Lightning and fire rained down upon the other objectors, so fast the crowd was stunned into silence, the guards closing in, forcing them closer together.

"Enough!" Rivvek shouted, a hand signal letting Bhaeshal know to make it even louder with her Aeromancy. His next words came as calm whispers raised to the level on an irkanth's roar. "I did not doom you. Nor did my father, Grivek, or brother, Dolvek. Even Uled was not alone in his blame. Some here have not 'held the leash' as the Aern say, but some of us—"

"We did nothing wrong!" one of them shouted. An older Eldrennai, with the look of a retired soldier. "Nothing!"

"That! That is exactly what you did!" Rivvek tore off his crown, going off script even though he knew it was unwise. "You never let the people see you take off your crown," his father would have said, but he'd been rehearsing this argument in his head ever since Dolvek had first started showing signs of denial. All at once he had the words he'd been trying to find for all those years. "I . . . I have heard many Eldrennai, too many, say they did not hold the leash. Claim they never abused a Vael. Some even say they knew what the king was doing was wrong all along. But what you did with that knowledge was—" he shook his crown at them, "—nothing!

"You stood by and let Uled make not one race of slaves, but two. You could have risen up against my grandfather. Perhaps you would have died, but you would have done something! It could have made a difference. What it might have changed, we will never know, but maybe the Aern would have thought differently of the Eldrennai.

"Perhaps this crown," he said, as he held it aloft, "would still be on my father's brow and we might have had six hundred years of true peace rather than the uneasy cessation of hostilities we have enjoyed. Vael might walk our cities alongside Aern who had forgiven us. . . .

"You did nothing and thus, you failed. This crown?" He handed the crown to Emma's son and picked up his helm. "This crown must be exchanged for armor. Kind words to stir the heart must become hard, stinging breaths grasping at faint hope.

"You failed the Aern and the Vael. You failed yourselves. Do not fail your children. Two great leaders have died to buy you a chance. If we do not seize this final opportunity to make amends, we, our whole race, will vanish from the face of Barrone and we will not be fondly remembered.

"I have sentenced all of those Eldrennai whom the Aern find unacceptable to death." Rivvek saw some in the crowd open their mouths, with anger in their eyes, but no sound escaped their throats. A few understood what was happening and held their tongues, but those who actually protested fell dead, the air ripped from their lungs courtesy of Lady Air and her Aeromancers. *And if I wasn't a monster before, I am become one now.* "But it is a sentence I hope to commute. When I met Kholster at the Grand Conjunction," Rivvek said, "I understood what many of you cannot. There is no way we can atone for what we did, but I tried to find a way.

"I was young and arrogant, in my own way, and I believed there was a chance to bring back some of those we cost the Aern. The Lost Command marched armorless through the Port Gates, led by Wylant's father Kyland to hold back the Ghaiattri long enough for the Port Gates that could be sealed to be sealed and those that could not to be destroyed. Their sacrifice, like that of the Elementalists who wrapped the Eldren Plains in an impenetrable field of magic that even the Ghaiattri could not pierce, holding them here rather than letting them overrun the whole of Barrone, was true sacrifice. . . . They were not ordered to go, but, to protect us all, they went.

"So, I decided to go into the Never Dark after them, to find their remains and retrieve their bones. I did not make it far before the Ghaiattri found me, but for those of you who have wondered, that is where I got my scars. Therefore, I now charge you, my people whom the Aern do not accept, those called Oathbreaker or Leash Holder, to atone! Come with me and help me prove we have changed and are willing to die to make things right. I will lead as many as will come through the Port Gates. We will return the Lost Legion to the Aern . . . or die trying.

"For it is truly a death sentence." Rivvek coughed. "But if any should return, I challenge the Aern to call them by a different name. Call them Vhoulk, the Redeemed, or Tesset, the Forgiven. And then, with no Eldrennai left who claims that name, let us be at peace."

Among the sea of faces, some believed him, wanted to make amends, others pinned him with baleful eyes.

"You are angry. I understand. You are afraid. So am I. You need someone to blame. Blame me. Hate me." Rivvek held the demonic helm over his head. "I am scarred. I am the loathsome one who will kill those he cannot save. Call me a murderer. When this is done, assassinate me. Curse my name for all time!"

He donned the helm, blinking fiercely at the transition from the mundane world to the shadowed overlap of the Ghaiattri's dimension, the Never Dark that bled over into it under his demon-hooded gaze. Magic was beautiful, the only thing of beauty in that realm beyond, the mystic art of those around him coursing through the crowd. Lady Flame and the other Pyromancers lit up with the power of their fire; the Aeromancers, shimmering as the elemental air they controlled, glimmered in his sight. Veins of granite crisscrossed the skin of his Geomancers. All the Hydromancers' pale skin shone blue.

"Do whatever you like when this is ended, but know—" as he spoke, heart pounding, face hot, his scars pulsing, purple light flared behind him casting all around him in the lambent shadow of wings composed entirely of violet flame, "—you will wait until I am done saving you. Until the last Eldrennai has fallen, surrendered, died, or been claimed . . . I! Am! Your! King!"

*

Kazan knew a terrible thing had happened when he failed to open his eyes. One eye, his left, functioned well enough—a little blurry, perhaps. All attempts to open his right eye, however, generated the most amazing jolts of agony he had ever experienced. Leaves of an ancient blood oak rustled above in the cold breeze, and the coppery tang of human blood scented the air. As he watched, one of the seed-bearing leaves dropped free of the branch, spiraling off to find purchase. He remembered there had been a second attack, a group of knights falling on them in the night as they hobbled along the path toward Port Ammond, but after that first crush of combat his memories were fuzzy.

I'm not thinking straight.

Breath came in labored, uneven pulls.

I'm lying down. His thoughts were unsteady as his breath. *My mouth is dry, too.* He smacked his lips, and that felt . . . odd as well. Not painful like the eyes, but strange. *Some stupid um . . .* The word he wanted escaped him, so he moved past it . . . *left a dead knight on top of me. Is that why it's hard to breathe?*

Guys? He reached out for the others.

"Over here!" Joose shouted both in his head and in his brain.

Part of Kazan's mental map repopulated when Joose came into range. M'jynn and Arbokk were okay even though the Arvash'ae-influenced end of the battle had spread them far afield from each other. Two humans, Cadence and Tyree, outlined in gold to mark them as allies, were north of Kazan next to each other. Blurring, the map smeared itself across his vision until he banished it with a thought. What were the others thinking, covering up his whole field of vision like that?

Kazan tried to shift the knight off of himself, but his left arm wouldn't move and his right arm barely managed to nudge the heavily armored corpse. Even that slight movement lit a fire of pain in Kazan's belly, spreading along nerve pathways in a single pulse of agony, vanishing once Kazan had registered it.

That's not good, he thought, twitching his eye again to check and see if the pain there behaved the same. It did.

There was a human saying: "Pain is your body's way of letting you know you're still alive." For Aern the saying was even more accurate. Small irritations like cold or heat the body ignored up to a point, reading them as warning signs then dismissing them. Pain did the same thing, but it persisted. You felt pain so you'd know where you were hurt . . . and continued to feel it to help avoid further injury. But for a wound, a bad one, to stop hurting . . . flicker then fade . . . Kazan had never heard of that. Well, not in any good context.

"Bird squirt." Joose hissed the words, horror-stricken. Pinioned with arrows and dotted with lacerations that were quickly vanishing now that Joose had eaten his fill, Kazan's fellow Overwatch displayed a few notable injuries. He had lost a hand during the fighting and had it tucked into the top of his pants, the fingers poking out above the top of his belt. His nostrils hung flayed wide open and raw where one of the knights had sliced away a large chunk of his nose. The sight made Kazan want to wince, but doing so would have taken too much of an effort.

"Hrrgl." Whatever was wrong with Kazan's jaw kept him from speaking audibly with any real chance of being understood, the words coming out as more of a liquid gurgle.

Trying to look in the direction of the others sent another sharp barb through Kazan's head and ended in failure.

Why won't it turn?

One by one the other Overwatches arrived. Arbokk seemed none the worse for wear, or would have if Kazan didn't know Arbokk had had a full head of hair at the beginning of the fight. A melted patch or two still dotted his pate, but Kazan bet there was a story behind that one. Once they got all the nasty bits shaved off, Kazan was sure Arbokk would be more than happy to tell his tale.

"Kholster's name!" Arbokk took one look at Kazan and tripped over a root.

"It can't be all that ba—" M'jynn froze. He was still picking arrows out of himself as best he could while trying to stay mounted on one of the chargers the knights had been riding. His left leg had been hacked off above the knee—which had to have been painful. Kazan couldn't see the leg and wondered whether they were going to have to scour the roadside looking for it or if M'jynn already had it in his saddlebags. He'd hate for a Bone Finder to have to come out here just to get it.

It was not the eyes of his friends or even those of the two humans that told Kazan exactly how bad his injuries actually were; it was the shadow of a warsuit leaning over him.

"Kholster?" he asked.

"Hello, Overwatch," the death god said.

PART FOUR
THE OLD SKULL LAUGHS

"In my studies of my father's creations and the interconnectivity of their souls, in particular those of the Aern, I have studied many of the gnomish philosophical works relating to the soul. Specifically, those texts regarding reincarnation have led me to wonder to what extent the individual is submerged when an Aern's soul is spread among his or her fellow soldiers. Having spoken with three of the Incarna among the One Hundred, I have heard them describe the experience of receiving their father's spirit as a flood of knowledge and memory, but always filtered through their own beliefs and opinions, enhancing, informing, but not supplanting themselves.

"Would such a thing be possible, I wonder? To, through reincarnation or the Aernese sharing of spirit, allow one soul to influence another directly, to maintain some sort of consciousness apart from the new being it inhabits? If so, what would that be like? Would it remain behind the filter of awareness? Would the two fight for control? Or would it manifest as a sort of madness? Whispers of the departed, a maddening voice in one's head that no drink, alchemy, or meditation could alleviate? Now you know the secret dread that haunts my thoughts: If anyone could accomplish such a return, it would be my father."

From the introduction to
Ramblings on the Nature of the Created Soul by Sargus

CHAPTER 29

NOT SO HIGH AND MIGHTY

Guest rooms within Hashan and Warrune lacked the elaborate decor found back in Port Ammond, but it was wonderful to again be surrounded by a room full of living wood. The spirals and flourishes here had been shaped by the twin trees, every mural the work of years of careful growing. The balance of each room between form and function was delicate, peaceful, and pure.

Yavi watched Gloomy pacing the room Queen Kari had granted him, his heavy feet crushing the mossy green carpet provided by the twin trees. Dolvek, as oblivious to the subtle scent cues the trees were giving him as he seemed to be to so much of the world around him, showed no sign of removing his boots. Ears twitching, Yavi stepped in front of him, the over-head illumination brightening.

"Yes," Yavi spoke at the ceiling. "I'm going to tell him, Dads."

"Wha—?" Prince Dolvek started.

"So . . ." Yavi kicked the side of his boot with her bare foot. "The boots. Take them off. My dads provide seriously skoosherized moss carpet in the sleep chambers and guest rooms. It's not proper grass, or it wouldn't feel so luxurious, but it also can't hold up long to rude obnoxious stompy people."

"Dads?!"

"I ask you to stop killing the carpet." Yavi twisted her lips into a wry smile. "The part you get stuck on is pollination?" Her next kick was aimed at his shin level.

"Ow!" the prince yelped.

"Boots!" Yavi put the knuckles of both fists against his chest and gave him a soft shove. "Off! Now! You are killing the carpet."

"I am not going unarmored while that . . . that thing is left to roll about in the garden as if it is some honored guest!" Dolvek muttered the words under his breath, his spirit opening a gateway to the realm of elemental air so tiny Yavi could barely catch a glimpse of it with her spirit sight. "I will, however, protect your mossy floor covering . . . even if I refuse to accept it as carpet."

Bobbing up a hand's breadth above the floor, Prince Dolvek floated, boots clear of the carpet. Yavi knelt down, eyeing the space between the sole of his boots and the moss that began to spring slowly back into shape.

No lasting harm done, Yavi thought, *and I only had to kick him twice and shout at him once.*

"She is an honored guest, you know," Yavi said.

"She's wha—?"

"A Zaur." Yavi pushed down with her palms in the soft, cool grass, moving to a sitting position. "Well—a Sri'Zaur in her case—with an offer of peace? The only thing as surprising as that would be a bone thief who said, 'Here ya go,' when a Bone Finder did his whole 'I've come for the bones' thing."

"I can't even picture that." A seed of a smile lit on Dolvek's lips. Drifting over to the desk and chair the twin trees had provided, Dolvek settled on top of the desk, feet in the seat of the chair as he pulled off his boots. "And . . . I apologize, both to you and to your Root Trees. It seems I will be forever apologizing."

Yavi gawked at him, mouth and eyes wide open in amazement. She squinted at his spirit, but he was no imposter. This was the same Eldrennai who had been with her at Oot, who had denied all that the Eldrennai had done to her people and to the Aern, now flecked with shades of gold she had never before seen in him.

"What?" Dolvek lowered one boot gently to the floor then began to pull at the other. "Am I too heavy for the desk or—?"

"What happened?" Yavi asked. "Since I saw you last, there is a change. You were, I don't know—closed—but now you're open, slow to open, but you're listening . . . conscious of others . . . you apologized about the carpet!"

"It *is* a living carpet." Dolvek set his other boot down next to the first. Hesitating, he began to peel off his socks, too, tapping into the planes of fire, water, and air to wash and dry both his feet and the woolen socks.

"That," Yavi said, "is the most useful thing I have ever seen you do with magic. How do you use all three so easily?"

"All of the royals can . . . except my brother," Dolvek answered. "And he could, too, could use it better than me before he came back all scarred from wherever he went after his Grand Conjunction."

"Wylant's destruction of the Life Forge did not affect us, or her. I can only think of a very small number of other elemancers who did not have to accept elemental foci. All either ancient relics like Hasimak or from the few surviving bloodlines that predate the Test of Four and the unification of the elemantic schools."

Struggling out of his brigandine, revealing the gambeson beneath, he laughed bitterly. "I didn't bring any other clothes."

"We can loan you something. . . ." Yavi offered.

"That would be most kind." Dolvek moved from the desk to the chair.

"Thank you. What did I think I was doing, flying off like that to rage at my brother? Then, barging in here, demanding things . . ."

"What happened?" Yavi rose to her feet and moved closer, pressing the knuckles of her left hand against his shoulder.

"When I outlined my plan to attack the Zaur," Dolvek said, closing his eyes as if he saw it all again, "Bloodmane mocked me. He demoted me and put Jolsit in my place. I remember thinking how unfair he was being and that he was just angry and being petty because Kholster hated me so much, but—when the Ghaiattri came through the Port Gates and the warsuit needed someone to step in and lead the crews in destroying the Port Gates, he had me do it. Just gave me the order and I did it. When that happened I realized Bloodmane wasn't being cruel or spiteful, he was trying to get through to me, to let me know that you use your soldiers in the best way you can. He knew what I could do and he had me do it, which meant . . . my plan of attack had actually been stupid."

Dolvek opened his eyes and looked at Yavi. "He . . . you said I was open. I'm not, but I am trying. It's like . . . Jolsit. He fought in the last Demon War with Kholster, impressed him enough for Kholster to make him Demon Armor out of Ghaiattri hide. He's this magnificent person, but if I asked, I know you would tell me he has a Litany because I saw its effect on him. He told me about a Vael named Merri who realized she could stop the fighting after the Sundering. He mentioned how the guards used to abuse her, and I assume he did, too, and . . . it . . . it was a happy memory for him until he looked at it in the context of the present.

"Viewed through eyes centuries old—" Dolvek's voice quivered, "—he was ashamed at how he had behaved. I was embarrassed for him. I . . . I didn't know what to say, but I am trying to use that lens of awareness to look at my own actions and . . . it's hard to like what I see. I wanted to kill Zaur because they are dirty monsters who deserve to die, but what if they aren't? Is Queen Kari right to entertain peace with this . . . Tsan person? And if she is, then . . ."

Dolvek grew silent, gazing down at where his toes touched the moss and grass carpet. Yavi kissed him on the cheek, slipping three steps away before he could react, just in case her scent and the physical contact were enough to summon the (Was "old Dolvek" the right name for someone who had changed so much in such a short span?) old Dolvek's instincts.

"I'll get you some spare clothes," she said from the door. "And, Prince?"

He looked up at her, hope in his eyes. She hoped it wasn't hope for some sort of relationship with her but for his own personal growth to continue, allowing him to become as tolerable an Oathbreaker as he could be.

"Keep thinking the way you are thinking," Yavi said. "It suits you."
Then she vanished into the corridors of the Root Tree.

*

Coal blinked, crusted rocklike nuggets of sleep crumbling and dropping free of his eyelids. Stretching the kinks out of his artificially rejuvenated muscles, he spat fire into the air to greet the dawn, only to realize it wasn't dawn. Gone were the sounds of elemancers flitting about and drilling. Around him for a quarter jun or more the ground was frozen over where he'd leeched heat in the night. A thin layer of ice over charred earth was enough to wake a chortle in his throat. How long had it been since he'd seen such a sight? How long since he'd had the heat to squander when he was not hip deep in a lava pool?

"Mighty Coal," said a warsuit he did not recognize, its helm two seahawks conjoined with three eyes, one on the outward side of each beak and a third in the center of the helm, the beaks pointing out at roughly a thirty-degree angle from each other.

"I do not like your helmet." Coal cleared his throat, coughing a few random splats of molten rock upon the ravaged soil. "Who made you?"

"We could not awaken you from your slumber," the warsuit said, "so I was tasked to await your awakening and send you to Fort Sunder."

"I missed whatever it was you wanted me to do here, then." Coal sniffed. "How did it go?"

"Please, Mighty Coal—" The warsuit's voice shook.

Was it afraid?

What scared warsuits?

Coal presumed he was the cause, but he also could not abide such rudeness.

"I asked you a question!" Coal roared. Ignorant little warsuit, to make demands of a dragon without so much as a please, a thank you, or an introduction.

"He is Twin Beak," an Eldrennai voice answered, "Mighty Coal."

Coal blinked, craning his neck around to spot the speaker. It was the same demon-armored knight who'd impressed him earlier. Joe something? Or was it Joe-el? Jessup?

"My apologies for speaking out of turn, Great Wyrm," the elf continued, gliding in to stand next to the warsuit, only to drop to one knee, fist on the ground, head bowed. "We spoke before, but I of course would not expect such a grand and glorious being as yourself to have spared any effort in remembering me. I am Jolsit and, if it pleases you, I would be happy to answer any questions you may have."

"Ah, yes, Jolsit," Coal purred. "Of course I remember—"

"There is no time for any of this!" the warsuit roared. "You have to go t—"

"Carst, rein Twin Beak in, now!" Jolsit rounded on the warsuit, going from a kneeling position to striking a closed fist backhand with a level of prowess Coal was used to seeing in Aern. "He is out of line and offending the dragon."

"But they are in danger, Jolsit and—" The warsuit stopped in mid-sentence as if he were a puppet whose puppeteer had jerked it upright, back straight, hand at its sides.

"Taking the time to grant the elder wyrm his due respect is not something one casts aside out of fear or urgency," Jolsit snarled. "I know you are frightened, but a dragon cannot be ordered about like a common soldier. His aid must be requested and, hopefully, granted. It cannot be assumed.

"My apologies," Jolsit turned back to Coal. "I—"

"What does the warsuit fear?" Coal narrowed his eyes, the concentration fanning the flames within even brighter.

"The Zaur," Jolsit answered, "have found a way to kill warsuits. All of the Armored in the Aernese army have been withdrawn from the field. One group is heading to . . . or has now arrived at . . . Fort Sunder, and another is present at Port Ammond to defend the Overwatches and kholster Rae'en, while a third group is escorting Eyes of Vengeance to meet Vander at the Halls of Healing."

"Kill warsuits? Escorting?" Coal pulled himself up to his full height, glossy black wings spread out behind him, lines of fire tracing their edges. "Why would Vander be at the Halls of Healing? Who was injured?"

"He was." Jolsit stood in the shadow of the dragon, unflinching. "Whatever the Zaur used has killed several warsuits by slaying their makers. Vander has survived for the moment, but . . . as I understand it, his connection to the Aern has been broken. Glayne has stepped in as Prime Overwatch until . . . well, until."

"But . . . how would . . . ?" Coal jolted as the realization struck him. "Pieces of the Life Forge! Yes . . . they've found some of the shrapnel from its sundering and made weapons of them. Clever little cold-blooded schemers, aren't they? Where is Kholster's little girl?" He eyed Jolsit, leaning close enough to see the elf wince at the heat.

"At Port Ammond, but they respectfully request that you fly to Fort—"

"Bah!" Coal snorted. "You go to Fort Sunder. I've seen it. Your watch cities are likely already fallen, so you should be safest there. The Zaur have scared you and drawn you away from the sites you once protected and gathered you conveniently in two spots. Where is Kholster's wife? Where is Wylant?"

"She stands atop the wall at Fort Sunder," Twin Beak answered, "but—"

"Ah, then you won't need a dragon there." Before he'd slain the hurricane and stolen its heat, prompting the return to youthful vigor—albeit a brief last gasp before the grave—taking off had required flexing and preparation. When taking off from the surface of the ship the Aern had built to carry him, he had sunk it, but now . . .

Coal sprung into the air with ease, powerful wingbeats taking him aloft. The warsuit shouted after him, a voice that was lost in the snap and shake of the wind beneath his wings. If the Eldrennai followed after him, he outpaced him, because when Coal looked back after a few jun, he was alone in the air, flying free. In a few hours he would be at Port Ammond. How long had it been since the capital city of the Eldrennai had seen a dragon? Had it been before the other dragons had departed, before he was called Betrayer? It did not seem like it could be, but then again, who among the elves had lived so long? Hasimak, perhaps?

*

<<Attack!>> Dryga ordered, seething as he waited for the Lurker to relay the command. But the booming, squealing sound came faster than he anticipated, and the Zaur were in motion. Had the Eldrennai expected them to attack by land? Foolish warmbloods. They would die for their ignorance. Teams of borers swam in first with a synchronization that reminded Dryga of the tales he'd heard of human dances, where whole lines of the stupid creatures moved as one to music. Teams of five grasped the hull of their designated target with their hind claws, drawing in the augurs strapped to their backs, and once all were in place and had signaled their readiness with a high-pitched squeaking message, the lead Lurker announced the next phase. Zaur and Sri'Zaur swam for the same ships that the borers were holing or to the edge of wood or stone and piers and berths.

A mass of Lurkers skirted along the seafloor into their own predetermined spots, ready to swim from the bottom and break the war, leaping like sharks upon the dock proper.

Dryga swam to the pier closest to the warehouse Asvrin's Shades had located, filled with thoughts of junpowder and victory, of handing Warlord Xastix not only the third vial of blood he required but also a barrel of the Dwarven secret of death. Young and eager, he swam forward, obsessed with the idea of training a squad, not just of crossbow wielders but Zaur fighting with junpowder, Zaur wielding weapons that hurled slugs of metal powered by a dash of pink powder.

*

Walking his standard patrol route along the docks, Private Jevin stopped and sniffed the air. Overhead the clouds hung heavy, promising rain before nightfall, but he smelled something else. The docks always had loads of different odors, but this wasn't fish exactly. Wrinkling his nose, he put it out of his mind.

Two sets of ten Grudgebearers stood out front of the Bimley Brothers warehouse guarding whatever cargo the Dwarf and his carnivorous friends found so blasted important. With predominantly their own ships in port it seemed a waste to have an Eldrennai patrol, but then again, it wouldn't do to let their guests feel like they could do whatever they pleased in Port Ammond, even if the new king was hells-bent on doing just that.

Rounding to the port master's office, open but unoccupied given the current state of things, Private Jevin saw a clawed, scale-covered paw reach up over the edge of the docked Aernese warship. By the time he opened his mouth to shout the alarm, he saw a dozen others. Some climbed the piers and walkways, while others disappeared into the docked vessels themselves.

"Zaur!" he shouted, wishing he was a Thunder Speaker or possessed of some other elemental magic. Merely a Geomancer grunt with little enough talent, he grabbed for his alarm whistle, put it to his lips, and blew one loud, shrill blast.

Any thought of fighting vanished. There were too many. He'd raised the alarm and done his best. He ran for the harbormaster's office. If he got inside, maybe he and the others could barricade the doors and windows. That one thought locked firmly in mind, Private Jevin reversed course, boots skidding on the damp wood.

It landed on the edge of the walkway, a gray shark-skinned horror, bigger than a Zaur but obviously related to them. Dead eyes, like on the doll he'd given his niece last birthday, stared at him as it drew two Skreel knifes from thigh-hugging sheaths. Jevin grabbed for the hilt of his sword, managing to draw it and hold it shakily.

The thing dropped to all fours and charged. *How does it run on its front paws while holding the Skreel blades like that, knobby knuckles bare on the hard wood?* He was still thinking that as it opened his belly and throat, charging on with more Zaur than Private Jevin had ever imagined he might see in its wake, Zaur after Zaur pouring upward out of the bay.

"Well," Kholster told him as he seized his soul, "at least you got your sword out even if you didn't actually do anything with it."

"Am I dead?" Jevin asked the armored figure.

"You certainly aren't alive."

"Do I go to paradise?" Jevin asked. "The white towers? I've always longed to see them. Please, even if I don't get to go there, can I have a glimpse of them?"

Kholster dragged him by the neck and took a single step. Shimmering towers of pure white glistened in the golden light of eternity. White pennants flew over fields of amber grass. Jevin gaped in awe. It was not as he imagined it. It was better, except . . .

"Where is the singing?" he asked.

"There is no singing."

"Why?" Jevin met the red crystal gaze of the death god's warsuit.

"Because there is no one here but us."

"I am the only one who made it?" Jevin could not believe that. He'd spent the last moments of his life in abject terror, trying to do nothing more than get away.

"No." The warsuit's helm opened, as if the entire irkanth's skull "face" were a cleverly constructed visor. Amber pupils rimmed by jade irises in pools of black were waiting for him. "Torgrimm sent them all back before I fought him."

"Back?"

"Reincarnation," Kholster told him.

"Like the gnomes?"

"Yes."

"But why?" Paradise could not be empty. It was impossible, but in every direction Jevin looked, he saw no sign of the revered souls he'd expected to find. He pulled free of Kholster, running toward the central tower where Shidarva or Aldo, it was said, would greet the most valiant of the dead, but the grand hall was empty. "No!" Jevin shouted. "No!"

"It's not as bad as it seems, Jevin." Kholster appeared next to the soul, already holding him by the arm. "You won't be staying here either, but you wanted to see it. So here it is."

"But why?" Jevin asked again. "Why would he send them all back?"

"Because." Kholster's grin bared doubled canines. "He was afraid of what I, or one of me, might do to them if he did not." With a wave of Kholster's gauntlet, Jevin found himself in the hands of a different god, one clad in farmer's garb, and soon he was being born to a human mother in a Guild City home.

CHAPTER 30
THE MASTER
OF ELEMENTS

Glayne got word of the attack on the harbor to Rae'en while she was still out on the Lane of Review. Hasimak had caught her eye when he returned from the Tower of Elementals. Had he sensed he would somehow be needed? In memories she'd been shown, Rae'en had seen snatches of how many of the Oathbreakers revered the Elementalist . . . as some wizened old master teacher. While she could tell that he was very old, he seemed so . . .

What did it matter? She could stand there all day studying the way the Oathbreakers and Aiannai interacted with each other—scrutinize the subtle glances that the four Elemental Nobles cast at Hasimak as if they were waiting for him to react to what King Rivvek was doing. The old Elementalist himself remained utterly neutral in a way that even Kholster had seldom managed.

Unflappable in the face of all this slaughter—wasted meat—yet this was the same Oathbreaker who had screeched and shouted when the warsuits had destroyed the Port Gates when the Ghaiattri had tried to come through. Lingering on that memory, shared with her via Eyes of Vengeance at a time when she'd taken a breath between frantic dives to find her father's bones beneath the waves of the Bay of Balsiph, Rae'en could not help but relive that moment, seeing her father burning, falling into the water.

How had it happened? How had her father's invasion resulted in this strange succession of events? Death for one king meant life for his people. But what had Kholster's death accomplished? She couldn't imagine her father wanting to be a god. Could not conceive of him striking out at Torgrimm unless there were some greater plan, but she did not know what it was.

She knew her father had planned for her to be First, but he could have appointed her First anytime he wanted to! He hadn't needed to die, so why—

A muffled cry escaped one of the Oathbreakers no Aern would claim. "But I only ever gave one order," the elf wearing a chef's apron cried. "Please!"

"You held the leash," Rae'en snapped. "Consider the years of life from then til now as merciful gift. . . . And if you want to go charging into a Port Gate to try and rescue the Lost Command, and you survive, we might even call you something interesting."

She wished King Rivvek could do this himself, though she knew she had to be there, or Bloodmane did. It was better than hiding in the castle, even if she did have to listen to Oathbreakers begging as they were dragged off to a common barracks to decide whether they wanted to die filling a Ghaiattri's belly or an Aern's.

How many of these Oathbreakers are going to turn out to be Aiannai? she thought at Bloodmane.

Many of the Leash Holders died in the Demon Wars or on Freedom Day or the war that followed, Bloodmane answered. **More than half of their current population has been born in the last six hundred years. Even among those who lived while the Aern were enslaved, there are a large number who were peasantry or who never had the occasion or authority to hold the leash.**

The warsuit gestured for those newly named Aiannai in the prince's current group to follow a cadre of knights to different barracks to receive their scars. Tears streamed down their faces, and Rae'en kept expecting to feel happy about it. Vindicated. If she had to put a name to her emotions, though, she would have picked embarrassment or shame.

They had this coming, Rae'en thought at her warsuit.

I have never argued that they did not, Bloodmane acknowledged. **I have merely argued that one need not always get what one deserves. There is no shame in mercy if no oath is broken in its granting.**

"This is mercy," Rae'en growled, drawing the looks of the king and his Elemental Nobles.

After a fashion, kholster Rae'en, Bloodmane thought. **I believe I feel about mercy the same way you might when you've finished eating a slab of your favorite meat.**

Full? Rae'en thought back at him.

I wish there were more of it.

Kholster, Glayne interrupted. *You need to see this.*

Then show me, Rae'en thought. *This sad lot is making me wish for a good clean fight.*

Glayne sent the images, but Rae'en could not tell whence he was getting them. Unfolding before her was a scene from her last journey with her father wrought large. It had been one of the first nights when she and Kholster had set out for the Grand Conjunction. So recent, for so much to have changed. When they'd made a reluctant stop, Rae'en had started to lay out her bedroll when Kholster had called her over to him. He'd broken open a beetle-infested log, the hard, shiny bodies swarming over its surface covering every scrap of wood.

"They remind me of Issic-Gnoss," he said. "If you ever fight them, remember that the ones you see are only a meager serving of the whole dish. Always be sure you don't tuck into a meal you can't finish. Even blue wasps can take down an irkanth if they swarm."

Kholster'd thrown her a piece of liver and smiled.

Those had been long days of travel with liver at every opportunity Kholster could find. Rae'en missed it, wished she could relive it once more and pay better attention, but once your parents are gone, you only have the memories you made, not the ones for which you might wish.

Zaur swarmed the harbor in unfathomable number.

"How many are there?" Rae'en asked, then remembering Kholster's words, she revised it to "How many do you count?" When Glayne did not answer, she realized she had asked aloud instead of in her mind, but Bloodmane answered.

Approximately twice the number of the combined Aern and warsuit invasion force. Ten thousand. But, Bloodmane added, **if my advice is not unwelcome . . . where there are ten thousand Zaur, there are never** *only* **ten thousand Zaur. I think we have underestimated this Warlord Xastix.**

The warehouse guards Glinfolgo asked to have assigned to his warehouse are down, Glayne sent. *Awaiting orders, kholster Rae'en. You have a small window of decision. Do we engage?*

She wanted to give the order to attack, would have done so immediately if the stupid lizards hadn't found a way to kill Armored, but now . . . with Vander down and others truly dead . . . she knew they would not hesitate to give their lives, even permanently if it served the whole, but she couldn't see how dying defending Port Ammond served the Aern at all.

What does Vander think? Rae'en asked.

We should attack, kholster Rae'en, Glayne thought. *Vander is barely conscious and—*

Glayne, you are relieved of your duties as Prime Overwatch, Rae'en thought. *Thank you for standing in, and I may need you to resume that function very soon, but I need answers right now, not arguments.*

I . . . Glayne thought back, his stung ego clear in his thoughts, but he was just as shocked at the way he'd responded to his kholster as he was embarrassed by being replaced. *I apologize, kholster.*

Apology accepted, Rae'en thought back. *Now gather up your soul-bonded weapons and get ready to use them. I'm going to need you in top fighting form faster than I think will allow you the time to collect them all.*

She watched Glayne's thoughts for a response to that and was glad to see him leap at the challenge. He was a good soldier, and it wasn't as if any Aern other than her Overwatches would have any idea what had happened . . . and even then, she had a perfectly acceptable excuse for Glayne to hide behind, if he chose to use it.

Amber! Rae'en thought hard. *I'm rotating Glayne out of the Prime slot because I need a different perspective on this and I need it now.*

I think we should retreat to Fort Sunder, Amber answered. *All the warsuits who aren't here or there already are on their way to one of the two places. We'll pull back and let the Oathbreakers handle the Zaur. Port Ammond is their city.*

Noted. Rae'en turned to Bloodmane and waved him over. *Can we move Vander?*

As Amber delivered the bad news, Rae'en pulled off her glove and placed a bare palm on Bloodmane's chest. When Kholster had touched Bloodmane's surface upon their reunion after six hundred years of exile, their fundamental differences in opinion over the fate of the Oathbreakers had caused a physical wound. But now, only a handful of days later, Rae'en's hand did not burn, did not blister as her father's had. Did this mean she had forgiven the Oathbreakers, or was it evidence Bloodmane had come to accept what must be done? Either way . . . no burn.

Are you up to being worn? Rae'en thought.

Yes.

Do you mind being worn by me?

I would be honored. You are my rightful occupant.

King Rivvek bit his lip when Bloodmane turned and split open at the back. Rae'en stepped forward and was enveloped, Bloodmane's senses and hers becoming one. If being Armored had made her feel strong and powerful, being physically one with Bloodmane brought with it a sensation of unadulterated invincibility.

Rae'en had already been wearing Wylant's bridal armor when she stepped within the warsuit, but she couldn't feel it.

How di—?

A moment, kholster, Bloodmane sent. **I am still adjusting.**

Rae'en felt a sense of inner movement as if her skin were simultaneously being stretched and shrunk. She felt trapped, unable to move; she was suffocating and then . . .

All is well, kholster Rae'en, the armor told her, and she could breathe again. **Try to move now, please.**

She rubbed the fingers of Bloodmane's gauntlets together, and it felt like skin on skin. When she breathed, Rae'en felt her nostrils flaring, the slight movement of air across her philtrum as if her face were completely uncovered.

Will it feel that way every time? Rae'en asked.

The discomfort? No. Bloodmane's thoughts were colored with shades of amusement and traces of sorrow. **You are your father's daughter, but you are not his physical duplicate. Adjustments were required. I have made them.**

How different do you look?

Fractionally smaller with slight proportional differences. Do not worry. I am quite recognizable.

But you're okay? Rae'en asked. *I didn't even think about—*

Bloodmane laughed. **It was nothing compared to the dismay I felt the first time your father decided he wanted to take off my helmet. At the time, I was not designed to allow it.**

How many Armored can wear their warsuits now? She thought, and the answer came to her. She knew the information originated from Bloodmane, but this wasn't like a conversation—it was as though there were no difference between them, as if Bloodmane were subsumed by her. The lack of an all-out war against the Oathbreakers, combined with the death of Armored and the threat to the remainder, had worked a fundamental change.

This was what Kholster's death had bought the Aern: freedom from their old oaths and the return of their warsuits.

Bloodmane's mind sank deeper and deeper within her as if he were willing to allow all that he had become to fade so that she could—

No! Rae'en thought. *If it is okay with you, unless we're in battle and don't have time, talk to me. We know you are your own people now. Kholster would have never wanted me to endanger or belittle that.*

I am never belittled by my rightful occupant, Rae'en. Love and a fierce desire to protect and aid coursed from Bloodmane to Rae'en, and she understood why the Armored referred to the warsuits as their true skins. **If you learn nothing more of me, please, know that.**

Rae'en turned her mind to Amber and saw through her eyes.

*

"—wants to know what you think?" Amber asked.

"I think . . ." Vander licked his lips, his tongue sandpaper, his breath coming in shallow wheezes. All around him, worried faces looked on. The Oathbreaker healer had gone away when Glinfolgo had started stitching him up—stitches! Vander could not believe he'd needed such things—but Amber and Feagus had not gone anywhere, even though now he could see that they wanted to. "I think . . ." He tried to find his train of thought, but it was hard to focus when he was cold.

Since when did an Armored shiver?

"Since you got stabbed by a piece of the Life Forge," he whispered to himself.

But I didn't have to whisper to keep my thoughts to myself, did I? Vander thought. *Hello! Hello!*

Blue light from Glinfolgo's floating pyramid of runestones shined in his eyes, but Glinfolgo's attention turned elsewhere. Still bent over at Vander's side, the Dwarf's thoughts and mind were otherwise occupied.

Did those green-lensed goggles let Glinfolgo see somewhere else? Vandal wondered. Dwarves had little flying spies, like dragonflies with round shiny faces they could look through in some fashion.

"I think we should ask Glin what he's seeing in those Reading Glasses of his," Vander said. "Are they connected to a Dwarven Scrystone or dragonspy?"

"Just a little bit closer," the Dwarf spoke slowly, his voice tense with concentration. "Drat! I can't get it to respond!"

"What to respond?"

"The dragonspy!" Glin growled. "I set things up so, if the warehouse were to become compromised, I could ignite the junpowder and destroy the lot, but one of those cursed Zaur knocked it out of the air, before I could set off the first Hearth Stone!"

"How many Zaur would that kill?" Amber asked.

Good, Vander thought, *we're hunting along the same path there. Amber, Feagus, and Glayne could sort it all out.* He closed his eyes and stared at the black, listening to fluttered beats of his own heart.

Kholster? he thought, and not at kholster Rae'en, but at his best friend, Kholster the death god with a capital "K."

Nothing.

Kholster, please answer me.

"Yes, Overwatch?"

*

"King Rivvek, Port Ammond is now under attack by an immense force of Zaur," Rae'en Bloodmane said, her voice sounding much sterner and more commanding when it came from behind Bloodmane's faceplate. Rivvek could not decide exactly how it worked. The armor had obviously been too large for her, yet it moved as if she were comfortable within. Was Bloodmane shorter? It had seemed to ripple for a moment. . . . "Glinfolgo attempted to destroy the warehouse full of junpowder he unloaded from our ships, but the attempt failed. We have decided to regroup at Fort Sunder. Will the Aiannai accompany the Aern?"

Great Aldo, Rivvek swore. *What a cavalier way to tell a king he's lost his capital city and you don't intend to help him keep it.*

"Will the Aern allow . . ." Rivvek began asking the question before he even knew what he was going to ask. He knew he had to make a request quickly, to use the moment to gain whatever aid he could from the Aern, but . . . it came to him. "Will the Aern allow the Eldrennai who have yet to be properly . . . sorted . . . and those who have agreed to my rescue mission . . . to accompany them to Fort Sunder along with the Aiannai?"

"As many of them as you can evacuate, but I don't see how you will mobilize them in time," Rae'en said. "How many Port Gates do you have left? And can we even use them without—"

"No, we can't use them here, the Ghaiattri are still paying too much attention, but if you would grant us access to the Port Gate at Fort Sunder—"

Hollis cleared his throat rather loudly.

Hasimak shot him a warning look, one Rivvek remembered well from his own time studying with the elder elemancer.

"You would interject, Sea Lord?" Rivvek asked.

"He would not deign to bother the king," Hasimak offered calmly. "Perhaps he requires a cup of *jallek* root tea."

"Hollis?" Rivvek asked, but the Sea Lord gave a careful shake of his head.

"My apologies, kholster Rae'en, you were say—"

Ferris and Klerris cleared their throats in unison, the twin Elementalists looking directly at Hasimak, eyes full of a message Rivvek could not decipher.

"Three cups of tea seem to be required." Smiling sweetly as if chastising a pet he knew could learn nothing from shouting, Hasimak spoke softly. "Perhaps I should go and fetch a pot. Would you or kholster Rae'en require anything, Highness?"

"He's a new king, teacher," the Stone Lord pleaded. "Ask him. Tell him."

"It is unseemly." Hasimak's voice came soft and musical as always, but he observed the Geomancer with eyes half-lidded. A smile touched those eyes, but it was a false one, born of fondness for the individual, not for his actions. It was a tricky smile. If Rivvek had not made such a study of Hasi-mak's behavior in court in preparation for the Test of Four manipulation he would have missed it, but . . .

"You have advice, High Elementalist?" Rivvek asked, a hint of amuse-ment in his voice mixed with equal parts curiosity. On the one hand, the timing was abominable . . . but in a different light who knew what color it might be. . . . These were the four who had sold the lives of the many to secure a future for their children. They had kept their king's secrets before he had truly become their king, and if any of the four of them had wanted to do so, they could have bogged the whole thing down in a civil war . . . so, mindful of the sounds of fighting just beginning to be heard from the docks, Rivvek paused to consider.

"No, Your Highness," Hasimak answered. "Another time, perhaps, when it suits the king to grant an old elf a private audience."

"There may not be time for that, Hasimak," Rivvek pressed.

"As you say, Highness."

"I mean ever."

"I understand, sire." Hasimak bowed low. "I will not press the matter."

"No," Rivvek breathed. "I do not believe you do understand. There may be no private audience because some or all of us may die escaping Port Ammond, but I believe I know my four Elemental Nobles at least well enough to know that if they would pause in the midst of an invasion to draw you out into the open about whatever this . . . is . . . it must be of grave import."

Especially since I know they were prepared to kill me if I ordered Sargus to execute you back in the throne room.

"It is a delicate matter." Hasimak dropped to his knees. "I pray let it wait until some distant day when—"

"Ask permission to defend the kingdom with your magic, Teacher," the Stone Lord growled. "I have promised not to raise the other matter. We all have, but at least—"

"I will never ask permission to use magic beyond the scope of educating my students or advising the king or his forces as required." Hasimak sighed. "The Aern are not the only ones with promises to keep or who take them as a mortal matter."

"You require permission to defend the kingdom?" Rae'en asked.

Hasimak remained tight-lipped and silent.

"Answer her, please," Rivvek said.

"Is this a royal command?" Hasimak asked.

"Must it be—yes." Rivvek shifted direction. "It is a royal command."

"And is this command meant as capital punishment, or does it supersede other relevant commands?" Hasimak's eyes were wary, cautious.

"Should it?"

"That is a question I cannot answer, sire."

"Who placed you under such restrictions, Hasimak?"

"Nor can I answer that question, at present," Hasimak trilled. "But it is a silly matter. Let us put it out of our heads. Why don't I show you an interesting bit of magic instead?" The elder elf waved the conversation away with his hand as if it were an errant puppy. "Even with your . . . noted . . . challenges in the field of elemental magic, I believe we could, if Sire were willing, help you master the ability now available to you. Would you like that?"

"He's spellsworn," Rae'en shouted, aiming an accusing gauntlet at Hasimak, "and he's been ordered not to reveal it, to lie about it if he has to do so!"

"Nonsense." Hasimak laughed. "I did not want to answer in front of the Aern, true, but it is a matter of Royal Secrets and of little interest in the middle of our current crises, so I'm sure—"

Could it be true? Could the oldest known elf have been a prisoner for all these millennia to the same magic that had bound the Aern?

"Let it be known," Rivvek began. "By Royal Proclamation, that on this date, Hasimak, Master of the Tower of Elementals, is free from all bonds, oaths, and responsibilities both private and public superseding all previous orders, proclamations, writs, and contracts. All that binds him, I revoke. Any laws restricting him in a way other than that applying to all Eldrennai citizens, I abolish. Do the Elemental Nobles concur?"

"We do," they said as one.

"I was fine. Perhaps better off. But . . . very well." Sitting down on the ground, Hasimak reached under the hem of his robes exposing heavily runed anklets on each leg that he carefully removed and set aside. Still seated, he withdrew similar pieces of jewelry from his upper arms and wrists. As he cast the articles aside, magic swelled within the ancient elf. His veins coursed with stone to the king's Ghaiattri-helmed vision. The air about Hasimak shimmered and popped. Flames rolled over and through him even as his skin took on a watery aspect.

Sighing with relief, Hasimak shed seven heavy necklaces studded with gems Rivvek did not recognize, which had hung beneath the neckline of his robes. Finally, with a delicate working of Hydromancy and Aeromancy Hasimak regurgitated an obsidian sphere the size of his fist.

Starlight shone from behind the Elementalist's eyes, his very essence thrumming with a power Rivvek did not recognize . . . not elemancy but another magic that rippled the air and set the king's teeth to humming. Just like a Port Gate? Rivvek remembered the reports he'd been given about Hasimak's shrieks when the Port Gates had been destroyed when the Armored had used them to spread themselves quickly to the watch cities. Had there been more to it than had met the eye?

"Am I required to allow those artifacts to continue to exist, Highness?" Gray bled from Hasimak's hair, leaving it a lambent white even as he gestured to the pile at his feet.

The objects themselves held dark, blood-tinged magic of a type Rivvek had only ever heard described . . . the sort of dark arts that had been used to create the Life Forge's aetheric soul hooks . . .

"No," King Rivvek answered, "you are not."

Expecting a dramatic blaze of light and color, Rivvek swallowed hard as the restraints, for that was all they could have been, withered under Hasimak's gaze, drying up like grapes unpicked on the vine until, shrunken and raisin-like, they collapsed to powder and scattered on the breeze.

"Thank you, Highness." Hasimak closed his eyes, smiling as he breathed deeply. "I would have understood if you had desired them preserved for Sargus to study, and though I still believe we might all have been better off if you had done otherwise, I must admit I am exceedingly gratified you did not so instruct."

"But, how——" Rae'en started. "I mean. This prey doesn't track at all. You're an . . . Eldrennai." Rivvek blinked at the use of the word from Aernese lips. "You don't enslave each other."

"Uled was a gifted lunatic," Hasimak said without opening his eyes. "He was a serial defiler of all the virtues and morals my people hold dear. Such creatures start with the destruction of that which is closest to them before their interests wander into more exotic pursuits."

"When your people are older," Hasimak said, looking to the Tower of Elementals as if it made his point, "you may begin to comprehend how rare the combination of genius and madness that were his curse (and his gift) truly are. But we may yet have time to discuss such things. Let me say just this, since I have so long been prevented from so doing.

"Not all of the Eldrennai remained silent, kholster Rae'en." Neither Hasimak's robes nor hair moved out of place as he lifted himself from the pavement. "I opposed your creation just as I attempted to stop Uled from experimenting with soul-binding magic and as I tried to stop his twisting of an entire species into a new one. Slavery was wrong then as it is now, and, though many thought nothing of it, I was not alone among my people. We who objected suffered for our beliefs."

"But should the question arise, do not expect me to ask for your scars upon my back. I am Eldrennai, and though you recall only the recent inglorious fourth act of my people's time upon Barrone, I can recall our golden age, our triumphs of ages past, and I shall never lose hope that we might once again rise to be all that we were . . . rise to a glory seasoned in its maturity with wisdom, mercy, and enlightenment."

"Remember this moment." He reached out with his hand, and kholster Rae'en, warsuit and all, rose into the air. "I hold you in my hand with magic too ancient for your vaunted invulnerability to defeat and yet, just as despite all those—" he gestured at the spot where his mystic chains had blown away, "—ways in which I was bound, I could not be forced to turn my magic against the innocent, I will not, now, when nothing but my conscience binds me, use it to harm a single living being. One day you may understand the mercy strength requires."

With another wave of his hand, Rae'en dropped gently to the ground.

"Hasimak—" Rivvek began.

"Lead the rescue efforts, King Rivvek." Hasimak looked upon his monarch with warmth and affection. "My apprentices and I will buy you time."

"Students." Hasimak flared his hands outward catching the Elemental Nobles up in waves of violet light.

CHAPTER 31

BAY WATCH

Five Eldrennai flew over the sprawling melee below. Non-casters, both human conscripts or Eldrennai of limited magical ability, charged down from guard stations and the lower barracks. Crews of various ships or dockworkers tried to fight for their city or to merely make it out alive. No warm-blooded beings jumped into the bay in an attempt to swim for it as gray, black, and brown-scaled reptiles swarmed out of the water in a seemingly endless stream.

Aernese ships sank in the bay, holed by crews of the gray-skinned Sri'Zaur and broken apart by others from within. As the living ceased to be called so, Kholster reaped them. Whether they were reptilian or human, he sent the souls to Minapsis. Oathbreakers went on to Torgrimm for reincarnation.

Several Zaur fell, few at the hands of the motley defensive force, but several via misadventure. Sinking a ship from within was dangerous even for creatures who could hold their breath or breathe underwater.

Fulfilling his deific purpose became a secondary concern; Kholster could do it thoughtlessly. Perhaps rote performance was the nettle of concern growing at the back of Kholster's mind in addition to his other more pressing issues. Torgrimm had been thoughtful in the execution of his duties. Kholster pushed the thought aside and watched for signs of interference. He looked through the eyes of other Kholsters, too, but it didn't work as well as it had when Vander—"That hasn't been seen for nigh on a thousand years." Nomi, her hair composed of living fire and hanging down to the middle of her back, appeared next to Kholster, who walked through the combatants even as others of him watched from the tops of buildings.

How did she decide which one was the primary Kholster, he wondered. *And does she know she got it wrong?*

Nomi wore loose-fitting trousers, her sandal-clad feet hovering two hands above the ground, putting her close to eye level with the eighteen-hands-tall Aern. She was still the same apparent age as when she'd stolen a portion of Dienox's godhood. Based on appearance alone, Kholster would have guessed she had not quite hit her second decade of life. Strikingly beautiful in an aggressive way, her eyes were warm but calculating, as if she could not help but take the measure of everyone and everything and felt discomforted by that trait. Her top was actually a wide scarf vest over a silk blouse.

Kholster did not know why it surprised him that she rarely donned reds or oranges to match her hair, favoring natural, earthy tones instead. A mix of ethnicities played in her features, but they were from a time before Kholster had been forged, and he only recognized some of the influences. Being a goddess had not changed her. Which was part of the problem, he realized. If it was a problem. Kholster had not yet decided if he had the right to declare such. Nomi was his senior, even if the thousands of years she had spent as a goddess had done little to expand her horizons.

Horizons.

One Kholster argued with Kilke. Another tracked Dienox's every movement. Another spoke with Aldo, and elsewhere, not far from here, the prime Kholster spoke to an old friend and tried to ignore the pain in his head and the way the world had shifted to black and white with so many different Kholsters going about their duties and so many other Kholsters doing things that did not involve the collection of mortal souls at all.

He'd had such grand notions of the conflict his apotheosis would necessitate, but the gods acted like spoiled nobility, plotting and scheming and committing their dirty deeds through intermediaries. They did not, unfortunately, all deserve to die. Xalistan and Gromma still did what they had done since their creations. They had taken on mortal aspects but rarely used them. Yhask and Queelay were largely guiltless as well. But the more human the god, the more that being had forgotten his or her role of guiding and enlightening mortals rather than playing games with them.

One last test, the Prime Kholster told him. *We've questioned Aldo about the levels of interference that are acceptable. Tested them with Wylant. Now we need to know how much he's holding back. Can you do it?*

You ought to know the answer to that, Kholster thought back. *You're me.*

Our divergent perceptions are taking longer and longer to combine. Your plan should resolve the issues before we end up irreconcilable like we did with Bloodmane.

Are you going to take the Overwa—? Kholster asked.

I am going to take one of them.

Kholster hated to think of the choice he had to make, but he needed assistance or more power . . . and the laws governing ascendancy precluded personal power grabs outside of the game they all seemed so interested in playing. Thousands of years of mystic enslavement, the need to work within the confines of his orders (or rules) while accomplishing as much of what he needed to get done as possible, even the need to find a loophole in an oath he or one of his soldiers had taken, had left Kholster with a surprising skill he had not realized he possessed until—

In short, there were rules, but there was also room for interpretation.

"Hello, Overwatch," more than one of him said at the same time. It was almost time for the first god to fall. Just a few tests first to see if his suppositions were correct . . .

Perception shifting, Kholster noticed only distantly when the five Eldrennai, Hasimak accompanied by four Elemental Nobles, flew overhead on a wave of dimensional magic. Ozone and iron scented the air, carried on an unseasonably warm breeze. Klerris always had preferred summer air, and it left Kholster wondering if that was because her sister favored flame.

Flames . . .

Nomi's hand rested on Kholster's shoulder, warm and inviting. The sensation shocked him, sending him back to his first studding before his skin had adjusted completely to filter out variations of temperature. He wanted her, but that went without saying. Nomi was that sort of female; it was in the way she moved and breathed. Fortunately it had been millennia since Kholster had been unable to control such urges . . . and he was beginning to suspect that Wylant would prefer it if he saved that type of physical affection for her alone.

"I don't want your hands on me," Kholster said simply. "We are not married and I am overfond of the sensation."

Between steps he both summoned and was clad in Harvester, putting a nice safe layer of bone-steel between himself and the fiery goddess.

Are we reaping Nomi, sir? Harvester asked.

Not her, Kholster sent. *Not yet. Not at all if she behaves as I think she may.*

"I think I'll take that as a compliment." Nomi rubbed the fingers of the offending hand together as if feeling traces of him on the tips of them. "How are you doing? Torgrimm asked me to check in on you from time to time, and the last time I tried you were busy being married and before that, you were still getting settled in."

Hasimak thrust out his hands, sprays of power invisible to the mortals below, but obvious to Kholster and Nomi, lurched forth to generate a rapidly developing shield. Gaining prismatic iridescence, the barrier spread from the edges of his palms, fanning outward and flowing down to seal off the docks. Some Zaur made it through, but the bulk of them crashed into the barrier.

Kholster, one of him, examined the source of Hasimak's power: a tightly woven cord spooling out as the ancient Eldrennai moved into position. Pulsing with dimensional energy from the few Port Gates that remained intact, the crackling thrum of the magic disturbed any being who passed through it. Birds flew around the cord, which stretched not only to the gates at Port Ammond, but also one lonely strand led back to Fort Sunder, and three others flowed Kholster knew not where. He could have known, but that was a snake's trail down which he felt no need to hunt.

Being able to know most anything so easily led to vanishing off on journeys of discovery, which left him wondering what he had intended to accomplish by seeking the answer out.

"Knowledge is not always empowering," he whispered. "Too much can paralyze."

"That does not sound like the answer to my question." Nomi cocked her head, attempting to decode him.

One Kholster distracted Torgrimm. Another flew alongside Dienox pretending to marvel at the sight of Coal in flight. A third waited for Aldo to swap out his eyes to see the fight differently.

"How am I? My wife still loves me." Kholster smiled. "My half-born son is happy. My warsuit is getting along very well with Irka, my artistic son, even though the two of them think I do not know. My daughter is coming into her own in a much different world than I imagined for her, but she wears my old friend and makes her own decisions. She could have enslaved him, but she did not. I am a proud father."

"That's good." Nomi narrowed her gaze. "But it sounds like you're leaving a few things out. Want to talk about it?"

"With Aldo listening?" Kholster shook his head. "No. I think I will take action instead."

"Action?" Nomi turned at the first shout of "Kholster" that went up among the combatants. "You just became visible to the mortals."

"Did I?" Kholster asked. "Should I do something meaningless for them to ponder?" He pointed at the warehouse hosting Glinfolgo's junpowder with one finger and at Nomi's flaming hair with the other. Eyes fixed upon the five elemancers, Kholster caught Hollis's eye first. "See how they react?"

"Did you just make me visible?" Nomi raised an eyebrow. "How?"

"You touched me," Kholster answered. "Until you leave my proximity, if I'm visible, then you are as well."

"I didn't know that," Nomi said.

"Most don't seem to know it," Kholster said as casually as he could.

*

In a semi-dark square of stone, Aldo took out his Aernese eyes and dropped them into the box. When he reached for the next pair of eyes he wanted, the box was gone.

Are you going to tell her how it works? Harvester asked.

No.

Or how you made such a discovery?

No. Kholster let amusement color his response. *Why? Do you think I should?*

You do seem fond of her, sir.

Don't get too attached, Kholster sent. *I've killed a lot of people I liked.*

Kholster pointed overhead at the spot in the air over the warehouse upon which he and Nomi stood. Kholster grinned when Dienox became visible, trying to shift the Hydromancer's attention (Kholster assumed) only to become briefly visible as one of Kholster appeared in the air between them, watching. Nomi traced his gaze and gasped to see one of Kholster standing next to each living being, walking with them, keeping guard.

"Can they see all of you?" Nomi asked.

"No." Kholster's answer was softly spoken, his eyes on Hollis signaling to Zerris and Klerris. "Only one of me at a time is subject to the visibility phase-matching."

The twin Aeromancer and Pyromancer diverged, Klerris breaking off after Hollis, and Zerris heading straight for the warehouse. Lady Air and the Sea Lord flew over the open bay, a column of water rising up to meet them. Zaur and Sri'Zaur swam into the column, trying to disrupt its magic, but the Sea Lord ignored the implied threat, ice forming in a thin layer at the top, pushing down and out to establish a stable platform from which to cast. Sri'Zaur swam up the stream, attempting to break through the layer of ice.

Working together with Klerris, the two began to funnel a mass of water into a skyward funnel. While Hasimak hung in the air, maintaining his mystical blockade, Zerris swept down at the warehouse, unleashing a cone of fire.

"You told her to do that." Nomi nudged Kholster. "That's cheating."

"Demand that I be penalized." Flames engulfed the gods but did not touch them. "Though I believe you'd be surprised by what is and is not considered breaking the rules of your game."

"Why don't we ask him at least," Nomi said.

"Go ahead." Kholster nodded.

"Aldo?" Nomi asked.

When the god did not appear at once, Nomi chewed her bottom lip.

"Did you truly believe that would blind me?" Aldo chuckled, golden light pouring from his empty eye sockets. Kholster stood across from him, a slight smile on his lips, baring one set of doubled canines.

"No," Kholster told him.

"Then why did you do it?" Aldo asked.

*

Kholster dropped through the ceiling of the warehouse intangibly, leaving Nomi blinking on the roof. Inside, several Zaur grabbed armloads of rifles and shot, and two sets of two carried junpowder barrels between them. At the entrance two more Sri'Zaur stood, holding the doors closed until the time was right to dash out with their haul.

Crossing the scuffed and well-used floorboards, Kholster passed directly through the bed Glinfolgo had set up for himself. Leaning against the doors, Kholster waited for Nomi to join him.

"What do you mean by that?" Nomi dropped to the floor. "There are rules, Kholster. They lost Kilke one of his heads, they—"

Flames licked their way through the ceiling.

*

<<We have to go. Now!>> one of the Sri'Zaur pounded with its tail. <<There are shadows waiting at either end of the harbor. All of the Zaur on my left head left. Zaur on my right, head right.>>

When they ran to the door, the black-scaled Sri'Zaur on either side tried to throw it open, but the door did not move.

*

"If you aren't going to answer me," Aldo chided, "then perhaps there is some way in which I can be of service. Did you want to watch the assault on Port Ammond? It has been ages since Hasimak was off the leash. Coal headed that way, so perhaps we will have a rematch?"

Aldo had grown slightly taller in response to Kholster's tomfoolery, but subsided to his more gnomish proportions as he regained self-control.

"We may, but I am not here to watch your scrying mirrors."

Around them, Aldo's study reappeared in its former state of impressive size and contents. Wherever Kholster turned his attention, the spot he'd just been watching filled with the necessary details.

*

"Kholster," Nomi asked. "What are you doing?"

"Do you know why beheading Kilke's center head failed to kill him?" Kholster asked.

"Because they didn't specifically state that he would have to give up his life," Nomi said. "So Aldo ruled that—"

"Torgrimm did not reap him," Kholster interjected. "I would argue the agreement between the gods, not some binding set of universal rules, was what worked. Kilke submitted to the punishment, but only out of an (ironic) sense of honoring the game. Good sportsmanship."

"Kholster, what are you doing?" Torgrimm appeared out of thin air, bringing with him the scent of fresh rained-upon grass and the warm scent of the planting season. His ears, even after such a short span after the separation of Sower and Reaper, had already begun to shift to a more human shape. His garb was that of a Hulsite farmer: simple but well made and often mended. There was even dirt under his fingernails.

"Testing an idea I have." Kholster unslung his warpick. "I did not break the rules by appearing to a crowd because gods do that sometimes." He hefted Reaper in his hands and watched as, toward the center of the ware-house, the roof collapsed, one of the falling timbers killing one half of a two-person barrel-carrying team. Torgrimm flinched as the Zaur's soul was reaped and sent to Minapsis all without the Kholster to whom he was speaking missing a syllable.

"But all gods are bound by oaths that—" Torgrimm began.

"I died," Kholster answered. He swung his warpick into the soul of a Sri'Zaur trying to force open the warehouse door. "And in death—" Kholster seized the Sri'Zaur soul one-handed, slinging Reaper onto his back without breaking eye contact. "—all oaths are redeemed. I wondered, at first, if, perhaps, it hadn't counted as death, but if it hadn't, then the Aern would still be bound by my oaths.

"But I can feel the oaths by which I am bound, and I feel nothing."

"What is this?" hissed the Sri'Zaur. "Why are you here? Where is Kilke?"

"You have my apologies." Kholster shifted his grip to the spirit's throat, choking it into silence, its claws raising sparks as it scraped at Harvester's armor. ". . . but I am making a point." His fist growing tighter around the Sri'Zaur's neck, the spirit deformed, head distending.

Around them, Aldo's array of scrying surfaces, the twirling mercury-like liquid mirrors, prisms, reflective surfaces in all shapes, sizes, and construction swarmed around the god of knowledge. Multiple images of Port Ammond, Fort Sunder, a chamber in Hearth, where the Twin Trees hosted their first Sri'Zaur general. Even images of Coal, the great black dragon, could be found.

"Are you watching Port Ammond?" Kholster set the box of eyes back down on Aldo's desk.

"Of course," Aldo said. "Why?"

"Because one of me appears to have gone rogue."

*

"No!" Torgrimm leapt toward Kholster, clutching at his arm.

"If I hated the Sri'Zaur in my grasp," Kholster spoke softly, "I suspect you could stop me from harming it, but I am death. I am the reaper. When Reaper and Sower were united, it would have been unthinkable, but in allowing this to happen, you have altered one of the few fundamental lynchpins of reality. Death need not be a cycle. Death can be an end." Closing his fist, Kholster felt the Sri'Zaur's spirit burst beneath his gauntleted hands. "Death may nullify life."

Taking two steps back, Nomi summoned a sword and shield of flame, but Kholster remained where he was.

"I thought you would have mercy," Torgrimm wept.

"I do." Kholster felt the warmth of tears on his own cheeks and was glad the Sower could not see them. It made the next step easier for the other gods to believe. "But there is less of it than there was. Bloodmane, as you may recall, was a part of me. While joined, even though we were physically separate, we shared a soul in a way I did not fully comprehend. In a sense, my warsuit forgave the Eldrennai because part of me wanted to forgive them. The trouble we had connecting was a sign of that conflict: one part ready, trying to move on, and the other part, the Oathbound portion, unwilling and unable to release its grip on the past."

Kholster's gauntlet opened, and the shattered spirit of the Sri'Zaur scattered into ether.

*

"What are you—?" Aldo gasped. "No. What is he thinking, this rogue self of yours?"

"Don't you know?" Kholster shrugged.

Grabbing a pair of eyes worked in obsidian, amber, and jade, Aldo popped them into his eye sockets. He blinked, brows furrowed. "I can't see."

*

"Aldo," Torgrimm shouted, "I demand an amercement!"

*

Now? a familiar presence thought at Kholster.

Now, Kholster sent. It was so good to hear his thoughts again.

The warpick's point sank deep into the gnome-like god's skull. Star trails burst forth in semi-liquid streams, flowing through the air like colored oil through water. Eyes blinking blindly, mouth agape, Aldo hurled bolts of light at Kholster, one burning a hole through his shoulder and another through his thigh, but the death god stood still, waiting for Aldo's death throes to subside, before taking two balls of obsidian, jade, and amber from his pocket and placing them back in the box.

Kholster left the nonmagical eyes, perfect replicas Irka had made, in Aldo's eye sockets, not wanting to interrupt the power exchange that was underway. By the time the bald-headed Aern who'd wielded Reaper knelt over the helpless body of the god of knowledge, doubled canines breaking the skin as he began to eat, Kholster had already pulled Aldo's soul free. No need to prolong his pain.

"What are you going to do with me?" Aldo's spirit asked.

Kholster, one of him, took Aldo with him without answering, leaving the new god of knowledge to his gruesome meal.

*

"Aldo?" In answer to Torgrimm's cry, Kholster concentrated on the fragments of the burst soul, eyes narrowing, amber pupils glowing as the spirit flowed back together. He handed the confused creature to Torgrimm. "I don't think he handles that sort of thing anymore. But if you'd like to speak to his successor, I'll call him."

Vander, the new god of knowledge, formerly Second of One Hundred, stepped into the light.

At that moment, the warehouse exploded.

CHAPTER 32
OVERWATCH

Gazing back at the shield of force blocking off the harbor as she ran, Rae'en couldn't help but jump at the sound of the explosion that came from beyond its quasi-visible arc. Around her, Oathbreakers screamed, covering their ears. A human child fell onto the cobbles, abrading his hands and knees. Rae'en scooped him up from the path of a carriage carrying people important or rich enough to afford one and tossed the squawking, bleeding thing to the human female who looked the most concerned by his fate.

Such a strange sensation to realize even though she'd been startled and slow to react, Bloodmane hadn't, so to a non-Aern observer, Rae'en suspected she seemed an unfazed creature, more bone-steel than flesh, of the sort others had come to fear when they pictured the Armored. The grooved bone-steel boots of Bloodmane wreaked havoc on the street, but no one was complaining to her.

A second explosion shook the ground and rattled the air, but Rae'en scarcely paid it any heed. Things were too busy. Working with Rivvek's forces, the Aern, Eldrennai, Aiannai, and humans were evacuating Port Ammond, the parts of it they could reach, as quickly as they could. It helped that the guards had already been gathering the citizenry into small groups for the multiple audiences with the king—the deadly game of live, serve, or die with which King Rivvek had been presenting them.

There was fighting beyond the city gates, too. A large force of Zaur and Sri'Zaur crossbowmen as well as a sizable infantry was in place, but they hadn't been prepared for the Aern not to try to hold the city, so the warsuits had pushed through and waged a fluid war of unknowable formations, breaking into splinters to re-form or break off again as needed.

I ought to be out there, she thought.

The tokens in the corner of her mind map flashed black for disagreement, but Amber spoke up from where she and a small force were preparing Vander for transport.

It's up to you, kholster, Amber thought, *but the warsuits are fighting so hard because they've already lost some Makers and they are terrified of losing you. None of us will tell you not to do it, but this isn't a charge. If it were, you would lead it. This is a strategic withdrawal . . .*

Vander is gone, Bloodmane interrupted.

In the same instant, Amber and Feagus both transmitted images of what had happened in the Hall of Healing. Vander had lain on his stretcher, strapped in as gently and safely as Glinfolgo could manage, his breathing slow, nigh imperceptible when . . . it stopped. His eyes snapped open, wide amber pupils blazing with light and then . . . the sheets and straps collapsed upon an empty frame. Glinfolgo, whose elbows had rested heavily at the injured Aern's side, slid forward and snapped one of the carrying poles as he struggled for balance.

Kholster . . . uh . . . Kholster Rae'en? called a friendly and familiar mind. *I'm sorry we're running so late. After your father ascended, these knights started chasing us . . . a lot of knights really. We got—well, we had help—only two people, but one of them is a really powerful crystal twist and the other is this dubiously trustworthy human who says he knows you.*

Kazan? Rae'en stopped dead in the road, ignoring the thump as a human behind her tripped as he tried to swerve around and avoid her.

Me and . . . um.

I am here as well, kholster Rae'en, Eyes of Vengeance sent. **It is my duty to inform you that Kazan is now Second of One Hundred.**

Another explosion went off in the distance, but this time Rae'en had no urge at all to glance back at the smoke rising beyond the shield. Up ahead, King Rivvek was calling her name, but she didn't care about him either.

Are you all—? Rae'en began.

I think I can link us, Kazan thought. And then Arbokk, M'jynn, and Joose were all there, their tokens alongside those of her current Overwatches.

Bloodmane, Rae'en thought, *can you?*

She tried to come up with the words for what she wanted but could not decide how exactly one asked one's warsuit if it could take over for the present and keep you running where you were supposed to be running and give a shout if something required your attention.

Yes, kholster Rae'en, Bloodmane answered. **I will take the lead for the moment. You will be notified should anything arise requiring your attention.**

Thanks, Bloodmane. Rae'en thought, then to Kazan: *Are you all okay?*

*

Rae'en cursed at the long list of Kazan's injuries. They impressed Kazan, too. He could picture the fight in his head but couldn't reconcile how he'd let himself get cornered as he had. Eye punctured, lower jaw literally ripped loose by a kick from a horse, disemboweled by his final opponent even as he killed the knight in return. When the left arm had come off he couldn't pinpoint. Rae'en assured him the memory would return, and though he didn't know how she knew that, he believed her.

What are they going to do for your jaw? Rae'en asked. *They did find your jaw, didn't they?*

Still looking.

How many knights did you kill? Rae'en asked.

Kazan wanted to quip back at her, but suddenly there were other Overwatches in his head as if he were present in two different conversations at once. He continued the one with Rae'en, giving her the information she requested, while simultaneously relaying and responding to appropriate requests from the Armored in the field, taking all the guidance Eyes of Vengeance had to offer. He didn't follow all of the warsuit's advice, but with Eyes, he made sure to explain his reasons for not doing so, giving the warsuit a chance to refine, agree, or dispute his calls. Kazan kept waiting for Eyes of Vengeance to ask about Vander, but the warsuit reacted as if it was not at all disturbed to have lost Vander and have a young little biter in his place.

She wants total kills, Amber told him. *Don't give her a hard time.*

I think I know how to talk to Rae'en, Kazan sent back, closing his good eye to get rid of the overlap created by seeing through the eyes of Eyes of Vengeance via his missing eye. The warsuit, escorted by a small squad, had detoured to an Oathbreaker farm so that he could "**Better deal with your injuries, Kazan,**" whatever that meant.

Kholster Rae'en, Amber corrected. *She is your kholster, not your childhood playmate to—*

She's both, Kazan snapped. *And we've been out of contact for quite a long time for Aern our age. Rae'en is stressed. She lost her father and then got him back, but not the way she wants.*

He became a god! Feagus thought, pride painting his thoughts.

And she would rather have her father back, Kazan sent, *here and in charge where she could talk to him and learn from him.*

Eyes of Vengeance was talking to a terrified old human hired hand in homespun garb when the farmer came in shouting.

You don't know that, Amber thought, *and I'm Prime at the moment, so . . .*

Actually. Kazan sent a mental challenge, startling Glayne, Feagus, and Amber as their tokens rearranged themselves on one of Kazan's mental maps. He had several now: one for each grouping of Armored Aern. Kholster's old Overwatches were immediately reshuffled and relegated to the same positions they'd held Vander had been Prime. *I'm Second and that means I'm automatically Prime Overwatch unless Rae'en decides otherwise. Sorry you had such a short time of it, but none of you know Rae'en as well as me and my other Overwatches do.*

It might not be wise to antagonize them, Kazan, Eyes of Vengeance spoke in his thoughts.

Bird squirt, Kazan thought. *Thanks. Sorry. Wait. What?*

One of his maps appeared to flash purple behind the others, needing his attention. Not seeing the immediate problem faced by the group of warsuits, he popped into Crimson Smile's point of view and directed the armor to scan back to the southwest.

Smoke rose in the distance. Kazan pulled back, assembling the maps as best he could to guess the location of the fire. In The Parliament of Ages, between South Watch and Silver Leaf City. He sent the information to Amber, Feagus, Glayne, and their warsuits.

I don't have a recent map of the area, Kazan added, *but is that close to anything important other than the Oathbreaker watchtower and the human city? It feels like one of the Armored knows something about it, but you know them better than me, so you might find it faster.*

Never mind, Eyes of Vengeance thought at him. **They will respect that, too.**

Respect what?

Your scope of vision, Eyes of Vengeance answered. Kazan spared the warsuit a moment, watching as the now subdued farmer was hung by his feet from a branch outside his home.

Whoa! Ask him again before you do that, Kazan ordered. *Um, please.*

You think he will have changed his mind?

Replaying the events in his display triple-time so he could get the gist of them—it wasn't as if he'd been listening to the whole exchange at the time—Kazan laughed. Laughing hurt, but that the pain remained, an ever-present status report, was a pleasure and a wonder.

Will he let you kill his only cow instead of killing him? Uh . . . yeah.

But he said his family would starve . . . Eyes of Vengeance replied.

Trust me, Kazan thought. *He'll have become more creative since you gagged him. Why did you gag him?*

His cries were disturbing the cow . . .

In the back of his mind, Kazan argued with Kholster's Overwatches, but Eyes of Vengeance was correct. Apparently his way of looking at the river of perception that now flowed through the warsuits was unique enough an approach that they found it impressive.

All I'm doing is applying what kholster Malmung taught us, Kazan sent to his other set of Overwatches: Arbokk, Joose, and M'jynn.

That and what we worked out on the way up, Arbokk sent.

Who knew we were so mold-breaking? Joose asked.

Everyone was hoping your mold was broken, M'jynn teased.

You are correct, Eyes of Vengeance interrupted, he is now quite willing to let us purchase the animal.

Why do you need the cow? Kazan asked.

You are not used to being Armored, Kazan, by Mraskr, out of Serah. Eyes of Vengeance told him. Now it is your turn to trust me.

CHAPTER 33
THE THING

Winter was off its leash for the day, roaming the Broken Plain ahead of schedule. Nothing unusual for a part of the kingdom where, ever since the Sundering, there could be snow in summer or unbearable heat in the midst of winter. Wylant noticed the cold only because she'd asked Clemency to allow it for the moment. The experience of being one of the Armored took adjustment.

Below, in the courtyard of pearlescent bone, she could feel the eyes of soldier and Bone Finder alike. Who knew what they thought of her now. Worse than wondering would have been asking them. They would have told her, she was certain of that, but she didn't want to know. Knowing would have made it all too solid.

"I will never have to fight my king again," she told the air, and it carried her words away without comment, seeking vulnerable creatures to freeze.

Off in the little village not far from the mesa upon which Fort Sunder stood, a handful of village children gazed up at the Fort and told tales of what might go on behind those walls. From her place upon the battlements, Wylant wondered if any but the sharpest-eyed among them would notice she was not one of the Aern.

You may find out soon enough, Wylant thought, eyes squinting against the wind as it changed direction erratically.

"Hard to hunt in this kind of weather," she imagined Kholster saying, "have to guess which direction is going to be upwind or down from your prey and for how long."

Helmet off and cradled under one arm, Wylant watched the path from Port Ammond, wondering how long until the refugees began to arrive and how far behind or ahead of them the Zaur force would arrive. Vax slid out of her sheath, slithering up to coil and perch on Wylant's shoulder. This was not how she had hoped to watch the suns set with her son the times she had imagined it over the years, but her eyes watered all the same.

Do we want to tell them? Clemency asked.

"Tell who what?" Wylant asked.

Kazan, the new Second of One Hundred, is attempting to determine the source of a fire, Vax thought, *in The Parliament of Ages to the southeast of Fort Sunder between South Watch and Silverleaf.*

Based on what I've seen the times you've flown back and forth in the last thirteen years, Vax thought, *and when you encountered him when you went to approve the Vael representative to the final Grand Conjunction, Clem and I think it is near the Root Tree Tranduvallu.*

Wylant took a deep breath, opening her mouth to curse, and sneezed. While her mind processed the Zaur scent in her nostrils, Vax was already moving along her arm. Dropping low, sweeping her leg out and trusting Clemency to keep her from tumbling off the wall, Wylant grunted as her calf struck a meaty reptilian limb. Wielding a dagger-shaped Vax, she struck at the unseen creature, blade cutting deep, the edge scraping bone.

There are two, Clemency shouted in her head. **Permission to mark your vision, ma'am?**

Do it, Vax ordered before Wylant could respond.

Wondering where she'd dropped Clemency's helm when she spun, Wylant chuffed to find the helmet still attached to the side of her armor. Wylant sneezed twice more in rapid succession, then her vision blurred as she fought to keep her eyes open despite the sneezing. Two Sri'Zaur shaded into view before her eyes, like smoke filling a shaped glass but rimmed with firelight as if the glass were still hot and being blown.

I'll mark them as I see them, then.

No time to wonder why her allergies were back or whether she'd always had them and it was now only the divinely enhanced aspect of them that was gone, she snapped on her helm as Clemency and Vax more than Wylant parried a stab from one of her Sri'Zaur assailants.

Hey, Vax shouted in her head, *I think I've felt that metal before! Parry another one with me, Mom. See if you can get into a clinch with it and—*

"Why don't I just kill them and you can examine the weapons after, eh?" Wylant coughed.

With Clemency's helmet securely in place it was easier to breathe, which seemed counterintuitive. Wylant had always found full helms stifling. Even if they were well ventilated, there was always that moment when she found herself gasping for breath and wanting to tear the thing off her head.

One of the two assassins leapt and so did Wylant. Grasping at her magic, she took flight just long enough to dodge and pivot, her feet shooting past the edge of the battlements over empty space, then back onto solid ground. Her would-be killer found its balance quickly, readying for another strike. Its partner gawped for the briefest of moments but more than long enough for Wylant to sling Vax out from dagger (his excess metal coiled around her forearm) to a long sword, cleaving the beast's head in twain: bisected a half inch above its jaw.

Nice shot, Mother! Vax laughed. *I don't think we've ever inflicted that death-blow before.*

"Have you sent the alarm to the other warsuits, Clemency?" Wylant asked.

No, ma'am, Clemency answered, **but I am certain they are aware.** The crossbow bolt suddenly jutting out of the back of the second Sri'Zaur's neck confirmed that readily enough. **They don't know what to think of us.**

"It doesn't matter what they think." Wylant smiled then sneezed inside her helm. "And yes, tell this Kazan whatever he wants to know about your theories." She sneezed again, breath coming in a series of tight wheezes. "And please, help me find some *jallek* root?"

*

Acrid relief arrived in the form of a bit of shredded *jallek* root so old and shriveled Wylant wondered if it was a dose she had left behind on her last trip to Fort Sunder all those years ago. Wylant watched as, along the walls and battlements and in the courtyards and buildings of Fort Sunder, warsuits patrolled in grid-like patterns looking for more hidden reptiles. They hadn't found any other assassins, but that did not stop them from patrolling in greater numbers and more actively than before, even to the point of shifting their coverage at apparently random intervals to make it harder for stealthy infiltrators to go undetected. It actually seemed to have lifted their spirits. She had to chuckle at that. Give an Aern or a warsuit a problem to solve or an enemy to hunt, and they're happy.

Vax, far more prone to wandering since their link had been completed, rested in her lap looking like a crudely fashioned figure of a metal cat. Lacking a proper sense of the importance of a good mattress, the billet in which she sat was appointed with a hard metal berth, little more than a flat bench attached to the wall, a chair, and a worktable. There was likely a bed in her old quarters, the ones she had shared with Kholster. He would have thought of that long before she completed her trip from Port Ammond.

I should fly out to meet the king, she thought for the hundredth time. *Mazik and the Sidearms have it handled*, she countered. He had Bash, too, and the combined might of the Eldrennai and Aernese Armored military—as far as that went—and Sargus would look after the king in a way Wylant knew he would no other. Hard to believe any seed of Uled's could find praise in her thoughts, but Sargus was proof that there was no such thing as bad blood. She pitied the Zaur who tried to kill the king Sargus protected.

Still she thrummed her gauntleted fingers on the worktable, trying to put herself in the mindset not only of Warlord Xastix or Kholster but also King Rivvek. Xastix had attacked the Overwatches with assassins. Cutting off enemy lines of communication made sense. More so with the Aern because it had so rarely been managed in anything but a temporary manner and even then only through tricks or extremely unlikely circumstances.

Attacking Port Ammond from the sea made sense as well.

"But what do they have to gain from letting the Eldrennai evacuate to Fort Sunder?" Wylant sucked at a wiry strand of *jallek* root that had worked itself between two teeth as she chewed thoughtfully. "Why not crush them at Port Ammond? Pierce the irkanth's heart and be done, as it were?"

Had it been a matter of them failing to account for Hasimak's power? Even she had not known the extent of his abilities. Now the armor network was alive with assembled memories, any interaction the High Elementalist had had with any of the Armored compiled together as a batch of recollections to be explored and examined freely by one and all. There wasn't much there other than to confirm Hasimak had never held the leash. He'd kept to himself and his students unless forced to appear at state functions. She'd always respected the old elf, known he was old, but not quite how ancient—

"Hasimak held off the Zaur with the help of the Elemental Nobles?"

Yes, Clemency answered. **Glayne left one of his soul-bonded weapons behind to continue to observe.**

"And then what?" Wylant steepled her hands, eyes closed. When she still saw through Clemency's eyes she imagined the sensation of shutting her eyelids again, the second time bringing the inner dark she wanted.

They remain in place and continue resisting, Clemency said. **The Elementalists traveling with the evacuees are weaker without their assistance, but King Rivvek and Kholster Rae'en's combined forces have been able to successfully repel all attempts to hinder the retreat to Fort Sunder.**

"Can you show me one of them, please?" Wylant watched the harrying attacks unfold. After the fourth, she cursed. "Are you doing what I think you're doing, Warlord?"

Ma'am? Clemency's thoughts were tinged with mild confusion.

She knows he can't hear her, Vax sent. *She's just working it through. Like a kholster whispering into her hands.*

"The Zaur are resistant to magic." Wylant leaned back in her chair, drawing a deep breath and picturing the path from the port to Fort Sunder. "But not immune like the Aern."

Correct, Mother, Vax chortled. *I must admit I respect their ingenuity.*

I do not follow.

I do, a young male voice whispered in her mind. *Well done, kholster Wylant. Are you available to lead an escort to intercept the evacuees?*

"Who the—?"

It is the Prime Overwatch, Kazan, Clemency explained. **You said you did not mind if I shared information with him.**

"Two things." Wylant stood, eyes snapping open, and sheathed Vax. "He read your mind, not mine?"

Of course.

"I have no objection to that, if you don't." Striding for the door, she asked the second thing, it only now dawning on her that they'd referred to this Kazan person as the new "Second of One Hundred." "Wait. What happened to Vander?"

He died and passed on his warsuit, Eyes of Vengeance, to Rae'en's initial Prime Overwatch.

"Just his warsuit?" Wylant floated down the hallway and out on to the ramparts again, exactly where she had stood when the assassins attacked.

"Tell Kazan I may be needed here, please." Wylant muttered.

You could think to him, if you wished.

"I don't wish." Wylant ran gauntlets over the black stubble on her scalp. Soon she'd have to attempt a hairstyle again. "Vander, though. He gave Kazan his warsuit?"

Yes.

"His warpick, too?"

Yes.

"His memories or skills?"

Neither.

"So, like Kholster then?"

I suppose. Clemency paused. The sensation of that break in conversation, the conveyed knowledge that more words were coming, but the warsuit needed a moment or two to think things through was one of the best things about mental communication. Never having to guess what the other person grasped or didn't . . . never being unsure about whether or not to fill a silence.

Down in Bark's Bend, the village at the edge of the Shard River, Wylant spotted the tiny shapes of villagers. What did they make of the renewed life breathed into the fortress so nearby? Did they worry? Were they reassured? Did they wonder if they would once again be paid in bone-steel for cattle ranching? The news of King Rivvek's death sentence would not have reached them, yet, but then . . . how many of Bark's Bend's simple folks would have ever had the chance to give any Aern an order?

There are no warsuits at Oot, Clemency answered eventually, to allow me to fully answer the question of how closely the actions of Vander, post-death, have mimicked those of your husband.

"I could always ask him . . ." Even at that simple thought, not naming him but speaking and thinking of Kholster, she felt him nearby, awaiting her call. But did she need him? Certainly he could slay the whole of the Zaur and Sri'Zaur in existence if he wanted . . . and might do so . . . if she asked. But what would that kind of interference do to him? To meddle in the affairs of those who remained mortal. He had interfered on her behalf with Dienox, and with Vax, but Kholster . . .

"Gods, but you are infuriating," Wylant hissed. His name lingered on her tongue unsaid. For their entire marriage she had avoided giving him an order. Why then, now that he was finally free, would she do so? *No, I may be the one person who could order him to slay my foes no matter how numerous, but I will not do so. I am Wylant. I defeated the Aern. As distasteful as it may be, there is always a way . . .*

You're close, Mom, Vax told her, the pommel of his hilt resembling a snake, eyes upturned to watch her.

Close to what? Wylant thought back.

To figuring out what Father wanted you to know.

"The Vander thing, the finding a way thing, or . . ." Annoyed at the ambiguity, she flung her hand out to indicate the Eldrennai hamlet below. ". . . this view?"

At a thought, Clemency increased the magnification of her vision. The Eldrennai in the village. What about them struck her as so unusual ? Not all of them could cast, but at least two of them could. Two children played tag in the air, young Aeromancers zipping in and out around the small buildings, zooming close to farm animals that were no longer spooked by their antics. That close to the northern edge of Fort Sunder, the shrubland and jagged terrain of the Broken Plain met a withered mirror of its former lushness. Drinkable water flowed from the river, and crops would grow . . . there the elemental magic of the Eldrennai functioned properly for those who were not protected, as she was or those of royal blood were, from the aftermath of the Sundering of the Life Forge . . .

"Hells." Wylant grasped Vax's hilt. Hard.

Why would a warlord, a demonstrably clever one capable of building a vast network of tunnels right under their careless gazes, invade from the sea while possessing a superior land force? Why not surround and hem in the Eldrennai? Why allow them to flee to a place of martial power, well fortified, where they would have strong allies to assist them?

"It has to be in your strategic interest, Warlord. And I think I see your plan or part of it. . . ."

Fort Sunder, to the reptilian warlord, had to be a preferable place to engage the Eldrennai. A place of strength for the Aern that would prove a weakness for the Eldrennai. Wylant watched again those images Glayne had observed: Five elves (the most powerful and well-trained Elementalists to be sure, but still only five) slew hundreds, even thousands of troops. But take any one of them and remove his or her arcane might, and that left four well-trained combatants and an old schoolmaster who might slay tens, even hundreds with luck and good weather, but never thousands.

Lack of magic aside, what would the cramped conditions do to the refugees? Down below, warsuits moved about the courtyard, training ground, and every scrap of available space, making preparations for the incoming flood of evacuees. Poles were being laid out and tents assembled. Had Kholster completely restocked the fort when he, for lack of a better word . . . reforged it? No. She saw no animal pens. No livestock. Just physical equipment, then?

"The tents won't be enough." Fort Sunder was large, with walls now made of bone-steel after Kholster's bit of divine remodeling, but even if the refugees camped on every scrap of training ground between the main gates and the rise of steps up the butte to the fortress proper, Wylant couldn't imagine things would go well. Fort Sunder had once been home to more than a quarter of a million Aern, but . . .

Dropping over the lip of the wall, Wylant eyed the berths built into the fortification. Thirty feet thick and just over forty feet tall, the wall surrounding Fort Sunder ran just under a quarter of a jun from one side of the butte upon which the fortress proper stood to the other, and it was honeycombed with berths for the Aern, two thousand, two hundred and fifty in all with no ladder leading from berth to berth. One just used the berth below or above and climbed.

No Eldrennai would sleep there.

She had done it once, to prove that she could, but it was not her idea of comfort. To be fair, Mazik and some of Lancers might, but not many.

Wylant crossed to the nearest barracks building and stepped inside. Claustrophobic was an understatement. Twelve-foot ceilings were high and good, but with each set of bunks wrought of stone and going from floor to ceiling and only a space of five hands between one bunk and the bottom of the next (roughly the same distance from elbow to fingertip for an average

Aern) . . .

"Five-by-five-by-five." Wylant ran her gauntlets along stone, feeling its cool rough surface on her fingertips despite the intervening metal. Holding out her arms, Wylant could easily bridge the distance from one rack to the next. "By five again. Five bunks in a stack with five stacks in a shelf and five shelves to a single barracks . . . and only nine hands of clearance between each row of shelves . . . gods but it would get hot inside these things."

Six hundred and twenty-five Aern in such a confined space creates a lot of body heat, Clemency thought, but I fail to see why it would prove to be an issue. Isn't kholster Rae'en using the evacuation, the larger, stronger mobile force to ensure the maximum number of Aern survive any assassination attempts while they regroup?

"No." Wylant sniffed. "She's acting in good faith. I've never met a kholster who didn't . . . from their own point of reference."

Surely, Clemency argued, they will be willing to submit to minor discomfort . . . ?

"It's still insufficient." Even if the Eldrennai would sleep in such close quarters, since only one-fifth of the Aern on duty were asleep at any given time, there were only eighty barracks buildings, so they could only house fifty thousand people in them. True, there was space inside the main fortress itself, rooms that had been meant to serve as homes for the Eldrennai observers, visiting Eldrennai troops for training, and, of course, Uled's old chambers . . . and her own.

Exiting the barracks, she flew up to hover near the center of the courtyard. Could they defend it against the Zaur? There was no doubt that a proper Aernese force could do so, and had done so against Ghaiattri in the Demon Wars, but then the Aern had been supported by the full elemantic might of an unbroken Eldrennai people. A people who had not lost a full half of their population in the first Demon War, been halved again by the second, and a third time on Freedom Day and the days of rage that followed it. . . .

A few thousand Aern, even with warsuits, even assuming the bulk of the population of Port Ammond made it to Fort Sunder in fighting trim, wouldn't be much over one hundred thousand people, and only a tenth of those were active military. Perhaps another twenty percent would have served at one time or another. . . .

She could remember a time when fully half of the Eldrennai had great elemental powers, but the most gifted were also the most likely to be needed on the frontline, and the carnage had been greatest there . . .

The Armored could, over time, win against nearly any foe. But they were no longer immune to death.

"Kholster," Wylant sighed, "we'd need divine intervention to win if there are anywhere near as many Zaur as I expect there to be."

"That is likely, but do you believe the Harvester should do such a thing?" Kholster, clad as he was back in her chambers at Port Ammond, stepped into existence next to her. Muslin shirt and jeans. Those well-worn boots of his. No armor save a frown. But what other armor had he ever needed with the ones he loved?

"How else can we win?" Wylant asked.

"It is not my place to tell you how to win this war." Kholster touched Clemency's helm, and it was as if he stroked Wylant's cheek. "I can tell you this, however. You are correct and you can win . . . if you are willing to do whatever is necessary. That much I have arranged. Victory is not sure, not even likely, but it is possible."

"I don't see the solution, Kholster." Wylant touched his hand, holding it tightly against her helm, leaning into it.

"I have faith in you, wife." Kholster let his forehead rest against her own. "All conflicts are resolved eventually. It is their nature. It is yours to win at any cost. You have never needed my help." He smiled, baring those doubled canines wolfishly. "I cannot imagine that you ever truly will. From time to time you get it, but that is only because I love you and also because mundane tasks are more enjoyable when they are shared."

"But you implied you'd meddled." Wylant chewed over his words even as she spoke. "Victory is possible. You arranged it?"

"No husband is perfect," Kholster said, "especially me."

"Kiss me and begone with you then, if you like." Clemency's visor parted, revealing Wylant's smirk. "I have to think."

And so it was.

CHAPTER 34

SNAPDRAGON'S DILEMMA

Inside the twin temple to Xalistan and Gromma, Yavi took off her boots and sighed in relief, tension ebbing from her body at the touch of the blessed soil on her bare bark. Rich black soil covered the floor deep enough to shove in her toes and sink down to the knee if she wanted, but this wasn't for her . . . except in the sense that the temple was open to all Vael. A priestess of Gromma clad only in the thick bark with which she'd sprouted examined Arri's stump, applying a mixture of ground worms and other nutrients to it, before chanting a prayer to the goddess of growth and decay.

"May you grow straight and tall and feed mighty sproutlings when at last you are felled."

"I'll trust in Xalistan instead, priestess," Arri growled. Her Root Guard armor was so much a part of her identity she looked out of place in the casual leathers she wore. "May I hunt long and well and slay my hunter when hunted I become."

"Gah." Priestess Goumi waved the words away with a shake of her ever-green head petals, twisted into braided fronds. "Next time have Lallaya treat that little clipping of yours. I think you come in here just to admire my bark and leave footprints in my loam."

"How is she?" Yavi asked, deliberately cutting off the exchange. Arri's emotions ran raw with the loss of so many of her fellow Root Guard and the loss (though temporary) of Kholburran.

"Princess!" Face brightening, Goumi made her way across the room and touched the back of her hand to Yavi's, continuing on to the subject of Yavi's question, each step releasing a fragrant burst of fertilizer and pine. "We are doing the best we can for her. Queen Kari gave us strict instructions. We all know how special she is to the prince. How is he?" Goumi prodded. "I heard he made it back. Escaped, did he?"

"They let him go," Arri growled. "And followed him back to make sure no misadventure befell him on the return trip. Cursed reptiles, I can't under-stand them at all or why the queen listens to that forked-tongued envoy of theirs."

"Well." Yavi closed one eye and quirked her lips against the thought, but it didn't go anywhere. "It sounds like they want peace, but have a very . . . ah . . . competitive way of showing it. It's total wolf pack behavior in a way . . . rather like the grim and gory way irkanth males fight for leadership of the pride."

"We aren't animals," Arri muttered. "That's why girl-type persons lead us."

"Which may well be the problem when it comes to understanding the Sri'Zaur." Yavi placed the back of her fist gently against the small of Arri's back.

Eyes flashing, on the verge of anger, Arri did not step away, but Yavi sensed nothing had changed in Arri's spirit. The fury was dampened but not snuffed. Despite her innate desire for peace, Arri wanted to rip General Tsan to pieces and use her to fertilize her garden.

"If the prince is well . . . ?" Goumi let the question trail off.

"Mom won't let him out, yet." Yavi chewed her lip, wondering how much to say. "I think she wants to give Malli and Snapdragon a little time apart."

"It couldn't hurt." Goumi gestured at her patient. "She's healing well enough, but there is only so much we can do."

Overhead, stored sunlight shone down constantly on the temple's lone troubled patient, duplicating the long days of summer despite autumn's diminishing span outside in the real world.

Flat on the dark soil, Malli lay, eyes closed, concentrating on healing. Meditation wasn't Yavi's strong suit, but Malli was good at it. Even her spirit was a focused green mixed with gold. Wrapped tight with damp living moss, her air bladders inflated only minutely, enough to keep in practice, but they made a distressed sound when they did. A combination of the same moss, fishmeal and the substance Goumi had applied to Arri's stump filled up the cracks in Malli's trunk and held her together while Arborists sprinkled measured doses of animal blood on her outer layer to help sustain the fleshiest layers while her heartwood was taxed and normal nutrient routes were reduced due to the damage.

"Do you think she'll recover?" Yavi asked.

"If Snapdragon has his way," Goumi whispered, "I hear she'll be a Root Wife, and then we'll have done nothing here but make sure she lasts to her wedding day. He can fix the rest."

"And she will lose her place in the Root Guard," Arri scoffed, "not to mention her ability to travel or do anything outside of her husband's shade."

"My mother is a Root Wife," Yavi snapped. "She doesn't seem to find it such a hardship."

"But she traveled the breadth of Barrone first." Arri gave her a knowing look. "Was pollinated by Kholster . . ." The look she gave Yavi was one she'd seen far too much of since her return. Still clinging to a false spring, her body gave all the signs that more had happened between her and Kholster than a kiss. Denying that, even though it was fact, had proved to be a waste of air. "She lived full and free before settling down to watch over her people and live in the shade of her husbands."

"I—" Yavi began, only to hear a commotion in the chamber without.

"Malli?" Snapdragon's voice came tight and strained. "Look. I know she's in there, I just need to see her. I'll stand across the room, if you want, but I need to see her with my own eyes."

"I'll turn him away," Arri growled.

Yavi was opening her mouth to ask why they shouldn't just let him in—true, he was a boy-type person, but if he'd seen the injury when it was fresh, how could it hurt? Queen Kari might be against it, but—when Malli spoke.

"Let him in."

*

How easily Yavi could wave away the Root Guard who wouldn't let him in. Kholburran liked to think they listened to her for reasons other than her gender, but he was royalty, too, so the argument didn't track well enough to catch a rabbit. But he supposed that went with the same sort of logic that let Yavi walk around carrying her heartbow in the city and around the Root Trees when he wasn't allowed to carry his weapon. He'd brought that up once, but the queen had asked why he thought his Root Guard couldn't defend him in his own home and was someone picking on him . . . should she have a word with them?

"C'mon." Yavi motioned him in. "She doesn't look fabtastic, but she'll be fine."

"Princess." Seizal (one of the prince's Root Guard and one of the two who'd been blocking his path) stepped between him and the knot-like entrance to the temple—its entrance without door to symbolize an open welcome to all, which Kholburran found ironic given the circumstances. "The queen thinks it is unwise for—"

"Oh, who cares, Seizal?" Yavi stepped forward, palms toward the Root Guard. "The temple is supposed to be open to all. Yes, I know this one is mainly for royal use, but it hasn't got a door on it and if my brother saw the wound inflicted, then I don't understand what all this is about. Mom thinks he's going to pressure Malli into marriage? Hah. Is he going to be upset if she says no? Well, yes, but best make it a clean kill, as the Aern ought to say."

"Ought to say?" Seizal asked.

"I've never heard one say it, but it sounds like something they ought to say. Just like you should say, 'Yes, Princess,' and clear off. I'll take responsibility for this."

"We're only trying to look out for you, Prince." Seizal stepped slowly to the side. "You know that, right?"

*

Malli was clothed from hips to armpits in a tight wrap of moss and meal. Kholburran winced at the tell-tale blue of leaves plucked from Hasan's upper branches. He'd learned to make bandages out of them (all boy-type persons did; the ones suitable for Taking Root wound up having to practice even more) when he was just a sproutling mainly so he could render emergency aid to himself if he were to be injured and no girl-type person were around to take care of him.

Ground-level Vael probably never even saw them. They had to be carefully harvested to avoid harming Hashan . . . and Warrune, well, his leaves weren't good for anything. The healers said it was because his leaves had been harvested too roughly in the past and too often, but Kholburran suspected it had more to do with the rumor that Warrune hadn't wanted to Take Root in the first place and had only agreed on the condition that Hashan Take Root in the same spot and that Kari be their Root Wife.

I know the feeling, he thought.

Taking Root was not a thrilling thought. It was well and good for girl-type persons to talk about the honor, and Vael like Uncle Tran did seem to relish the opportunity to grow beyond the humanoid form and serve the whole rather than himself, but others . . .

It would be worth it to save her, Kholburran thought. He was double-checking the healing wrap and redistributing the mixture of worm and fish meal for more direct application before he felt Malli's eyes on him.

"Sorry," he coughed. "I'm sure Goumi is taking excellent care of you, but I . . . worry."

"'S cute." Malli spoke, her voice a strained whisper with a hint of flatness at the end of her words like a leaking bellows. Her air bladders hadn't been this bad back when she had first been injured.

"Hi." Kholburran looked into her eyes and tried to smile. *She's got a fungal infestation*, he thought, trying to think of the best way to treat it without doing more damage or alarming her. *We could remove her air bladders.* She didn't actually need them for much of anything, and, if everything else healed, they would grow back, but that meant she wouldn't be able to speak for the duration of her convalescence. "You look beautiful."

"Have Goumi check your head for injuries." Malli smiled briefly, the spots of animal blood on her skin giving her the look of someone stricken by rot or some other blight.

"Well." Kholburran lay the back of his hand against her cheek, trying not to jump at the coolness of her bark. Vael were only warm to appeal to the Aern, which was funny given that the Aern would never have noticed. Had Uled done it for his own people, then?

Never mind that, Kholburran berated himself, trying to home in on one topic, but his mind went off on a thousand different trails: how to treat her wounds, signs of body failure, how attractive she looked even covered in blood and moss, her beaded leggings replaced by a top soil that had been mounded over her lower extremities to help absorb nutrients . . .

Second behind Malli's health came the other thought, the thing that could correct the first problem while making so much of his future existence tolerable, joyful even.

Will she marry me?

Wincing, as if she could read his thoughts and did not like them, Malli shook her head.

"Not until this heals, Snapdragon."

"What?" He asked the question, feeling stupid even as he did it because he knew what she meant.

"No answer until then." Malli struggled through the words. "I can't marry you, become a Root Wife, to heal my wounds. Can't even think about it until after." He wanted to interrupt but held his tongue, not wanting to force her to start over. "Don't want to say yes or no without knowing I did it for the right reasons."

Eyes drooping closed, her body went still.

"She's turned her mind back to healing herself now, Prince Kholburran," Goumi told him. "Best leave her to it."

"Her breathing is worse than it was on the road." Kholburran stood. For all that he'd hated those lessons in self-treatment, he was glad to have them now. "Did you notice?"

"I have things well in hand," Goumi said.

Kholburran leaned over, pressing down ever so slightly on her chest to push out a little air. A certain amount of lichen was healthy. Each Vael's was different, but Malli's gave her breath a light violet odor. That odor was now tainted by the trace of an unpleasant meaty scent.

"Do you have any blue flower?" Kholburran asked.

"What sort of blue flower?" Goumi smiled, amused.

She doesn't understand. Kholburran growled in frustration. It wasn't her fault; it was rare enough to find in the wild, and importing gnome-made versions was expensive.

"Not an actual flower," Kholburran said. "It's a mineral you find around copper deposits."

Goumi stared at him blankly.

"Other names . . . blue vitriol, uh . . . there's another name, too."

"Do you mean blue stone?" Goumi asked. "We can get some from the Arborist Cache. They usually have some, probably the same chunk of crystal they showed you in your training, but we can only use it with royal . . ." Kholburran smiled at the priestess, baring his fang-like thorns, "permission . . . ah . . ."

"Arborist Cache?" Kholburran scoffed. "I always just told Malli what I needed."

"Well, where did you think the supplies came from, little brother?" Yavi waggled her ears at him.

"I didn't think about it."

Kneeling over Malli's still form, the priestess leaned in close, her head petal fronds brushing Malli's forehead. Forcefully enough to make Kholburran wish she'd been more careful, Goumi depressed Malli's chest, rough bark hand between Malli's breasts.

"Her breath smells okay to me," Goumi muttered.

"Trust me," Arri laughed. "Snapdragon is an expert on all of that one's parts. If he said her nose tasted funny, I wouldn't even bother to wonder how he knew."

Goumi's leer left him wanting to cover himself with a big, thick coat, but if a little embarrassment and ogling got him what he needed to help Malli heal, he resolved to persevere.

CHAPTER 35
ALCHEMICAL BONDING

Being escorted by a new group of Root Guard, these all uninjured and without blemish, gave Tsan the answer for which she had been waiting without the queen uttering a word. Thus far, all their conversations had taken place in the Arboretum with an air of informality Tsan had come to expect from the Weeds. Reports that the Weeds had no throne room proved to have been in error, for what else did one call a large space with a raised seat larger than everyone else's?

As in the Arboretum, both Hashan and Warrune were represented, intermingled roots becoming one throne of living wood upholstered in fabric of a rich dark green with the appearance of felt but holding the scent, like all Weed-wrought creations, of flora. Upon the throne Queen Kari sat, clothed in formal armor cast in white.

Some form of laminate?

She wore no crown, but as Tsan had learned, many of the non-evergreen Weeds were losing their head petals and that Kari had not (never did) served as its own regal display. Tsan did not pretend to understand what being a Root Wife entailed, but as Kari was one, and she was older than the other Weeds, it seemed to convey political advantage rather than the disadvantage brood Matrons endured.

Sunlight shone down as it had in the Arboretum, but here the over-head panes had been tinted to create an image of Kari and two male Weeds touching hands.

Hashan and Warrune, I presume?

Kari's solid red eyes met Tsan's slit-pupiled ones. Tsan prayed for insight from He Who Ruled in Secret and in Shadow. Life was preferable to death, and though Tsan had been allowed to fulfill so many of her lifelong dreams, the destruction of a Root Tree, the burning of a human city, even the killing of countless Weeds, there was more she wanted to accomplish: to be a female who was not forced to hatch a brood, to keep her name, and her rank . . .

Surreptitious sniffs and tongue flicks revealed a nervousness in those around her. Not fear of Tsan personally . . . surely not, but of her reaction. *They still hope for peace,* she thought. *Or at least to avoid open warfare. They are afraid this peace, this chance for it, is about to slip through their grubby little roots. How interesting. Maybe there is room for success despite the Weed queen's decision?*

Six Root Guard took positions at either side of the throne; another six positioned themselves on either side of General Tsan.

"Bad news?" Tsan stood on her hind legs, tail stretched out behind as she bobbed her head toward the assembled protectorate.

"You have my deepest regrets, General," Queen Kari said. "I cannot agree to a truce so readily. Please convey my regrets to Warlord Xastix and inform him that, while the Vael are happy to remain on peaceful terms with the Zaur and the Sri'Zaur, we have existing agreements with the Eldrennai and the Aern that preclude any such new arrangement without consulting them."

"Is that all?" Tsan chortled in the back of her throat, keeping very still, studying the queen. "May I be permitted to ask the queen why she declines to open such a dialogue?"

"I was under the impression you required an answer now, General," Kari said.

"Requiring and desiring are two different actions, Your Majesty." Tsan tasted the air, hoping for more olfactory cues, but it told her nothing other than there was a young Vael running down the exterior corridor. The prince? She could not tell. Not an Eldrennai . . . therefore not the idiot Prince Dolvek, though for him to barge in would have proved most useful. "Perhaps you would consider a temporary truce while you arrange discussions. As I have said, my people cannot accept peace with the Eldrennai, but we are not so close-minded as that requirement paints us. We are also an imaginative people. There exist, as your saying proclaims, more than one way to hunt an irkanth."

Kari's eyes narrowed. *Had colloquialism been inadvisable?*

If so, the mouse was in her mouth now, might as well swallow it, sick or not, eh?

"What do you propose?" Kari asked.

"Merely what I was hoping you might propose. We could be amenable to a war of mutual avoidance with the Aern: an array of territories that would be considered neutral ground, as it were, and others where any faction upon detecting the presence of the other would be completely within their rights to destroy the offending party. The Vael would serve as mutually trusted intermediaries and arbiters over any violations before the Aern come marching into our territory or we go tunneling into theirs."

While not the overwhelmingly one-sided treaty she knew Warlord Xastix would prefer, Tsan suspected he would go along with it, assuming the bulk of the Eldren Plains were ceded to the Zaur. . . .

"You could have opened with that suggestion," Queen Kari said.

"As could you, Highness," Tsan said.

Raising an eyebrow (eye petal?), the queen quirked her lips. "This new proposal appeals to the Vael at our heartwood. Peace is of tantamount import to us, as you know, and—"

"Mother." The young prince, Kholburran, burst into the audience chamber, and Tsan had to close her mouth tight to keep from hissing at the male or even ripping out its annoying throat. Of all the ill-timed, idiotic . . . were there simply not enough Root Guard left to keep the brat out of the adults' work period? To fail to delay him? Tsan had calculated she had a full minute or more before the Root Guard let him in. "I need permission to send a group of Root Guard to Kevari Pass. There is an old copper vein there where we have harvested blue stone in the past and—"

"Kholburran!" Kari said coldly. "As I am sure you can plainly see, I am in the midst of negotiating a truce that—"

"Malli needs it soon," Kholburran insisted, "or she might die!"

"Surely the Arborist—"

"With the war on, no one has been able to go out and gather any." Kholburran approached the throne, his entire posture marking him as prey by his supplication. Even so. Perhaps Kilke had a claw in this interruption after all. Blue flower. Copper. Did the boy mean copper sulfate? If so, why not simply have one of their alchemists create a batch? The Weeds did not appear to use much metal in their modes of construction, but did they smelt no metal at all? Surely they possessed some level of alchemical knowledge and metallurgy. . . .

"Ah." Queen Kari tuned to Tsan. "I beg your indulgence, Tsan, but the female in question is the one my son intends to wed, if she will have him, and—"

"Of course." Tsan held up a paw. "Though we understand alliances far better than we do these emotions like friendship and love that you possess, we are not unpracticed at making allowances for the perversion."

"Thank you," Kari said.

Pausing until the queen redirected her attention to her son, Tsan counted to ten in her head before interrupting.

"Were we allied," Tsan began, "I would surely be able to arrange an escort. But . . . I wouldn't want to use the treatment of the injured as a bargaining point."

"You wouldn't?" Kholburran blurted.

Of course I would, you whining thing, but it serves no useful purpose in the long term. Not if we want a lasting alliance.

"The destruction of the hale and strong in battle is a demonstration of strength." Tsan clenched her claws into a tight fist. "Persecution of the injured," she said, lingering on the word "injured," opening her fist and wiggling her claws as if flicking away the remains of some unseen crushed thing, "is evidence of cruelty."

General Tsan smiled, her attention fully on young Kholburran. The Weed's desperation flowed from him in a heady mix of pheromones as intoxicating when emitted by an enemy as they would have been repellant to emit herself. "This blue stone," Tsan asked. "Does it have other names? You said it came from copper?"

"Yes, a blue crystal that grows in copper—"

"Ah," Tsan's eyes flashed wider. They truly lacked such simple knowledge? What was another name they would know it by, one that would not reveal too much . . . she could not bring herself to call it blue flower . . . what did the humans call it? "Copper Vitriol?"

"Yes." The young Weed's hope-filled eyes locked with her own. *And here is where we show our superiority, yet again, but in a manner these foolish Weeds will find much more laudable.*

"Then, if you'll pardon me," Tsan said, interlacing her foreclaws, "have you no copper?"

"Yes, but—"

"Have you no oil of vitriol?" Tsan tried to keep her tone politely puzzled rather than condescending, but it was so hard when one considered the inferiority of the Weeds.

"It is possible we have that, but how will it help?" Kholburran asked.

"Queen Kari." General Tsan's tail twitched as her muzzle shifted directions. "Many think that because Kilke is god of secrets and shadows he delights in deception and trickery. And while we employee those methods tactically from time to time to defeat those unwilling, or unworthy, of alliance, our focus is on the value of secrecy, the power of knowing what others do not. It is not unusual for my kind to hoard knowledge or, on occasion, to reveal it as a sign of sacrifice. Does that make sense?"

"Yes." Queen Kari nodded. "I believe I track you."

"Then," Tsan let her volume drop, forcing the Weeds to lean a little closer, try a little harder to hear her, "allow me to make a gift to you of knowledge. The substance you require can be created, here, using only copper, the proper vitriols, and simple tools. Let me show the technique to your Arborist before I leave to take news of our temporary agreement to Warlord Xastix. You can come to specific terms and areas of territory with the representative

Xastix sends in my place, and in the interim, perhaps you could approach the Aern on our behalf?"

"And what of my people?" Prince Dolvek asked from the shadows. Had he been present all along and managed to remain silent?

Interesting. How did I not smell his arrogance?

Tsan opened her mouth wide, in a fang-baring yawn, eyes wide and flashing. "By now you are likely a very rare specimen indeed. Dryga's forces will have already taken Port Ammond, and the survivors will flee for safer havens. Except, I can assure you, Prince Dolvek, there are none. Nowhere on this entire continent is it now safe to be an Eldrennai."

Prince Dolvek's lips drew into a white line, but he said nothing. *No denials. No tirades? Unimaginable.*

"Your permission, Majesty?" Tsan asked, giving the Eldrennai her back.

If Kari's eyes flicked from Dolvek to her son, it was impossible for Tsan to discern. Silent and unreadable she sat, like a reptile soaking in heat, checking the distance to prey, waiting perhaps for them to cross the line of no return where they strayed too close to the waiting jaws of a Zaur to escape.

"You have it." Kari stood. "But I ask that you take with you a representative from my kingdom, one whom I trust to make agreements on my behalf. Few of my kind have had experience with the complexities inherent in negotiations between warring factions, but she has. Take Princess Yavi with you and we will accept her safe return as a token of the warlord's sincerity."

"I fear the environments in which we make our home may be unpleasant to a Vael." Tsan dropped lithely to all fours, stretching her hindquarters. *But if Warlord Xastix was pleased with the sample of Vael blood Kuort had delivered, would he not be amused, at the very least, by having his very own Weed? And if the negotiations went forward, so much the better. The Weeds, their appearances so much more pleasant to a warmblood's eyes, might serve as excellent intermediaries as the Sri'Zauran empire grew.* "But if you would prefer to expedite negotiations in this manner, I can guarantee her safety only so long as I hold my rank. And, as you may recall, I fully expect to be executed."

"Can you make the same promise to me?" Prince Dolvek asked. "If what you say is true, if my people have been crushed and scattered, I request they be allowed to abandon the Eldren Plains. We will do as the Aern did and flee beyond Bridgeland, never to return."

"The Eldrennai must die, Prince Dolvek." Tsan rolled her neck, peering back over her shoulder. He looked so resolute it was hard to laugh him off. Foolish, but brave. There was a glow about him, too. Was he god-touched? Tsan let her tongue flick out, nostrils flaring, and breathed deep. A blend of fire and blood lay buried in his scent. Could be Dienox. Could be nothing. But . . .

"My brother and others like him . . ." Dolvek walked forward with a different gait than before. The arrogance had gone out of his movements, replaced by . . . and then she recognized it. Where once there had been swaggering confidence, there was now only resoluteness and acceptance . . . an alteration with which Tsan could not help but identify. "These Eldrennai turned Aiannai, who understand the wrongs my people have committed, have been accepted as a new people by the Aern. In the past, have you not made peace with one set of humans who call themselves by one name, while despoiling humans who . . . taste and . . . smell the same but call themselves by another name?"

"We have," Tsan allowed with a nod. "We war with the people of Zaliz but know peace with the Holsvenians. Both nations are predominantly human."

"Then—" Prince Dolvek kneeled, "—if it is acceptable to the people of Queen Kari and those clans united by Warlord Xastix, allow me to do well what I once did poorly. Allow me to represent my people, my new people, and secure a peace or . . . at the very least a territorial arrangement between us." He hesitated on the final word. Whether by design or emotion, Tsan could not know. "Please."

Well, well, well, Tsan thought as she agreed, *as the saying goes, once the tunnel is dug one never knows what manner of creatures will try to crawl into it.*

"I can promise neither your safety, nor that you will be heard, Prince." Tsan dropped low, neck arched to look up at the Eldrennai from a lower vantage, a striking vantage. "But if you want to try, I welcome the attempt, if for no other reason than I may desire company when I am executed."

CHAPTER 36
FIRST BREATH

"Not that I'm trying to hurt your feelings here, Magic Sam." Tyree leaned over Kazan in the warm, steady light of Dwarven lanterns doing their best to push away the cavernous dark of the Zaur tunnel. Framed by locks of black hair, Tyree's face almost glowed in the lantern's light, his conspicuously white teeth and minty breath leaving Kazan wondering what this man knew that other humans didn't about taking care of his teeth. "But what did you just do?"

"Magic Sam?" Kazan wiped motes of sleep from his eyes.

"A traveling performer I know." Tyree put an ear to Kazan's chest, and the young Overwatch wondered when his chain shirt had been taken off. "He used to fake all kinds of injuries only to 'alchemically' heal them with a special potion he would then conveniently sell to any and all who were interested. Some of them would be ghastly in appearance, but they all healed."

My apologies for the discomfort, Eyes of Vengeance thought. I had never tried it that way before, therefore the results were uncertain.

Discomfort? Clearing his mind, Kazan felt the familiar contact of his fellow Overwatches as his mental map filled in. They were in a tunnel. He scrolled back along their path, grabbing information from the memories of M'jynn, Arbokk, and Joose for the time he'd been unconscious.

Blood.

He remembered blood.

A cow.

The blood raining down over Eyes of Vengeance as it opened wide to accept the flood.

A variation on a strip and dip, Eyes of Vengeance told him. It never occurred to us pre-Sundering because of our lack of independence. Given the circumstances, however, and the lack of real risk . . . the possibility became obvious. If we can breathe for you and burn for you, keep you from getting excessively tired . . .

Then why couldn't you, uh, feed for us and initiate the same kind of regeneration used when an Armored's bones are sealed within you and soaked in blood. Kazan ran his tongue along his bottom teeth. Everything was there. *All better. I track you there, Eyes. Makes sense. Thanks.*

This then was part of what it meant to be Armored and have friends, family, who were not. Kazan's wounds were gone, banished by his warsuit and the others still limped along, needing to down as much protein as they could to speed the healing. He knew he wasn't invincible, but he felt it. Stronger, faster; even his senses felt sharper, his mind more agile, and his link to the other Armored . . . had Vander felt like this?

I do not believe so, Eyes of Vengeance sent. **You have the benefit of all the wisdom and knowledge it took Vander years to accumulate and an outlook young enough to see alternate approaches more easily.**

"*Give me a moment*," Kazan thought and said at the same time. Clicking together like tiles of the mind, Kazan let his connections to the other Aern restore themselves. Splitting the task amongst his local Overwatches, as well as Rae'en's inherited core, by the time he could have counted to one thousand, the world made sense again. Absently directing an imperiled Aern on the road to Fort Sunder to duck and roll, thus avoiding a crossbow bolt, and apologizing to the Aern's Overwatch for stepping in on her behalf, Kazan found the other data he needed about his local status.

They'd gone down an air vent into a Zaur tunnel, hoping to avoid any further Knightly encounters. Reptilian patrols were marked on the map where they had opted to avoid them. Apparently there was a large force with the giant serpents the Zaur called Zaurruks and Sri'Zaur of more types than the Aern had ever seen, moving aboveground toward Silver Leaf. Tyree and Cadence had opted to avoid them too, despite M'jynn's suggestion that they speed up their pace and try to make it to the human settlement in time to warn them.

Taking the safer route was a plan to which Kazan did not think he would have agreed had he been conscious at the time, but it was underway now. Arbokk and M'jynn were taking turns ranging ahead and behind to avoid any surprises. Tyree kept having to calm the horses, but for the first time since the Knights had begun chasing them at Castleguard, Kazan felt calm and safe . . . in a snake hole.

"Fake injuries healed?" Kazan asked, remembering what Tyree had been saying about a cohort of his named Magic Sam.

"Oh, it isn't all that unusual for a few of the world's more devious beings," Captain Tyree began, "to take advantage of the less creative or intelligent. Not that I approve, of course, but . . ."

"Oh, you approve." Cadence sat, legs crossed, hovering above the cavern floor. The lantern's light picked out the varying colors in her hair and eyes. He'd never met a crystal twist before, but if they were all like her, it was no wonder humans disliked them so much.

Why would people pay for a potion that didn't work? he asked Eyes of Vengeance.

He is talking about a confidence game, Overwatch Kazan, the deep echoing voice boomed in his mind. Having never been injured, the human wiped away the false wounds as if by the magic of his elixir: often some combination of urine and an inexpensive pigment. He then sold the concoction at what appeared to his victims to be a low price and moved on to the next town with some urgency, hoping to be far out of reach of the local guards or angry customers by the time his deception was detected.

Often the dishonest individual (or individuals) rotate through more than one of these types of deceit, not performing the same crime in towns too close to one another.

You okay to walk now? Joose thought. *Or do I need to carry you some more? You started shifting around, which is why we stopped.*

I'm fine, Kazan sent. *Thanks for the assist.*

You're not all that heavy, Joose sent back, *just unwieldy.*

We have a lot of bodies up ahead, Arbokk sent. *As best I can tell, we're close to where they were holding Rae'en and Wylant when Tyree helped them escape. The human took us a bit out of our way, but my guess is he was trying to get his bearings, not deliberately throw us off.*

But it's passable? Kazan stood and began to pull off his blood-stained clothes, washing the muck away with water from his Dwarven canteen. He discarded the jeans, washed the bone-steel mail, and donned his spare pants (blue as opposed to black). One of the others had rescued his boots, so he donned them, too.

Of course. It stinks, but it's not like kholster Wylant is with us. Are either of the humans allergic?

"You scarbacks really don't have any problem with nudity, do you?" Cadence was chuckling to herself while Tyree shook his head.

"Are either of you allergic to Zaur?" Kazan asked, assuming Cadence's query to be rhetorical.

"No," Tyree answered. "I'd have noticed."

"It stinks like a snake pit in here—" Cadence wrinkled her nose, "—but I'm not throwing up."

Up and about? Rae'en thought at Kazan.

Yes, kholster. Her viewpoint (almost always running at one size or another in his view space) showed her on a nondescript section of the White Road en route to Fort Sunder. Working with the other Armored, he assembled an updated map with the location of all the Armored and their warsuits. Having been taken by surprise once when the Sri'Zaur assassins claimed the life of an Aern or a warsuit, Kazan intended that the Aernese army should never again be caught off guard by such an attack. *Sorry about the off-duty time. We should be able to pick up the pace now, but we're in a tunnel system and the others are not completely recovered yet.*

Prime, Glayne thought. *Do you recall what Twin Beak reported about Coal?*

The dragon? Kazan felt along the network of minds looking for Twin Beak and found him running toward Fort Sunder. The memory was recent enough, easy to find despite the guilt Twin Beak's behavior should have generated. He forwarded a quick note to Carst's kholster about it, leaving a little blinking icon in the corner of the kholster's map.

It's a note, Kazan explained in response to the near-immediate inquiry he got from Carst's kholster. *You read it and decide whether to take any action regarding Twin Beak's cowardice. You're his kholster, not me.* Then to Glayne: *I do now. Why?*

You'll want to see this.

Kazan flipped through Glayne's inputs before finding the one Glayne had left behind at Port Ammond. It was the point of view with the dragon in it.

Rae'en, Kazan sent, *you'll want to see this.*

Show me.

*

The first sign of a dragon attack is often the cold. Captain Dryga had heard those words before, whispered from the lips of his Matron when he was just a little biter, having managed to kill one of his brothers. As he'd chewed on sixth hatchling's heart, his mother cooed instructions to all the survivors, her pheromones quelling the need to fight, leaving them a mass of paranoid hatchlings eyeing each other, suspicious of the truce the presence of their Matron enforced.

Dragon tales had been his favorites of the stories his Matron told. Other lessons had application in reality, the here and now: tales of alliance now that they had reached the stalemate of being worthy enough to train. Rules of duels and how they were no longer allowed to eat one another unless in a formal combat, and even then only if she agreed the loser was no longer suitable for instruction. The winner instead typically took the loser's tail as his dinner (since it would grow back), and the loser had to endure the embarrassment of taillessness and limited Zaurtol while it regenerated over the next few months.

But as his breath blew white and sudden cold bit his scales, Dryga realized for the first time that all of his Matron's dragon stories had been education, too.

<<Dragon!>> was all he managed to tap before the cold shut down his thoughts, his blood spreading sugars through his body in reaction as his limbs froze.

*

Hasimak and his students had created a routine. As they meditated to restore their concentration, they did so in pairs. With the evacuees away, Kholster suspected the Elemental Nobles would be following suit. If so, they said nothing. Kholster stared at the ancient Elementalist, watching his meditations, and felt he understood the elf for the first time. In six thousand years, it had never occurred to him Hasimak might have also been a victim, a prisoner of Uled's magic. He'd known of Hasimak's link to Kyland, Wylant's father. He'd even known that the old elf had taken Kyland in as an orphan with high magical potential and raised him, just as he had Uled and countless others.

It had been considered a great honor. Kholster knew this in the osmotic way he knew many things about Oathbreaker politics and practices. Some he witnessed, and in the earliest of days, when he and his brother One Hundred were treated as little more than trained hounds, waiting at table for scraps or performing whatever tricks or amusements the elves devised, he recalled a discussion where one of the Elemental Nobles of the time had asked Hasimak to take his niece under his wing, to train her and let her stay with him as Hasimak had done in the past.

Hasimak had agreed to train Bhaeshal, to personally tutor her as he did many, but he had refused to name her his ward.

Standing in their midst, in the high chamber of the Tower of Elementals, with its meditation mats, pillows, and scrolls, Kholster could not help but notice how tired the nobles were. Zerris and Hollis took one watch, Klerris and Lord Stone (how strange that each Stone Lord surrendered his proper name when the other nobles did not) taking the other, while Hasimak meditated through both watches, sustaining even in his quietude the field of energy that now wrapped around the tower, effectively sealing it against the Sri'Zaur attack.

"Coal." Hasimak's eyes snapped open as the cold came. Blazing with violet light, the entire tower vanished, leaving Kholster standing in empty space for a hundred count as frost flowed over the city. Windows cracked.

Everything froze as the dragon stole its heat to power his fire. The worst damage came not with the cold but with heat's return. Soil, heaved upward by the expansion of the water turned ice within it, crumbled inward by the rapid temperature change at the onset of Coal's draconic fire.

Stone cracked or shattered. Structures weakened and collapsed as heat melted the flash-frozen water. The dragon roared its delight.

*

So Hasimak is here. Coal eyed the absent top quarter of the tower of High Elementals, soaring over the lower quarters and blazing with torrents of heat as he smote the glowing stone with his tremendous bulk, sending the tower tumbling sideways to crash through rows of close-by buildings. *How fun.*

The castle came next, each of its three towers sent down blazing atop the icy reptilian figures. Some shattered on impact, others, lucky enough to be near the super-heated stone and not under it, stirred as they began to thaw. Yes, this was definitely more amusing than assisting the Aern at Fort Sunder would have been. There, he would have needed to preserve the Aern-built infrastructure, but as far as he knew, the Aern, in their war with the Zaur and the Eldrennai, had no interest in Port Ammond with its haughty architecture . . . and if they had wanted the city intact Kholster or his daughter should have mentioned it to him well in advance.

Attacking Port Ammond allowed him to keep his word to assist the Aern while destroying several thousand Zaur and providing assistance to the warsuits as requested. Two elves in one maw, as the saying went.

As Coal spun around to ready another cycle of cold and heat, the upper portion of the tower reappeared, first tumbling from the sky over the empty space where the lower portion had been, then held in place by the mages within.

*

"The first blast is the worst," Hasimak hissed through gritted teeth immediately after jerking the tower away from the dragon, "as the frost-and-burn cycle of a dragon is imperfect. He absorbs heat from his surroundings, inflicting cold, but when unleashing the stored heat, the exchange is imperfect, only a bastard portion of that which he took in. By the third blast he is essentially breathing plain fire, and the cold effect is uncomfortable but not fatal."

"Where are we?" Lord Stone asked. All four apprentices looked out the windows at the roiling chaos beyond the tower walls.

"Between dimensions," Hasimak grunted. "He's probably toppled the tower, knocking the Port Gates out of alignment. I'll have to bring us back soon, and I may not be able to shift us out again unless at least two of the Port Gates are intact and in rough alignment. If we can wait him out, I may be able to convince him to leave. Dragons do not have the patience for a siege in the conventional sense. They find them too boring."

"But he's destroying Port Ammond," Klerris complained.

"The people are gone, except for us." Hasimak's voice was soft and tired. "I would dearly like to preserve as much of the tower as I can, because it has been my home for years beyond measure, but it can be rebuilt. It can all be rebuilt."

"And if you can't get the dragon to leave?" Hollis asked.

"I know the Betrayer of old." Hasimak's eyes lit up at the memory.

"The Betrayer?" Zerris asked.

"When he was still young," Hasimak said, "before the other dragons left Barrone, before Kevari fell, creating with her death throes the pass that bears her name . . . When his scales were black and his eyes were bright fire . . . that is what the other dragons called him."

"But if you can't talk him into going away . . ." Klerris pressed.

Hasimak closed his eyes, internal struggle playing out on his features as a series of grimaces and twitches. At last, he gave a long, low moan.

"Have I ever," Hasimak asked, absently pleating and re-pleating his robes, "told the four of you how to kill a dragon?"

*

Coal swooped over the rooftops of Port Ammond, belching a continuous stream of raw heat and energy, cutting a swathe through civilian, municipal, and military construction alike. Landing with the vigor of false youth atop the Royal Museum, the dragon chortled in low grumbling rumbles as it collapsed beneath his weight. Feeling the ebb of his inner heat, the dragon directed an irritated blast of rage at the museum's center, destroying exhibits old and new. Shattered cases from which the warsuits had emerged only days earlier caught fire. The wooden frames burned, and velvet pillows upon which warpicks had rested smoldered into ruin.

Wreathed in smoke, his fires blazing brightly throughout the port city, Coal dropped low into the center of the inferno he'd made of the Royal

Museum where all the trouble had been set into motion thirteen years earlier and spent the last of his tremendous heat melting the stone beneath his claws, the remains of the ceiling above him and the walls around him, so that the molten stone flowed over and enfolded him.

Kholster watched all of this without comment, several of him moving amongst the dead Zaur and Sri'Zaur, those who'd frozen incorrectly and died rather than entering a protective freeze, those who'd been crushed, and those who'd been burned. It no longer pained him to be in so many places at once. Being unified by Vander acting again as his Overwatch kept him all in sync, requiring him to focus only on a handful of things at once, with the rest sorting itself out in the back of his mind without the need for direct attention.

One by one, the primal gods joined him.

Xalistan arrived first, appearing in classic fashion with a lion's body, the trunk of a humanoid attached in place of the neck, and huge leathery wings springing from his back. He held a bone spear in his hands, tossing his horned head like a challenging buck, but Kholster paid him little heed other than to clad himself in Harvester, Reaper appearing on his back.

Are we going to reap him? Harvester asked.

No, Kholster thought. *We needed to take Aldo, and I may have to reap others so they have a chance to learn a few things, but the primals appear to understand for the most part.*

Understand?

That mortals are not toys, Vander answered.

Clad in dead leaves, mulch, and moss, her body composed of the carcasses of dead animals, mushrooms blooming from their hides, Gromma arrived in a cloud of dirt. Yhask and Queelay, the wind and sea, arrived together as a storm raging over the port, their heads formed of cloud and rain, gazing down upon the scene.

Minapsis and Kilke arrived together looking every bit the brother and sister they were, Kilke clothed in shadows, Minapsis in black furs. Their horns were bedecked with jewelry.

"My husband is angry with you," Minapsis told him.

"Then he should not have allowed me to fight him," Kholster said, eyes forward, watching the reptilian forces attempting to withdraw, those who were sufficiently thawed to do so. "I am doing exactly what he asked. That he may have underestimated what that would entail or how being reduced to one aspect would change his opinion on the matter is no fault of mine."

"You have to learn to abide by the rules, Kholster," Dienox said firmly, manifesting in a suit of black plate armor. He held a matching buckler in his left hand and a longsword in his right. "What you said earlier—if we don't follow rules, cosmically binding or not, then we'll destroy the Outwork in our squabbling and float in the Dragonwaste blaming each other."

"This destruction." Head bowed, Sedvinia appeared in a long-sleeved dress of dark gray, "It's both wonderful and terrible, the power of this one beast." Eyeing Kholster pointedly, she added. "The dragon, too."

"If he were a beast," Gromma rustled, "I would collect him."

"Or I," Xalistan growled.

"Are we talking about the dragon," Kilke's ram-horned head asked, "or the death god?"

"Both are problematic." Shidarva, the goddess of justice and retribution, four armed, a scimitar edged in blue fire wielded in each hand, burst into existence. Her armor flashed with the same fire. "Both must be dealt with."

"Oh?" A Dwarf in full plate armor, wielding a hammer arcing with electricity, rose up from the stones. "And what has the dragon done to offend?"

"Jun." Shidarva gestured with her swords, encompassing the destruction. "Do you not see what it has done to Port Ammond?"

"I see." Jun nodded. "And it is a mortal being whose redress must be handled by other mortal beings. Any deity who interferes with Coal will get to experience the joy of having his or her head between my hammer and my favorite anvil."

"The dragon is not the problem." Torgrimm, still in his farmer's clothes, pitchfork in hand, arrived next. "I may have made a mistake when I—"

"That you did," Kholster spoke. "But I do not believe you comprehend why it was a mistake to give a portion of your power to me, to make yourself vulnerable so I could take it . . . but you will. Aldo is learning now. I will deliver the same lesson to any of you who require it."

"Oh stop your posturing," Dienox bellowed. "The dragon is going to go off a few more times before it finishes. Can we at least watch that first?"

CHAPTER 37

THE THERMODYNAMICS OF DRAGONS

<<You're on your own,>> came the call from Asvrin and his thrice-cursed Shades. Captain Dryga, still slow from the cold and groggy from such a quick freeze and thaw, could not even tell how far away the master assassin was, only that the Zaurtol he used was blunted and inelegant, as if beaten on Zaurruk handler drums from far away.

Probably exactly what he did, the coward.

"Retreat!" Dryga croaked as the second wave of cold hit him. Some made it back into the water; other smacked their heads into ice too thick to break, skulls cracking and blood spilling on the ice.

"Hello, enemies of my favorite mortal-turned-deity," the dragon bellowed as its shadow fell over Dryga, its claws striking the ice of the harbor, intensifying the cold. "I'm afraid I got carried away with the destruction of the city on that first breath. I shall correct that oversight presently."

Dryga got his head turned around far enough that, as he froze in place, he had a clear view of the great wyrm, lines of fire racing along its pitch-black scales, eyes alive with flame, fang-rimmed maw filled with light.

When the blast of heat came, it was nothing like Dryga had ever imagined, not fire so much as a beam of heat so strong it set the air ablaze. Where it hit, stone shattered, scale, muscle, and bone flash-fried to cinders, blown away by the force of that terrible beam, even as it cooked them. The dragon's hate swept along a flat plane, clearing the dock of buildings and invaders alike.

Tracking upward in an arc, the flashing column of orange, yellow, and white clove the shattered base of Castle Ammond in twain again, dropping lower remnants of the towers atop the dead and dying. Steam flowed up from the boiling bay as the dragon aimed the last of its second breath down at those attempting to escape back into the waters, melting the very ice upon which it stood but jerking itself upward into the roiling storm overhead on its immense wings of destruction.

The last sound Dryga heard was a hiss, a pop, and the high-pitched whine of his organs sizzling inside his skin. Then he saw the god of death, and it was an Aern.

As some of Kholster gathered the souls of the dead, the Prime Kholster, the one who wore Harvester and unslung Reaper from his back, gauntlets tight around its bone-white grip, stood surrounded by all of the other gods save Nomi and the new god of knowledge. Distracted, the primals had eyes mainly for the dragon. Its destruction and glee were far more intriguing than yet another squabble among deities.

Shidarva and the others gave Kholster the entirety of their focus, weapons at the ready (though Dienox did seem torn between watching the dragon and watching Kholster . . . and Jun appeared to be on both sides or on the sides of mortals themselves rather than either side).

"You've gone too far," Shidarva breathed. "You acted as if there were no rules! You murdered Aldo and did who-knows-what with his soul!"

"It's in a safe place." Kholster's words came soft, sure, and unhurried. He turned with glacial slowness and profundity as if he were an Irkanth noticing a tiny creature upon which it might pounce. "And I did not murder him."

"You claim that you did not—" Shidarva took a step, the ground beneath her feet pulsing blue with each move.

"I loaned a soul my warpick." Kholster held Reaper up and out. "You need not be alarmed. He gave it back."

"But you tricked Aldo," Dienox growled, ignoring the dragon, who had settled amid the wreckage of Castle Ammond to bask in the glow of his own warmth before lashing out again. "You blinded him."

"The eye that spies on me," Kholster quoted, holding out two obsidian eyes with amber pupils surround by jade irises. He shook them in his left hand like a gambler throwing bones. "I shall pluck out."

Kilke tried and failed to stifle a laugh, the resulting snort drawing a disapproving glare from Minapsis and Torgrimm as he stepped free of the conflict and then, drawing a two-handed blade as long as he was tall, moved to Kholster's side.

"Could you quote what Aldo said to me the last time I caught him spying on me and confronted him about it, please, Harvester?"

"My friend, if pulling a few of my eyes out of their box and shaking them about would mollify you in any way—" Harvester recited.

"You claim this was all an ill-timed prank?" Torgrimm asked. "Is that it? You—!"

"Demoted him." Kholster held his left hand out and dropped the eyes. A box containing the others appeared beneath them, held by a bald Aern.

Vander wore no warsuit, clad as he was in life in bone-steel mail, jeans, and boots favored by so many Aern . . . a slight variation being the fedora he wore, with vents sewn in to better accommodate his ears.

"I'm standing in for the god of truth and lies until he's learned the lesson you all need to learn." Vander snapped the box shut and stuffed it into a pocket that, though the box fit seamlessly, was too small to contain it.

"And what lesson is that?" Dienox asked. "And what do you mean 'truth and lies'? Aldo was the god of knowledge! Kilke is the liar!"

"Secrets are not lies," sneered Kilke's leftmost head.

"Nor are shadows," said Kilke's rightmost head.

"Aldo was no more intended to be the god of knowledge, Dienox, than you are only intended to be the god of war." Kholster bared his teeth. "You are not what you are supposed to be. You play at being mortal and it simply makes you sad hoaxes, mockeries of what you should be. So I'm—"

"You're what?" Shidarva and Dienox brandished their weapons, flaming scimitars alongside a blackened longsword. "What is it you think you're going to do, new god?"

"We three," Vander said, "four, if you count Kilke, are going to explain it to you."

"What?" Dienox laughed. "With a lecture?"

"By whichever methods are required." Kholster spread his arms wide. "You want to play games with mortals? You like the idea of powerful beings toying with, rather than respecting, those weaker than themselves? Very well. I accept your challenge. Come then and play a game with me."

"Four gods," Dienox muttered, peering from one god to the other. "I only count three over here. Are you counting Jun?"

"No." Vander smiled. "No, he is not."

*

In the ruins of a broken tower, floating in a chaotic sea of sensory overload, Hasimak held the barrier in place, protecting himself and his wards, but the Ghaiattri were coming. A lone ram-horned creature with leather wings and a light-brown hide had noticed his intrusion, but one meant others would gather—moths to a flame.

"We don't have much longer." Hasimak breathed easily, still drawing enough power from the remaining Port Gates: one at Fort Sunder, one in the kingdom of the bug-like Issic-Gnoss, and a third in the frozen lands where the beings with whom he'd meant to keep a line of communication open had long since vanished from Barrone, slain by a menace he'd had never been allowed to investigate. Of the two local Port Gates that had remained in near alignment after the first dragon attack, now only one remained in partial alignment. It was like the destruction of Alt come again. A once thriving people, Shidarva's worshippers on Alt had given their lives and homeland to stop the threat to the World Crystal, and, at the last moment, Uled had forbidden Hasimak to let them escape through the Port Gates. Forced him to seal them off as they sank beneath the waves. It hadn't been murder in any technical sense, but it still felt like it. "Can you see the dragon?"

"All I see is madness," Zerris answered.

I've forgotten to open a view port.

A gesture opened a rift in the air.

"Look through it, but do not put any portion of yourselves, not even your magic, through it or we will be thrust back into the material world whether we are ready or not," Hasimak whispered. "And don't try to make it wider."

More Ghaiattri came, scrabbling against his protective shell. Whispering his name. *Did the others speak Ghaiattric?* He did not think so.

"Opener of doors!" the demons sang in their horrid tongue. "Weakener of walls! Shatterer! Bond breaker! Let us in!"

"No," Hasimak hissed back in the same language. "I. Will. Not. Never again!"

Hasimak only hoped that in drawing this many of the demons to him, he was drawing them away from Fort Sunder's gate as well. Geography in the Never Dark did not map itself with a strict one-to-one correlation onto the material plane that shadowed it. That was how the Port Gates functioned, effectively moving through one side of the gate, with the gate itself shifting location so that when one emerged, the other side of the gate had moved in the demon's world to where you wanted to emerge; the tricky bit was to hurl the traveler through a brief tear in dimensions and drop them safely at their destination without opening a gate into the demon realm itself.

So easy for so long and then . . . Alt.

The wise men and women of Shidarva's kingdom, those who studied stars and energy, worked magic and mystery . . . in their last desperate moments, they had tried to force their gates, to bull through into Port Ammond and thus reach safety . . .

"I see it," Klerris said. "Great Aldo, but he's destroyed the towers. The city burns!"

"Port Ammond has been razed and reborn nine times in my memory."

Hasimak smiled. "It can rise again so long as there are elves, whatever they call themselves, to take up the task. I've told you. It can all be built again."

"Focus." Beads of sweat rolled down his face, dampening his grayish hair. "Can you tell if he is on his third breath?"

"He is snuggled in amid the glowing slag that was Port Ammond," Hollis, the Sea Lord, said. "He crouches there. Waiting."

"Hasimak!" The dragon's voice shook the stones. "I've saved the third breath for you, old friend. Promises kept to the god of death and his daughter, I have slain thousands and ruined the capital of their ancient masters. Come then, crafty elf, eldest of the Eldrennai. Master of magicks! I await your pleasure. Let us duel one last time before I die!"

Under the gaze of his apprentices, with enemies from beyond the Port Gates calling him and the dragon challenging him, Hasimak felt as trapped as he had the day Uled had enslaved him. He could have killed Uled. Many would say he should have, but he had seen so much then, nations' rise and fall, Nomi's defeat of Dienox, the exodus of dragons. . . . How do you justify the shedding of blood? How many genocides did it take before killing was as thoughtless as breathing? For Hasimak, it had been three . . . and then his eyes had been opened, retribution, punishment from the goddess Shidarva. . . . He would always love her for that.

"When he is weak." Hasimak cleared his throat. "When I have taxed him and his breath is merely flame. Then he will be vulnerable."

"Then we should kill it?" Klerris asked, her face so intense, it was hard for him to look at her.

"Then you will have the option of slaying the dragon." Hasimak's voice was hoarse, choked with emotion.

"Why wouldn't we kill it?" Lord Stone asked.

"I can think of countless reasons." Hasimak patted him on the shoulder. "But you must provide your own."

"Hasimak!" The dragon bellowed.

"Dragons feed on heat," Hasimak said earnestly, looking from one student to the next, making eye contact. "Cold cannot normally harm them, but when they have spent their might in grand fashion like this, then they can be vulnerable to elemental ice."

"Hasimak!" Coal roared. "My years are numbered now in less than a century. I will not tire of waiting for you this time, old sneak. Death is my friend and will come to collect me. All my promises are kept. I have visited the mountains of my true home a final time. All the remaining years I grant to you, if need be. Wait as long as you like. With sufficient delay, I shall regain my strength. This area shall once more be rich with ambient heat upon which I shall feast, and then you can taste a First Breath."

"What now, teacher?" Zerris asked.

"Now I watch for it." Hasimak eyed the small rift he had opened into the material world. "A moment of distraction. A moment of inattention." His shields flickered, Ghaiattri beating against the magic shell.

I only hope I have enough time.

CHAPTER 38

PATHS OF LEAST RESISTANCE

If there were any Eldrennai in the whole of creation less comfortable than Dolvek was, he hoped their pain ended quickly. He enjoyed flight. Not as much as some did. He didn't know if it was because he associated flight with arguments with his father or with his realization at an early age that his brother could no longer do it. Flight was the reason Bhaeshal's eyes were permanently masked, the confines of the mask slowly taking up more and more surface area as she used her magic.

Were Dolvek honest with himself about his instinctive dislike and disrespect for General . . . no . . . for kholster Wylant, he might even admit it had its roots in the way she could use her Aeromancy with such casual disregard for the limitations her actions had brought upon others, and that without being angry, he often felt too guilty to fly.

It wasn't the view. Even in the autumn weather, the trees stretching out below him had their beauty. The Parliament of Ages, due to the interference of Hashan, Warrune, and the other Root Trees, perennially received optimum rainfall for the growing things below, and thus, even as they left the supernatural spring of Hearth that kept some non-evergreens green year round, flowing away from the Root Cities, the forest unrolled a canvas painted in rich golds and reds, even the occasional purple of magic-eating Genna Trees.

Pyromancy ablated the cold, working in tandem with his cloak and armor. A scar of black ran off to the left (was that northeast?), the forest fire begun by the destruction of Tranduvallu raging on. Yavi assured him it was a healthy blaze now, controlled and renewing, and if anyone knew about such things, he was certain the Vaelsilyn . . . the Vael did. But the black billowed for miles, a sight that, combined with the firelight from below, he imagined at night might be mistaken for the steady march of one hell or another.

Flying alongside Yavi was a thrill.

He'd given up on any chance at romance with her. The young Vael's heart was clearly set in a more Aernese direction, and while that wounded him, Dolvek could no longer pretend he did not understand. Were the Aern noble and brave? Well, in Dolvek's opinion, no. It was hardly brave to be a well-made engine of destruction and then destroy things; what they were was . . . admirable. He could not begin to understand what it was to be Aern, but he understood enough to view them as admirable.

Having been created as instruments of war, built to kill and eat their fill of their enemies created a cycle that could prove endless, yet they did not wage a constant war. They reasoned. They made allowances for the differences of others and tried, more often than not, to accommodate that diversity and function as a part, rather than as despoilers, of Barrone. What would the world be like if the Aern, like the Zaur, exercised no population control?

No . . . his thoughts, though occupied one moment by the bleakest of imaginings about his people, the slaves they had created, even the death of his father, were not the problem. He did not cry because, as foolish as he now understood it sounded, an Eldrennai prince did not cry tears, he cried havoc. A lesson, one of many, he'd been taught without realizing how much of his father's heart wasn't in them.

What ruined the trip for Dolvek was the same thing that made his back ache and his flesh crawl. He shuddered at the sensation and not, he hoped, solely because of the passenger riding on his back, tail trailing out behind them, occasionally slapping against his legs, forepaws on his shoulders, wedge-shaped head resting far too close to his ears.

"Am I bothering you, Prince?" The Sri'Zaur's breath was dank on his neck.

"I was lost in thought, General," Dolvek called over the wind.

"We could always walk," Tsan purred. "You must be getting tired. Does it tax you more to carry a magic-resistant being with you when you fly than it does to carry a more malleable individual?"

"I can fly on horseback," Dolvek scoffed. "You require far less effort than carrying a horse."

"It is much faster this way," Yavi whooped, a friendly wind spirit tossing her about the sky in wasteful arcs and dives. She shot low, dropping below the canopy, then arcing high above the clouds.

"Stay close enough for the prince to catch you should your elemental friend tire or grow bored," Tsan shouted to be heard over the wind. "We wouldn't want to lose you."

Every bone in Dolvek's body screamed for him to hurl the blasted lizard off his back and onto the hardest rock available, to let it smash to bits.

It wasn't jealousy, but Dolvek loathed the way Tsan spoke so solicitously to the Vael, tracking her, head darting in controlled motions up, up, down, down, left, right in response to her every move.

It wanted something from her, but Dolvek had no idea what and . . . if he had misjudged the Sri'Zaur as severely as he'd misjudged the Aern . . .

"How much longer do I fly this direction?" Dolvek asked.

"Keep heading northwest until you reach Rin'Saen Gorge." Tsan's forked tongue flicked his earlobe.

"How far is that?" Yavi asked. "Most wind spirits won't travel more than a hundred jun, give or take, and will slow down a little more every ten jun or so before that. This one is strong, but we'll start to lag behind between forty and sixty jun. . . . It takes bunches out of them to go so fast without a storm."

"Just shy of three hundred jun to the gorge," Tsan called. "Then another twenty or so by paws through the tunnels."

"And then where?" Dolvek asked.

"You know how your people have suspected for centuries that we were making our way into your lands through Rin'Saen Gorge?"

"Yes."

"For once, they were correct." Tsan's hind claws tightened. "You never dug deep enough."

Biting back a response, Dolvek turned his thoughts to the path ahead. He had not given much consideration to what would take place when he got to Tsan's home. Instinct had told him to go, to be at the table when the Sri'Zaur dealt with the Vaelsilyn, or the Eldrennai would never get a seat at all. If Yavi's magic failed, would she let him carry her, either on his back or . . . could he use his cloak? Let her sit on it while he carried the fabric? *In as little as a day*, he told himself, *you have to have a plan.*

*

"It's at least two hundred and fifty jun," Tyree leaned over and whispered.

Why he had to get so close, Cadence knew too well.

You fancy him, don't you, you faithless— Hap's voice rose and died, washing away in an echo of confidence not Cadence's own.

"Stop it," she told the handsome captain. "No one invited you inside my head."

"Sorry." Tyree's hands came up again, a gesture meant to imply surrender, but Cadence saw traces of potential movements, bracelets to daggers, daggers hurled. He meant the surrender, but Tyree never let his guard down enough that the possibility of attack faded from him. "Just trying to help."

"You're a dangerous man." Cadence picked at the mixture of dried fruit, nuts, and mushrooms in her pack. "Too dangerous to have in my head."

"I'm too much of a gentlemen to suggest other alternatives." Tyree's smile blazed at her, part an unconscious blast of charisma, and the rest wholly physical and behavioral. He was attractive, but she'd had her fill of outlaws. A farmer had more chance to bed her than he did, someone who could provide a normal home for Caius where he wouldn't grow up to— Another vision flashed through her head. Leather wings. A burning farm. Dead men hanging from an apple tree.

"Who is Caius?" Tyree asked.

"I told you to stay out, curse you." The Long Fist loomed at the edge of her mind.

"You think quite loudly." Tyree's eyes went cold. "If you don't want me to hear you, stop shouting. And that other thing . . ." His eyes flicked to her right, where she'd imagined a hand ready to grab him. "You'd likely win, but the real question is whether you'd be blind in both eyes or just in one by the time my brains have been bashed onto the tunnel wall."

It hung there between them, silence pregnant with delayed violence.

"C'mon," he whispered. "Whoever this Hap was, I'm not him. This Caius fellow . . . I'm not him either. I have no interest in hurting you, a moderate interest in getting to know you better, but mainly, I'm leading these Aern." He nodded, not breaking eye contact, toward Kazan and the others, farther up the tunnel, feeding on the bodies of the dead, stripping the livers, and sucking the marrow from the bones. "Back to their kholster, because I have every confidence she'll pay me again and I can see the size of the debt I'll owe Niorri—well, I hope Niorri, she is the best shipwright in Midian—on a new ship getting smaller and smaller with each chip of bone-steel or royal kandit they pay me."

"That," she said, catching the edge of a thought, "and you're afraid of what will happen if you try to make it through Castleguard's borders with Aernese coin on you while the Harvest Knights are stirred up."

"Now who's peeking?" Tyree lowered his hands, a calculated surrender. "And I wouldn't call it afraid. Appropriately wary." He said another thing too, about being able to smuggle himself through if he wanted, but not wanting to take needless risks with his horse, but Cadence had stopped listening.

In his eyes, Cadence beheld other visions. Some of her and Tyree together in ways she doubted would ever come to pass, others with him as dead as Sedric at the knife, pistol, or hands of her son. But there, amid the visions of death and murder, was a fleeting image of her son at the wheel of a ship, Tyree's hand on his shoulder, forearm touching the edge of those leathery wings, a bandage on her son's back, a healing wound. They met each other's gaze and laughed, sailing out to sea with Midian at their backs.

"Where did you go just then?" Tyree asked.

Leaning forward, ignoring the way his eyes darted to the neck of her blouse, Cadence grabbed his shirt and pulled him forward, eye to eye.

"I want to get a better look." Her nose touched his. "May I?"

"That all depends." But she could already see the march of days. A young boy orphaned by Aern, adopted by a Hulsite mercenary, only to lose him to an Aern as well. An uncle. The sea. So much hate and anger, yet he'd let it go, blaming no one, accepting others as he found them. Trustworthy to his friends. A man of his word, but also an unblinking killer if the situation arose. . . .

Maybe, she thought.

I'll take maybe, he thought back. "Now did you see whatever you need, or do I need to take my shirt off?"

She flinched, expecting him to take her in his arms and try to kiss her. Instead, he turned away, eyes on an approaching Aern. Kazan, the one she'd been sure would die.

"You two ready to move on?" Kazan said. "I think they've filled up on the least rotten bits."

"It's those least rotten bits that are so important." Tyree gently pulled his shirt from Cadence's grasp. As he stood, he winked at her. "Everybody has them."

"Actually . . ." Joose joined them, still wiping gore from his lips. "No, some of the older bodies are rotten through and through."

"Now." Tyree put his arm around Joose's shoulders. "As I was telling Cadence, it's around two hundred and fifty jun as best I could count from here to what the Zaur were using as a central tunnel. I'm no Dwarf, but I used to live with one in Midian and if what she taught me is correct—"

"Why would she teach you about tunnels?" Arbokk asked.

Tyree grinned at that. "As I was saying, I think they had staging areas near each watch city, so if I steer us well, we can come up under South Watch then cut overland from there. We'll be in the Eldren Plains proper and I don't see the Harvest Knights tracking us that far afield."

"South Watch is clear," Kazan told him. "They already killed the Zaur force there and Bloodmane feels it was a feint to begin with. I can have Eyes of Vengeance meet us there."

"Then let's go." Cadence sprang to her feet.

*

A ragged line of misery, the exiles pushed on. Rae'en and Glayne held a wagon in the air while the Oathbreakers who owned it tried to fit the mended wheel onto its axle.

Strange to be helping them, Amber thought at Rae'en.

Yes, Kazan sent, *but they might be Aiannai tomorrow. Why not assume that and not worry?*

If they are not accepted as Aiannai, Bloodmane added, **it is quite possible they will go on the prince's mission to recover the Lost Command.**

In which case, Rae'en sent, *we want them to succeed. So a little assistance now is no meat off my table. What I want to know—* Rae'en looked back in the direction of Port Ammond, though it was miles distant and long out of sight, *—is what happened with Coal.*

Inconclusive. Glayne shrugged, lowering the wagon. *You saw what I saw before the dragon melted my weapon.*

We'll get an update from the Bone Finders Zhan dispatches to recover the bone-steel, won't we? Kazan asked.

Who is he sending? Rae'en asked.

Teru and Whaar, Kazan answered. Rae'en's map zoomed out as if she were on dragon back, and two dots among a sea of them flared bright gold. *See?*

Looks like they are headed this way, Rae'en sent. *Not to Port Ammond.*

Another dot, this one moving by itself, along the White Road from Fort Sunder flared.

Alysaundra is meeting them here so she can join them after they deliver your ring, Eyes of Vengeance said.

Should I send someone with them? Rae'en asked.

Why would you? Eyes of Vengeance asked. **You could offer, but Hasimak and the nobles, if they yet live, will not attack them and Coal is our ally, so neither will he.**

I guess. Rae'en dropped her side of the wagon back to the ground, the wheel in place and having withstood the weight of Glayne's portion of the wagon back on it.

It's hard to sit back and let Zhan run his Ossuary, Amber sent, *isn't it?*

Yes.

Teams of Aiannai, Eldrennai, and Aern ranged out from the long trail of cold, complaining evacuees to hunt more game to feed them. Reports of their progress scrolled through kholster Rae'en's mind in exhaustive lists pared down by Kazan as best he could.

She didn't know how he kept it all straight in his head, holding the location of all the Armored and tracking their positions moment to moment. Kholster had often joked about how much more effective Overwatches were than kholsters at that sort of thing. He could talk to them all at once. He was the one who had linked them, but he only came close to feeling the kinds of things an Overwatch did at the start and finish of an All Know or an All Recall.

Each time they stopped, a sally from the Zaur would begin, usually within hours, forcing them to press on, to barely sleep. This was no problem for the Armored; Rae'en had even learned the art of warsuit rack time—sleeping inside Bloodmane while he soldiered tirelessly on when she wanted a nap.

On the first night out, a group of rebels had tried to assassinate King Rivvek only to be brutally beaten back by the king's Lancers and the Sidearms temporarily under Brigadier Bhaeshal's command. As effective at cowing rebellion as the presence of so many Aern had been, many found the sight of the night sky alight with lightning strikes as Mazik and Bash struck, sending the twelve would-be murderers dead and burning into the air as Geomancers summoned a protective ring around the king, to be more so. Pyromancers limned in flame had stood at the ready, not even moving to strike, alongside Hydromancers showing the same restraint.

But the words Rae'en heard repeated over and over again by the Oathbreakers as they struggled on were the trepidatious words "Are the Aern getting hungry, kholster Rae'en?"

Hundreds had slipped away before morning, deciding to take their chances with the Zaur. Their screams had started less than a jun from camp. On the second night no one had deserted, and though the grumbling increased, it lessened with each day as the king and his soldiers moved through the line of refugees at dawn, noon, and dusk ensuring all had adequate food and water, that the sick or injured were cared for as best as conditions allowed. With each Zaur attack repelled, his people began to trust him more, cursing him in one breath and then thanking him in the next when he tended their needs.

By the third night, Alysaundra and her ex-husbands had returned Rae'en's ring and headed on to Port Ammond. Rae'en wore the ring of silvered bone-steel and vowed never to take it off unless it was to read her father's inscription. If the return of the ring lightened her mood, she did not seem to be the only one.

Older elves had begun to recount tales of King Villok's bloody rise to power and of the abuses of King Zillek's reign. Not many openly praised

Rivvek, but some began to argue about what more he could possibly have done to spare them. Had he not managed to secure the help of the Aern? Had he not spared as many as he could? What else could one expect of a mage-cripple than to grab at what allies he could? That brother of his hadn't shown up with a plan to save anyone, had he? And him with all the magic an elf could ask for? Didn't even show up to his own father's funeral. . . .

On the fourth night, Rae'en walked with her Overwatches, patrolling a circuit around the group, listening to the sounds of elves sleeping, moaning, and crying in the night. Laughter was scarce, but so were screams.

He seems to be winning them over, Rae'en thought.

Maybe it's the leisurely pace he's setting, Amber thought. *We've only covered half the distance in almost four days of walking. They stop at dusk and don't start until dawn. We could have been to Fort Sunder and back several times over.*

Why haven't the Zaur overtaken us? Glayne asked. *That is what bothers me the most.*

Maybe they think if they keep us in close quarters with them long enough, Amber sent, *we'll eat the Oathbreakers ourselves.*

What do you think, kholster Rae'en? Feagus asked.

I don't care. Rae'en closed her eyes, enjoying the feeling but still seeing what was in front of her through Bloodmane's eyes. *Whatever reasons they have, whether it's that they don't want the Eldrennai to be able to use their magic, or they want us to kill each other for them, we're going to win. The Aern held Fort Sunder against a full Ghaiattri invasion. We can hold it against the Zaur.*

We did have a larger force then, Bloodmane sent only to Rae'en.

But now we have a dragon, or should. Rae'en thought of the dragon, and anger grew in the pit of her stomach. *Both Coal and the Oathbreakers should have rejoined us by now. They can't still be holding Port Ammond. There were only five Oathbreakers and even if they died, there is no way the Zaur killed Coal.*

It is not unusual for a dragon to sleep for several days after a large expenditure of energy. . . .

Show me the dragon attack again, Rae'en thought at Bloodmane. *Right up until Coal slagged Glayne's dagger.*

Of course.

As she watched, Rae'en sensed she was missing a vital aspect of unfolding events, but viewing the sequence over and over did nothing other than to make her wish Coal were with her army. She knew dragons were capricious beasts, but she wished this one cared a little more about how she wanted his help, rather than how he wanted to grant it.

CHAPTER 39

ANYTHING TO WIN

Sedric sat at Castleguard, shivering despite the heavy robes he wore and the cup of soup he'd been offered. He had missed the noon Changing of the Gods and passed beyond North Gate near dinner time. Even as a Master Long Speaker, there were things best viewed with one's own eyes. Cassandra, Revered Master Long Speaker and controller of the Castleguard Relay, sat next to him in the crush of people gathered around the statues of the gods.

"Is it always this crowded?" Sedric asked as a young boy jostled him.

"More and more since the new death god arose." Cassandra, a pleasant woman with a pleasant face, who eschewed normal Long Speaker garb, preferring the warm wool dresses, fur-lined gloves, and boots popular among the lesser nobles in the King's Court, did not give the impression of being a human who could tear out one's mind with a thought. She patted a child on the head and shooed him away. "And once that happened," she said, rolling her eyes at the statue of Vander that occupied Aldo's former position, "the Knights had to force less influential supplicants to watch from the bottom of Pilgrim's Hill."

Sedric sipped at the soup, mostly to warm himself. Everything in Castleguard tasted of boiled potato. Normally in an organized arrangement, the statues themselves had shifted. Vander, Kholster, and Kilke stood on one side. Jun stood in the middle, hands outspread as if keeping the factions apart. Shidarva, Torgrimm, Sedvinia, and Minapsis were on the other side with Xalistan, Gromma, Queelay, and Yhask standing clear of the conflict, nominally seeming to favor Shidarva's forces but wary of both.

"Has anyone spotted Nomi's statue?" Sedric frowned down at his broth before sipping at it again.

"Oh, for Shidarva's sake, Sedric," Cassandra laughed. "It's not spiced like they do in the south so that your eyes water and your bowels run, but it tastes fine."

Waving over one of a group of guards (half from the college at the Guild Cities and half from the Castleguard relay), Cassandra sent for mulled spice wine.

"They found her in the woods," Cassandra said once the guard had run off to the Long Speaker Tower.

"Nomi?" Sedric asked.

"Yes." Cassandra nodded. "A huntsman did. Hiding behind a tree; the statue of the goddess, not the huntsman. I have a few of the acolytes out there tracking her."

Sedric raised a brushy gray eyebrow.

"Oh." Cassandra leaned in close. "She's in a different direction noon and midnight. Always hiding."

"And this . . . standoff?" Sedric asked.

"For seven Changings now." Cassandra smiled as the guard returned with the wine, accepting a portion for herself and for Sedric. "The priests don't know what to say about it anymore. Try to keep the people calm, most of them, but—"

—But, she continued in his thoughts, *King Mioden is talking about raising an army and marching south to kill the Aern and stop them from slaying gods.*

As if that would do anything. Sedric groaned at the thought but sighed pleasantly at the heat, both temperature and spice, of the wine.

You don't have to tell me! The Token Hundred down at the gate can't even come into town now without risking a fight with the Harvest Knights. I'd considered killing the old bear, Cassandra thought, *but we'd have to assassinate so many before we got to a reasonable heir, there is no chance it would go unnoticed.*

Kholster, Sedric prayed. *Vander, I hope you both know what you are doing.*

"Two minutes to midnight," a Harvest Knight in brigandine bellowed. "Two minutes."

All conversation wound down as the assembled watched the stones around them to see what their gods would do.

*

Nomi ran. Kholster was coming for her next. He had to be. She was the obvious choice. But where on all Barrone could one hide from the Harvester?

Through forest and mountains, never feeling safe. Yes, she had flaming hair and immortality, but her power was at its core merely an extension of a part of Dienox's responsibilities he did not want. But if Kholster decided to kill Dienox, attacking the god of war while possessing a portion of Dienox's former power could only hasten his victory.

She'd thought herself safe; she'd never played in any of the games the other gods and goddesses played, never participated in their wars and intrigues. Life as a goddess had been fun, gadding about the halls of power, taking different shapes and walking among mortals, exploring the Outwork, Barrone below, and even the Dragonwaste beyond before she'd come to accept that it truly was empty.

Vibrations of power rose in the ether, though. She heard what the other gods were saying, had been able to hear anything said within Dienox's hearing ever since she'd taken his hair, and they all kept mentioning a battle destroying everything and leaving the gods alone amid the debris.

If only Kholster would give in a little bit, she thought, *then he might have no interest in further conquest. But if Vander and Torgrimm could not or would not weaken his resolve, get him to see reason, to play along with them until they calmed down, to make only small changes, or even convince Kholster to slay all of the others except for her, then who on Barrone could?*

Nomi stopped running.

"I'm an idiot," she swore. To whom did Kholster always listen? It was like a rule of the universe. If Wylant could be convinced that Kholster needed to stand down, then she would be able to make him do it, if anyone could.

*

Supervising the defensive preparations at Fort Sunder had swallowed Wylant's world. It had started with realizing how little room there was and then moved on to how they were planning to feed and water so many refugees. Beginning with the people of Bark's Bend, she'd told them to come with her to Fort Sunder and bring everything they could: animals, crops, clothes, food—and then to have the warsuits and the Bone Finders help harvest whatever crops they could as Wylant and representatives from the current village moved on to the next.

At all the Eldrennai villages, they did whatever she asked with the understanding that they would be allowed to take refuge at Fort Sunder when the Zaur came. And even though she did not see how she could house even the ones already on their way, she said yes because she needed the supplies and the help gathering them. She did not say whether she could protect them after.

Human villages went poorly until she started keeping the helmet on. When community elders thought she was an Aern, they were perfectly agreeable. "Just so long as your lot remember us when the lizards come and when you done killed those high an' mighty elves. Do you think you'll be using their Port and Watch cities when you done them in?"

We're misleading all of these people, Mother, Vax thought. *Or many of them.*

I know, Vax. Over the last few days, these were the conversations that broke her heart.

There isn't room for them all at Fort Sunder, not inside the walls, Vax thought. *I know.*

But you said you'd protect them, Vax said. *You promised.*

No, Vax. Wylant and Clemency had made it back to the fort, but it was so late, she would have been asleep in the saddle if not for Clemency. *I have promised to remember them. I have promised to try to protect them when the Zaur come, or in a nonspecific way. I have said I will allow them within the walls—but not when I would allow them within the walls.*

She waited for the hurt and betrayal. This was as hard of a push as Vax had ever made an—**That is correct, Clemency thought. I have tracked her oaths and you may review them, Vax. They were all prudently worded to allow flexibility.**

Oh. Vax was silent while Wylant directed a new batch of people to go down to Bark's Bend so the villagers could teach them how to gig for frogs or help weave mats. *Hey, Clem is right, Mother. I'm sorry for doubting you. You'd do more if you could, though. Right? It's not all loopholes in the oath with you, right?*

"Of course it isn't," she whispered. "But, Vax, even with a warsuit, there is only so much that is within my power. I'm not like your father. I'm not—"

Fire bloomed into existence next to her. Humans and Eldrennai fled, but the Aern and warsuits all looked to see who it was before resuming their tasks as if a goddess had not just manifested in their midst.

"You have to talk to Kholster," Nomi said. "I know you are busy here, but the gods are all taking sides and—"

"—a god."

Wylant took her head off with a single cross-body draw of Vax. Catching the head of the goddess in her free hand as she pivoted, Wylant brought Vax's blade up to Nomi's hairline, Vax already shrinking into a smaller knife for the scalping. Clemency's helm opened and fell back revealing Wylant's now-bare scalp. Settling the flaming tresses atop her skull, amazed that fire did not burn her, she willed the fire to be hers.

It can't be that easy, she thought.

It was.

A scream so full of emotions she could not tell them apart tore free of her throat, raw and ragged, and . . . triumphant. She jumped in shock as the Aern and warsuits echoed her victory with shouts of their own. She looked down at a small Eldrennai child, one of the two young Aeromancers she'd seen playing down in Bark's Bend, who stared up in fear and disbelief.

"How else was I going to keep you safe?" Wylant asked her.

Screaming, the little elf ran for her mother. That got a reaction from the assembled Aern and warsuits: A mixture of laughter, hoots, cheers, and applause.

That was all of the things, Mom, Vax thought.

What?

The things Dad wanted you to figure out, Vax said. *That there were way more of the enemy than you suspected, that they wanted the Eldrennai hemmed in at Fort Sunder so their magic would be unreliable, and that if you took Nomi's power, you might be able to win.*

"Your father," she swore nonspecifically, taking flight and trailing fire through the sky as she headed toward the remains of Port Ammond.

*

Sedric and Cassandra saw the statue of the new goddess flying over the tree line and began to move as quickly and as quietly as possible from the area. Fighting did not break out until they had made it to the bottom of the hill; then those assembled lost their minds. One god losing a portion of his power to a mortal had happened before. They knew how to react to it—stories and legends let them process the change—but to have two more gods thrown down in a scant space of days was too much. Nomi had been the only human god and was well-liked.

Cast as a mischief-maker in tales, Nomi was famous for stealing fire from the gods and showing humans that, though they were mortal and the shortest-lived of Barrone's races, they could take comfort in the knowledge they could rise to any heights.

Tower or Gate? Sedric thought at Cassandra.

Tower. Her teeth were gritted as Long Arms and Far Flames repelled the crowd. *It's closer and the Knights may make for the North Gate to attack the Token Hundred.*

Tense minutes later, safely behind the bolted and barred gates of the Castleguard Relay, Cassandra and Sedric sat in front of the fire in the common room staring at one another.

"Do we let the information out?" Sedric asked.

"I don't know how we can stop it." Cassandra looked into the fire, seeing Sedric knew not what within the flames.

It was still small enough that they could. Working together, they could offer discounted services, and while their customers came expecting to send messages, the Long Speakers could erase or alter memories. It would be barely feasible, and it would only delay the inevitable.

"People aren't as religious in the South," Sedric said finally. "I mean, they are, but not like in the North. They wouldn't go to war over it."

"No?" Cassandra asked.

"I hope not."

"We'll adjust to this, Sedric," Cassandra said. "Even if all the gods change, most people trust and fear the Aern as it is. They've viewed Kholster as a creature of legend for years."

"I hope you're right." Sedric held his hands before the flames. *I'm too old for this*, he thought, then laughed at himself. *Was anyone really young enough for times like these?* Caius came to mind. He would grow up in a different era. Uncertain, where even the gods seemed impermanent. What would that mean to the coming generations? How would it shape them?

"At least nothing worse can happen," one of the nearby guards offered.

Sedric did not strike the man, but he was pleased when Cassandra did.

*

Purple lit the sky of the smoking ruin of Port Ammond. Where nothing had been, the fractured top of the Tower of Elementals popped into place. It hung in the air long enough for Coal to perceive its existence and then, as he started drawing in heat, it exploded in a fine powder of debris, the last remnant of a once-great city's history dashed to pieces.

One being flew out of the cloud, white hair strung out behind him as he soared straight at the dragon, hands outlined in purple and gold. Vapor trails of breath spilled from the edges of Hasimak's mouth as the cold struck him. Coal thrilled at the sight of his old playmate, so much so he was tempted to ignore the four Eldrennai dropping out of the base of the clouds, heading for the Port Gates.

"No. No. No." Coal launched his bulk at the base of the fallen tower. "No fair fights."

*

"There will be no agreement." Shidarva's face contorted in rage, blue fire glowing within the veins of her cheeks and forehead. "No compromises until you tell us what you have done with Aldo! I want to see him."

She did it, Vander thought.

I know, Kholster sent. *I have Nomi. I'm healing her body and forcing her soul to stay in it until she's strong enough to live on her own.*

Is that guilt, sir? Harvester asked.

A little, Kholster sent. *She did exactly what I wanted and I knew what*

Wylant would do to her. Death is supposed to be on the side of the mortals. All the mortals. I shouldn't pick sides.

Truly? Harvester asked.

Of course, Kholster thought. *I can't always help, but I'm rooting for them. All of them. Just like Torgrimm would have if he hadn't broken himself on our behalf. This isn't just about Oathbreakers and Oathkeepers. It's about setting things right.*

By breaking them?

The road to victory and the road to defeat can look astonishingly similar until you reach the end, Vander told them.

And sometimes— Kholster cleared his throat *—you have to make sacrifices to draw your true opponent out of hiding. Pretend you don't see him.*

And then you kill him, sir?

I am powerless against him because Torgrimm thought he was fighting Kilke.

He isn't?

"They're back at it," Dienox shouted, excitedly pointing at Port Ammond. "Everyone be quiet, I want to see this."

*

Later, Kholster could not describe the battle. For Aern who wanted to hear the tale of Hasimak's battle with the Great Black Dragon, he would tell them to wait until Day Eleven of the New Year when he, with Rae'en's permission, would do an All Recall and share the memory. To any other being, mortal or immortal, he would only shake his head and tell them it was something about which he could not speak.

Coal went for the apprentices, and Hasimak stopped him, hurling a dimensional barrier between them. It shattered when Coal struck it, but then Hasimak was there with another and another, each growing smaller as his power ebbed. Zerris flew free with Klerris, fearing to feed the dragon's fire. Lord Stone raised the Tower of Elementals straight up into the air with his might, holding it in place as it once was, while Hollis flew inside to reach the Port Gates.

When the cold waned, Hasimak shouted a warning a heartbeat ahead of Coal's third breath. A small mountain formed of fallen buildings rose up between Lord Stone and the bright white beam. Hasimak threw up a shield, but he'd used too many, too often, and it was not enough. Stone evaporated, as did the Eldrennai who called himself its Lord.

The Tower of Elementals came crashing down again with Hollis, the Sea Lord, still inside. Hasimak's grief split the sky, lightning raining down upon

Coal, electrical arcs crackling around the dragon in a corona of blue-white. Then the beam hit Hasimak.

He did not vanish completely; perhaps he shielded himself at the last possible instant. Limp robes torn and tattered, the High Elementalist fluttered to the ground as if he were no more substantial than a leaf.

Spitting the last of his volcanic breath into the sky, a flare of triumph, Coal hovered above his old foe, wings flapping . . . and then the ice began to flow. Used to his own breath steaming, the great gray dragon did not see it until the crackle of the condensing ice was a full story tall. Rising like a sculpture carved from ice, the Tower of Elementals rose, transparent and beautiful, powered and wrought at its center by the Sea Lord's magic and his rage.

"Impressive, young water wizard," Coal chortled, "but I am tired of fighting today and I would not sully my old playmate's death with further injury to his students."

Wings flapping, Coal struggled to rise, but then came the wind bearing down on him as if it had a grudge, because it did. Searching the sky for some sign of the Aeromancer thwarting his grand exit, he found the elven lass with the red-trimmed robes easily enough but squinted seeking out her sister.

He spat a mouthful of molten liquid at the huge construction of ice flowing toward him, but it was like trying to smelt copper with a match. Drawing in the cold as much as he could to power his breath, Coal spotted a female figure clad in white.

"Wind Witch!" he howled, spraying her with fire, the bulk of his flame reaching all the way to the clouds, surrounding her with fiery death. She did not fall.

Again and again he spat, but though she smoked and sizzled, robes burning away, the wind would not stop. Turning at last to Hollis as the tower of ice grew close, Coal threw his bulk at the tower, claws scratching great chunks away, opening cracks—but then the wind pushed him away. Particles of ice fell from the top of the tower, covering Coal's skin, becoming steam as they hit, but soon, the sleet-like pellets only melted, and then they began to stick. As the dragon froze, Lady Air, Klerris, clad in her sister's red-trimmed robes, floated down from the clouds, her sister's smoldering body clutched in her arms. Zerris had held off the fire as best she could, but even weakened by Coal's earlier exertions, there was only so much one Pyromancer could do to ablate a dragon's fire.

A tremendous spike of ice formed at the center of the tower, and Coal laughed.

"Well done," he croaked in a hoarse roar as the tower toppled, the spike piercing his chest. "Well done."

CHAPTER 40
GATEWAYS AND SECRET PASSAGES

If riding through the air with a Sri'Zaur on his back was bad, crawling through the cramped tunnels Tsan called the Gorge Entrance to Xasti'Kul (the Shadow Home) was far worse. Was everything shadow something to these lizards? Kilke was lord of secrets, too. Couldn't there be a Secret City or a Secret Passage? A Secret Road? Even a secret Secret Road . . . redundancy could be fun, couldn't it?

Mucus ran from his nose. Eyes red and rimmed with tears, Prince Dolvek understood how General . . . kholster Wylant must have felt over the years. If this much concentrated Zaur stink could so affect him, it would surely have killed her. Yavi had even taken pity on him and plucked a few of her head petals, braiding them into a mask for him to wear over his nose and mouth. It helped, but her scent was so strong on it that crawling behind her in the tunnel added a different kind of torture to the mix.

I will not ask how much farther it is. Dolvek gagged, pulling aside his mask to spit phlegm onto the sticky tunnel floor. He thanked any gods who wanted his thanks for the gloves. *Not just hours of this*, he tormented himself. *We're on the second day.*

My robe idea worked for carrying Yavi . . . but being mystic piggyback champion of the trip, glorified sky horse to the influential, is all I've done. They'll likely kill me and eat me in front of Yavi, and her last thought of me will be how much better an Aern would have tasted.

*

Wylant had not returned when King Rivvek and his kingdom in exile arrived, but the Armored and the Eldrennai already in place knew what to do. Grand tents stitched from animal hide and whatever could be found, repurposed, or skinned dotted the area outside the wall of Fort Sunder.

"Sargus," Rivvek asked wearily, "is it just me or does it look like the Aern have made preparations to keep us alive and fed?"

"It does indeed, my king."

Mazik, Bash, and his other soldiers moved out among the people, helping the young, the old, and the sick find their places, keeping those the Aern had already rejected as unsuitable to be Aiannai in the same camp with the king. Hours later. Bash arrived with kholster Rae'en, and it came as a sigh of relief.

Almost over, he told himself. *Almost done.*

All his calculations, all the trignom tiles stacked in his mind had led to this moment. His people were at Fort Sunder. The Port Gate was near. They would be sorted. He would lead the unforgiven through the Port Gate, and whatever happened then his people and the Aern would be at peace with one another.

Tired but intent on making it through this last set of obstacles, Rivvek studied kholster Rae'en. She looked different now that she was Armored, as if the world could never touch her again as anything more than an inconvenience.

"Are your people settled in, King Rivvek?" Rae'en asked. She wore her father's warsuit, its helm under her arm, two warpicks on her back, the one made of pearlescent crystal and her father's first warpick, Hunger.

"Where is Grudge?" he asked, standing to offer her the lone chair.

"Entrusted to the Ossuary, for now." Rae'en shook her head, refusing the seat, but Rivvek remained standing as well.

"If only all grudges were so easily put aside," he said, rubbing the back of his neck. There was not an inch of him that did not hurt. Close quarters magnified the smell of days on the road, and since his Hydromancers could not use their magic here, he did not avail himself of the offers to wash until all of his people had been given the opportunity to go down to the river and bathe.

"Right," Rae'en sighed. "Okay. Look. How do you want to do this?"

"Sort us," King Rivvek said wearily. "Tell me who is Aiannai and who is not. Of those who are not, I wish permission to lead them into the Port Gate here."

"Why you?"

"I am their king." Rivvek shrugged. "Why would I not lead them? Yes, Mazik and Bash, many of my soldiers, in fact, are better fighters than I, more experienced leaders of men, but I have been there."

Of the two hundred thousand Eldrennai who made it to Fort Sunder after the destruction of Port Ammond, only twenty-seven thousand, two hundred and thirty-seven were unsuitable to be called Aiannai, at least provisionally . . . but that number comprised more than half of the trained soldiers and Elementalists.

They spent one night at Fort Sunder, said good-bye to their loved ones, and bathed in the half-mile section of river downstream from Bark's Bend, turning the river black. Packing as best they could for a long foray into enemy territory, they each took a blanket, a bedroll, two canteens of water, and whatever weapons or personal items they could carry in their packs. One in twenty had a Dwarven canteen. One in one hundred had an extra pair of shoes. Almost two hundred of them even had suits of Demon Armor like Jolsit and the king.

They rehearsed the Port Gate entry twice out on the training field in front of Fort Sunder's walls. Every other elf, alternating directions, left and right, moved forward and took up defensive positions to hold the gate if the Ghaiattri swarmed it.

"Let me go with you," Sargus said in the candle mark break they had between practice and departure. "I can help. If you run into any problems, I can—"

"Protect my brother." Rivvek put a finger to the other elf's lips. "Make sure he listens to Wylant or Bash. If he won't, I want you to kill him." He handed Sargus a sealed scroll. "This will pardon him and declare him king." He held out a second scroll. "This will renounce him and reveal Bhaeshal as my wife and heir."

"But she isn't your—" Sargus balked.

"Of course she isn't, but how many elves already suppose that she and I are secretly lovers?"

"Will you do it, Bash?" Rivvek raised his voice, knowing she was near enough to hear.

"I was going to ask permission to go with you as well," Bhaeshal moved closer to them so they could speak more quietly, "but this . . ."

"If Dolvek is not up to the task," Rivvek said, clasping her arms, "the people will need you. They won't follow Wylant. The Elemental Nobles, should they ever return, have killed too many to ever rule peacefully. Please?"

She nodded, and that was all it took.

Almost there.

He pictured his plans, each completed task a trignom tile, in a row of a thousand tiles, already falling. The click of each step he took now, at the end, was the sound of the last tiles falling, forming the pattern he'd envisioned. A few adjustments had been made along the way, but it was all down to the alignment of these last few tiles, these final calculations. If one tile was out of place now, and he had failed to take it into account, failed to adapt, then it could all still fail.

*

"Any sign of demons?" Rae'en asked the king as they stood outside the Port Gate.

"No," Rivvek, already clad in his demon armor, told her. "It is deserted, as if they all were drawn elsewhere."

"Lucky," she said.

"There is no such thing." He bowed formally. "May I have your permission to open the Port Gate?"

"Before you do . . ." Rae'en sighed. How to say this? There was no way to apologize for killing his father. She wasn't even sorry, but there also wasn't a good way to say how much she liked his scars and offer him a "hope you make it back alive" tumble either. Who knew how he would take that?

He might applaud, Amber thought, *and make everybody wait out in the hallway.*

I don't want to hear this, came from Kazan, Glayne, and the others.

Rae'en flushed.

"I hope you make it back alive," Rae'en said, "and not just because that means you will be returning with the Lost Command."

Rivvek narrowed his eyes.

"What?" Rae'en looked away.

"May I tell you something," Rivvek said, removing his helm, revealing sweat already running down the scarred side of his face, "before I go, and have your oath that to the best of your ability, if it angers you, you will try not to take it out on my people?"

I wouldn't take that oath, Bloodmane said.

"I will swear that it is currently my intent," Rae'en answered.

"Intent is insufficient," Rivvek said. "I am sorry, but I must take my words with me through the Port Gate unspoken."

"You have my oath then." Rae'en sighed. "Say it."

"Your father sacrificed his life to release your people from the oaths he swore, and he made a freeborn Aern First so that you could have a chance to be truly free, to show everyone that Aern are more than the corpse-eating death machines Uled made them to be."

Rae'en had never seen such fury in his eyes.

"My father gave his life so that he could appoint a king you would not immediately destroy." Rivvek put the helmet back on, giving the signal for Bhaeshal and Sargus to open the gate. "You took his life when there was nothing forcing you to do so. The agreement you have with me could have been made with him, but you were too busy trying to show the world that you are exactly the thoughtless killers people like my brother accuse you of being. You may not blame me for your father's death, but do not forget that you are responsible for the death of mine, for I never shall."

King Rivvek stepped first through the Port Gate, and his army of unforgiven followed him. Rae'en waited until the last of them were through the gate and it was safely sealed before slamming Hunger into the wall.

*

Well-lit was not something Yavi had expected of the Zaur and Sri'Zaur city. She'd been prepared for more cramped corridors and lizard stink, but the scent was mild in the city itself and if the Zaur and Sri'Zaur were a little strange, Yavi attributed that to the whole reptile/amphibian thing they had happening. Spirits here were comfortable and in good moods. This was not like living underground with Dwarves . . . from what she remembered of her mother's stories about the journey to return Irka to his father, the Dwarves shaped everything, taking advantage of the properties of stone but rarely letting a cavern remain natural solely for its pleasing aesthetic.

Here Yavi saw whole caverns of rock formations, not just stalagmites and stalactites but stone curtains, columns, flowstone, and walls of lace-thin helictites. Tsan knew all about them, leading Yavi and Dolvek through the central gardens where various mosses and fungi grew . . . some for food and others for display.

Carefully placed reflectors filled caverns with sunlight during the day and amplified torchlight at night except for sections of cave where bioluminescent plant life cast its own arboreal brilliance. Mineral-rich air brought a symphony of smells to Yavi, some familiar, others strange and mysterious. Dolvek said he couldn't smell anything but Zaur and roses, but he did not say it in a spiteful way, which she hoped Tsan appreciated.

He was making progress. Maybe it was the blood he'd swallowed back at the Grand Conjunction when he'd been poisoned by the Zaur and saved by a concoction whose main ingredient had been Kholster's blood. Conversation in Zaurtol went on all around them, so much so that Yavi wished she could speak or at least understand it. She wasn't sure if you could make all the right noises and vibrations without a tail, but Queen Kari had learned a little, so Yavi hoped she would teach her what she could when they got back to The Parliament of Ages.

"Warlord Xastix says he would be pleased to entertain you in the throne room," Tsan purred.

She sure was padding along awfully cheerfully for someone who expected to be executed, but given what she'd heard the former general say about the cheapness of life from a Sri'Zauran point of view, maybe they looked forward to it. Yavi could see that, too, in a way. She wasn't in any hurry to die, but when she did, it wasn't like she wouldn't be happy to see Kholster again.

*

Kuort missing. Dryga dead. Asvrin having lost half of his Shades. The bad news rolled in via the echoing vibrations of Zaurtol all around General Tsan. She kept up a running commentary, walking her guests in meandering scenic trails . . . because no one could get the warlord out of his bath? Seriously?

"I should warn you," Tsan prattled on, not knowing what else to say but trying to arrange for multiple eventualities, "that Warlord Xastix will want us all to shed blood as a sign we are sincere in our intent to reach an alliance before the negotiations begin."

"How much blood?" Dolvek gasped, struggling to breathe.

"Not much," Tsan said smoothly. "You can use your own blade, or a Skreel knife can be made available to you."

"Fine." Dolvek coughed. "Thank you for warning us and for including me in these talks."

"Does the warlord have a preference?" Yavi asked.

"It is a sign of trust to use a Skreel knife provided by your host," Tsan said, improvising as rapidly as she could, "but it should not be a large impediment to our endeavor—"

"Skreel knife," Dolvek wheezed. "Polite."

"Me, too," Yavi chirped.

<<He's making his way to the throne room,>> a newly Named Sri'Zaur, whose Zaurtol was insufficiently crisp for Tsan's tastes, tapped in a hesitant cadence. She tried to catch the scent, but he was so new his pheromones were too easily masked by the others who'd worked this section of cavern more regularly. Braja? Brana? She couldn't make it out.

<<And should we head there as well?>> Tsan tapped, trying to conceal her irritation both from any who would overhear and from her guests.

<<I . . . yes . . . I think so . . . probably.>>

Probably?! Tsan guided the two in a circuitous route to the throne room so they couldn't find the way to or from it easily without a guide. She did it more out of habit than the belief that they might cause problems, the same habit that had made her take them through winding loops for an extra day in the tunnel from Rin'Saen Gorge.

Claws clicking angrily on the stone, she tried to keep a measured pace, finally standing on her hind legs to check her gait more naturally. *Hard to believe anyone walking on two legs is in a hurry.*

*

Get up, the voice shouted, *your General Tsan has the blood of a Vaelsilyn with her.*

"Her?" Xastix thrashed, muscles rigid as his attendants struggled to apply salve to the foul-smelling ruin his back had become. What scales remained were curled and dry, flaking away or matted with dark blood or salve. Seizing the smallest of the two fawning creatures, Xastix sank his teeth into its throat to stifle a scream.

"Should we try armor, Warlord?" the survivor asked, trembling. Pulsing between his shoulder blades, the once blue shard had taken on a red glow, the flesh around it black and necrotic, pustules oozing a yellowish miasma. He had, at times, believed the voice in his head to be his Ghaiattri patron. Each shard-slotted being had one, whether they were ever connected by the filling of the slot with a shard of the World Crystal or not. He decided it no longer mattered. Kilke had commanded him to make an offering of the blood of an Aern, an Eldrennai, and a Vaelsilyn. Two of those samples were in sealed vials awaiting the arrival of the third.

Kilke had promised him an increase in all things: strength, stamina, dexterity, mental acuity, if he only poured out the blood as an offering. Forefront in Xastix's mind was the promise of an end to the torment inflicted upon him by the shard in his back.

"You will need," Xastix panted, "four strong . . . Sri'Zaur. My personal guard. Tell them Kilke . . . tests. My. Faith. Here at. The final step. Of my. Ascension."

We are so close to victory, you weak, pathetic reptile! the voice berated him. *Help with your armor. Can't even stand under your own power and be steady. Must I do everything?*

Four guards entered, but Xastix dismissed them imperiously. Pain still ruled his back, but an extra measure of will ruled the rest of him. As the voice commanded, Xastix felt his body obey.

Put the armor on! No screaming, screeching, or mewling. That's right. Over your head. Do it!

Girded in blue-tinted armor made from the scales of the Great Dragon Serphyn, Warlord Xastix could imagine himself in a world without pain. His inner tyrant gave him focus, demon or not, pushing him forward.

Its insults kept him moving, one paw ahead of the other. Reaching the throne room deserved a pounding of drums and the declaration of a feast. It was too bright. Light flowed in from inset reflectors, illuminating the two long quartz tables lining the walls, displaying war plunder and artifacts of previous ages. Against the rear wall, the head of a decapitated god sat upon the Throne of Scale. Gold-colored flesh was accented by two curling crimson horns on its brow, Kilke's reptilian eyes, so reassuring despite the human cast to his facial features, tracked Xastix as the warlord rested the bulk of his weight on one marble table. Claws rested close to one of his favorite treasures, the skull of an Eldrennai, teeth replaced with a full set of Aernese teeth. Almost as an afterthought, he picked it up, carrying it with him to the throne made from the bones of conquered foes and upholstered with the scaly skins of defeated warlords. At its base sat two of the three samples of blood his god required.

"I have the last sample," Xastix said weakly. "Your test will be completed faithfully according to your secret purpose." Falling to all fours before the throne, Xastix set the skull between the blood samples and knelt before his god.

Kilke did not comment, but looking into his fathomless eyes calmed the warlord. By the time he heard the familiar tapping of Tsan requesting entry, he was composed enough to stand.

*

Tsan struggled to conceal her surprise at the condition of the warlord. Once strong and hale, he seemed gaunt and wasted, and the red blotch of scales between Xastix's eye ridges had turned black and now wept a milky substance. Eyes like those of a wild beast in a trap greeted Tsan's gaze, rolling in an unfocused manner as if the warlord were trying to track the flight of a very swift insect.

"You may approach," Xastix hissed.

"Warlord Xastix." Tsan dipped low, baring her throat submissively. "May I present representatives from The Parliament of Ages and the Eldren Plains. Princess Yavi of the Vael and Prince Dolvek of the Eldrennai."

Silence.

Princess Yavi, eyes down out of respect, waited patiently to be recognized. Dolvek gawped openly both at Kilke's head and at the warlord's obvious ill health, before his manners asserted themselves and he bowed low.

Silence.

"I have informed them of the requirement to shed blood as a sign of sincerity before any further discussion of treaties can begin."

"Blood," Xastix muttered. "Yes, the blood is . . . required."

<<A Skreel knife,>> Tsan tapped with her tail, <<so I might provide the warlord with his blood sample.>>

Four black-scaled Sri'Zaur entered; two took positions on either side of the throne, and the other two stood between the guests and the warlord. One of them offered Tsan his own Skreel knife.

"Princess Yavi." Tsan took the blade, offering it to her hilt first. "Would you do us the honor of opening our talks?"

Yavi nodded, reaching for the Skreel knife, opening her mouth to speak as she lifted her head to find the eyes of the warlord, but what came out instead of pleasantries was a scream.

*

"It's a demon, Dolvek," Yavi shouted, "and a monster and something I don't even have a word for!"

More than anything, Dolvek wanted Yavi to be wrong—for this all to be some mistake, but it was Yavi who had looked at the unawakened Aernese Prototype and seen the tortured spirit, driven mad by pain, still clinging to it. It had been Yavi who had looked at the warsuits in that same display and known they were alive and sentient. He wished, in the split instant of decision, that she were some silly, pretty thing who hadn't killed more Zaur at Oot, faster, better, and more tactically than he had.

But she had done all of those things, and despite how much he needed this to work, how much he wanted to establish a treaty, to have some tangible proof he was worthy of the blood of his father that had spilled out at Oot for his people . . . possibly because Dolvek himself had been too arrogant, too stupid, too tied up in his own false little world to do anything remotely useful for the entirety of his existence. While Yavi, though silly and happy and so desirous of peace, had been willing to take even him, Dolvek, into her kingdom to try and save him.

For all those reasons and a thousand more he could not articulate, Dolvek did not question. Instead, throwing open his connection to the elemental planes of earth and air, Dolvek acted.

What he did not do was grab the knife.

*

"I apologize, Princess," Dolvek shouted as he seized her by the waist and shot for the ceiling. A sharp yelp ripped through her as the Skreel knife, slapped harshly by the ascent, slashed the back of her arm. Too shocked to even process she had been grabbed, Yavi gawped, eyes wide as the rock ceiling tore itself apart, making way for their rapid exit. Fire blazed from Dolvek's outstretched palm, filling the hole left in their wake with flame.

"I very much need you to tell me," Dolvek said, his voice shaking as they reached the open air, slamming the earth behind them back together with a closed fist, "that you were not joking about the monster."

Yavi tore his mask off and twisted around to kiss him full on the mouth, which she hoped even a male-type person as thick-headed as Dolvek would understand as a very firm yes.

"Thank you for rescuing me," Dolvek told her, chest heaving as his breath came in ragged pants, almost falling from the sky except that then he might have dropped her.

"I *did* thank you." Yavi quirked her lips at him, brows furrowed. "That's what the kissing was about."

"It wasn't a prompt," Dolvek laughed. "The thanks was genuine. Whatever that thing was, I would have stood there like an idiot and been eaten, hoping all the while it would sign a treaty with me."

"Warlord Xastix is tied to a Ghaiattri, and his shard of the world crystal has gone terribly insane." Yavi kissed him again. "And there is another soul inside him, like a parasite, belonging but evil. I've never seen anything, even a Ghaiattri, that was actually pure evil before, but whatever is inside the warlord . . . it wants nothing good."

"I'll set us down and then you can ride on my back so you won't have to endure being held," Dolvek told her.

"No." She put the backs of her hands on either side of his face, wrists crossed beneath his chin. "You must not land on that mountain. Get us out of here as fast as you can. Take us . . . take us . . ."

"Back to Hashan and Warrune?"

"Fort Sunder first." Yavi wrapped her arms around him. "Here, just so it is easier to carry me. Once we're free of the mountain, I'll be able to fly with the spirits for a while."

"Yes, Princess," Dolvek answered. *So that*, he thought, *is what it feels like to do one thing right. It's a start.*

CHAPTER 41
THE TRUE ENEMY

Tsan grabbed for the Skreel knife, leaping free of the fire and rubble. Neither as lucky nor as quick, the two guards nearest her lay crushed under a small mound of rubble. Rocks had cracked one marble table; the artifacts displayed upon it lay broken or scattered. On either side of Warlord Xastix, his guards moved to get him out of the chamber only to find themselves hurled against the walls, like string-cut marionettes.

"The blood?" Xastix hissed.

Checking the blade, Tsan prayed she had been right. She thought the knife had slashed the Weed during her rapid ascent with the Eldrennai. And . . . yes . . . there it was on the blade—a trace of blood running down the length of the edge.

"Is it enough?" Tsan asked, offering the blade to her warlord.

"Yes!" Xastix danced on his hind legs, twirling amid the remains of his guards and laughing wildly. "Now for the offering."

"What offering, you fool?" said an entirely different voice, using the warlord's throat. "You'll put the blood on the skull, you won't pour it out for some useless god!"

"But he'll make the pain stop," Xastix said in his own voice.

"I'll make the pain stop," the other voice snapped. "Now do it."

Wedged-shaped head cocked at an angle, Tsan began to back away from her warlord.

"Well done," Kilke's head said from its place on the Throne of Scale. "Pour the blood upon the throne and I will bless you with—"

"You lie," the other voice spat. Xastix snatched up the Eldrennai skull and the vials moments before lightning fired from Kilke's eyes, hurling Xastix across the room. Crushed between his chest and the skull, the two vials broke, smearing the skull with blood. Where they mixed, lines beneath the surface of the bone shone silver.

"Don't!" Kilke shouted.

"Last sample." Xastix wiped the blade across the skull, then spat his own blood upon the bone.

Flesh ripped itself from the warlord's body in ragged strips. Jagged lances of bone thrust through skin and organs on its way out of the mighty Sri'Zaur's body, his screams filling the auditory receptors and mind of General

369

Tsan. Nothing, in Tsan's estimation, could have been worse than the sound of the skull's laughter.

"Reptilian error? That's what the boy called you all?" A cruel voice croaked from lips formed of stolen skin and cartilage with a tongue still as forked and gray as it had been in the mouth of its previous owner. "Error?"

General Tsan's eyes widened.

The Weed was right, she thought desperately. *It's time to get the hells out of here.*

She tried to run, knew she should, but her body would not turn. Her slit-pupiled eyes could not help but watch as a crude yet increasingly elegant skeleton wove itself together from the flailing near-corpse of her warlord.

"Error?!" the thing taking shape before her shrieked. "I make no mistakes! I make discoveries!" It nodded to itself, raising a hand held together by veins and wriggling ligaments into the air. "Such things I have learned no other being on the whole of Barrone was brave enough to master. Not before me and not after!

"Hasimak may have discovered the Port Gates, but I have created a new state of being!" Parts of the warlord's scales flowed like liquid, settling into an approximation of smooth Eldrennai flesh, but not all of it. One eye transformed into a perfect elfin eye with a dark-brown iris then settled itself into the ocular orbit, muscle and nerve endings reattaching themselves like snakes latching hold of their prey. The creature's left eye stopped mid-transformation with two pupils off center in the orb, one matching its elfin mate, the other bright green with a slit pupil.

Tossing its head back in triumphant joy, the thing shook its head as long trails of thick, black head petals sprouted from the skin and muscle attempting to cleave to the skull. As Warlord Xastix's screams died away, first in her auditory receptors and lastly in her mind, General Tsan's body began to move: first the shifting of one hind leg, then the other, and the spell was broken.

"Dead, am I?" the creature roared. "Dead once. Born twice, but now . . . something new." The warlord's lovely scales had become a hybrid of Zaur and elf hide, with dark-brown scaly patches outlined in pale, perfect Eldrennai skin slipping into place with a soft sucking sound where the interior assembly of meat and bones was complete. "Neither dead nor alive. Beyond the reach of Sower or Reaper!"

General Tsan backed away as the entity stuck out its forked gray tongue past a newly grown nose, narrowing its gaze as the forked ends melded together, the whole mass of muscle thickening and becoming more elfin without losing its color.

An odor like burning hair and sizzling fat hit Tsan's nostrils, joined by the sickly sweet aroma of decaying meat.

Smiling with rictus glee, revealing a mouth full of bone-steel teeth, the being waved its skinless hands in time to music Tsan could not hear, humming snatches of the music, as it conducted its own construction, nodding, swaying, and gesturing to different points in the throne room as if keeping time for an unseen orchestra. Using the reflection it saw in the polished bronze mirror that lined one wall of the throne room, the coalescing thing shifted to accept organ after organ.

Tsan's tail twitched nervously as the intestines coiled, spewing out their contents onto the floor of what had once been the seat of Zauran and Sri'Zauran rule.

No more, Tsan thought. *We are all lost now.*

Not quite, Kilke's voice whispered in her mind. *Take me and flee. Take with you as many soldiers as you can. You are Warlord . . . No, Warleader. I don't care what gender you are, so long as you can plot and scheme and strike. Can you do this? He will only be distracted for a little while longer.*

What is he? Tsan thought, leaping over the churning remains of the warlord, claws scrabbling for purchase on the blood- and fluid-slick tile. One false start, and Tsan landed on the throne, hovering over the severed head with its golden scales and curled ram's horns.

An abomination, the god purred. *No time for reverence and obeisance now*, Kilke urged. *Pick me up and run.*

Can't you protect me? Tsan asked.

I can make you stronger, faster. I can even let you remain female for the rest of the unnaturally long life I will grant you, Kilke promised, *but first you have to get me away from that creature of death. He is new, and my power over him will remain limited until I understand exactly how this came to pass. Torgrimm is an unbroken circle of death and birth.*

Nearby on the lone surviving table of artifacts, several items drew Tsan's attention in quick succession. Brssti's Axe, forged from metal that fell from the sky, worked by Kilke himself. Made to be wielded in two hands when standing upright, yet capable of splitting into twin hand axes for quadrupedal strikes.

Mere legend-making, Kilke hissed in her mind, *It's made from a rare Dwarven alloy. I only told Brssti how to work the metal and design the apparatus that allows it to come apart and rejoin.*

Tsan seized the axe, the silk beneath sliding under her touch to reveal the naked quartz tables underneath. Gathering in the air over the still-shifting form of the thing composed of Tsan's warlord's corpse, the silk cut itself with delicate precision, unraveling in strips to form thread with which to sew itself.

He's almost complete, Kilke shouted in Tsan's mind. *The pack Warlord Viax used, it skidded behind the throne when the Vael and the Eldrennai escaped. It can hold more than it appears to hold, at one-tenth the weight. Put me in it so your fore-paws will be free. Bring the axe and grab Warlord Ryyk's armor, if you want—it's the necklace that looks silver and has the sapphires—just trust me, I'll explain how to use it later.*

"But the armor of Warlord Ryyk was lost," Tsan muttered as she snatched up the necklace. Slipping the necklace on, she dropped behind the Throne of Scale and found Viax's pack exactly where Kilke had said it would be. She tore open the flap before unceremoniously snatching the head of her god from the throne and thrusting him inside, muttering apologies as she did so.

Actually, Kilke thought at her, *the armor only works properly for a Justicar of Kilke. Which brings us to my offer from earlier. You know any Sri'Zaur who might like the strength of ten, an immensely long and gender-locked life, and the gratitude of their god?*

"And all I have to do?" Tsan hissed as she ran through the tunnels of home.

Is agree to accept it, Kilke answered. *I led Warlord Xastix along the fool's path because I wasn't sure what was wrong with him. His soul was twisted, that I could see, but I'm not the god my other heads are.*

"Other heads?" Tsan lost her footing as a loud explosion shook the tunnel. She dove over falling debris, twisting clear of a huge mass of bronze as it rocked free of its mounting and crashed to the floor. "But you are Kilke."

I'm One-Headed Kilke. Kilke's thoughts were angry and bitter, causing bile to rise in the back of Tsan's throat. *The gods have (or had) multiple natures. Before Shidarva took my throne I was Three-Headed Kilke, the god of secrets, shadow, and one other thing: The reason I was cut off and thrown from the heavens, the reason Shidarva feared to rule with me still amongst the gods.*

So, Tsan thought back at the god in her backpack, *what were you the god of?*

Power, One-Headed Kilke whispered.

Tsan burst out into the grand auditorium where relays waited with ready tails to send forth the commands of their warlord. Staring at her with frightened eyes, they shook, their gray-scaled bodies quivering.

"The warlord?" asked the bravest of them.

Tsan looked out upon the cavern, chosen for its pristine acoustics, knowing that below in other tunnels were other Relays waiting to issue commands.

You will never have a better chance to seize power, Kilke tempted. *You can lead them out of here. Regroup. Prepare and then come back to drive out that thing that clothed itself with your warlord's meat.*

She closed her eyes and shook her head at the Relay.

"What happened?"

"I don't know, but I do know this." She paused. "We need to run. I can lead you to safety, but we must go now."

I accept, Tsan thought to her god.

*

Cadence Vindalius and Randall Tyree found themselves sitting in yet another part of the Zaur tunnel system. Very close to South Watch according to Tyree, but he'd been saying the same thing for the last two hours. Dead Zaur lay about it, rotting in the stale air. Kazan stood next to them, waiting for the other Overwatches to pick through the corpses for any remaining good meat.

"I guess that's it," M'jynn yelled. "All of this is too rotten."

"Not all of it," Joose said with a mouthful of questionable meat.

"I'm done, too," Arbokk said, standing up from rooting around in a Zaur's abdomen for liver.

No one expected the dead Zaur to sit up, but it did.

Arbokk jumped free, swinging Charming, his soul-bonded mace, at its skull, knocking it away. It was not the only body on the rise. Alberta whinnied nervously, and Tyree's pack animal ran headlong down the tunnel, not looking back or slowing when Tyree called.

"Have you ever—?" Cadence asked.

"I was going to ask you the same thing," Tyree quipped.

"The dead don't just get up and walk around." Cadence jumped up and was already putting distance between her and the dead. "Torgrimm wouldn't . . . stand . . . for it."

"Maybe Kholster hasn't read that far in the training booklet," Tyree said. "I like to think they have one. You know, after Nomi became a goddess, I picture Shidarva and Aldo getting together and writing out a guide."

One by one, the fallen reptiles rose, some picking up their weapons, others their missing body parts, reattaching them when possible.

"Run?" Tyree asked. "My plan is run."

"Run," Cadence agreed.

Behind them in the tunnel, the Aern ran and the dead walked.

*

Miles away, Teru, Whaar, and Alysaundra scouted among the ruins of Port Ammond, gathering the melted bone metal that had comprised Glayne's weapon. Finding the bones of the Aern who had fallen defending the dockside warehouse had been easy, but Glayne's weapon had been airborne when it melted, and droplets of bone-steel appeared to have scattered far afield.

"Do we have to get all of it?" Whaar asked.

"Only what you can sense," Alysaundra answered, using her warsuit Bone Harvest's fists as sledgehammers to break up a section of wall under which a large part of the weapon lay.

"But we can sense all of it," Teru groused.

"Then you have your answer." Alysaundra laughed.

Stopping a moment to let the dust settle more than to rest, Alysaundra caught herself looking out of the city to where the body of Coal, the great black dragon lay. She wondered what had dealt him such a blow.

"Hey," Whaar said, pointing at three grave markers, "these are new. After the evacuation, I think."

Someone had water-etched the stone.

"Zerris, Lord Stone, and Hasimak," Whaar read. "Dragon slayers."

Teru heard the first scrabbling sounds of fingernails on stone, as if someone were trapped, trying to claw their way to the surface.

"Hey, Alys," he called. "I think someone's trapped under here."

"Wharf rats," she said. "Keep looking."

"Okay," Whaar said. "Now I'm hearing it."

More scrabbling.

Dead Zaur came from the sea, struggling out from under the rubble whole or in pieces, covered in dirt and detritus, some caked in dried blood, others still tacky. They made no sound other than the scrape of limbs that should not move scraping along the ground.

"Alys," Teru shouted. "Let's move."

Tell Zhan's End Song we're going to have to come back for the bone-steel, okay? she thought at her armor.

He wants to know why, Bone Harvest intoned.

Alysaundra heard a tremendous shifting and turned to face it. There, in the rubble, Coal was struggling onto his side, the dragon's heart still and unbeating, plainly visible through the massive hole in its chest. Like flickering candles, its eyes lit once more with a guttering blue flame that spread along its scales until its wings began to stir.

"Coal?" Alysaundra asked.

"Yes," the dragon slowly croaked, "but you should run, little Aern. Run fast and far, for I fear I am not my own."

*

The gods watched as the dead rose, turning as one to Shidarva, Kholster, and Wylant. She had come in shouting and giving orders, chastising all parties, truly a goddess of Resolution.

As soon as he'd seen her, Kholster's grin had threatened to expand beyond the confines of his face. As much as he'd suspected Wylant might associate her flaming tresses with Dienox's "blessing," Kholster hoped she liked them because she looked stunning with the waist length locks trailing behind her as she flew.

Wylant landed like a comet, Vax drawn and at the ready, her flames visible despite her warsuit's helm, as if the magic desired the optimum display and adapted to the helm by mimicking in fire the same type of look achieved by the mane on Bloodmane's helm.

"You all stay over there," Wylant ordered the gods who sided with Shidarva. "And you shut up," she told Dienox as his eyes brightened in astonishment and he opened his mouth to speak. "And you—" she pointed two fingers at Kholster and Vander, "—are both in trouble."

"I just got stabbed with a piece of the Life Forge." Vander had taken a step back. "Everything else was Kholster's idea."

Betraying me to my wife, I see, Kholster teased.

It seems to make her happy, Kholster, Vander sent, his thoughts brimming with mirth. *Permission to continue?*

Within reason, Overwatch.

I do not understand the cause of all this amusement, sir. Harvester thought. Your wife is a formidable opponent and she seems very angry with you.

You presume that I intend to fight her? Kholster thought.

"Another betrayal," Shidarva screeched. "For whom shall you come next, Harvester? Do you have your eyes on the throne, perhaps?"

"At this point . . ." Kholster, still grinning from wolf-like ear to wolf-like ear behind his helm, lowered his warpick. "I would like to apologize for my behavior. I put Aldo's spirit inside an ant colony. Thus placed, it will be Gromma who collects his spirit next . . . as she handles the deaths of the less-sentient beings."

From there it had been a matter of finding one reasonable voice, and Wylant had been elected. As the dead dragon flapped its wings, rising into the air on a breeze of magic, Gromma and the other primals turned to face the risen dead.

They feel it, Vander thought. *The wrongness of it.*

"Gromma," Shidarva called to the goddess, but she did not answer. "Gromma, is what Kholster claims true?"

"Aldo?" Gromma muttered. "Yes, I have him. I will give him to Minapsis when he dies. . . . Unless he doesn't stay that way." Springing up beneath her garb of leaves and hide, a steed of equine cast but built of vines and moss and other living things rose so that Gromma was already mounted. She rode to the city's edge.

"I think I understand, Kholster." Xalistan growled. "You are right. This must not be allowed."

Shidarva frowned at Kholster, and Kholster frowned back.

"Truce?" suggested two-headed Kilke.

"For now," Shidarva said, and Kholster repeated. "For now."

One by one the gods of Barrone left, each curious to spy out his or her favorite places and people to see if the dead rose to threaten them as well, until only Wylant, Kholster, and Vander remained hovering over Port Ammond, watching the waves of undead Zaur and Sri'Zaur freeing themselves from the ice and rubble, lining up in rows upon the broken span that had once been called the Lane of Review. Captain Dryga's body, its scaly hide parboiled and split open, stood atop the cracked steps that had once led up to the royal premises. Coal landed next to him, lowering his head to let the Sri'Zauran captain climb aboard.

"Is Coal's soul in there?" Wylant asked.

"No," Kholster took his wife's hand, smiling when she swatted him on the arm. "None of those things have souls . . . except their master."

"Uled?" Wylant asked after she thought for a moment. It was possible some other being might have conceived such an abomination, but she remembered what he'd said before she'd killed him, about a plan to fight the Aern, a plan that had involved altering Torgrimm. . . . "But how do we stop him?"

"I was hoping," Kholster said softly, "that you would have a few ideas. When I realized what was happening, I could only think of one solution."

"Well?" Wylant motioned for him to continue, relieved to know he had a plan. "What is the plan?"

"You are," Kholster answered. "You always win."

"Bird squirt," Wylant cursed. Closing her eyes, Wylant took a deep breath and asked herself one question: How do I kill what is already dead?

Kholster Wylant, Clemency thought. **If you have a moment, I believe Vax and I might have an idea.**

ACKNOWLEDGMENTS

This is all Richard Iversen's fault.

Almost a decade ago, Rich said he was going to run a role-playing game and didn't. As a result, the character I was going to play ran rampant in my imagination until a world was populated with new races, cultures, and a pantheon all its own. I didn't wind up using my character as the focus of the trilogy, but Caius does make a small appearance. You can also blame Rich for the thermodynamics of my dragons. When I asked what would need to happen to extinguish a hurricane, Rich answered me. Thank you, sir.

I was given so much help and understanding from so many people I will undoubtedly omit someone, but I'll do my best. Thanks to Rene, my editor, for extreme patience. Thanks as well to Rob and Mary Ann for being my alpha readers on this one when I was so far behind they only had a week to do it. The debt of gratitude I owe my wife, Janet, would require its own volume to complete. It was love at first sight, and she is still putting up with my hijinks two decades later. Thank you to the Friday Night Crew (all of the above plus Amy, Dan, and Karen) for cheerfully accepting many canceled and/or abbreviated Friday evenings so that I could take extra time to write. My sons get a special thanks. They have taught me so much and I love them so dearly. Thanks to my mom and dad, because existence is a requirement for writing, and without them, I wouldn't.

Lastly, I would like to thank the readers. I would tell these stories anyway, but without you, I'm just scribbling in the dark.

ABOUT THE AUTHOR

J. F. Lewis is the author of the Grudgebearer Trilogy and The Void City series. Jeremy is an internationally published author and thinks it's pretty cool that his books have been translated into other languages. He doesn't eat people, but some of his characters do. After dark, he can usually be found typing into the wee hours of the morning while his wife, kids, and dog sleep soundly.

Track him down at www.authoratlarge.com.

Photo by Janet Lewis